In *Confessions to a Stranger*, Danielle Grandinetti weaves a tale that is at once mysterious, suspenseful, romantic, and inspiring. I was drawn into Adaleigh's story and her admirable strength ... Filled with truths that made me ponder my own life, this novel is a lovely start to what is sure to be a wonderful series!

—Heidi Chiavaroli,
Carol Award-Winning Author of *The Orchard House*

Danielle Grandinetti has crafted a wonderful tale of suspense and romance that will keep you on the edge of your seat. With well-drawn characters authentic to the era, a gripping plot, and a strong message of hope, *Confessions to a Stranger* is a read I recommend!

—Misty M. Beller,
USA Today bestselling author of the *Sisters of the Rockies* series

Riveting from the first scene, *As Silent as the Night* offers a unique, edge-of-your-seat Christmas read ... A beautiful, gripping, and romantically suspenseful Christmas story you wouldn't be able to put down if you tried.

—Chautona Havig,
author of *The Stars of New Cheltenham*

Sweet and suspenseful, *As Silent as the Night* takes readers on a twisty ride that will keep pages turning ... Her captivating characters, heart-warming families, and Christmas traditions aplenty check all the boxes for a fabulous holiday read.

—Beth Pugh,
Selah Awards Finalist and author of the *Pine Valley Holiday Series*

A Strike to the Heart is a compelling story. From the very first page, I was immersed into the thrilling action and remained gripped with intrigue until the satisfying ending. The romance escalated right along with the winding plot, creating a layered mystery that is sure to delight readers.

—Rachel Scott McDaniel,
Award-winning author of *The Mobster's Daughter*

Strike to the Heart is an entertaining story that grabs you on the first page with its intriguing plot, as Grandinetti expertly balances action with the tender stirrings of a romance that will woo your senses until the very end.

—Natalie Walters,
award winning author of *Lights Out*

"Inheritance battles, labor strikes, and a sweet Irish romance to root for ... *To Stand in the Breach* is the Depression-era tale you won't want to end."

- Kelsey Gietl,
author of *Broken Lines*.

"A page-turner, *To Stand in the Breach* combines suspense and romance that leads the reader through a thoroughly engrossing tale of what it means to stand with those you love."

- Ann Elizabeth Fryer,
author of *Of Needles and Haystacks*

CONFESSIONS TO A STRANGER

Danielle's Books

CONFESSIONS TO A STRANGER

DANIELLE GRANDINETTI

HEARTH SPOT PRESS

CONFESSIONS TO A STRANGER

Published by Hearth Spot Press
Printed in the United States of America
© 2023 Danielle Grandinetti

Scripture quotations are taken from the King James Version of the Bible

Kindle Book ISBN: 978-1-956098-07-5
Paperback ISBN: 978-1-956098-06-8

Cover Art: Roseanna White Designs
Author Picture: Abby Mae Tindal at Maeflower Photography
Editor: Denise Weimer

To my husband
who showed me the magic of the waterfront and joy of fishing

When thou passest through the waters,
I will be with thee;
and through the rivers,
they shall not overflow thee:
when thou walkest through the fire,
thou shalt not be burned;
neither shall the flame kindle upon thee.

Isaiah 43:2 (KJV)

CHAPTER ONE

Friday, May 30, 1930, Memorial Day
Crow's Nest, Wisconsin

T he caw of a seagull yanked Adaleigh Sirland's gaze from her worn journal. Her pulse kicked up, and she gripped her mechanical pencil as she searched for the bird. It sat atop the uppermost spire of a boat docked ten feet away. Dark and murky, the water lapped at her shoes.

Relax. No one knows you're here.

Behind her lay Crow's Nest. A bright, bustling place for a secluded inlet town on the western banks of Lake Michigan. Children raced. Mothers attempted to contain them. Chains clanked as boats came in and out of the harbor, creating a gentle surf. Seagulls fought with the pigeons. The evening sun dodged the clouds as it warmed her back. The summer heat soothed the ache in her soul.

Another scream tore her out of her reverie. A child's scream this time. Not of excitement, but terror. Adaleigh stuffed her journal, pocket Bible, and pencil into her knapsack as she bounced to her feet. To the left, a young woman with pinned-up blonde hair pointed at the water as if it would jump out at her. Two school-aged boys tugged a rope closer to the edge of the boardwalk. The boy who had fallen into the water barely bobbed above the surface three feet from shore.

In an instant, Adaleigh tossed her bag on the dock that jutted out from the boardwalk, kicked out of her black Oxfords, and jumped feet first into the harbor. Her knee-length skirt flew over her face, and air leapt out of her lungs as she hit the frigid water.

Come on, Adaleigh, focus. She shoved the fabric out of her way.

The boy floated facedown, inches from a large boat's hull. *Please, God, not a child.* Practiced strokes quickly brought her closer. The boy didn't move, didn't call for help, didn't struggle with the water. She maneuvered around him, attempting to come up behind so she wouldn't startle him into drowning her. That's when she saw the blood.

She flashed to another scene. The one that haunted her nights and dogged her by day. *God, not here, please.* She hauled herself back to the present before panic made her useless.

Adaleigh quickened her stroke, wrapped an arm around the boy's shoulders, and pulled his head above water. His chest didn't rise against the pressure of her grip.

"Take this!" Someone called, and a red life preserver ring landed by her elbow.

A crowd had gathered along the edge of the water. She hesitated. Not only was she inappropriately attired to be in the water, her life depended on staying unnoticed. One look at the boy whose chin she kept above the surface pushed back her fear. He needed help. Her help. That didn't require a second thought.

She clutched the life preserver, kicking to help the bystanders pull them in. Eager hands reached down to lift the boy onto hard ground. A man in a cowboy hat held out a hand to her, but the warning in her head, the one reminding her that her own life was at stake, had her shaking her head. Getting out of the water with a dress plastered to her body in front of a growing crowd ... no.

She eased back toward where she had left her shoes, treading water and clenching her chattering teeth as Cowboy Hat performed resuscitation on the boy. He had him on his stomach, arms extended over his head, and pressed on his upper back. One ... two... three ... The man counted to ten before the boy choked for air. Thank God. He was alive!

Now, time to disappear. Again.

With no ladder to climb up and the water barely lifting her high enough to grasp the top of the planks she'd so quickly jumped off of to rescue the boy, she would now have to pull herself up without leverage—and without help since she didn't want to attract any undo notice. No easy feat, but she could do it. She had to.

She grabbed the edge and kicked at the water for momentum. *Almost.* The fabric stuck to her stomach caught the rough boards as she fell back into the water. A shiver skittered over her body. Maybe she should have taken the help when it was offered, even if it led to embarrassment. But discovery ...?

The county ambulance's horn stopped the crowd's commotion for a moment, then the onlookers redoubled their interest as two men in white coats pushed their way to the boy. No one seemed to notice her in the water. That's what she wanted, right? To stay hidden? To stay ... alive?

Cold wrapped its icy fingers around her chest. Or was it fear? *Don't panic. Don't panic.* Again she reached for the dock, gave a kick. And lost her grip.

David Martins left the pullover and flat cap he'd shed while setting up for tonight's Memorial Day festivities on board the deck of his boss's lead fishing boat, the *Tuna Mann*. Nor did he bother with the suspenders that hung at his hips as he leapt to the dock. With a single ambulance to cover the county, seeing it head for the boardwalk never meant anything good.

Pausing at the edge of the crowd, he squinted against the sunlight, trying to make out the scene. Couldn't from this far away. His instinct to help someone in need launched him forward. He easily maneuvered through the crowd in time to see a woman treading water as she handed off a boy to the waiting arms of his friend Silas Ward—easily recognizable by that ridiculous cowboy hat he insisted on wearing since his return from a ranch out west. David didn't recognize the woman, but the boy was Matthew Hitchens, and his nanny, Amy Littleburg, stood nearby, furiously wringing her hands.

David's adrenaline eased as the ambulance personnel took over the scene. The relaxed expressions suggested Matthew would be all right, despite the blood matting his hair. As a fisherman, David knew all too well that a day on the lake could quickly turn to tragedy. Several of the younger fishermen were trained in basic water rescue, thanks to the local Red Cross Life Saving Corps, but not being able to save a life when one had the power to do so made it all the more difficult.

Thankfully, the woman had acted so promptly. He scanned the water for her. Had she gotten out already? Not if the shoes and knapsack on the dock were hers. He jogged over to them. Two decades on the water warned him she needed help.

He dropped to his knees beside her belongings. Just below the surface, the woman's brown hair swirled. His heart pounded. God wouldn't take the life of someone who'd just saved a child, right? He leaned over the edge and plunged his hand into the frigid water, hoping he wasn't too late to pull her out.

Adaleigh forced her cold limbs to cooperate. Powerful kicks propelled her to the surface. This time, a hand grabbed the back of her dress and hauled her onto the dock. She lay still for a second, teeth freely chattering, before she opened her eyes.

Above her appeared a clean-shaven face topped by wavy brown hair. She scrambled back, pulling her sopping-wet dress over her knees and putting distance between them.

"Thank you for assisting me," she said, forcing the polite, yet casual words past stiff lips.

The man rocked back on his heels. His mouth firmed, but before he could speak, an older gentleman, probably close to seventy, with a large-brimmed hat, stark blue eyes, and a gray mustache pressed a hand on his shoulder.

The narrow dock left Adaleigh no escape except back into the water. She'd have to let bravado be her shield. She clamped her teeth to manage an easy smile. On the boardwalk, the boy had been placed in the ambulance, and the crowd parted in anticipation of its leaving. Time to get out of there. If these two men would let her.

She tugged her Oxfords onto wet, stockinged feet. Mustache stuck out a bony hand to help her up as Handsome leapt to his feet in one lithe movement.

"You saved that kid," said Mustache, the gravel in his voice further showing his age.

"Someone had to." Adaleigh ignored his offer and stood unassisted after gathering her belongings. She smoothed her dress, well aware the wet fabric clung to every curve and Handsome studied her from beyond Mustache's thin shoulders. She raised her chin. Saving a life trumped propriety in most anyone's book, yet her cheeks warmed nonetheless.

"You're not from around here." The older man's appraising eyes ran over her from under bushy eyebrows, then he removed his coat and held it out to her. "Let me buy you coffee while you dry out."

"No need." Adaleigh gave a practiced smile and pushed past the older man only to find herself sandwiched between the two. Her ears pounded. Handsome's eyes darkened in concern as he shifted to the edge of the dock, giving her space to escape.

"I insist." The authority in Mustache's voice pinned her feet. She looked over her shoulder, and he pulled a police detective's badge from his pocket.

Fear squeezed her throat. Her sister wouldn't have contacted the police, would she? No way. Not with how they left things.

Mustache set the jacket over her shoulders, eyebrow raised. Fine. She would go along with him. A police detective was supposed to be safe. Right?

Intrigued, David considered the woman he'd pulled from the water. She was definitely scared of something, even if she seemed determined to hide it. Tempted as he was to join them for that cup of coffee, to satiate his curiosity and see what else he could learn about her, as Captain Mann's first mate and fleet manager, duty pulled him in other directions. He loved the work, but the hours were long during fishing season, especially since the economic crash last fall.

He parted with the lovely stranger and her detective escort at the edge of the dissipating crowd, snapping up his suspenders, then turning his steps toward Mann's fish shanty set up beside the Wharfside Café, the hub for all of Crow's Nest's independent fishermen and direct competition for Buck Wilson's Crow's Nest Conglomerate. He needed to speak with his boss before he finished preparing the boat. The holiday meant he could be home for a late supper with his grandmother, brother, and sister before daylight slipped away. However, a glance at the sun told him he'd have to finish up quickly if he wanted to make it tonight.

It took a moment for his eyes to adjust as he stepped into the dim interior of the wooden structure. Empty. He could have sworn his boss planned to come straight here after leaving the boat. Captain Mann was a cantankerous enigma. Rotund and jolly, often jawing the day away, yet a stubborn old man who'd built his own business out of nothing but fish. He'd given David his first and only job back when David was just a teen. Now David basically ran the company, even if Captain Mann wouldn't admit it. The man usually returned to the shop like a homing pigeon, but today, perhaps the excitement outside had distracted him.

Before David could turn around and head out the front door, Captain Mann's raised voice came from the back room. "I will not—"

David paused, his hand pressed to the closed door. He barely made out the rumble of a second voice.

"You city boys are all the same," Captain Mann said, launching into his typical tirade about the wealthy businessmen who sought to regulate the fishing waters and those who wished to claim the same waters for sport. The Great Lakes fish population seemed to be declining, and no one could agree on fixing the problem. Something would need to give soon, whether his boss liked it or not.

Ever since the financial crash, bitterness crept into his boss's voice more often than not. His mentor's succumbing to the growing divide among the fisherman weighed on David. Buck Wilson's conglomerate was supposed to bring the small businesses of Crow's Nest together, give them a voice in the national and international—Canada bordered the Great Lakes, too—fishing conversation. It did the opposite.

"I'd take my business elsewhere, but yours is the boat I need." A man in a dark suit and red tie emerged from the back room ahead of Captain Mann, who wore his usual overalls. "Though this place is as old and dusty as I expected."

David bristled. He swept the wooden floor every night before he closed up and dusted the shelves whenever he restocked the various goods they kept on hand for fishermen to purchase.

"I assure you ..." Mann stopped beside the counter, not making eye contact with David and cracking his knuckles. "Our boats are kept to the highest standards."

"Humph. I need the boat every afternoon next week."

How were they supposed to fish if this man commandeered their boat?

"Put it under *Guy Spelding*." He pulled out more money than David had seen in the past six months combined. "I'll make it worth your while."

"Make it happen, Martins." Mann gave a definitive nod.

David reluctantly slipped behind the counter. Mr. Spelding glanced over at a red-faced Mann with an air of derision. Or was it conquest? David swallowed down his protest. He loved the lake, loved fishing, loved being a first mate, and hated the injustice of pretentious snobs thinking their money made them better than everyone else. Even if money was getting hard to come by these days.

Adaleigh and her detective companion stayed silent as they approached The Wharfside Café, an old weather-beaten building with seven outdoor tables. It made Adaleigh think Ishmael could have eaten here before sailing off on the *Pequod*, like in Mr. Melville's tale. A large mastiff got to its feet, its hind quarters wagging in an undignified fashion.

"Have you been a good boy?" The detective rubbed the dog's massive head and untied the leash, which was wrapped around one of the fence posts that sectioned off the outdoor tables, with ropes slung between them, and the public area.

The dog barked—a sound that shook the beams of the board-walk—and pressed close against the detective's legs.

"Easy. I'll get something for you."

The dog whined but plopped down under the table they neared. The detective suggested she use the water closet inside to change out of her wet clothing. For a moment, she considered slipping out the back. But she was chilled and had nowhere warm to go. When she returned outside, the detective held out a chair on the far side for her to sit in. He took the one next to the dog.

Adaleigh leaned against the chair back, the warmth of its wooden surface seeping into her skin, then slipped off her shoes, letting the wood beams of the boardwalk heat her stockinged feet. As her shivering stopped, Adaleigh's hypervigilance began to relax, and curiosity popped out its head. Why had this detective invited her for coffee?

Before she could ask, a young waitress with a catching smile appeared, carrying a notepad. "Coffee, Mr. O'Connor?"

"Please, Mindy." The detective's voice was deep and calm like a tidal pool.

"The usual?" Mindy asked. "And water for Samson?"

"It's my day off, so let's shake it up." Dozens of tiny lines broke out over Detective O'Connor's face.

Mindy smiled. "We have all but the cranberry muffins left. How about a cinnamon roll?"

"That'll do. Warmed up, too, if you would."

"And for you, miss?" the waitress asked. Adaleigh guessed her to be about her same age, early twenties. It appeared Mindy lacked the ostentatiousness of most of the girls Adaleigh knew; perhaps they'd even be friends in another life.

"The same for my guest." The detective tossed his hat on the chair between them.

Adaleigh rubbed her bare arms. "A muffin please, any flavor." While she occasionally enjoyed a gentleman ordering for her, she couldn't let the detective get the upper hand. Who was she kidding? One of the highlights of growing up as she did was being treated like a lady, and the detective had just won major brownie points.

Before Adaleigh could launch into a full internal debate on the subject of male chivalry, out of the building next to the café, the one with the hanging sign that read *Captain Mann's Fishing Shanty*, stepped a man dressed too well for the setting.

Of medium height with an impeccably tailored suit, he had jet-black hair, a closely trimmed beard, and sculpted facial features. He reminded Adaleigh so much of her next-door neighbor that she not-so-surreptitiously watched him round the old fence to enter the café seating.

He took a table two over from where they sat, unbuttoning his suit and letting the red tie swing loose.

A throat clearing brought Adaleigh back to her own table. "Sorry." She rested folded hands in her lap and zeroed her attention onto the man across from her.

Detective O'Connor's blue eyes felt like light beams, reading every message she intentionally, or unintentionally, sent him. His gray hair was matted, and he wore a blue-and-gray-plaid dress shirt under a navy vest—a conventional appearance, neither striking nor haphazard.

"Your name?"

Adaleigh blinked. "Pardon?"

"We have not had the pleasure of exchanging names." He smirked.

Adaleigh straightened her shoulders. She couldn't tell him, so how could she redirect?

The muscle below his left eye twitched.

"Here is your coffee." Mindy set a cup of the steaming liquid on the table in front of each of them. Then she placed a bowl on the ground for Samson. He lapped at it lazily, spreading more slobber than water.

Mindy moved to the table where the smartly dressed gentleman sat.

"Got a little sugar for my coffee?" The man's sultry baritone drifted over. He intrigued Adaleigh more than she cared to admit. Could her sister have sent him?

"I'm working, Guy." Mindy swatted his hand away, but he slapped her backside. *Not everything is about you, Adaleigh.* Those two had history. Not the good kind.

"Your turn." Detective O'Connor's voice pulled her back.

Goodness gracious. Adaleigh had never been this distracted by a good-looking man before. But she'd been off ever since—

"You have not told me your name." Detective O'Connor looked at her from under those bushy eyebrows, making her squirm.

"It's Leigh," she lied. Well, partially.

That muscle under his eye twitched again.

Regret stung. She loved her name, her full name. Adaleigh Grace Sirland. With her two newly minted college degrees in psychology and rhetoric from the University of Illinois.

Adaleigh switched gears. "You're with the police here?"

"Special investigations."

"Special?" Mercy. Once he returned to his station, he would no doubt track down her whole history. Family drama, educational independence, general philosophical leanings, and spiritual practices. So much for the anonymity she craved.

A smile lurked under the detective's mustache.

"Mr. O'Connor." Mindy appeared, placed the pastries on the table. "Anything else?"

"Thank you, Mindy." Detective O'Connor smiled at her, bringing out all his wrinkles again. "A little trouble with the customers today?"

Adaleigh used her fork to break up the blueberry muffin, letting the air cool it.

Mindy fumbled for her notepad. "It's nothing."

Detective O'Connor touched her arm and gave her a look of father-ly concern, then she gave a faltering smile and turned away. Emotion clutched Adaleigh's throat. Why in all creation did she have to lose everyone who cared for her like that? She was on her own. But she was a fighter, a survivor, and she believed in God, even if He seemed rather silent when she needed Him most.

"Okay, time to tell me everything," Detective O'Connor said before tossing Samson a bite of cinnamon roll. "I've seen people like you before.

You didn't give me your real name because you don't want anyone to know you're here. Beau trouble?"

"No."

"Family trouble." It wasn't a question.

Adaleigh folded her arms. "What do you want from me?"

He laughed. A jolly, good-natured, crazy uncle laugh. The kind that clears a person's head and makes them feel good inside. "I want you to finish eating."

Adaleigh stared at her plate. Her recent lack of sleep left her helpless to sort out the concoction of emotions bubbling in her stomach.

"You can be safe with me." He reached a weathered hand across the table. "It's not about how far away you go, it's how little a trail you leave behind."

CHAPTER TWO

T he detective's large mastiff loped ahead of them, sniffing at fire hydrants and tree trunks. Detective O'Connor walked beside Adaleigh with easy strides, leading her over cracked roads that wove north of the boardwalk. She found she liked the quaint town of Crow's Nest.

With the lure of a home-cooked dinner, the detective had managed to convince Adaleigh to at least go along to his sister's house, a simple frame structure set back on a shady lot, as it turned out. He also said she had a spare room she'd let in exchange for light housework. Adaleigh's stomach growled at the thought of food—the muffin hadn't touched her hunger—and her muscles ached at the idea of a soft bed. She had no experience with housework, but how hard could it be for a few days? And surely, she could keep her guard up while obtaining much-needed rest and still be out of Crow's Nest before her sister was any the wiser.

"Afternoon, Em." Detective O'Connor beamed at the woman who answered the door.

Short, plump, and with a bob of silvery hair, Marie Martins did not look one bit like her brother. Except for the eyes. They both had those squinty, smiley eyes with creases at the corners. Unlike her brother, who had studied and interpreted Adaleigh, Mrs. Martins seemed to know everything from a simple glance.

Adaleigh recoiled at how exposed Mrs. Martins made her feel, but the older woman planted her hands on Adaleigh's shoulders. "What have you brought me, Michael?"

"The girl needs a place to stay."

"What's your name, dearie?"

Adaleigh stammered.

"Leigh is new to town." Detective O'Connor nodded, encouraging her to pick up the explanation. What story could she give them? How much of the truth did she want to share? She'd already lied to the detective about her name.

"Michael, be nice. She'll tell us in her own time."

The detective leaned closer to Adaleigh. "I told you my sister takes in everyone."

Mrs. Martins harrumphed. "The Lord said to welcome the stranger, so I do what I can."

Detective O'Connor rested his hands on his belt. "Like that one pickpocket who just needed a little guidance."

The two stared at one another for a few moments, silent conversation passing between them, until Detective O'Connor grinned. Mrs. Martins gave a martyr's sigh.

"Come with me." She spun around and headed down the long hall. "We're just about to have supper."

"Why do you think we're here?" Detective O'Connor called after her, winking at Adaleigh before following his sister.

Adaleigh entered the kitchen. Its beige, marbled linoleum separated it from the front room's tan carpet, which peeked through a wide doorway. Cracked cupboards, a wood stove, an electric refrigerator, and a large sink with a hand pump surrounded the large wooden table on three sides. Two people stood near the table: a lanky man with a mop of blondish hair and scraggly whiskers and a fresh-faced woman holding the cone of the wall phone to her ear.

"Who's she?" The woman glared at Adaleigh, voice full of annoyance, eerily reminding Adaleigh of her sister.

Samson moved underfoot, Mrs. Martins shooing him away as she put bowls full of food on the table.

"Leigh, meet my sister's adult granchildren." Detective O'Connor pointed at each in turn. "Patrick and Samantha."

Adaleigh nodded, apprehensive with all the eyes staring at her.

Samson let out a howl. Adaleigh barely contained the yelp that bubbled out of her throat. Detective O'Connor squinted at her as the dog raced toward the opening front door.

"Thank heavens." Mrs. Martins placed a bowl of potatoes on the table. "I didn't think he'd make it before the food got cold."

"Grandma, it smells amazing!" A cheerful voice echoed down the hallway followed by the man who'd pulled her out of the lake this afternoon. He ran his fingers through short brown hair as his gaze landed on Adaleigh.

"Leigh, this is my other grandnephew, David Martins." Detective O'Connor made formal introductions.

David—Mr. Martins felt too formal in her head—bowed slightly. "Happy to officially meet you, Miss Leigh. I'll forgive my uncle for not allowing us the pleasure earlier."

Adaleigh kicked herself into turning an unusually shy smile into a genuine one, especially when she met his gaze. She was struck by the kindness in his eyes, like his grandmother's. A deep brown. A hint of sadness added to their depth, though humor flashed for a moment while he spoke. A few freckles attempted to peek from under the tan that covered his shaven face. And the faint whiff of water, sun, and fish reminded her of how easily he'd pulled her from the water.

"But what's she doing *here*?" Samantha replaced the receiver on the phone and flipped her bobbed black hair as she placed a well-emphasized whine in her words. It snapped Adaleigh's attention away from David.

"Will you be staying with us?" David asked before he placed a kiss on his grandmother's cheek en route to carry over the platter of fish before the older lady could do so. Lean and lithe, he moved easily, as if accustomed to being in the kitchen. Intriguing.

"Wait." Patrick squinted at Adaleigh. "You match the description of the girl who saved Matt."

Heat infused Adaleigh's body. She hadn't considered people would make note of her description. Wouldn't that just make her sister's day? She already had her Pinkerton boyfriend searching for her. A news article would lead him here in days.

"It was Amy's fault, wasn't it?" Samantha's charcoal-lined eyes stared at her.

Adaleigh had to do a double-take to assure herself it wasn't her sister standing there. Fear tightened every muscle in her body. She couldn't stay here. Couldn't bring danger to this family. She had to get out of Crow's Nest. Now.

"Nonsense." Mrs. Martins stirred something in a pot on the stove.

"What do you mean? This is exciting." Patrick pushed past his sister, reaching for the house phone. "Wait until I tell—"

"Sit down!" Detective O'Connor growled, stopping Patrick—a grown man—in his tracks.

Warmth heated Adaleigh's left arm, drawing her attention. David had materialized beside her and placed a hand on her arm as he watched her with a mixture of question and concern. He undoubtedly had the same disconcerting ability to read her that his uncle and grandmother had. Yet ... he grounded her—perhaps because of his touch—more than either his uncle or grandmother had done. More than anyone in a long while.

"Patrick, that's enough." Mrs. Martins snapped a towel at her grandson. "You *children* need to learn to respect a person's privacy. Leigh is our guest. She is not an exhibit, and my house is not a zoo. You treat her right. Is that clear?"

"Yes, ma'am." Both bowed their heads.

"Even a hero needs to eat," David whispered in Adaleigh's ear as he nodded to a chair at the table. "Impressive rescue, by the way."

The warmth rose to her hairline and her stomach grumbled as David held her chair. So much for leaving. She'd stay for dinner, then decide what to do. Food made for a clearer brain.

"Enough antics now. It's suppertime." Mrs. Martins set the last bowl—cooked carrots—on the table and settled at its head. David sat opposite her with Patrick to his left. Detective O'Connor took the chair beside Patrick, Samson underneath, and Samantha sat across from him so that Adaleigh found herself with Samantha on her right and David at her left.

After Mrs. Martins insisted upon saying grace, people dove into the food. Platters passed every which way. Empty plates were handed off, then returned, overflowing. Butter dish, salt, bread ... all distributed in no certain order. It took Adaleigh a minute to catch on to the chaos. Actually, it took David handing her the breadbasket with a look that said, *jump in before nothing's left.*

Baked fish, boiled potatoes, cooked carrots, fresh bread ... everything smelled so delicious. It baffled her on where to begin. Fortunately, the manners that had been ingrained in her head for as long as she could remember kept her from shoveling the food into her mouth at an un-ladylike rate, no matter how much her stomach complained over how little she'd consumed over the past few weeks.

As Adaleigh took one purposeful bite after another, she watched the Martins family. Patrick ate and talked at the same time—all about Adaleigh's rescue of young Matt, who had apparently suffered only a minor concussion. Samantha responded to his tale with eye rolls and dramatic sighs. David ate silently, his eyes on his plate, though sometimes he'd glance at Adaleigh with a smile timed well with one of Patrick's outrageous comments, which kept her from fully panicking. Mrs. Martins and Detective O'Connor seemed to talk without saying a word, letting Patrick's voice fill the silence, even though Adaleigh wished they would make him stop.

It was something like dinner at home the last several years. Mom and Dad would silently communicate from across the table. If Ashley was present, she would tell fabricated stories aimed to wound Adaleigh in their parents' eyes, no matter what scolding, threatening, or cajoling Mom and Dad would do. Adaleigh limited herself to reporting on her day, then kept quiet. It wasn't like it used to be. Nothing was like it used to be.

"Leigh?" It was Detective O'Connor. "Ah, you are with us."

Adaleigh smiled, quickly tucking away her embarrassment.

"He just wanted the potatoes." David winked at her, looking like she imagined his uncle would have forty-odd years ago.

"Hey!" Patrick swatted at the potato bowl David held over his plate.

Mrs. Martin cast warm eyes on Adaleigh. "Now, tell us, dearie, what's brought you to Crow's Nest?"

What could she say? That, for the second time in her life, she was now penniless? Mrs. Martins would probably brush that aside. How about that her sister ran her off from the only home she knew? The dear lady would surely start to wonder about her then.

Thankfully, Detective O'Connor took the potatoes and redirected the conversation. "David, who was the man, about thirty, black suit, red tie, who came out of the Shanty after Leigh's rescue? Saw him at the Wharfside."

Adaleigh's head turned. The Shanty? Captain Mann's Fishing Shanty? The old building next to the restaurant Detective O'Connor had taken her to?

"Gave his name as Guy Spelding." David rested his fork on his plate. "The hotshot made me feel like he *deigned* to step foot inside the Shanty."

"Need you conduct business at the table, Michael?" Mrs. Martins snatched the potato bowl out of her brother's hand. "Let our guest talk."

Detective O'Connor's mustache bobbed. Adaleigh ducked her chin.

"Spelding met with Captain Mann," David said between swallows of water. "Then insisted on using our boat all next week."

"You work too much," Samantha mumbled around a bite of potatoes.

"Meeting up with friends." Patrick pushed away from the table.

"And where do you think you're going?" Mrs. Martins called after him, then shook her head. "He's all grown up and I can't manage him anymore. I'm afraid he'll ..." She stopped with a glance at David.

"Become like Dad?" David wiped his mouth with his napkin.

The silence stiffened like muscles held still too long.

Samantha broke it, scooting her chair back with a scrape. "I'm meeting friends, too. Don't wait up."

"Young lady!" Mrs. Martins called after her, but Samantha was gone.

Adaleigh's wasn't the only dysfunctional family.

Detective O'Connor leaned back in his chair and tossed Samson a crust of bread. "This is why I don't come to supper, Em. You and I have a lovely time, but your grandchildren ..."

"They'll be the death of me, Michael." Her face aged suddenly, making her appear closer to ninety than the seventy-some Adaleigh had guessed earlier.

"Regardless, the meal was delightful." Detective O'Connor's voice changed the mood in the room, as if the curtain closed and the play ended. "I've got to report bright and early tomorrow."

Out of the corner of her eye, Adaleigh saw David shift. He looked as if he wanted to leave, too, but something kept him there.

"You also work too much." Mrs. Martins glared at her brother.

He stretched and stood. Samson followed suit. "The Conglomerate has been making more serious power moves since the new kid kicked out old man Baxter. Buck is a cunning devil and a pain in the—the hindquarters. I don't like it."

"Do be careful, Michael."

"You know I will." He kissed her cheek. "David, let me know when you see more of that Spelding character."

"Of course, Uncle Mike."

"Leigh, you're in good hands." He patted his sister's shoulders, then whistled for Samson to follow him out.

"Grandma, what can I do?" David stood.

"Be a lad and clean the table for me." She unfolded herself from the chair rather slowly. "This old body can't do what it used to. I'm going to bed. Leigh, will you be in need of anything? It is a struggle for me to climb the stairs much anymore, and with Samantha gone, I'm afraid David will have to show you to your room."

"I'm sure it will all be lovely. Thank you." Adaleigh half stood, then sat again, unsure what to do next, but needing to know the answer to one question. "Mrs. Martins, why let a stranger stay in your house?"

"You can tell a lot from someone by watching them." Mrs. Martins smiled. "I think you need a safe place. A harbor to moor your boat for a while, if I may use the analogy."

Adaleigh blinked away prickly tears.

"Ah, well, dearie, these old bones are done for today. David can see that you're settled. But, if you ever need to talk, I've got two fine, listening ears."

Mrs. Martins tottered down the hall, leaving Adaleigh alone with David.

David focused on peeling off whatever meat was left on the remaining salmon instead of letting his eyes wander to the stranger he'd pulled from the water only a few hours ago.

Melinda "Mindy" Zahn, a waitress at the Wharfside, was the only other woman he felt this comfortable around, but their friendship—and that's all it had ever been—lacked the spark he felt around Leigh, which couldn't be her real name. Who would name their daughter a boy's name, for heaven's sake? This Leigh seemed cloaked in a mystery he wanted to uncover. If only he'd gotten home early enough to wash up before supper. He hadn't expected to see her again, let alone for his uncle to bring her home.

Leigh grabbed her empty plate and Samantha's, setting hers on the countertop to use both hands to manage Samantha's leftover food. The fish into the stock pot, the potatoes into a bowl for later. Still, David cringed at the amount of food his adult siblings wasted. As the primary breadwinner in the house during the recent economic downturn, he knew the cost of things all too well.

"Need help?" David asked, unsure how else to start a conversation with her.

Leigh must have been lost in her own thoughts, since she had stalled, potatoes half in the bowl. She seemed so self-contained, and his curiosity warred with her signals to leave her alone.

She glanced down. "Distracted, I guess," she said, then finished emptying the plate.

He could sense a crack in her walls—or maybe he just wanted to hear her talk. Regardless, he tried again, adding in a teasing tone with the hopes it would help her to open up. "So, other than being a beautiful lady who heroically rescues children, will you tell me about yourself?"

She pursed her lips, hazel eyes twinkling for the first time. "I do believe you're a flirt."

A flirt! A laugh exploded from his belly, warming his chest on the way out. How long had it been since he'd let out such a hearty laugh, let alone flirted with a girl?

"I'm sorry," he said, wiping good tears from his eyes. "I'm just so rarely accused of being a flirt these days. Not at all, really. I guess I just didn't expect to pull someone as pretty as you out of the lake."

"See? You did it again. You're incorrigible," she said, but her tone seemed to say she liked that about him. In fact, was that a glimpse of a smile lifting the corner of her mouth before she turned to the table to gather two more plates? The pleasure filling his chest held an addictive quality that made him want to coax her smile out of hiding more than ever.

"So how did you end up at our supper table?"

She bobbed her shoulders, still collecting utensils without looking at him. "Your uncle insisted."

"He's like that, knows a good person when he sees one. Grandma too. They read people."

"Rather unnervingly so."

David chuckled. She was right about that.

"What about you?" Finally, she turned to separate Patrick's leftovers into their proper containers. "How did you end up here with your grandma? You and your siblings."

That question. He hated answering it. But the way Leigh avoided his gaze as she worked told him she wouldn't divulge more until he did. She circled the table, gathering utensils that she placed in the wash bucket. Each move was graceful and purposeful. She didn't fit in a worn down town like Crow's Nest, but her bravery at rescuing Matt, her discomfiture when he pulled her from the water, her willingness to stay here ... his curiosity hadn't been peaked this much in ages.

He lifted the fish carcass and dropped it into Grandma's garden bucket. She'd use the bones in her garden. "Grandma adopted us while we were all still rather young." He could have moved out when he finished school, gone on with his life, but Grandma needed him here. His family needed him. So he'd put his dreams on hold to be the provider his dad couldn't be.

Leigh wrung out a dish rag. "No parents?"

"Mom died when I was twelve. Dad ..." He shrugged. What else could he say?

"I don't mean to pry."

Of course she didn't. She was diverting from herself. Knowing that didn't make his own story any easier to tell. There was an awkward silence as they worked in tandem to place the rest of the dishes into the washbasin. He wrestled his emotions back into their box. He should be able to handle questions about his parents by now, but no, he had to make everyone uncomfortable with how the whole situation still affected him.

Enough. He didn't need to burden her with his family's troubles, even if she managed to get him to share more easily than other people. He wanted to know more about this beautiful stranger, and he might only get one night to do so. Memorial Day Night, no less.

"Have you seen much of Crow's Nest?" David asked as he scrubbed the dirty dishes.

She grabbed a towel to dry them. "I only discovered your town this morning."

She reached for another plate, her shoulder brushing his arm, wisps of her brown hair escaping her braid and catching on her sleeve. A feeling he barely recognized—longing, if he had to name it—skidded through him. He needed to tread carefully, for both their sakes, but his curiosity was too strong to ignore.

"To honor Memorial Day—after the parade and speeches this morning, the decorating of the gravestones this afternoon—the boats put on a nighttime light show. Captains hang lanterns from the prows and wheelhouses of their boats, illuminating the harbor, so it's as if the wharf comes alive, celebrating life after a day of mourning. There's music, dancing ..."

"Sounds magical."

He didn't miss the wistfulness in her voice. "Come for a walk with me? I'll show you."

"Really?" She narrowed her eyes as she studied him, but was that a flicker of interest he detected?

"No obligations." He held up his hand as if swearing on the Bible in a court of law. "I'll have you back before ten. I do have to work in the morning."

She stared at him a beat longer and his hope rose. Then she smiled. "I'd be delighted to join you. Thank you."

He grinned. Perhaps he could finally get *her* talking.

Chapter Three

A daleigh grabbed her cream sweater from her bag and followed David out the front door as he slapped on his flat cap. He'd taken five minutes to change into a collared shirt, dark dress pants, and a gray sweater jacket. He cut as handsome a look as he did in just his shirtsleeves. Not that she was looking.

Outside, stars blinked in the pink sky, and a stiff breeze blew in from the lake. The air, though still warm from the day, had Adaleigh pulling her sweater tighter around her shoulders. For the first time in weeks, she felt ... normal, which is why she'd ignored caution and accepted David's suggestion.

They walked three blocks east and two blocks south before they reached the northern end of the wharf—or boardwalk, as Adaleigh considered it. It stretched half a mile south, if she'd judged the distance correctly this afternoon. Bordered by shops, restaurants, and boat docks, it had seemed a tame place by day, but tonight, it pulsed with energy, as David had said it would.

Gas lamps Adaleigh hadn't noticed before lined the boardwalk, casting a flickering glow that reflected on the pale yellow of her cotton dress. Light also spilled from every doorway, along with music and voices. On the water side, the docked boats swayed, brightening up the night with song, light, and laughter.

... When sorrows like sea billows roll ... Thou hast taught me to say ... it is well with my soul. Horacio Spafford's hymn danced through Adaleigh's thoughts, causing hope to whisper for the first time since the fateful day that landed her here.

"Great, isn't it?" The light reflected in David's light-brown eyes, making them sparkle.

Adaleigh smiled back, caught up in how relaxed this stranger made her feel. Perhaps it was a connection built from his rescue of her, but perhaps it was something deeper. He made her forget her troubles. Gave her hope that she might be safe again someday. A dream, when hiding meant survival, but she could indulge the daydream for a night. Right?

David directed her down the boardwalk, one hand lightly resting on her back to aid in dodging other pedestrians, the other indicating various points of reference—the police boat dock, the lighthouse at the mouth of the harbor, places his mother would take them as kids to play. People they passed called out a rowdy hello. Most knew David's name. There was something special about small towns.

Technically, Adaleigh grew up in a small town not far from Chicago. It had possessed the outward charm while lacking substantial reality. With every house a sweeping monolith to wealth, what could a person expect? Every couple weeks, they would attend a party at one of those houses. They'd wear their Paris-designed dresses, their hair perfectly curled, everything elegant and refined. Money created an alluring facade, but pretentiousness drained any essence of a small town. Any kindness.

Tears sprouted and Adaleigh quickly blinked them away.

"You sure you're up for this?" David rubbed the back of his neck. "I meant what I said. No obligations. I work eighty hours a week, so it is unusual for me—"

Adaleigh took his arm to stop his rambling. "I'm glad you asked me. Honest."

The bustling boardwalk faded as he studied her, his eyes squinting, gazing into hers before glancing at her hand resting on his muscled forearm, then to her lips, and back to her eyes. She held her breath. Would he really like what he saw if he knew all about her?

"What were you thinking about?" He leaned a shoulder against the gaslight post beside them, his stature casual, but Adaleigh wasn't fooled by the laid-back air. Nevertheless, the light cocooned them in a world all their own and, heaven help her, she wanted to tell him.

Adaleigh fidgeted with the button on her sweater. "I was thinking about my mom."

"I know a thing or two about missing a mother. Tell me about yours?"

She raised her head to find David's expression full of compassion. Gracious, she was going to cry! She forced the emotion back and focused on the water lapping at the boardwalk. "She was like a fairy godmother, you know, from the tales? She could turn little ol' me into someone resembling a princess." Once she scrubbed off the remnants of tomboy and athlete of course.

"Little ol' you?"

Adaleigh shrugged. "I wasn't much for tea and needlepoint. As much as Mom tried, I was usually more comfortable outside." Following the gardener around or exploring the stables. "But she would cajole me into a lacy dress, especially once I became old enough to attend fancy parties. Those nights were magical." Designed to introduce her to a prince.

"And yet ..." David shook his head. "Not my place to pry."

"And yet I left. That's what you were going to say. You're right." She couldn't prevent a tinge of bitterness in her response.

A lively tune sung by occupants of one of the boats behind her dueled with the cacophony of voices from the crowd that suddenly hemmed them in. Adaleigh's lungs constricted, as if the lake breeze had been swept out to sea, taking the air with it.

She gripped David's wrist, steeling herself against the rising panic. She couldn't let it take hold. Not now. Not here. She didn't want to lose the moment.

It took quick maneuvering, but David broke them free of the cluster of people. Something had scared Leigh. The past or the present, he wasn't sure. Since she reached out to him for what he guessed was security, he pried his wrist free in order to weave his callused fingers between her smooth ones, and squeezed. She closed her eyes. Raised her face to the cool air.

He couldn't help noticing she fit perfectly beside him. Though tall in her own right, she stood several inches shorter than him. Long brown hair, mostly held back in a thick braid, wisped across her face as she turned her head.

When was the last time he'd taken a lady on a date? His admission to Leigh was all too true—eighty hours a week was a low estimate of how much he worked. But, honestly, no one had interested him enough to give him reason to take a day off. Until Leigh.

She seemed oblivious to him now, as if she had transported herself to another time and place. Maybe revisiting those magical moments with her mom. He could relate to those wistful memories.

A smile played about her lips. Suddenly, a tear slipped down her cheek and she shuddered. Her eyes popped open, apprehension filling them.

Words caught on his tongue.

"You sure act fast." Samantha appeared from behind them, wrapping her arms around David's neck, which heated at her words. Sometimes his sister had no sense. He relinquished Leigh's hand to grab Samantha's, twirling her to stand opposite him and Leigh. The girl had on a too-short dress with no sleeves and a low back. When had she changed clothes?

He barely contained a growl. "Does Grandma know you own such scandalous clothing?"

Samantha gave a sarcastic curtsy, but her face quickly turned into a pout. David followed her gaze to a young man with hair splayed in every direction, dressed only in his shirtsleeves, and standing under a nearby lamppost. Sean Green, if he wasn't mistaken.

"Hey." He sauntered over, looking Samantha up and down.

David stuffed his fists in his pockets instead of using them to end Sean's perusal of his sister.

"Whatcha doin'?" Sean asked Samantha.

She shrugged her shoulders as she cast a flirty sideways glance at him.

David inhaled a deep breath, caught Leigh's slight shake of her head, and clamped his mouth shut.

"Have you seen Amy?" Sean's gaze left Samantha to scan the boardwalk.

"No ..." Samantha started, but Sean sauntered away without another word.

David exchanged a look with Leigh, baffled by the young man's strange behavior. "Sam, don't you think—"

She glared at him. "I'm an adult, David. I can make my own choices. Stop hovering."

"I would if you made adult choices."

"You mean dull choices. Like you. Though tonight is out of character."

More heat on his neck. He could only hope Leigh didn't take that the wrong way. Sam was right. He wasn't the type of man to play with a girl's emotions. If that made him dull, then so be it.

Leigh nudged him with an elbow. "Samantha?" David followed their gazes again. In the shadows between two buildings, Sean was kissing Amy Littleburg—Matt's babysitter—right there in the open. Apparently, he'd found who he'd been looking for, and David didn't regret it wasn't his sister.

Mouth turning down, Samantha looked between David and Leigh. "I don't understand why he's seeing her."

"Why do you care?" David asked, unable to keep annoyance out of his tone. Obviously, Sean was taken, and Samantha had no right to barge into his relationship with Amy. Even if Sean had eyeballed Sam like a piece of saltwater taffy.

"Amy is so popular." Samantha sighed. "She's got the most perfect skin. Big eyes. Every guy wants to be with her and every girl hates her."

Wants her? Hates her? What? David wasn't that old, but he felt like a curmudgeon ready to wallop some sense into these kids, er adults.

"So Sean's not acceptable?" Leigh clasped her hands together at her waist, the picture of calm.

Samantha snorted. "He's too good for her. He's not usually the type she goes for. So what is he doing with her?"

Oh God, help. David closed his eyes. How was he supposed to handle this? Samantha wasn't a child any longer, and he wasn't her father, but she needed guidance. She needed a mother. Obviously, not even their grandma had managed to assume that role, and it left Samantha floundering.

David met Leigh's look of understanding. Then she tipped her head back toward Sean and Amy. Amy was making her way through the crowd, leaving Sean trailing after her and Samantha shifting to keep him in her sight, edging away as if she'd forgotten about David and Leigh until she waved to a group of girls and hurried over to join them.

David sighed. Nothing he could do about any of that tonight, not without causing them all too much embarrassment, which would not fix the problem. Best to hope Samantha kept her head about her until he and Grandma could get her alone to talk.

"I have that to look forward to?" A familiar voice pulled him from his thoughts

"Silas!" David's mood lightened instantly. "Good to see you."

He tipped his cowboy hat toward Leigh. "I'm glad to see you fared all right after your rescue."

Leigh gave a nod. "You're the one who got him to cough up the water."

Silas waved her off. "My nieces are the same age, so I made sure to be prepared for anything." He glanced over his shoulder toward where Samantha had disappeared. "Except for them growing up."

David understood exactly. He and Silas had much in common these days. David had lost his mother, Silas, his father and brother. His brother's death is what brought him home to help care for his mother, sister-in-law, and two nieces. Speaking of Silas's nieces ... the two young girls dodged through the crowd to fling their arms around Silas's legs, brown braids flowing out behind them. David shared a smile with Leigh.

"Oh thank goodness!" Marian Ward, Silas's sister-in-law, appeared, hand pressed to her chest. "Girls, you don't run off like that."

Silas crouched. "You girls need to listen to your mother." The girls nodded.

Marian initiated greetings with Leigh before offering an apology. "I wish we could stay to talk more, but it's getting much too late for the girls."

"Of course." Silas tipped his Stenson to Leigh and clapped David on the back with a wink. "Enjoy the night."

David pushed the embarrassment away, but not in time to speak before Silas, Marian, and the girls disappeared into the crowd. Instead, he gave a gentle nudge to Leigh's shoulder, and she wrapped a hand around his offered arm. They stayed quiet, walking shoulder to shoulder. Soon the sounds and lights of the dock eased his angst. Comfort between him and Leigh returned, and he found himself watching her. She seemed to relax the farther from the crowds they walked. Her breathing grew even. Her eyes widened with a look of wonder. The tense ridge of her shoulders softened.

What brought this mysterious woman to Crow's Nest? What caused the fear that seemed to creep in at unexpected times? How come she was the one who jumped into the lake to save Matt when a slew of fishermen were at the dock? He opened his mouth to speak when another voice beat him to it.

"Why, if it isn't Mann's sheepdog's first mate." Guy Spelding pushed off the wall of the Crow's Nest Grill—which used to serve alcohol, and probably still did—and blocked their path.

David groaned. He did not want to talk with Spelding, especially with Leigh on his arm.

Adaleigh closed her eyes and grasped at the peace she'd had moments ago. She shouldn't have let her guard down, but the lake's magic ... how could she tune it out? The sparkle of lights on the water. The quiet music drifting in from the boats and buildings. The lanterns swinging from masts and posts, and in the hands of passersby. The odd mix of prepared food, fish, and dampness. She had entered another dimension—like the Time Traveler in Wells's *The Time Machine*—one where she could forget where she had come from and reinvent herself into whoever she wanted to be.

Her sister would never find her in such a small town if Adaleigh kept to herself. Ashley would probably never think to look in a place like Crow's Nest. A Sirland daughter hoofing it in a backwoods fishing town? Not likely. Not to mention how nice it would be to enjoy the company of a family for a while.

Or so she thought ... before the well-dressed man stepped from the shadows and shattered all her illusions. The gaslights from the boardwalk highlighted his suave features. He wore the same tailored suit and red tie he had earlier that day. The darkness made him appear more sinister. She didn't trust him.

"What do you want, Spelding?" David stopped, planting himself as if in preparation for a gale-force wind, his shoulder just in front of her. Protective, without being overbearing.

"Just making small talk." Mr. Spelding turned appraising eyes on Adaleigh just as Sean had done to Samantha. "How'd you attract such a doll? She's a right fine Sheba."

Adaleigh had observed that certain personalities had the capability, like that of a sun, to pull people into their gravitational orbit, causing the typically perceptive to lose their senses, if just for a moment. Employing a charisma that charms even while it manipulates. Adaleigh's father had that ability, especially in the boardroom. People would agree to anything he proposed no matter how absurd, unwise, or brilliant the idea. His words cast aside apprehension.

In that moment, as Mr. Spelding's barb flew toward David, Adaleigh recognized it—and him—for what it was. Mr. Spelding wielded an un-refined version of her father's magnetism mixed with a base flirtation, wrapping crude behavior in a glittering robe. Adaleigh blinked, repelled, seeing through Mr. Spelding's outward appearance to the real intentions of the man.

"Really?" David's voice held the same disgust Adaleigh felt. "Is no one going to treat a woman like a human being today?"

Good point.

Mr. Spelding laughed. "I said I think she's good-looking."

"You don't get it, do you?" David's voice rose. "Women aren't just play things for a night, easily discarded the next morning."

"Ha." Mr. Spelding crossed his arms. "I was going to call you a homely specimen, but now you're just pathetic. Only a blue-nose spouts such self-righteous talk. Really ... how did you get her to go out with you?"

"David." Adaleigh pulled him back. As much as she appreciated him standing up for her, this would not dissolve into a profitable argument. Not with someone like Guy Spelding.

David failed to yield, glaring at the interloper. "Just because you're new to our town doesn't make you better. We have a fine community here. Good people who know how to treat people right. We don't need your—"

"David." Adaleigh interrupted. "May I have a word?"

Spelding smirked. Adaleigh knew that look—the smugness of a man who knows his arrow not only pricked a sore spot, but that its poison had already begun to seep into its victim.

"Take a breath." Adaleigh took one herself as she pushed David several steps farther away from Mr. Spelding. She spoke softly. "You don't want to lose your job over the likes of him. He's only trying to needle you, and you have to deal with him all next week, so don't make things worse for yourself. He's a paying customer."

He muffled a growl. "I just hate it when people try to intimidate others because they think they're better."

Adaleigh's heart cracked open.

The angry light in David's eyes dimmed. "And then for him to insult you in the process. I'm sorry."

"I can stand up for myself pretty well." Adaleigh lowered him onto a bench, steeling herself against the appreciation growing for this man. "But thank you."

He sank his chin to his chest.

She glanced over her shoulder at Mr. Spelding. "Can you wait here? I need to finish something."

"Leigh, wait." David tried to catch her arm, but she dodged him.

"Stay here. Please." She gave him a smile. "I promise I'll be right back."

Guy Spelding might be a detestable worm, but he could also be playing her. Her sister would send someone just like him.

"Nice moves." Mr. Spelding grinned at Adaleigh upon her return, as if he could melt her into a puddle of water. He held no power over her. She saw him for what he really was, thank God. David, on the other hand ...

"Do you know a woman named Ashley?" Adaleigh demanded, watching his eyes for signs of the truth.

"I know lots of women, sweetheart." Mr. Spelding stepped closer, lust shining clear as the moon above.

Adaleigh didn't budge. "Do you know my name?"

Mr. Spelding rocked back on his heels. "I don't need it to have a good time." The man was as shallow as they came, but it didn't appear as if he knew anything about her or her sister. She read no deception in his tone, posture, or expression, only arrogance.

"Mr. Spelding, I would suggest learning how to treat people nicely if you're going to stay in Crow's Nest. Valuing people matters in a little town like this."

"Hey, now." He caught up to her as she turned to leave. "You're not from here either."

"So?" Adaleigh forced her hands to remain at her sides. She could've bitten off her lower lip after letting that little hint escape.

"Why defend it? You've got more to offer than this place will ever appreciate."

Adaleigh's suspicion rose. "You do know me."

He laughed. "I know your type. You come from education, power, and money. It's obvious. No one says *no* to you, and you always get your way. That's why my charms aren't working on you."

"Oh, please." She rolled her eyes.

"Fine, then." He grabbed her hand, forcing Adaleigh to face him. "How about a proper date? Dinner."

"For heaven's sake!" Adaleigh yanked her hand from his. "I'm not having this conversation with you."

"You're the one who came back to talk to me," he called after her as she marched toward David.

"Good night, Mr. Spelding."

"Don't ever let me doubt whether you can handle yourself." David stood now, watching the scene with arms folded, leaning his hip against the bench. "Next time, should I defend you, or would you prefer that I stay out of it?"

"Is your manliness hurt now, too?" she snapped.

"Nah, I'm impressed." David relaxed, gave her a smile. "Come on, let's finish our walk. There are less boats this way, so we shouldn't run into any more trouble."

Huh. Trouble stood before her, all neat and innocent with brown hair and a pullover.

Sure, part of her wanted to go back to the Martins' home, give up on an ill-fated evening, but David intrigued her more and more. He had none of the charisma of a guy like Guy or the authority of a man like her father. No bravado or grandstanding. Just the good-hearted kindness of the boy next door. She'd never met someone like that.

"There's my boss's fishing shanty." David stopped, pointed. He'd spent the last few minutes keeping the atmosphere light. Leigh seemed tightly coiled after her confrontation with Guy Spelding, and David felt no calmer. But he could deal with his emotions later. For now, Leigh deserved a pleasant remainder of the evening, and he aimed to give her that much. If she up and left, he hated the idea of her remembering him with a negative perspective.

"Fishing shanty?" Leigh prompted.

"I'm first mate on the *Tuna Mann*, but I also manage the three boats that make up Captain Mann's fishing fleet. So it's our headquarters, at least. About half of the other independent fishermen use our shanty too. Out back is a fish-cleaning area. Inside is gear for purchase. I oversee most of that."

"Your family must be right about you having a heavy workload. Did you mean it when you said eighty hours a week?"

David nodded. "Up before the sun."

"I like a quiet, early morning." Leigh ran her fingers over the ropes that hung along the edge of the dock to keep people from falling in by accident. The shadows of night contrasted with her quiet words. "Those are the moments when the world holds the most hope."

"And mercy." He stared out at the blackness of the water. It drew him like a soft whisper. Only out there could he find the peace and healing his soul craved. Him and God. He could no more deny its pull than a piece of metal could fight a magnet.

He shook himself and returned to a safer topic. "Most of our fishing captains are all old men who know Lake Michigan better than they know the roads west of here. They usually find the fish."

"Which makes happy bosses," she said. "Money makes the world go 'round."

He cocked his head. "You say that cynically."

"I'm not convinced money is all that." She pulled the edges of her sweater closed against the early summer breeze.

"There really isn't much money in fishing. Boats are expensive to keep up, and weather dictates when we can go out, then if the markets are bad ... Do you need my pullover?"

She shook her head and they continued sauntering, crowds and lights left behind. They should turn back, but David was loathe to end the evening, especially after they regained their comfortable footing. It might not be as magical as before, but it was good.

"Is it dangerous?" she asked.

"Fishing? At times. It's necessary to stay smart, sober, and pay attention to the weather. Not respecting her—Lake Michigan—is the biggest danger. She can give the illusion of tranquility even while harboring deadly riptides and swells. Yet when land disappears and it's just me sitting in a boat with nothing but water and sky for as far as the eye can see, I feel the most alive. Small and insignificant, sure, but it's like the boat is the palm of God's hand. The same God whose voice calmed the wind and sea."

"Yes," she whispered, a catch in her voice.

"That's just me." He bumped her arm, not sure why he shared so much. "I guess I find it hard to see God on land sometimes."

She brushed a tear that slipped down her cheek, then spoke before he knew what to say. "Tell me more? About life here."

"Here in Crow's Nest, water is our blood. We live in a ..." He gestured, attempting to help himself come up with the word. "You know, we live because of each other. My mother used to say it."

"Symbiotic?"

"That sounds right. Without the water, we cannot make a living. We would have no food, no money, no community. It can feel like we are at her mercy."

"The weather too?"

"The old captains anticipate the weather better than the weather reports half the time, but, yes, the weather too. The raw power of the wind and waves, yet God is even more powerful." David braced himself for the yearning that always overwhelmed him when he thought of God's strength. So many times, God could have intervened and hadn't. The only way he kept his faith was on the water.

"Is fishing ... fun?"

Fun? "Oh yeah." David felt himself light up like a little boy at Christmas. "I grew up going out with the old captains. They'd take me along on their boats, teach me everything from how to set a line and clean a fish to where the unspoken fishing territories. Captain Mann said I also have a good head for the business side of fishing, so maybe I'll be a captain someday."

"You really do love fishing, don't you?" She looked up at him with eyes full of wonder.

"Yeah." He hesitated a moment, but maybe she needed to hear this too. "It's the only way I survived losing my mom and managed when our dad left us. I meet God on the water. It's weird, I suppose, but I couldn't live without it." He gave a laugh. "You must think I'm a loon."

"Not at all. You remind me of *The Call of the Wild*." Leigh's soft voice soothed the pain in his heart. "Only instead of the arctic life of a wolf drawing you, it's the call of the water. I may see God's beautiful handiwork in its waves and colors, but the water brings out something in you the rest of us don't possess."

Call of the Water? God's beautiful handiwork? His pulse pounded in his throat. Only if it had brown hair and hazel eyes with a voice as magnetic as the sea. When her cheeks reddened, David swallowed. He'd moved within inches of her, and before he did something impulsive, like cup her cheek in his hand, or, even crazier, kiss her, he stuffed his hands in his pockets and stepped back.

He really needed to get his head on straight. They'd just met. He had no business thinking such things about her. It made him no better than a man like Spelding. *God, help me protect her, even from myself.* Because her presence here alone indicated she needed shelter from something or someone.

Leigh tugged on her sweater sleeves, pulling the fabric over her hands.

"What a long-winded fool I am, keeping you out so late and letting you get chilled." David yanked off his pullover, leaving him with just his gray shirtsleeves, and draped it over her shoulders. "Let's head back."

"I'm okay," she said, stopped, then opened her mouth as if to speak again when suddenly a sadness he knew all too well doused the light in her eyes and she shivered. "The magic of the evening must be muddling my head."

"Is that good or bad?" David held his breath. He shouldn't go there, but her response mattered to him.

Before she could answer, David caught movement beside a nearby building. Fear like he hadn't known since his mother's final days overcame him. He stumbled forward. Barely felt Leigh's steadying hand.

"Shhh." He put his arm up to keep her behind him.

Next to one of the buildings, a large, dark shape stooped over another shadowy form. David knew that middle-aged man—his rounded belly and brown unkempt hair. The front of his shirt looked wet, as if something had been poured down his chest.

The man staggered to his feet, and the light from the gas lamp behind them illuminated the lump he had been leaning over. It was a woman. Amy Littleburg. And the hilt of a knife rose from her stomach.

Air seeped out of his lungs. "Dad?"

Chapter Four

A daleigh shuddered, her flight instinct urging her to turn tail and run as David took another step forward.

"What have you done?" His face washed pale in the light of the gas lamps.

Dad? Done? Adaleigh blinked. Her heart accelerated as memories of another knife began invading her consciousness.

The man in the shadows hacked, bringing her back. "Wilson needs his dues, ya know."

"Wilson? Buck Wilson?" David's surprisingly calm voice had a stern edge.

"See, you understand." The man stumbled near enough now to smell the whiskey on his clothes. Bootlegged whiskey, most likely.

Claustrophobia closed in as his bad breath surrounded her. Adaleigh stepped back, but the man closed the gap. Only the young woman, lying there alone and still, kept her from running.

"I done do handyman stuff for them." The man huffed. "Ain't much. But it's a fair wage, ya know. A fair wage, and I put in a hard day's labor. A hard day's labor, ya know?"

"Dad!" David brushed past him, headed for the young woman. "Is Amy alive?"

"Who? This pretty woman?" The man leered at Adaleigh, sending ice skittering into her stomach. The man leaned into her personal space. "Ya got cash or jewelry ya could spare for an old man? I ain't flush, ya know."

Panic nipped at her heart the farther away David walked. She gulped in quick breaths, but his dad's stench suffocated her.

"You his girl?" The man breathed into Adaleigh's face. "David ain't done told me about his little lady."

She clung to the sound of the waves lapping the boardwalk until the blast of a horn overwhelmed the calming of the water. She could still run, right? Keep running until no one could ever find her. If only she could get her feet to move.

"Ain't ya gunna speak to me? Or ain't I good enough for ya?" The drunken man swayed before her. "Well?

Adaleigh closed her eyes against the whiskey-infused breeze, which was just the chance he needed to grab her wrist with his blood-stained hand. Panic surged. Had this man killed Amy, and was he now about to do the same to her?

He pulled her closer. "Ain't ya gunna say somethin'?"

Headlights from approaching emergency vehicles bounced off the buildings, a glaring brightness at odds with the darkness. Who called them? How were they here already? Adaleigh grasped at the frayed edges of her courage and gave Mr. Martins's instep a decisive stomp.

"Yowch!" he shrieked, jumping away from her like she was a scorpion. "Ya little—"

"Dad!" David jogged back, inserting himself between them. "What in heaven's name are you doing? Stay away from her."

"I didn't mean no harm, ya know." Mr. Martins dragged a dirty sleeve across his nose with a sniff. "No harm."

David set his hands on his father's shoulders. "Don't you realize what's going on? This doesn't look good ..."

Adaleigh folded her arms, drawing David's pullover tight across her shoulders. With his broad back to focus on, she was fine now. She could handle this situation. Just like the last time she came face to face with a venomous attack.

Oh, who was she kidding? David's voice faded. Two police cars skidded to a halt, encircling them. Four officers leapt out with guns drawn.

Adaleigh's heart raced like a horse's at the Kentucky Derby while her lungs dipped themselves in hot lava. Shaking overtook her whole body. Then, as if she could see it happening, her knees buckled, and she landed on the cold planks of the boardwalk.

Out of the corner of his eye, David saw Leigh's legs collapse and dropped to his knees to catch her before her head hit the ground. His elbow scraped against the rough boards as he cushioned her landing. Then he pressed two fingers to her carotid artery.

"Hands!" one of the responding officers shouted at them.

"She fainted." David raised his free hand, eyes on Leigh. "Heart racing. Rapid breathing."

"Martins?" The officer holstered his gun while two others hauled his dad away.

"Palmson." David puffed out a breath as he recognized his old high school buddy. "I think she hyperventilated."

"I gotta check you for a weapon first." Caleb Palmson ran his hands over David's arms, down his torso.

"My Swiss is in my left pocket."

"Got it." Palmson checked David's ankles, then knelt beside him. "Friend of yours?"

"Leigh. She's staying with us." David lowered Leigh's head and opened her mouth to check her airway. "Paramedics here?"

"They're coming. Who is she?"

"She saved Matt this afternoon."

"Really?" Palmson leaned forward to get a better view of Leigh, and an unfamiliar emotion twisted deep in David's stomach.

He pushed the feeling away, put a hand to Leigh's cheek, gave it a gentle pat. "Leigh, can you hear me? It's David. You're safe now. The cops are here."

Her eyes flickered.

"That's it. Just follow my voice." He kept it as calm as he could, though his body wanted to shake like a tree in a hail storm.

Palmson clapped David's shoulder. "I need to ask you some questions."

David frowned.

"I need to know what happened."

"Am I giving you my official statement?"

"Nope." Another voice cut in. "I'm taking it."

David held in a sigh. Chief Albert Sebastian. The man had a chip on his shoulder the size of Gibraltar and seemed to have it out for anyone related to Uncle Mike. Why? Because the rotund, gray haired man had been on the force as long as Uncle Mike, but the previous chief awarded Uncle Mike the special investigations position, not Sebastian. Then Sebastian became chief and never let anyone forget it.

Palmson gave David an apologetic shrug before deserting him.

David protested leaving Leigh—who was waking without aid of smelling salts—with the paramedic who followed in Sebastian's wake, but the officer gave David no choice. With a hand to the elbow, Sebastian directed David to a quiet area near the water, and David rested his hands on his hips, bracing for the questions.

Sebastian poised a pencil over a small notepad. "Start from the beginning."

"Leigh and I were walking—"

"Who's Leigh?"

David nodded behind him. The paramedic had her sitting up, and she appeared fully conscious, at least from this distance.

"And who *is* she?" Sebastian raised his eyebrows.

David kept a tight grip on his tone. "A visitor. She's staying with us. And she's also the one who rescued Matt earlier today."

"So she had a run-in with the victim." Statement, not question.

"A what!" David bit back a growl. He couldn't make these worse by losing his temper. "I cannot speak to that, Chief."

"The stranger rescued Amy's charge. That's a run-in and a motive."

David inhaled the fishy scent of water. This was why Uncle Mike made Special Investigations and Sebastian did not. The man was an idiot. "Honestly, I doubt they met at all. I saw Leigh in the water, nowhere near Miss Littleburg, after rescuing Matt." And nearly drowning, too.

"Precisely. Matt, who the victim was employed as a babysitter to watch over."

David sighed. *God, give me patience with this man.*

Sebastian tapped his pencil on the paper. "How do you know Leigh?"

"Why are you asking so much about Leigh?"

"I ask the questions, Martins. Tell me about Leigh."

"I have, and she had nothing to do with Amy's death." David splayed his hands, then dropped them to his sides.

"How would you know? She's a stranger here."

"Because I'm her alibi. And unless you ask me relevant questions, we're finished talking."

"Don't obstruct my investigation, Martins."

"Then ask me a—" David swallowed back the adjective he wanted to use. Being a sailor didn't mean talking like one. "Just ask me a legitimate question."

Sebastian still frowned at David's choice of words. "Why were you and Leigh on the wharf?"

"We were out for a walk." David glanced back at where the paramedics had moved Leigh to sit in the open doorway of the back of the ambulance. "Like everyone else this Memorial Day. Honestly, I still have no idea what this—"

Sebastian held up a hand. "When you first saw the victim, what did you see?"

David blew out a breath. "She was laying on the ground, and my father was leaning over her." *What were you doing, Dad?*

"So you saw him murder her?"

"That is not what I said."

"You saw him put the knife in her."

"No." David clenched his jaw, as if that could bite back the sting in his eyes.

"Then what did you see?"

"He was leaning over her." David blinked the image away. "Maybe he was trying to save her."

Sebastian rolled his eyes. "He's drunk, Martins. That alone proves he's a criminal. How was he supposed to save her?"

"Look, Chief, I will not make subjective observations. Opinions that could be misconstrued. I'll only report the facts as I experienced them."

One of the man's brows shot up. "Do not get testy with me."

David stared back.

"What did you do when you saw your father standing over the murdered woman?"

"I called out to him, and he came over to me and Leigh."

"And?"

"And then I went to check on Amy."

"Because?"

"Because? Really, Chief?" He waved his arm. "What was I supposed to do? I have first-aid training, and if she was alive, I wanted to help her."

"Did you?"

David ran a hand over his head. "She had no pulse and no respirations."

"So she was dead."

"I am not qualified to make that call."

"But you just said—"

"That I detected no pulse and no respirations."

"That means she's dead."

David clenched his teeth. Only a doctor could make that call.

"Fine." The man made a note, seeming pleased with himself. "Then what?"

He wasn't about to add a nail to his dad's coffin, so he skipped over the cause of what he noticed next. "I heard Leigh breathing erratically, so I returned to where she and my dad stood."

"And?"

"And she fainted." David pressed his lips together. He recognized her condition for what it was—overwhelming fear, but he refused to say a word about it. Felt guilty he hadn't paid close enough attention to stop her from losing consciousness, even though he'd seen it before in other people.

"Martins."

"Then you all showed up. End of story."

"I doubt it, but okay, I'll let it go for now. I need a written statement."

"I need to speak with my father." And Leigh.

"I cannot allow you to do that."

"Why not?"

"Because we're arresting him for the murder of Amy Littleburg."

Fortunately, Adaleigh's awareness fully returned before the paramedics could whisk her off to a hospital she didn't know. When she insisted she was fine, they let her sit on the back bumper of the ambulance while she waited for David.

Her body shivered even though she now had a blanket over her shoulders in addition to her sweater and David's pullover, which she now wore. She forced her breathing to slow. She was alive. She would be okay.

The hubbub breached her cocoon. Someone covered the woman's body with a sheet. Two officers pushed a fighting Mr. Martins into the back of a police car. A murmuring crowd gathered on the periphery. Adaleigh kept scanning until she found David. He was talking with an officer near the water. David's frown said enough.

That's when she heard a familiar—and surprisingly welcome—voice. Detective O'Connor. "This had better be good, waking me at this time of night for something that shouldn't requi ..." He surveyed the scene and removed his hat. "For the love of all that is holy."

He briefly made the rounds, talking first with David, then the detective, then the paramedics. Finally, he came to sit next to Adaleigh.

"Not the most pleasant welcome to Crow's Nest." He swung his hat between his legs.

Adaleigh managed a smile.

"Your fainting spell doesn't make you the most reliable witness, I'm afraid, but I'd like your statement, and Chief Sebastian won't let me take it without him."

She worked her tongue around her dry mouth. "Are you taking the case?"

He studied her with those all-seeing eyes. Finally, he shrugged. "Family is involved."

Right. She shivered.

His mustache bobbed, then he stood. "I'll have David take you to my sister's tonight. I'll bring Sebastian over to talk tomorrow. I've convinced him to wait that long, at least." He waved for David to come over.

"Uncle Mike, Dad might be blundering drunk, but I won't leave him take the rap for murder," David said as soon as he was within earshot. Honestly, he looked like a porcupine, hair sticking up and all sharp edges, ready to strike if anyone, friend or foe, made the wrong move.

"I'll take care of your dad." Detective O'Connor took the blanket from Adaleigh's shoulders. "You need to take her home."

"But—"

"David." Detective O'Connor glared David's quills into submission. "We'll find out what happened, but right now, the best thing you can do is take Leigh back to my sister's."

David's expressions varied as his internal battle waged. Adaleigh tried not to take his reluctance personally. Finally, he nodded and held out a hand to help her to her feet. "You look beat."

"Be nice to the woman." Detective O'Conner slapped the back of David's head with his hat. "She had to deal with your father tonight."

David looked sheepish, and Adaleigh couldn't help but smile.

For the first several minutes, David and Leigh walked silently, side-by-side. His mind raced with implications and questions. It made him nauseous, something being on a boat had never done, even in the worst storms. If only he could escape to the water now, find the peace he needed.

Uncle Mike had helped them dodge the crowd, and David led Leigh along quiet streets. The dampening air chilled his back through his cotton shirt. He pushed the cold aside when he noticed Leigh folding her arms tight against her chest.

"You okay?" He should have asked sooner.

Leigh nodded. She wore his pullover now, instead of resting it over her shoulders. It made her appear small, fragile, and he had the overwhelming urge to pull her next to him, tuck her under his arm.

Instead, he said, "I wish I had another coat to offer."

She turned warm eyes on him. "Perhaps your grandma has something warm to drink?"

"I'm sure she—" *Oh God, no.* How could he tell her about his father? Sam, Patrick, they didn't deserve this. What was he going to do?

"Hey." Leigh's hand touched his forearm. "It's going to be okay."

"How do you know that?" He pulled away even while wanting to desperately reach for Leigh's comfort as the reality of his father's situation rent his heart. "Leigh, *I'm* the witness. *I'm* the one who has to say that I found him there, like that. Me. His own son."

"We." Leigh caught his rough hands. "*We* saw him. I'm a witness too."

"I'm sorry about tonight." He clasped her fingers. "I shouldn't have asked—"

"How were you to know tonight would end as it has? Only God has that power. None of it was your fault." Her voice caught and she yanked back, slipping her hands inside the large sleeves of his pullover.

David blinked at her rapid withdrawal.

A sniff. A quick breath. And Leigh flashed him a winsome smile that went nowhere near her eyes. "I'm still holding out for that warm drink, so the night's not over yet."

No, no it wasn't.

The empty room Mrs. Martins lent to Adaleigh was up two flights of stairs in what was actually the attic. The edges of the ceiling touched the floor, leaving little room to stand upright except in the middle. A bed was tucked into one corner, opposite a short wardrobe and a washstand, with a pitcher and bowl covered in painted roses. One dormer window gave a view over several blocks of houses to the lake. The water gaped like an empty black hole, sucking the horizon into its depths. She shuddered.

"This should give you enough privacy," David explained as he leaned on the doorframe. "Sam, Patrick, and I sleep on the second floor. Grandma's room is on the first floor. Do you have any luggage I can bring up?"

"Just this." Adaleigh swung the knapsack off her shoulder and onto the bed. It had a soft-looking pillow and a faded quilt that matched the large braided rug. It felt like ages since she'd slept on a real bed, though it had only been a month. "I left my JD tucked away on the other side of town. I can get it tomorrow."

"Your what?"

"Motorcycle." Adaleigh plopped down next to her knapsack. The bed creaked, and the mattress was nowhere near the quality of the one she'd grown up sleeping on, but after the last few weeks—after the last hour—it felt like a giant cloud, reaching its gooey arms around her and taunting her with a warmth that couldn't reach her soul. She needed that tea or she'd never sleep.

"Didn't expect that."

"Huh?" Adaleigh shook herself. Right. Person—man—still in the room.

"You're a ... " —David tapped the toe of his shoe on the floor— "... girl."

She chuckled but didn't reply. Sure, she could have explained it was just her rebellious side or berated him for thinking less of her mode of transportation based on her gender or urged him to get tea started so she could finally warm up, but she waited in silence, knowing he had something else he wanted to say.

Finally, he let out a quick breath. "Thanks for going out tonight, even with the way it ended." Without waiting for a reply, he thumped the doorframe. "I'll get that tea started."

Without moving, she listened to his footsteps fade down the steps. Tonight had proved a good reminder she wasn't the only hurting person in the world, in this house. After waiting a few minutes to feel fully chastised for her selfishness, she wandered downstairs to find David holding two cups of tea, the smell of peppermint reaching her from across the room. The summer night was still too beautiful to stay inside, especially after the tragic events of the evening, so they sat in the backyard; him on the chair, her in the rocker.

Adaleigh gripped her cup with both hands and held it to her nose. The steam finally warmed her, the cool mint calmed her. The breeze rustled the top of the large oak standing guard next door. The clouds parted and a few stars peeped out. Crickets chirped. Surely, she could hear waves crashing if she stayed perfectly still. It was a moment she would remember for a long time.

David let out a deep sigh. "I have resented my father ever since he left. Never understood why he would abandon us so soon after Mom died. I get that he started drinking, but what about us?"

Her heart filled with a kindred pain. She let him go on.

"He's become a good-for-nothing man, but he's not a murderer. He wouldn't have killed her. He couldn't have. Right?"

Adaleigh tightened her grip on her cup as if it were the emotions rolling in her chest.

"I just can't help thinking, what if ..."

What could she say? That she knew exactly how he felt? That she understood his guilt? The pain. The questions.

"People know my dad and all his rough edges," David said, staring out into the darkness. "Lots of people get drunk here, despite the prohibition on it, so mostly people look the other way."

She hadn't obtained her degree in psychology without learning to easily identify when someone needed a listening ear, and David showed a classic case. Sometimes it was easier spilling personal thoughts to a stranger than a friend, so she settled back, rocking gently.

He set his mug on the table between them and put his head in his hands. "Now I learn he's been doing work for Buck Wilson. Of all things."

"Who's Buck Wilson?" Her question barely above a whisper.

"You heard Uncle Mike talk about the Crow's Nest Conglomerate? It started as a good thing." David relaxed into his chair, seemingly grateful to leave the emotional behind. "About a decade ago, Perry Baxter managed to bring together several small businesses to create a type of union. The businesses, including shops, mechanics, even fishermen, paid into the conglomerate in exchange for help with legal fees, or whatever type of protection they needed.

"About a year ago, a cocky up-and-comer, Buck Wilson, deposed old Perry and has turned the Crow's Nest Conglomerate into a power-hungry organism with some questionable practices. He expects members of the conglomerate to pay higher dues in exchange for his services, but if anyone wants out, he runs their business into the ground."

"That's horrible and can't be legal."

"Uncle Mike has been trying to close it down, but nothing sticks. It began as a legitimate business, so it's hard to prove otherwise, even if everyone knows what's going on. Nobody will talk on the record, and Buck retains the best lawyers. That's why Uncle Mike was called in tonight."

"He seems really good at his job, David. He'll figure this out."

"Uncle Mike can only follow the conglomerate angle, and the other officers, especially the chief, Sebastian, won't look past my dad." He rubbed his thumb. "Part of me wants to let him rot, but I can't. I've been taking care of this family for too long to let his reputation burn us even more."

Adaleigh understood too well.

Perhaps she could help, use her psychology and rhetoric skills to aid this family who took her in. As a witness, the cops probably wouldn't let her leave town for a couple days, anyway. She'd need to keep her head down to stay out of her sister's search area, but if she was truly honest with herself, she'd always regret not trying to help. She would do anything to reverse what happened to her family. Perhaps God was giving her a second chance.

The curiosity Leigh ignited in David flared with her offer to help. So many questions leapt to mind, but he didn't want her to feel like he was cross-examining her. Especially after tonight. So when she simply nodded instead of answering him when he clarified that she was willing to help perfect strangers, he didn't push.

He also wanted to start planning how to exonerate his dad, but Leigh's yawn reminded him he needed to be on the dock at three-thirty in the morning. Four hours from now. And people wondered why he didn't date or party or do anything but go to bed early on a Friday night.

How the other first mates functioned on no sleep, he didn't know. Maybe they took naps midday. He didn't have that luxury, not as Mann's office manager. The hours not fishing were spent at the shanty. Even on the weekend. He'd find time, though, and he'd figure this out. With Leigh's help. If she stayed that long.

For now, he escorted her upstairs, bidding her goodnight at the steps leading to the attic. As he lay in bed, however, she invaded his thoughts. How could someone wedge herself into his heart within a few hours? *God, I need wisdom here. I'm in way over my head ... in more ways than one ... and I don't know what to do.*

CHAPTER FIVE

Saturday, May 31

The next morning, Adaleigh walked quietly down the stairs, unsure what she would meet. Would David be there? Would they have the same level of comfortableness in the light of day? Had he told his grandmother and siblings about his dad? Would there be anger? Tears? Or would they all have forgotten about her and left for the courthouse?

"Good morning," Mrs. Martins, the lone occupant of the kitchen, greeted Adaleigh from the stove. She wore a black dress broken by panels of a floral pattern, as if attired for church, not the Saturday morning after learning one's son was the prime suspect in a murder investigation.

"Good—"

"Can I make you breakfast?" Mrs. Martins interrupted her greeting.

"Par ... don?" Adaleigh blinked at the rapid question.

Mrs. Martins pulled a loaf of bread from the breadbox, cut off a thick slice, and stuck it on the electric toaster. Then she grabbed a Ball jar half filled with jam from the refrigerator, a plate from the cupboard, and a butter knife from the drawer next to the wash sink—all with frightening efficiency.

Adaleigh shook out of her incredulity.

"I cook," Mrs. Martins said. "It helps me manage, especially after what's happened. Breakfast is simple. Toast, butter, and jam." Her hand shook as she spread the butter. "You and I should cook together, how about? Maybe dinner. I also have jam to make. This is my last jar. You could help me with that, but the garden needs weeding. Today is better for gardening."

Adaleigh stood beside the table. "Sure?"

"It'll be warm outside, so drink plenty of water, remember." Mrs. Martins poured coffee into a cup. Adaleigh hoped it was meant for her, not her hostess. She needed a brain boost to keep up with the woman.

"My old knees can't do the work as well anymore, and the grandkids ..." She faltered.

Adaleigh let out a slow breath, giving a natural beat before she eased the awkward silence. "What do they do on a Saturday?"

Mrs. Martins slid the coffee mug toward her. "David works, and the younger two are either with friends or sometimes working." She toyed with her wedding ring, tarnished and loose on her left hand. "I don't blame them. What young person wants to spend their Saturday with an old lady like me?"

What could she say? Adaleigh took the mug and held it under her nose, letting the steam finish waking her. Maybe it would lessen the disappointment that rose upon learning she'd have to wait all day to see David again.

Mrs. Martins handed her the plate of toast. "My brother will be here later this morning for the interview. Eat. Then garden in the meantime."

Yes, she must focus on how to help this family. Not her unwelcome feelings toward this woman's grandson.

David stifled a yawn and knocked back a chug of coffee from the mug he'd just filled from the jug they kept in the wheelhouse. Captain Mann steered the *Tuna Mann* toward deeper water, the shoreline long gone. Water surrounded them on all sides now. If only it could wash away his troubles ... and thoughts of Leigh.

He had this nagging suspicion that if something spooked her again, she'd dash out of Crow's Nest faster than a rabbit from a dog, investigation besides. He hoped he'd find her at home when his day ended. Or at least that she'd leave him a way to reach her if she vanished. Not that he'd blame her for skipping town after the way last night went.

A strong breeze came from the west. Cold spray left water droplets on his rubber Macintosh. He shivered, regardless of the wool sweater he wore beneath. Hopefully, the higher the sun climbed, the warmer he would feel. He doubted it, not with the turmoil awaiting him on shore.

Raised voices came from the wheelhouse. The captain had hired on two greenhorns—didn't need to pay them much. David ran his hands over the thick silk line, double-checking the clips where each snood—a short length of line with a hook at the bottom—was attached to the main trotline. Another month and they'd switch to gillnets.

"We fishing yet or what?" The older of the two greenhorns, O'Brien, emerged from the wheelhouse.

"Bait these lines." David nudged the bucket of herring toward the surly man.

"This needs to be a productive morning." He plopped down on an overturned crate. "I need the pay, so you need to hook the fish. Got it?"

David raised his eyebrows but stayed quiet. The other greenhorn, Randell, kept his head down as he baited the other trotline. O'Brien would be trouble, he knew it, especially if the fish didn't bite right away, as often happened.

"Do you always have to use such smelly bait?" O'Brien asked, patting his forehead with a handkerchief.

"We don't use any with the nets, but the trotlines need bait." David hooked a herring on the line. "Fishing is dependent on the weather, the currents, food availability, and much more. It's not a sure way of making an income."

"You'd better hope your captain can find the fish. or I'll go elsewhere."

David didn't bother answering the threat. They'd just find another fisherman to replace him. Not hard to do. But if word got around that Captain Mann couldn't find the fish, which meant a smaller catch and lower pay, things could get more difficult. Not what he needed right now.

He left the greenhorn to his work and leaned on the edge of the boat, looking out toward the horizon, breathing in the freshwater air. Usually the water brought him peace. Today, it did nothing to calm his desire to check in with Uncle Mike, to see if there was news on his dad. How was his grandmother handling the news? Had she told his siblings yet? And then there was Leigh.

He pushed the thoughts away, for supporting his family depended on finding the fish. He had to keep focused on his livelihood. Captain Mann slowed the thirty-foot Mackinaw boat. David eyed the lines, assuring himself they were ready to be tossed into the water.

Waves lapped at the hull, the rumble of the old Hicks Marine engine—new nearly a decade ago now—beneath his feet, clouds chasing the sun ... a perfect fishing day. David carefully took up a trotline and fed it into the water. If only he could cast his cares just as easily.

Adaleigh stood beside the rocker where she'd sat last night, gaping at the garden the darkness had hidden. It stretched wide and deep. She'd helped the gardener back home, so she wasn't without reference, but never had she worked with vegetable plants. Couldn't be too much different than Mom's prize roses, could it?

Nothing for it other than to get started. She found garden tools in the shed, then assessed where to begin. The muggy air caused her cotton dress to cling to her skin, but a wonderful breeze lifted the wisps of hair that fell out of her braid.

In the far left corner, Mrs. Martins had a nine-foot-by-nine-foot block of corn, which peeked through the ground as if wondering whether to stick around. Next to it was a patch of green beans, the tiny vines barely reaching out far enough to touch the spikes they would eventually crawl up. In front of the corn, Mrs. Martins had planted tomatoes, and beside the tomato patch was a row each of cucumbers, carrots, onions, zucchini, and squash, each labeled by neat signs. The rows seemed endless.

This was only the end of May so the little plants had a lot of growing left to do, but weeds could stifle them—or so Mrs. Martins said. Adaleigh wiped her forehead with her gloved hand. She had no green thumb, so she admired the woman's courage in letting her anywhere near her beloved garden.

As Adaleigh bent over, skirt muddied from the dirt, she recited Shakespeare. Growing up, she'd read several of his plays, but in college, she fell in love with the old language. It also kept her from stressing about tests or papers or speeches or anything else that caused her mind to get in a tangle.

Today, she felt trapped at the house, waiting for Detective O'Connor, but she wouldn't leave the Martins family in the lurch, especially if she could hide out here for a while. So she plucked weeds and quoted the bard, pulled and recited, growing steadily warmer in the rising summer sun.

Shall I compare thee to a summer's day?
Thou art more lovely and more temperate:
Rough winds do shake the darling buds of May,
And summer's lease hath . . .

Adaleigh felt his eyes before she heard his step. She stood quickly, dusting the dirt from her hands. Expectant. Detective O'Connor removed his hat, his smile half hidden by the mustache. Samson wasn't with him, but another man was. Short, plump, and bald. She recognized him from the crime scene and guessed this was Chief Albert Sebastian.

"I see my sister didn't waste any time putting you to work," Detective O'Connor said as the pair reached her. Both were dressed in simple dark suits, shoes, and hats, badges prominent on their coats.

Adaleigh looked down at her mud-covered dress. The only times she could recall being this dirty, she'd fought with her sister and hid in a nearby park until her father found her. Not a pleasant memory, that. Her parents never let her do anything that would make her clothes this dirty. It just wasn't done.

"Yoo-hoo." Detective O'Connor waved his hat in front of Adaleigh's face. "We let you recover, but we need an official statement from you today."

Adaleigh frowned.

"I'm Chief Sebastian." The bald man held out his hand. "I hope you are feeling better after last night."

Whether caused by sweat from the noonday sun or Chief Sebastian's saccharine greeting, a shiver skidded over Adaleigh's neck.

Chief Sebastian started toward the house. "Perhaps start by telling me why you don't want us to know who you are."

Detective O'Connor shook his head but motioned that they should follow.

"Sir?" Adaleigh pressed her heart, telling it to slow down.

Chief Sebastian spun to face her as he reached the back porch. "You're known as Leigh No-Last-Name, visiting from"—he scanned his notebook— "unknown. Care to tell me who you really are?"

Adaleigh glanced at Detective O'Connor. Last night, when she told David she would help, she'd forgotten that the police would want her full name, that they would search through her life, that her true identity would be discovered. She couldn't risk that. She couldn't let her sister find her. She—

"When we passed through the house, Marie was elbow-deep in pastry dough, so we've got plenty of time." Detective O'Connor lowered himself onto the lounge chair David had sat in last evening, resting his hat on his knee. "Al, why don't we revisit last night."

Chief Sebastian glared at Detective O'Connor, then sat in the rocker, leaving his hat on.

"I know this is your investigation, but we need cooperative witnesses if we're going to get to the truth."

"If you're covering—"

Detective O'Connor's eyebrow twitched like an electrocuted cornstalk.

"Gentlemen." Adaleigh planted her hands on her hips, stared at the two men as if they were the two unruly neighbor boys she'd had to deal with during her youth. "Would you ask your questions?"

Chief Sebastian registered surprise on his pudgy face. Detective O'Connor's mustache barely hid his smirk.

"Why are you in Crow's Nest?" Chief Sebastian demanded, obviously trying to regain what little authority he had between the three of them.

Adaleigh fiddled with the side seam of her dress, then clamped her fist closed. She knew all the nonverbal techniques they'd be watching for. She needed to keep the upper hand. With her pent-up nerves, pacing would be better than sitting.

"Leigh?" Detective Sebastian drew out the name.

Adaleigh squared off on him. "I left to start over. My sister and I had a falling out, which is not relevant to an official statement."

"I'll be the judge of that." Chief Sebastian crossed his legs as he leaned back in his chair with a Cheshire grin. "You can level with me, Adaleigh Sirland."

Adaleigh's head shot up. "How did you find out my name?"

"It didn't take much to recognize your face," the chief said. "Your family made the news recently thanks to some big advertising deal. You come from quite the wealthy background."

Adaleigh snorted. "How far did you dig?"

"I, personally, got sidetracked by your education," Detective O'Connor cut in. He sat with hands folded, legs outstretched, and the blankest of expressions under his bushy facial hair. He appeared relaxed, but Adaleigh would guess he was anything but.

"Yeah. What's a woman do with a pa-see-chol—or whatever it's called—degree?" Chief Sebastian rolled his eyes. "In my day, women didn't get educated."

"Psychology and rhetoric." Adaleigh folded her arms. If he wanted to read body language, then read this—*she ain't talkin'*.

Chief Sebastian opened his mouth, but Mrs. Martins stepped from the back door and interrupted. "Hot scones and coffee. The muffins will be out soon." She planted the tray of goodies on the small side table between the detectives.

"We don't need all this food, Em." Detective O'Connor caught her hand.

"Just eat." She brushed flour off her apron.

Detective O'Connor frowned. "It'll be all right, Em. I'm going to figure this out."

"My son is not a—Oh, never mind. Just eat." She waved a dismissive hand in their direction.

Detective O'Connor waited until she had closed the door. "She's not taking this well. Leigh, did you see him actually stab Amy Littleburg?"

"I'll—" Chief Sebastian attempted to say, but Adaleigh was already shaking her head.

"He seemed drunk." She focused on Detective O'Connor. His questions, she'd answer. "I doubt he realized she was dead."

"I wish that was enough." Detective O'Connor poured himself a cup of coffee.

"Why were you on the boardwalk with the suspect's son?" Chief Sebastian cut in.

Adaleigh ignored him, spoke to Detective O'Connor. "There were lots of people out last night, so surely someone saw something more than we did. She must have screamed or made a racket that would have drawn attention. Or maybe a time of death would help? Who called the ambulance?"

Detective O'Connor shook his head. "An anonymous person heard the scuffle but nobody saw anything." *Except you and David.* His unspoken words were clear.

Adaleigh hesitated. Did she really want to let herself be dragged into the middle of this? But then again, wasn't she already there?

"Do you know who did this?" Chief Sebastian stared her down.

Adaleigh took three calming breaths. She understood what David meant by wanting to clear his dad's name himself. Would Chief Sebastian stop with Mr. Martins, or would he dig deeper? Her experience with men like him—men who were stuck on themselves—said he'd take the easy way out to make himself look good.

"Walk us through your night," Detective O'Connor said.

She could do that. "We stopped outside the Lightning Bug, I think it was called. I saw Amy there, but I didn't speak with her."

"Did David?" Chief Sebastian asked before biting into a scone. He huffed as if it burned his mouth. Good.

"I can't say who all spoke with her," Adaleigh said.

"Where did you go next?" Detective Sebastian finally settled in his chair, ignoring the rest of his scone.

"David and I wandered down the boardwalk."

"Did you talk to anyone else?"

"Just a guy in a red tie." Adaleigh glanced at Detective O'Connor, knowing he'd catch her meaning.

"From the shop?" He leaned forward, eager.

"What shop?" The edge in Chief Sebastian's voice returned, as if he was afraid of being left out.

"New guy in town, a Guy Spelding." Detective O'Connor spoke quickly, like he wanted to get back to his own questions. "He might be a key in my investigation."

"You think he's with Wilson?" Chief Sebastian asked.

"I don't know." Detective O'Connor turned back to Adaleigh. "Did you speak with him?"

"A few minutes." Adaleigh shrugged, not wanting to go into it, especially with Chief Sebastian sitting there.

Detective O'Connor studied her for a minute. Could Spelding have harassed Amy too? Did it turn ugly when his advances were not received?

"How soon after did you see the suspect and the victim?" Chief Sebastian tapped his notebook.

"Not sure."

"What do you mean?"

"Just that. I'm not sure how long after. David and I were talking, so I wasn't paying attention to the time."

Detective O'Connor's mustache bobbed. Adaleigh blushed. What did he think of her, that she'd been out with his grandnephew and lost track of time? Why did she care?

"How did you realize there was a crime in progress?" Detective Sebastian asked.

"I didn't." Focus. Don't hyperventilate again. "David recognized his dad. Then we saw someone was hurt."

"Did the suspect say anything?"

Adaleigh tensed as she mentally transported back to last night. She could smell the alcohol on Mr. Martins's breath. Feel the grip of his hand on her wrist. Her heart began pounding against her ribs. Numbness crept into her cheeks.

"Do you believe David and Frank Martins were in cahoots to murder Amy Littleburg?"

"What?" Adaleigh stared at Chief Sebastian. The man was certifiable. "I think I'm done answering your questions." She needed to get away from him before she broke down completely—or shared something that would only hurt David.

"Did you have any other dealings with Amy Littleburg?" Chief Sebastian stood, intimidating in his stance. Funny that his action should instead bring clarity through her panic. Intimidating men didn't scare her, they reminded her of her past life.

Her rescue of young Matt was common knowledge, and now she had no patience left for the pudgy man. For the first time since she left home, Adaleigh wished she could contact the family attorney, Harold Binatari. He'd eat this small-town chief alive.

"Ms. Sirland, I asked you a question."

"Good day, Mr. Sebastian." Adaleigh nearly ran into Mrs. Martins at the back door as she made her dramatic exit.

CHAPTER SIX

Monday, June 2

Adaleigh tentatively left her hiding spot on the third floor. David had worked all weekend, including Sunday, and she hadn't seen him, nor his siblings. Even Detective O'Connor hadn't been by again. If Adaleigh was tempted to bolt, her hostess's vulnerable state kept her in Crow's Nest. It bothered Adaleigh that she—a stranger—seemed the only person to comfort Mrs. Martins. Or perhaps, no one saw the need to help the mother of a suspected murderer.

Mrs. Martins roved the kitchen, cleaning, sampling, gathering more supplies. Muffins and cookies already cooled on racks, and she was now kneading more dough.

"Whatcha making?" Adaleigh approached cautiously. The woman had red-rimmed eyes and a firm set to her mouth. Seemed like she was taking out her frustration on the poor dough.

"Dinner rolls." She plopped the blob onto the floured countertop and divided it into smaller sections—sorrow and anger in motion.

Adaleigh might conceal her own turmoil, but she couldn't let a needy soul fester in agony when she had the tools to get someone talking. She ran a finger along the cool tile of the countertop. "How are you holding up?"

Mrs. Martins sighed. "I'm baking more than I know what to do with. Bread goods only last for so long before they go stale."

"But if it helps you feel better ..." The memory of how frugally David had saved scraps the other night prevented her from finishing her suggestion. This family had no money to waste, not like hers had once upon a time.

Mrs. Martins shaped the little dough blobs onto a baking sheet. "Want a cookie? Or muffin?"

"Sure." Her stomach growled its approval.

After stoking the wood and sliding the rolls into the oven, Mrs. Martins delivered two still-steaming blueberry muffins on a plate, then slid over the butter dish.

"What's your favorite food to bake?" Adaleigh asked as she slathered butter on half a muffin.

"That's a good question." Mrs. Martins leaned her bare forearms on the flour-covered counter. "Pies. I truly enjoy making pies. In fact, that might be something we could make together." She hesitated before adding, "You'll be staying, right?"

The muffin hung between plate and mouth as Adaleigh cocked her head, the desire to spend more time with Mrs. Martins—and David—warring with the fear that hummed below the surface. "Do you want me to stay?"

Mrs. Martins gathered up her baking supplies. "It's foolish of me to ask."

"Of course not. I'm your guest ... or renter ... or visitor." *What am I, anyway?* "I suppose I should have asked if you would let me stay, considering what happened Friday night. I don't have to—"

"Nonsense." She slapped a wet cloth onto the floury mess. "You're good for our family. David needs a friend like you."

Adaleigh's cheeks heated.

"And perhaps I do too." She turned away, but not before Adaleigh caught a tearful sniffle.

"Mrs. Martins, has anyone come by to bring food or to talk or ..."

Brusquely, she shook her head and Adaleigh suddenly understood. Each day, Mrs. Martins had dressed up for visitors, to show a strong front, but no one had called. Now the poor woman felt deserted by her friends, her community, all because her son was accused of a crime he probably didn't commit. It must've devastated her so much that it caused her to reach out to the only friend at hand—a stranger who hadn't even shared her real name.

"Rose and Elaine—Mrs. Wittlebush and Mrs. Ward—stopped me at church yesterday. The three of us usually manage any funerals, but seeing as the situation is what it is, I am not helping, which means they are down a person and have their own businesses to run." She rinsed the rag and muttered, "I hate feeling useless."

Adaleigh could understand that. She'd been working to prove her worth to her family for years because being useless meant her life had no meaning. What sort of existence was that?

"You look as much in need of a friend as I do." Mrs. Martins's voice cut through Adaleigh's thoughts. Adaleigh had been tapping her knife on her plate. So much for being there for someone else.

"I guess I do," Adaleigh swallowed her unease at the idea of opening up to her hostess.

"I'll put the kettle on. Get my mind off ..." She waved her hands. "Now tell me about you."

"I don't know if I can," Adaleigh whispered, staring at her plate.

Mrs. Martins chucked her under her chin. "And if I promise not to tell a soul?"

Adaleigh grinned. "Will Detective O'Connor get it out of you?"

She laughed. "I'm still the older sister, no matter what he says."

What could it hurt to share her secrets? Maybe it would help if someone, somewhere knew the truth. The police already knew her name, her family. How well would Chief Sebastian keep her identity quiet? If he didn't, Adaleigh would have to go on the run again ... and she was awfully tired of running.

Mrs. Martins moved the kettle to a hotter spot on the stove where the water started to rumble, then she motioned for Adaleigh to sit with her at the kitchen table. She nodded at Adaleigh's dress, which was the same she'd worn yesterday. "Did I notice correctly that you came with nothing more than a knapsack?"

Adaleigh's escape from home had not been a smooth one. She'd left everything behind except for two changes of clothes—one of which had dirt stains from the garden, the other smelled like fish—and the coins she'd had on hand. She'd hopped on her motorcycle and driven north, out of state, until she ran out of money, fuel, and energy.

"I've found a church charity or two, but my clothing could use a laundry. Might I do that here?"

"Of course." Mrs. Martins waved a hand in dismissal. "But traveling on your own, visiting charities ... Leigh, for a woman, it is not safe."

Adaleigh shrugged. "Free food and safe lodging could only last for so long before I had to move on." If only she could find a permanent hideaway. Things weren't easy, but she'd felt settled while growing up.

Yet the adventure her sister's actions had forced on her fit with the part of her that had joined the all-female swim team —part of her high school's Girls Athletic Association—or went backpacking on a family trip to Europe. Asking for charity in exchange for work was one thing; now she'd gone and complicated things with the Martins by possibly witnessing a murder.

"Is there no hope for you to return home?" Mrs. Martins asked as the tea kettle whistled.

Adaleigh waited for her to pour two steaming cups of cinnamon tea. She stared into the black liquid. "Honestly, I don't know what home is anymore."

"Oh, child." Mrs. Martins covered Adaleigh's hand with her own.

The older woman's rough, nearly translucent skin contrasted sharply with her own smooth but darker skin—something for which Adaleigh's mother would have *tsk*ed at her. Ladies cultivated their hands, and they certainly didn't look like those of a working-class woman. If she stayed here much longer, her hands would become as rough as Mrs. Martins—and somehow, that felt right and good.

"You know a home is not about the walls that make a house, right?" Mrs. Martins gently shook their hands as if to make sure she had Adaleigh's full attention. "Home is built first on the foundation of God and His word. Its structure is made of wisdom and understanding. This home no one can take away from you. Storms will try to wash it away, but it will stand. Hide yourself in this shelter, Leigh."

Adaleigh gripped Mrs. Martins's hand as hard as she dared squeeze the woman's fragile bones, trying to keep the tears at bay. If only she could trust that hiding in God would physically keep her safe.

David ran the mop over the deck of the *Tuna Mann*. The morning's catch proved less profitable than any of them hoped and resulted in O'Brien quitting. Randell kept quietly busy repairing a line. Captain Mann muttered to himself as he rearranged crates around David's mop.

What David couldn't understand is why Captain Mann would let someone rent out his boat in the middle of fishing season. He'd made them fish early—earlier—this morning, not ideal, but manageable. However, without the afternoon, cleaning and preparing for the next day would keep them late into the evening, which would make the following early mornings increasingly difficult. Was the extra money worth the extra hours? Didn't seem like it in David's accounting eyes.

David glanced at Randell. His head was down, his jaw tense. With Randell distracted, seemingly by his task, David would risk it—he needed to know what his boss was thinking.

He sidled closer to the captain and lowered his voice. "Why is Guy Spelding booked this week?"

Captain Mann huffed and moved another crate.

David tried again. "We're down a man, and going out in the afternoon means more hours. Not to mention I didn't get the impression you were too happy about Spelding taking over the boat."

"Well, you're right, I ain't happy about it, but it ain't your business neither. In fact, I won't need you to join us today." Captain Mann hauled himself over the side of the boat, dropping onto the boardwalk. "Make sure the boat shines."

David frowned as he watched his boss disappear in the Monday evening crowd. Something was going on with him and Spelding, something that David was beginning to believe was very much his business.

"Lines are set for tomorrow." Randell appeared at his side. "What else do you need me to do?"

David handed him the mop handle. "Finish here, then get some sleep. It'll be a long few days."

"Aye, aye, sir."

David hid a grin as he leapt to the dock. Maybe Randell would turn out to be an okay hand.

He checked on the other two boats in the fleet, then made his way to the shanty, hoping he would run into his boss on the way. Perhaps if he approached the captain in a different way, he could get a straight answer about Spelding. Not having to go out on the boat tonight, however, meant he could be home for supper. He needed to check on his grandma and he missed Leigh.

Mindy Zahn waved at David from the outdoor area of the Wharfside, her skirt swishing as she wove between the tables. "You look like you need a cup of coffee."

Did he ever. "You treat me too well, Minds."

Her smile faded. "You doing okay? I heard about ... everything."

David leaned his elbows on one of the fence posts, swinging his hat in his fingers. "I don't know what to think. My dad can't be a murderer."

"It's hard to believe anyone related to you would be a murderer."

His neck heated. "I appreciate that."

Mindy patted his hand. "There's not a better guy around than you."

David eyed her. "More guy trouble, huh?"

"Someday I'll learn my choice in men is rotten." A light blush covered her cheeks. "I can't seem to get it right. I mean, I know you're a catch, but why can't I find someone as nice as you?"

He turned his wrist to capture her hand in his. "Because you need more adventure than someone as plain as me can provide." Would the same prove true of Leigh? Was he too simple for someone as sophisticated as her?

"But why?" Tears glistened in her hazel eyes. "Why can't I settle?"

David tightened his grip on her. "Don't you dare settle, you hear me?"

She dashed at her cheeks, then cocked her head. "What's that look for?"

"What look?" David bluffed. Mindy could always read his mind, and he didn't want her to know he'd just been thinking about Leigh.

"You're thinking of someone. A girl. David Martins, are you calling on someone and didn't tell me?"

"Shh!" He couldn't stop the heat from rising all the way to his ears.

"Oh, you are!"

"I'm not. I just met her."

"Wait, the stranger?" Mindy's sadness evaporated into excitement. "The one who rescued Matt and was with you—" She clapped a hand over her mouth. "You were on a date when you found your dad. Oh David, that's horrible! Do you think she'll say yes to going out with you again?"

Frankly, David hoped she'd still be at his grandmother's by the time he arrived home. It'd been three days since she arrived, and each day he doubted she'd be there. But she hadn't left. Yet. "How about I introduce you two sometime?"

"Of course! Wait a minute. Was she with your uncle after Matt's incident? Brown hair. Nice dress."

"Probably." He knew Uncle Mike planned to take Leigh for coffee.

"I liked her. She could manage your uncle too. I got the impression she could handle a lot of things."

David agreed on that point. But would it be enough to get her to stick around? Why did that matter to him so much? Maybe he needed to think on his own motives before doing anything rash, like asking Leigh to go on another walk with him and scaring her out of town for good.

After a supper shared between just Mrs. Martins and Adaleigh—none of the grandchildren had come home, again—Adaleigh grabbed her journal and found a comfy spot on the front porch step. Her conversation with Mrs. Martins earlier that day had her thinking, and the best way for her to get thoughts out of her head was to write them down.

The night air had a warmer feel than the previous nights. The breeze felt lighter, too, and pink clouds reflected the setting sun. An idyllic summer's night. With a smile on her lips, Adaleigh put her pencil to paper in an attempt to sort out the chaos that clouded her brain. Half a page into writing, she found herself writing about David.

Adaleigh hadn't courted much in the past. Her sister went out enough for both of them. Frankly, the young men in her wealthy family's circle of friends were too stuffy and full of themselves for her way of thinking. In college, Adaleigh went on a couple dates. But most of the men there looked down on a woman who felt the need to get a college education. Every time she risked going out with one of them, it failed miserably. Finally, and after so many hilariously awful attempts, she pushed relationships aside in favor of her career. Once in awhile, one brave soul would invite her out, roommates would urge her to go, but she found herself doing all the listening and none of the talking.

Anyway, why get serious with someone if she didn't know what she wanted for her own future? What did God have in mind for her life? Would she become the wife of a wealthy businessman? Work in psychology and become a spinster? Travel the world and be her own woman? There had been enough money in the family for her to keep on doing whatever it was she loved without having to worry about everyday concerns like a house or food, no matter where she decided to live or whom she married. *Follow your dreams* had been the mantra of her parents.

So much for that. It took only a few moments for those dreams to be crushed, literally. All Mom and Dad had hoped for, planned for, invested for ... it disappeared because of one man's illegal behavior.

Adaleigh had stopped writing, the hurt inside coursing into her fingers, freezing them in a tight grip around the pencil. To go from all the bright hope in the world to running for her life ... it was a hard pill to swallow. She closed her journal. She needed to get out of her head. Spend some time *doing* something. That's why she swam. It was action. It was purpose. It gave an outlet for all the words she read.

As the sunlight faded, the stars beckoned. *He leadeth me beside the still waters. He restoreth my soul* ... The phrases of the twenty-third Psalm floated through her mind. Yes, she needed to find her way to the lake. Have a long talk with the Almighty.

Adaleigh traded her journal for her sweater and followed the same path she and David had taken the other evening. Closer to the lake, the air cooled, bringing with it a distinctly fishy smell. The lake itself was a darkening pool of emptiness, as if it swallowed the light, even the light of the stars. The path here would lead to the boardwalk, and Adaleigh found herself walking more quickly. The inkiness of the lake pulled at her. If she wasn't careful, it would trip her up, yanking her into the abyss.

With a breath of relief, Adaleigh reached the boardwalk only to find the magic from Friday night had disappeared, leaving the shadows dark and clanking boats empty. She got a couple whistles of seeming appreciation as she walked down the boardwalk. Unease had her increasing her pace. She shouldn't have gone out alone, but she'd expected at least the presence of families and the feeling of safety in such a small town.

"Leigh?" A voice called from behind five steps later.

Adaleigh spun around, pulse pounding.

David turned the key to the door of the shanty where he worked. "What are you doing out and about tonight?"

"Clearing my head." Relief swept through her, followed by appreciation at seeing how handsome he looked in his gray pullover and flat cap.

"May I walk with you?"

Her heart betrayed her with joy at his suggestion. "Perhaps we can walk toward your grandmother's home?"

He held out his arm for her to grasp. They strolled side by side in comfortable harmony. Dark waves licked at the boat hulls. Fishy smells wafted through the air—a smell that didn't wrinkle her nose the way it likely would have a month ago—and a breeze ruffled loose strands of her hair. What had felt sinister now felt homely.

"Good day?" she finally asked.

He sighed. "I like fishing because it's a generally quiet venture. I missed supper because we had to hire on another new man, and he would not stop talking. Someday I'll be master of my time and captain of my own boat and can make my own hires." His eyes sparked.

Adaleigh held his arm a little tighter. "What's it like out there?"

"On the lake?"

She nodded.

David's muscles relaxed under her touch. "Water stretches as far as the eye can see. Soft waves sparkle like tiny stars. Lines bob in the water, waiting for a fish to bite. The dull hum of the boat motor mixes with the thump of the water against the hull. Then a fish catches the hook, then another, and another, until we have a whole trotline to haul into the boat. It's the best feeling in the world!"

Adaleigh widened her eyes as she stared at him, drawn into his description. The man had a way with words.

"Then comes a battle of wits." He winked. "Hauling in a line fish takes finesse and calculation. If you allow any slack in the line, fish can spit out the hook, but if you're too aggressive, the line can snap, and you'll lose the whole catch. But sure as shootin', I get 'em."

Adaleigh laughed and he grinned down at her.

"I'd be honored if you would ..." He stopped, tension bursting from him as his callused hand grabbed for hers. And then he yanked.

"This way," David hissed, pulling Leigh after him, grateful she didn't balk. He dashed through the narrow alley between two weathered buildings.

As the light from the wharf's gas lamps grew smaller behind them, Leigh finally resisted. "What's going on?" she whispered.

"Conglomerate people."

A damp wind tunneled through the alley. Leigh rubbed her sweatered arm with her free hand. "Why are we hiding?"

"They were looking at the crime scene."

"Wait. Conglomerate? You mean that Buck person? His people? The people your dad was working for? They are at the crime scene?"

David scrunched his eyebrows as he processed all her questions.

"I didn't realize we'd gone as far as the crime scene already. Why would they be looking at the crime scene? Is it still marked off? Is—" She darted back toward the boardwalk, slipping from his grasp.

"Leigh, wait." He ran after her.

"I have nothing to fear from these Conglomerate people, David. They don't know me, and I'm not a business owner. What they want with the crime scene, now that I want to know. Not to mention, I blacked out before I got a look at what really happened. If I'm going to help you clear your father, I need to see what I missed the other night."

The words passed too quickly for David to come up with a response, so he had no choice but to follow her. They emerged onto the boardwalk to find it empty, and David breathed a sigh of relief. Not Leigh. She planted hands on her hips. The crime scene lay ahead of them, and with the memory of his father leaning over Amy, blood on his shirt, still so fresh, he shivered.

Beside him, however, Leigh stood still, her breath hitching, and David moved his attention to her. Her eyes had glazed over, as if she saw a scene not currently in front of her. She was likely reliving Friday night, just as he had been. The sounds, the smells, the feelings. He hated to see such a strong woman plagued by horrors she shouldn't have witnessed.

He gently wrapped his fingers around her upper arm. "Leigh?"

She yelped. "Don't scare a girl like that." She pressed a hand against her chest as if that could slow her heart rate.

"You okay?" David leaned forward, trying to get on her eye level. Assure himself of the truth.

"I'm fine." Adaleigh hugged her middle. "Would you take me to your grandmother's house?"

David nodded. He stuffed his hands into his pockets, and they walked side by side, back the way they'd come. He wanted to put his arm around her, but what right had he to be so familiar? Especially when he was the one who got her into this predicament. He should never have asked her out that first night. He knew better. His life was far too messy to invite a woman into it.

"I'm sorry," he said, meaning so much more than those simple words.

Leigh stopped. "For what?"

"All this." He flopped his hands as if to encompass existence itself. "Near drownings, drunken men, murder. My dad. I can't believe you haven't run screaming for your life." Any other girl would have, and Leigh seemed to have an exponentially greater reason. Whatever it may be.

She chewed on her lip, moonlight casting shadows on her face. David held his breath.

Adaleigh considered her words as her nerves returned to a more natural level of alertness. David's uncertainty tugged at her. She had it in her power to reassure him. But was she brave enough to tell him the truth? That she enjoyed spending time with him despite the unplanned excitement?

"You're an intriguing person, Leigh." David jumped into the silence she'd let hang too long. "Somehow you've pulled out of me things I haven't told many people."

Adaleigh prided herself in her ability to read people, and having a degree that supplied the labels for what she tended to notice naturally only deepened that confidence. However, the look in David's eyes reflected something much deeper. Somehow, this stranger cared about her. She'd never met a man who took the time to see her for who she really was.

"Then you should know something more about me." She moved casually up the boardwalk. As innocuous as her forthcoming truth might be, her heart still beat wildly at the idea of sharing her secrets with someone. Other men had rejected her for less. "I'm a swimmer and a member of the Women's Athletic Club in Chicago."

"Wait." He stopped square in front of her. "You're a swimmer? As in, for recreation?"

"Not just recreation." Adaleigh laughed. "I competed in high school. Won a few times too."

"No wonder you felt confident rescuing Matt." He cracked a smile. "I have a feeling there are more surprises you're hiding."

"Perhaps." Adaleigh started walking again. His positive reaction urged her to share more. Could she?

"Okay." David jogged to catch up. "Besides swimming, what else do you like to do?"

Adaleigh hesitated.

"C'mon." David nudged her. "Just tell me one little thing that you enjoy besides athletics. I told you about fishing."

Adaleigh looked out past the bobbing lights of the boats to the inky water beyond. "I also—"

"Boy, howdy," someone shouted from the door of a building to her left. "Aren't you the gal who saved the Hitchens boy?"

Adaleigh froze.

"It is." Another guy barged past the first one. "She also witnessed Martins murder that girl."

Three more burly guys, swarthier versions of the largest men she'd ever met, joined the first two, blocking her way and separating her from David. The grainy scent of hops swirled around her. Why weren't the police stopping all this illegal activity at the docks?

"You sure that's the dame?" Another guy, probably the soberest of the group, managed to part the circle and meet her gaze. "You're her? What's your name?"

Her mouth bobbed open, but no sound emerged.

"She's the one," the first guy said.

"Never seen her before today," the second said. "Where you from, doll?"

"Yeah, what's a pretty gal like you doing here in Crow's Nest?" another asked.

"How'd you feel, saving the Hitchens kid?" The soberest guy pressed close, sweat overcoming the smell of alcohol. "Did you plan on being a heroine? Did you know Matt beforehand? Did you know Amy? Did you see Martins murder her?"

With every question, he edged Adaleigh toward the side of the board-walk, the lake at her back. Closer and closer to the rolling abyss. The gas lamp above shown down like a spotlight, casting her in full display. The collective surge of men was too strong for her to push them back, and David was nowhere to be seen.

"My editor would kill me if I don't get a shot." The sober man pulled a folding camera from his vest pocket.

Pictures! No, no, no. She couldn't be in a picture. But the words still wouldn't come. Her chest tightened, quickening her breathing. Black edged her vision. Trapped. Again. Two choices ... which would it be—the snapping of the camera or the lapping of the dark water behind her?

CHAPTER SEVEN

"**B**ack up!" David's shout penetrated the crowd, and he shouldered through to put himself between them and Leigh.

"Aw, we're just havin' a bit o' fun," one of the drunken men muttered.

"She's a right nice 'un," another said.

"Nice? This is gold." Greg Alistar, a reporter with the *Crow's Nest Gazette*, loosed a maniacal laugh. Or did David only imagine it?

Someone hollered something about beer, and the crowd dispersed, the newspaperman vanishing into the night before David could stop him. Beer. A decade of the Eighteenth Amendment hadn't changed a thing. Wisconsin beer companies made ice cream or some other product, but they also sold hops and make-your-own-beer kits. And pharmacies sold medicinal beer. Though these men must have access to a more prolific stash.

He felt Leigh sink to her knees behind him, dousing his anger. He set his hand on her shoulder and squatted beside her. She didn't acknowledge him. Instead, an evolution of emotion charged across her countenance until she slowly raised her chin, determination replacing all the others.

"I have to go," she whispered, her gaze over his shoulder.

"It's okay, I'll walk you home." He clasped her elbow to help her to her feet but froze as she kept muttering as if he weren't there.

"If I leave now, I can make it to the next county by morning."

"Next county?" A stone dropped into David's stomach.

"No money left." She stood without his help. "I'll only be able to go as far as my tank will hold out."

"Tank?" Her motorcycle?

"Then I'll ditch the bike and—"

"Leigh!" He didn't mean to shout at her, but she was talking nonsense.

Red climbed her cheeks as she looked up at David as if seeing him for the first time. Had she not realized she spoke aloud? No matter. Those men had scared her. He'd do his best to keep his voice calm and focus on helping her.

"You're safe, Leigh. We'll go back to my grandmother's house—"

"He took my picture." Her hazel eyes sparkled with tears in the gas lamplight. "I can't be found."

"Hey, hey." David tightened his grip on her shoulders. "It's going to be fine. We'll figure this out together"

"You don't understand. I—"

"Come here." He pulled her into his arms. Couldn't help himself. She looked so broken, so in need of someone to care. Tears dripped onto his shirt as her body shuddered against him. Fierce protectiveness battled his usual calm propriety. He rested his chin on her head. "Tell me what's scared you so badly. Let me help."

Suddenly, she pulled away, her eyes darting like a cornered rabbit's.

He clasped her hand and she didn't move. "You don't need to tell me, but my uncle can help. Before you do anything rash, please, at least talk to him."

She met his gaze, the trust in her eyes hooking his heart. "Can we go now?"

"Absolutely." In that moment, he'd have escorted her halfway around the world.

"What's this?" Detective O'Connor answered his door carrying a lamp and wearing jeans and an old green flannel shirt, looking to Adaleigh like a scruffy lumberjack straight out of the Northwoods. He raised his chin to look at her and David through the spectacles perched on his nose. Samson poked his nose past his master's legs.

"Should we or the mosquitoes come inside?" David said, his hand resting lightly at the small of her back as if ready to catch her if she turned to run.

Detective O'Connor stuffed his spectacles into his shirt pocket as he raised a bushy eyebrow. "Come in. Coffee's hot." He left David to close the door.

Adaleigh stood in the entry, her thoughts jumping like popping corn. She closed her eyes and let out a long breath. Until she felt David shift closer and she opened her eyes. He gave a concerned smile but stayed quiet as he led her to an old couch next to the fiery hole of a burning fireplace. Across from the sofa stood two upholstered chairs, and between was a coffee table made of a slice of sanded tree trunk

David left her there and she used the time to take in the rest of the small house. On the other side of the room was a woodstove—where David talked with his uncle—an icebox, a pump sink, a small table, and only two straight-back chairs. A narrow door behind her must be the door to his sleeping quarters. There were no decorations to speak of, just the knotted wood of the walls and ceiling. Not one inkling of a feminine touch appeared in the woodsy place. Had the man never married?

Despite its lack of femininity, the house had a warmth about it, like the house was an extension of the great fir trees that filled his yard and lined the drive. He lived off an old, narrow, winding road, only seven minutes from town—she had counted each minute since David retrieved his grandmother's Chevrolet—but with no neighbors that she could detect in the dark.

David sat next to her, sliding a cup along the coffee table until it was within her reach. Detective O'Connor settled himself in one of the chairs. He stretched out his legs and seemed to be studying Adaleigh. Her hands had stopped shaking, so she reached for her mug. This house definitely had a settling quality. The mantel clock ticked. Samson licked his paws, grunted, then rolled over on the hearth rug.

Finally, she broke the silence, repeating what she'd told David. "I need to leave."

"But your coffee ..." Detective O'Connor met her gaze, daring her to be completely forthcoming.

"I mean Crow's Nest."

"I know." Detective O'Connor slurped his coffee. "David told me what happened while he poured your coffee."

"Then you know why I've got to leave tonight."

He raised a long, bony finger. "First tell me the real reason you left home. Why is having your picture in our little newspaper so bad?"

"I can't be found." The panicked feeling returned, and she set the mug down with a slight clatter.

"By whom?"

Nothing seemed to faze the man. Drat him.

Out of the corner of her eye, Adaleigh could see David's face. His kindness, interest, and concern. Just like on the boardwalk. She could still feel his strong arms around her. The impropriety of him holding her in sight of anyone who walked by couldn't shake the comfort it gave her. She took a deep breath. "You won't tell anyone?"

"My badge is over there somewhere." He waved generally toward the kitchen, and she took him to mean he wasn't listening to her story as a policeman.

David shifted to the edge of the sofa, gripping his mug with both hands, his attention fully on her.

"It's about my sister. I need to stay away from Ashley." Adaleigh could tell them that much without getting her in trouble, right?

Detective O'Connor laughed outright, nearly spilling his coffee and sending a spike of hurt through her middle. She should have kept her mouth shut.

"Start from the beginning, ma'am." Detective O'Connor's laughter subsided, but the creases by his eyes didn't go away.

Adaleigh glanced at David, who now wore a suitably serious, if somewhat confused, expression. Whatever Detective O'Connor found amusing, at least David wanted to know. He deserved to know.

She picked up her coffee mug again, needing the security of holding something. "It started on commencement day at university." If she told them everything, she'd have to say the words she'd been avoiding since then.

"Go on," Detective O'Connor said.

Adaleigh looked at David before continuing. He nodded his reassurance.

"My parents ..." She couldn't. The words caught somewhere between her stomach and her mouth. She couldn't say what happened to them, not yet. Saying it made it real. She didn't want it to be real. Surely, these two men didn't need to know *everything*.

Detective O'Connor cleared his throat.

Adaleigh straightened her shoulders. She could do this. As long as she switched the angle of her story. Even still, she avoided both men's eyes. "My sister has always been jealous of me, but we've managed to live in the same house, which wasn't hard considering we had suites all to ourselves."

"Suites?" David interrupted this time.

"Big house." Adaleigh shrugged. She had to stay focused. "After my commencement, my sister ... she ..."

How does a girl actually say the words, *she tried to kill me*?

She'd overcome her sister's jealousy before. Ashley was who she was, and Adaleigh would make the best of it. If that meant running away and beginning again as a penniless stranger in a new place, then so be it. What did it matter that she left home and family? Then the heartache could stay there in the past.

Except, if Ashley found her ... Adaleigh shuddered.

Detective O'Connor let out a big puff of air. "Just say it. How'd she hurt you?"

"What?" The word was out of Adaleigh's mouth before she could stop it.

"Who hurt you?" David seemed as shocked as Adaleigh felt.

"Your sister." Detective O'Connor leaned his elbows on his knees, his eyes narrowed as though he could see her soul. "Knife, wasn't it?"

"H-How did you know?"

"Your reaction at the crime scene." Detective O'Connor flipped his hand. "You're not squeamish—you saved a kid from drowning. But a reminder of nearly being murdered will cause the strongest individual to swoon."

Strongest? Tears jumped to Adaleigh's eyes. No one had ever called her emotionally strong before. Rebellious, stubborn, willful ... emotional, reactionary ...

Detective O'Connor steepled his fingers. "Now you're running away from her because you think the next time you see her, she'll do the job right."

Her body went cold. Then a little jitter started at the top of her spine and worked its way down, like a chunk of snow slipping underneath one's coat on a winter's day.

"Leigh, is he right?" David, already on the edge of the sofa, leaned closer, as if his presence could offer her security.

Adaleigh nodded.

"Why didn't you report your sister?" Consternation colored David's voice.

"It's not worth it." She stared at the fire, suddenly exhausted, all fight gone. She just wanted to curl up next to Samson and fall asleep. Maybe when she woke up, it would all be over.

"Adaleigh!" Detective O'Connor's voice, sharp and accompanied by a snap in front of her face, brought her to attention. As it did David. "The adrenaline is wearing off. You can tell us more later. For now, you need to sleep."

"But the picture in the newspaper?"

Detective O'Connor smiled as he crouched on one knee in front of her and took her hands in his scraggly ones, handing her mug to David. "People may not have believed you before, but they do now. No more running. We're going to get to the bottom of this so you can go home."

"You'd do that for me?"

"I'm a policeman, remember? It's kinda in the job description."

Adaleigh's laugh came out more like a cough. "You said you left your badge in the kitchen."

Detective O'Connor grunted as he pushed himself to sit on the edge of the tree table. "I knew you didn't murder anyone, so it didn't matter. Now let's get you back to my sister's house so you can get a good night's sleep. I'll have a good long talk with that reporter in the morning. You'll be safe until then, I promise."

Grandma met David and Leigh at the front door. She took Leigh's face in her hands, ran her eyes over her expression, and nodded. "David, take her upstairs while I make her a cup of tea."

"But—" He didn't want to leave her, but he wouldn't ruin her reputation by being in the attic room alone with her.

Mrs. Martins turned on her heels down the hallway. "You will do exactly what I asked."

Leigh patted his arm. "It'll be fine."

David held in his protest. She sagged and he wrapped an arm around her waist. Funny thing with fear, once it ebbed, a person wanted to curl up in a ball somewhere safe in order to weather the storm. He knew that from experience. He also knew that once Leigh regained her strength, her fight would roar back like a tidal wave.

They reached the foot of the stairs leading to the third floor, and David slowed, reluctant to let go of her. "I wish there was something I could do or say to make things better."

"You're a good man, David." She rested her head on his shoulder. "Thank you for caring for me tonight."

He stuffed his free hand into his pocket to keep from wrapping her in another embrace. "Is it strange that it feels like we've known each other a lot longer than a couple days?"

"Is that all? Seems like much longer after all we've been through."

"I have tea." Grandma's voice came from the end of the hallway. David and Leigh stepped apart as she appeared with a tray containing a teapot and two cups.

"Let me carry that." David took it from her and led the way up to Leigh's attic room.

"Put it on the bed and git. I'll stay with Leigh." Grandma's voice followed him. "After a fright, I find a cup of tea calms the nerves and helps one sleep. As does a bit of company."

David set the tray on the bed and backed toward the door as Grandma escorted Leigh across the room.

"I'm a bit embarrassed that I reacted so strongly." Leigh tucked her legs under her as she sat on the bed. Her shoulders sagged and she wrapped one arm around her middle as she slipped a loose strand of hair behind her ear. Mercy, how was he supposed to leave the room? "Did Detective O'Connor tell you what happened, Mrs. Martins?"

"He didn't need to. When he called as David drove you home, he only told me to greet you at the door." Grandma poured tea into a cup with a large daisy on the front and handed it to Leigh before pouring tea for herself in the second cup. "I knew as soon as we met, there was more going on with you and it seems to have caught up to you. When you're ready, I'd like to hear about it."

"I—"

She wagged a finger. "Not now. Tomorrow. After you've slept."

Leigh glanced between David and his grandma, her cup resting in her lap. "Are you sure it's safe to stay here? I don't want to put anyone in danger."

"Dearie, there are a lot of frightful things in the world." Grandma sipped her tea. "We cannot live in constant fear. We put up reasonable safeguards and trust the good Lord with the rest."

Leigh frowned.

David drew a breath to underscore what Grandma said, but she kept speaking. "I'm an old woman, Leigh. I've learned that we cannot worry about what we cannot control or we'll go mad, surrounded only by our self-made fortresses."

"What's worse than knowing someone wants to kill you?" Leigh's words were more of a desperate cry and it pierced David's heart.

Grandma set her cup down beside the pot with a slight rattle. "Do not fear, child, we will be vigilant so you are safe to sleep."

Emotion clogged David's throat. How often had his grandmother said those same words to him after his mother died?

Leigh sniffed as she set her full cup beside Grandma's. "Thank you for taking me in."

"It does my heart good to help a bright young woman like you." Grandma tucked the tray against her hip as she pulled down the blankets—David's cue to leave. "You give me hope, and in the midst of pain, I must hope."

As David quietly closed the door, he heard Leigh ask, "Why does Detective O'Connor want to help me?"

"Oh, I suppose you remind him of someone."

A frown twitched David's brows downward. Who would that be?

Tuesday, June 3

The next morning, David hated leaving the house without first check-ing on Leigh, but he left too early, especially this week, and he couldn't be late.

Now he sat on the rocking *Tuna Mann*, thermos of coffee beside him, mending hooks along the trotlines, and trying not to think of the mysterious woman he wanted to protect. His uncle had called her *Adaleigh* last night. A beautiful name and it fit her better than Leigh. It also made sense that she didn't want anyone to know her real name, not after the story she told.

Adaleigh. He ran her name through his mind again.

The sun rose before the bow, leaving the stern cloaked in the shadow of the wheelhouse. David lowered his flatcap as he watched the shore-line recede. Leigh—Adaleigh—said she liked mornings. Because of their hope.

God, help her wake to that hope when she opens her eyes. Show her the new mercies You give her each new morning. Let her know of Your great faithfulness.

"David, your name is, right?" The new man, Weber, plopped down next to him. A stout man who lumbered as he crossed the bobbing deck.

David didn't have the energy for idle gossip or irritating greenhorns. "Whatcha need?"

"Teach me what's you're doing. I'm here to learn."

The man might talk a lot, but what a nice change to actually have a little willing help about the boat. "Alrighty then, here's what you do ..."

Just as David, Detective O'Connor, and Mrs. Martins promised, Adaleigh woke the next morning alive and well in the bed on the third floor of Mrs. Martins's house. Light streamed in the east window like a warm hug. She snuggled under the quilt. The details of all that followed the photographer ambush were a little fuzzy, but she knew she owed her current state to David.

Her heart panged. He had seen the raw side of her. Sirlands did not reveal that type of information to anyone, especially someone of a different gender. It wasn't proper. It wasn't refined. Adaleigh sighed, recalling the safety of David's arms again. Who was she to ever follow those rules, anyway? It wasn't in her blood.

But... *What if David doesn't like me now?*

Adaleigh sat straight up in bed. What in grasshoppers did she just say? No way would she ever think such a girlish thought if she were operating in her right mind. Those words had to be some other voice talking because the whole wishy-washy female thing wasn't her. And, God help her, it never would be.

She tossed back the covers. They were coarser than she was used to, but they kept her warm, so what did it matter? People mattered. Yet a few-day friendship was just an acquaintance. It couldn't mean anything, and she wouldn't tell him any more about herself.

Right.

Adaleigh flopped back on her pillow. The man had managed to get into her head the first moment she met him, when he pulled her out of the water as panic threatened to drown her, and that made the decision to leave even harder.

Reality said to run. Logic said to draw danger away from such a nice family. Then why did her heart not want to listen? Why was she willing to risk sacrificing her safety—and theirs—to stay? Did finding a home, a family, really mean that much to her?

What did she even know about this family? They seemed as broken as her own. The dad was arrested for murder, for heaven's sake. Yet Mrs. Martins took her in without question. Detective O'Connor looked out for her. And David cared about her.

Was she willing to give that up? Maybe the events of the past few weeks had her more vulnerable than usual, but having a friend right now meant more than she wanted to admit. In the light of day, the terror of last night seemed but a shadow. Detective O'Connor was right—decisions like this were best made in sunlight.

She let her thoughts coalesce as she dressed. It came down to whether Detective O'Connor convinced the reporter to not print her picture. Then she could decide if she would stay in Crow's Nest.

First step in place, Adaleigh peered out the east window. Was David's boat already out on that sparkling water? Seemed like a good fishing day. Not only was the sun shining brightly, but the air appeared fresh and the sky cloud-free. Seagulls floated over the water. A sailboat headed out of the harbor. Even *the gloomiest night will wear on to a morning*, Stowe said in *Uncle Tom's Cabin*.

The nagging thought that had played in her mind while she dressed rose more strongly. At first, she hadn't lent much credence to it, but what if it had merit?

What if Detective O'Connor was right and Ashley just wanted to scare her and wouldn't track her down to kingdom come? What if the safest place for Adaleigh was right here in Crow's Nest where she could live with a good family?

What if he was wrong?

Leaving that nerve-wracking train of thought behind, she made her way downstairs to find Detective O'Connor himself sitting at the kitchen table and sipping his coffee. Samson raised his head from his paws at her arrival.

"Mornin'." Detective O'Connor nodded as she walked over.

Samson stretched, then stood, his head at her hand. Adaleigh scratched behind his ear.

"Well?" It was the best prompt she could verbalize before her morning coffee.

Detective O'Connor's eye twitched. He took a slurp. Adaleigh waited.

"Marie is at the church for Amy's burial, so you'll have to make your own."

Burial. She hated the thought and never wanted to attend another. Not after having to survive burying her parents. "Why aren't you there?"

"Because I'm here. Now get yourself breakfast while you're at it."

Detective O'Connor and his cryptic answers. She was not awake enough to deal with any of this. She fumbled in the kitchen for a good two minutes before she got a new pot brewing on the stove and bread in the oven. Then she pulled out the chair across from the detective.

Detective O'Connor smiled from under that mustache. "Take a breath. Wake up."

Adaleigh rested folded hands on the table.

He chuckled. "This afternoon, I've arranged for you to join me as Alistar interviews Lizzy and Mark Hitchens."

Hitchens? Matt's parents? "Why?"

"Matt is fully recovered, and his parents insist on meeting you. They're the type of people who get what they want."

That type of family did not intimidate her. Her parents were that type of couple. "I didn't save the child because I wanted praise," Adaleigh said. "There is no need to meet them. I—"

"I know." Detective O'Connor stopped her. "But without you, their little boy may have died. You should meet them."

Heat rose in her face, and her lungs tightened. "So much for hiding out. My sister is going to find me. You said you'd help, but meeting this family is only going to make it worse."

Detective O'Connor set down his mug to give her his full attention. "The reporter agreed to keep your picture out of the paper in return for this exclusive. Meeting with Mr. and Mrs. Hitchens gives the added benefit of keeping Matt's near-drowning in its proper place. In other words, not blown out of proportion."

"And being a murder witness?"

"I warned the reporter to keep that off the record." Detective O'Connor paused.

Adaleigh suspected he had much more to say on the subject, but she wasn't prepared to drag it out of him, not this early in the morning, anyway. "As a witness, could I leave town?"

"Let's not worry about that right now."

Adaleigh rose to get her coffee. "I promise I'm not making this a bigger deal than it is."

"I know. You're scared. But work with me to package your story. You're the heroine who saved Matt Hitchens, not a witness to a murder. With that framework, attention on you should blow over after the interview. Then the focus will turn to the murder investigation, not you. You'll be safe here until then." He tapped the table to make her look at him. "There's one road in and one road out of Crow's Nest, and everyone here recognizes a stranger. If your sister shows up, we will both hear her coming."

Adaleigh nodded, digesting this information. Rhetoric was a powerful tool. Done right and it could shape a narrative. If the people of Crow's Nest associated her with being Matt's rescuer, then they wouldn't necessarily connect her with the ongoing investigation, which should keep her in a good light, a protective light. She blew out a breath. This could work.

"Good." Detective O'Connor smiled and resumed relaxing with his coffee. "Interview is at three this afternoon."

Interview? The word finally snapped into place. This wasn't about her or the reporter. Adaleigh returned to the table with her coffee. "You're using this as an opportunity to talk to Mr. and Mrs. Hitchens about Amy. She was their babysitter. This so-called interview is just a ruse, isn't it?"

Detective O'Connor's mustache twitched.

"Why do you want me—and worse, a reporter—present while you interrogate them about Amy?"

"You are too smart for your own good." Detective O'Connor took another sip. "Don't I smell your toast burning?"

Adaleigh rolled her eyes but hopped up to rescue her bread. "Could David's dad have killed Amy?"

"I can't talk about the case," Detective O'Connor said. "But I will say that Frank has caused Marie heartache most of his adult life. He's her only child."

"Do you think he's innocent?"

"Marie is convinced."

"Are you?"

Detective O'Connor turned to face her straight on. "I'm never convinced of anything until there is proof."

Adaleigh frowned. Now she understood why David was so anxious to find out the truth for himself. Getting any details out of Detective O'Connor took every ounce of her rhetorical and psychological abilities, and she still couldn't manage to come away with any significant information.

She buttered her toast and switched tacks. "How about telling me about the Hitchens family?"

Detective O'Connor looked at her sideways, as if he knew she was aiming at more than information about the family whose boy she saved. "Mark is a successful businessman. Lizzy is active in the community. They have two kids, Matthew and Sarah."

She waited for more, but Detective O'Connor changed the subject. She'd just have to pay close attention this afternoon at his "interview." Maybe she'd learn something to help David, seeing that he'd helped her so much already.

CHAPTER EIGHT

C aptain Mann looked up from the papers sprawled over the front counter as David entered the shop after finishing cleanup from the morning outing. "Martins, I need you to pull up records from last summer."

David tugged off his flatcap, blinking to adjust his eyes to the semi-darkness. He should've just kept walking if he wanted to go home for lunch. Instead, he'd followed his responsible nature and peeked his head into the shop to let his boss know where he could find him.

"I want to compare cost and profit from last year to this year."

Since when did Mann want to study numbers? He left that to David for a reason. Did it have something to do with Spelding? "It's early in the season, but I can plot a projected profit for the summer."

"No. I want hard figures." Mann ambled away from the counter, toward the back room. "And I need it before supper."

So David wouldn't make it home for lunch after all. No chance to check whether Adaleigh decided to stay or flee nor how his grandmother fared after attending Amy's burial. "Why do you need these numbers, sir?" he called after his boss.

"It ain't your place to ask why, Martins. Just get 'em for me." Mann slammed the door behind him.

Of course, word got out about Adaleigh's meeting with the Hitchens family. Crow's Nest was a typical small town, and gossip seemed to spread like wildfire in a small town. The reality of this struck when Samantha poked her head in at the attic door just after lunch.

Adaleigh had already tended the garden and and laundered her clothes as Mrs. Martins taught her yesterday, so while the older lady retreated to her own room for a rest from her emotional day, leaving the downstairs empty, Adaleigh curled onto her bed with a book from the Martins' bookcase. That's how Samantha found her.

Adaleigh sat up. "What can I do for you?"

From the doorway, Samantha gave a condescending glare. "This." She waved a finger around in a circle encompassing all of Adaleigh. "This must change."

"Pardon?"

She let out an exasperated sigh. "Since we have an association, you cannot be dressed like *that*." Again, the all-encompassing circle.

"Samantha." Adaleigh shifted so she sat on the edge of her bed. "I have a change of clothes I plan to wear."

The young woman raised a black eyebrow. "It's better than ..." She circled her finger again.

"This? Yes."

Samantha snatched the book out of Adaleigh's hands, tossed it aside, and grabbed her arms. "Still. You need something fresh, so come with me, or I will ..." She stopped, obviously thinking of the worst thing she could do.

She must've never come up with what it was because instead of giving Adaleigh another chance to refuse, Samantha practically dragged her out the door.

A short walk brought them to a bank of storefronts located along what locals considered Main Street, one block inland from the board-walk. Growing up, Adaleigh hated being fitted for clothes. Standing like a statue for some critical-eyed woman to take one's measurements felt like standing before a judgment seat. She had such an average body type—five foot six, slim waist, slight hips, and a somewhat small bust—the seamstresses were always and forever trying to add padding and shaping to make her appear more feminine in the right places.

"My friend is apprenticed here." Samantha held open the door to Rose Wittlebush's seamstress shop. Rose—wasn't that Mrs. Martins's friend?

Samantha tossed her bobbed hair as she waltzed inside with swinging hips. It was as if the young woman transformed into a daring flapper right before Adaleigh's eyes. Adaleigh expected an older woman to greet them, so surprise shot through her when a young man with blond hair and a blue pinstripe suit appeared. Sean, Amy's boyfriend ... and Samantha's crush.

David ran his fingers over his hair, knowing the action would leave it in disarray, but that's exactly how these numbers looked to him.

He'd been at the task for over an hour now. Pulling out last year's books had been simple. Only they didn't match up to what he'd recorded in his accounting pages—records Mann didn't know he kept. The locked drawer was just behind the counter, but since Mann left the bookkeeping to David and David believed in redundancy for just such a situation as this, the documents stayed untouched after year's end.

Now, however, David dragged out last year's record box and set it on the counter. Then he pulled out the master sheet and compared it to the one he'd gathered that afternoon. As he'd suspected, the profit lines didn't match. In fact, not only did they not match—his copy said they were in the black, but the shop's copy showed a rather large red number.

Unease settled in David's gut. Why would there be such a discrepancy? Other than himself and Captain Mann, who else had access to the books? Were they really so much in debt that Mann could lose the business?

David meticulously copied the relevant information from both sheets, replaced the box and the books, double-checked the locks, then placed the folded copies in his inner coat pocket. Mann would be irate if he found out, but financial integrity mattered to David, leaving him no choice but to show the information to Uncle Mike, even if doing so cost David his job.

"Good afternoon." Sean nodded at Adaleigh and Samantha, looking Samantha up and down. "How may I help you?"

"We're here for Leigh." Samantha smiled at him.

Adaleigh resisted rolling her eyes. Barely. They were not here for any other reason than Samantha wanted to see Sean.

"I have just the dress." Sean disappeared into the back.

Samantha wandered over to a mannequin displaying a pink dress in the latest fashion. Straight lines, skirt ending at the knee, slight sleeves. "What do you think?" she asked.

"Pretty." Adaleigh smiled at her. No doubt the young woman was working up to her real question.

"Do you think Sean would like it?" Pink dots appeared on her cheekbones.

Ah, there it was. Adaleigh waited. Samantha would talk if given space. Samantha moved to the other mannequin. This one wore a light-blue dress with a deep-V neckline. Before Samantha could say more, Sean returned.

"Come this way." He took them to a privacy area and left them with the garment. Adaleigh immediately knew it would be perfect. It had a modest collar, the skirt ending at the knees, with swaths of deep olive green over a creamy white. It would go well with her hair and eye color. She quickly made work of undressing, then slipped into the new dress. For a ready-made dress, the fabric was soft and cool. It draped in a straight line down her sides, made to conceal the curves other women had and so fit her just right.

Adaleigh turned before the mirror. "Samantha, what do you think?" No answer. "Samantha?"

She stood next to Adaleigh, but her face had grown cloudy. Adaleigh followed her gaze, stepping to see around the privacy screen. Sean was looking at a picture. Deep grooves marred his face, giving him an aged look that was even less attractive than the old men who visited Adaleigh's father. Yet Adaleigh recognized Sean's expression. The frown. The water that pooled in the corners of his eyes. The slump of the shoulders. Adaleigh felt awkward watching—no, spying—on his moment of grief. Had he really loved Amy, even while flirting with another woman?

"Samantha?" Adaleigh whispered.

She finally disengaged her eyes to look at Adaleigh. "Why did he court her?" Samantha glanced back at Sean's private grief. "He was too good for her. He's one of the nice men. Not proud or overbearing, like the kind she usually chased. Amy was destined to hurt Sean. We tried to warn him, but he wouldn't listen. Now she's dead and Sean is crushed."

"You care about him."

She nodded. "In a small town like this, your school friends are your social circle until you die." She rolled her eyes. "And isn't that just a cheery thought?"

"So your friends and Amy's friends didn't make up the same circles?"

She choked on a laugh. "No way! Are you going to buy that?"

Adaleigh ran her hands over her hips. Just a few weeks ago she wouldn't have thought twice about such a purchase, no matter that her mom would have thought it inferior. Now, without a penny to her name ... "I would love to, but I cannot today."

"Thanks for meeting me, Uncle Mike." David glanced around at who might be eavesdropping on their conversation. The boats on either side of the *Tuna Mann* also belonged to his boss, and their crews had finished for the day. Anyone else wouldn't think twice that David spoke with his uncle aboard the boat.

"What's got you so skittish?" Uncle Mike leaned against the side of the wheelhouse, crossed his ankles. Samson plopped down on the deck, massive jowls wagging as he panted.

David handed over the profit summaries. Waited for his uncle's reaction.

"They're from the same time frame." His bushy eyebrows scrunched together. "Which is the right one?"

"I thought the one where we made a profit was correct, but the books say the other one is."

"Did you talk to Mann about this?"

"Not yet. I'm worried it has something to do with why Guy Spelding booked the boat this week. Have you confirmed he has ties to the Conglomerate?"

"I'll dig into it." Uncle Mike rolled up the papers. "What are your plans for the rest of the afternoon?"

"I wanted to go home for lunch ..."

"Leigh is meeting with Mark and Lizzy Hitchens, Greg Alistar, and myself in twenty minutes."

David blew out a breath. She was still in town. *Thank you, God.* Not that meeting Greg sounded like a good plan.

"I'm sure she would appreciate it if you joined us afterwards," Uncle Mike said, an unmistakable gleam in his eyes.

David stopped himself from responding with a resounding yes, like he wanted to do. The grin playing under Uncle Mike's mustache said he read David's reaction perfectly. Fortunately, David spotted Mann ambling down the wharf.

"I gotta get back to work," he said.

Uncle Mike caught on and whistled for Samson to follow him off the boat. "Meet us at the Wharfside when you're finished."

"Making supper plans, Martins?" Mann ignored Uncle Mike and climbed aboard. "I trust you finished the project I asked of you?"

David held in a sigh. He might not be able to meet Adaleigh, after all.

The warm morning had given way to a muggy afternoon by the time Detective O'Connor escorted Adaleigh to the Wharfside. He'd left Samson with Mrs. Martins, whose spirits rose immensely at the news that one of her friends—Rose, the seamstress—planned to stop by. It made Adaleigh feel better about leaving her too.

"The reporter's name is Greg Alistar," Detective O'Connor explained as they sat at a corner table by the window. The inside of the Wharfside Café was decorated with a distinctly nautical theme. Nets covered the entrance side of the front desk, while fishing poles hung from the walls beside fish mounts and pictures of fishermen holding up their catch. The frame behind them showed a four-foot-long fish in the arms of one happy fisherman.

"Don't say anything you do not want printed." Detective O'Connor brought her back to the present.

No kidding. Adaleigh planned to keep her mouth shut. The less Mr. Alistar printed about her, the less likely it would help Ashley find her. *God, give me strength to hold my tongue.* She immediately recognized Mr. Alistar as he entered the café—short brownish-blond hair, closely shaved scruff, and a dopey expression. Regardless, he seemed shrewder than most. Perhaps more conniving. Either way, she didn't trust him.

He came with an entourage. The man behind him carried a tripod camera, had a mop of rusty brown hair, and looked to be in his late twenties. The lady held a notebook and pencil, had perfectly coiffed blonde hair, and looked to be even younger.

"Mr. O'Connor." Mr. Alistar held out his hand to the detective. His easy grin made Adaleigh dislike him even more.

"Mr. and Mrs. Hitchens have yet to arrive." Detective O'Connor waved Mr. Alistar to a seat.

"And you're our mysterious heroine." Mr. Alistar shook her hand. "I am dying to learn more about you. Let's start with your name."

"Anonymous, Greg," Detective O'Connor intoned.

"Ah, yes." He looked at her. "You agree?"

Adaleigh nodded emphatically.

He smoothed his lapels as he sat. "Were you at the crime scene the other night?"

She stared at him.

"Stick to the topic," Detective O'Connor nearly growled.

Adaleigh wanted to roll her eyes. She'd seen this move before with her father and his business associates. There would always be a few moments of posturing, like two wild bucks declaring their territory.

Mr. Alistar snapped his fingers. The young man set up his camera. The woman sat behind the reporter, pencil poised. An edge of panic took root in Adaleigh's lungs. This woman planned to record every word they spoke.

"No pictures, Greg." Detective O'Connor waved at the camera.

"You're tying my hands, O'Connor."

"No pictures. No names." Detective O'Connor spoke firmly, and Adaleigh released a quiet breath. She didn't have the energy to spar with Greg Alistar.

"How about a town, even a state where you're from?" Mr. Alistar looked at Adaleigh.

She shook her head.

"At least give me something!"

"You'll have plenty," Detective O'Connor said. "Here are Mr. and Mrs. Hitchens."

This was a powerful couple. Adaleigh blinked. Growing up in a wealthy circle, strong women didn't intimidate her, but Mrs. Hitchens gave them all a run for their money, especially with the way she dressed. She wore a fitted black skirt and jacket with a white shirtwaist. Her hair was wrapped up in a twist. And black pumps made her nearly as tall as her husband. However, Adaleigh also knew feigned quality when she saw it, and Mrs. Hitchens was trying too hard.

Mr. Hitchens, on the other hand, gave off the appearance of a relaxed businessman. His unbuttoned suit was a finely tailored gray one, with an embroidered vest. But Adaleigh spotted a scuff on his black-and-tan wingtips. Dad would have *tsk*-ed at that. Thinking of her parents' reactions to Mr. and Mrs. Hitchens relaxed her shoulders. She could handle this.

"Mrs. Hitchens, a delight. Mark, good to see you." The reporter pounced on them. They shook hands, exchanged pleasantries. "Thank you for coming out to The Wharfside."

When they finished, Detective O'Connor took his turn. "I'll be sitting in, Mrs. Hitchens. Mark." Mrs. Hitchens gave him a practiced smile. Mark, a nod. Detective O'Connor pointed his chin at me. "And this—"

"Such a pleasure!" Mrs. Hitchens circled the table to give Adaleigh a strong hug. The bulb of the camera popped as Mrs. Hitchens's perfume slapped Adaleigh across the face. She held her breath until the woman let go.

"Thank you." Mr. Hitchens reached across the table to shake her hand.

At the praise, Adaleigh shrank back into her seat. Sure, she did something many women wouldn't have done, something many men might not even be trained to do, yet she hadn't thought twice about saving a life. She had done a good thing, rescuing the boy, despite the unwelcome attention.

"Tell us about yourself." Mrs. Hitchens stole Detective O'Connor's chair. She leaned across the corner of the table, invading Adaleigh's space. "We want to know everything. Where are you from? How did you see Matthew? How did you know how to save him?"

Adaleigh glanced at Detective O'Connor. How was she supposed to answer this lady's questions with a note-taking secretary and nosy reporter hanging on her every word? Detective O'Connor only shrugged. Nice help he was.

Mrs. Hitchens set her purse on her lap. "When my husband told me you were still in town and that we had the opportunity to meet you, I dropped everything to be here. There is a Ladies' Aid Meeting this afternoon, but I told them they would just have to wait for me."

Adaleigh stifled a frown. She knew Mrs. Hitchens's type of woman—Mom had been one. Strong. Always in control. And managing the room like a puppet master.

"Now I must find a new babysitter. After Miss Littleburg let my boy fall in the water, I dismissed her immediately." Mrs. Hitchens pressed her lips together. "It's been impossible to find someone new. But you, do you babysit?"

Please don't ask me to take a dead woman's place. "No, ma'am."

A tragic sigh, then a flick of the wrist. "I do not know how I missed the signs. The girl obviously had better things to do than watch my children, and she always had her head turned when she needed both eyes on Matthew and Sarah."

Adaleigh raised her eyebrows. If she sat perfectly still, perhaps Mrs. Hitchens would talk herself to the end of the interview and tell them how Amy ... ended up the way she did. Detective O'Connor and Mr. Alistar must have had a similar idea because neither of them so much as twitched.

"Lizzy." Mr. Hitchens placed a hand over hers. Drat.

"Right, right." Mrs. Hitchens waved her husband away. "We must repay you for saving our son. Are you still in school?"

"You're a student?" Mr. Alistar leapt at the change in subjects. "What school? Did you know Amy before—"

"I'm not looking for any compensation." Adaleigh's back stiffened, but she refrained from rubbing her neck. "I know you are grateful, but please don't make too much of this. Anyone could have saved your boy."

"And what a great way to end this interview." Detective O'Connor clapped a hand on Mr. Hitchens's shoulder. "Alistar, thank you for documenting."

"I'm not—" the reporter protested.

"Mr. and Mrs. Hitchens"—Detective O'Connor ignored the reporter—"if I might get two minutes with you both?"

Caught off guard—exactly as O'Connor had no doubt intended—the others shifted, blinked, and looked around at one another. Adaleigh, of course, didn't mind at all. The focus had moved away from her, allowing her to relax a smidge. Not to mention, she was mighty curious what questions Detective O'Connor would ask the couple.

After a few moments of hemming and hawing on Mr. Alistar's part, Detective O'Connor got him and his posse to leave the café. Mindy arrived with coffee—God be thanked!—and the four of them sat comfortably around the table.

"Such a better environment for talking." Detective O'Connor sipped his coffee.

"Anything is better without Greg Alistar." Mr. Hitchens leaned back in his chair. "Man's got a burr up his hind end."

Detective O'Connor laughed. Adaleigh's cheeks heated, likely flushing as much as Mrs. Hitchens's.

The woman turned to Adaleigh, her shoulder angled to shut out her vulgar husband. "Is there any way I can thank you? Surely, there is some way."

Adaleigh smiled to set the woman at ease. "Nothing, ma'am. I'm glad it all ended well."

"What was Miss Littleburg doing when you first saw her?" Detective O'Connor asked Adaleigh, pulling her and Mrs. Hitchens from their private conversation. Adaleigh looked up to find him studying her as he had that very first day. Hmm. The Hitchens weren't the only ones being *questioned*? She had a mind to just ignore him, but her curiosity to discover what he was about was too strong to resist.

"The first I noticed her," Adaleigh said, "she looked scared because Matthew was already in the water."

Mrs. Hitchens huffed. "She said she'd been through the life-saving classes with the YMCA."

"Was she caught off-guard?" Detective O'Connor swirled his coffee.

"I couldn't say. I didn't see her before Matthew was in the water."

"You implied she has been distracted lately?" This question he directed at Mr. and Mrs. Hitchens.

"Didn't we answer these questions for the chief?" Mr. Hitchens grumbled.

"Hush." Mrs. Hitchens batted her husband's arm. "He's trying to help." She turned to Detective O'Connor. "She used our telephone more than I approved. She did not call the same residences, mind you, but all of them had young men."

"Several residences?" Detective O'Connor raised a bushy brow. "And how do you know this?"

Adaleigh scratched her cheek. Of course, Mrs. Hitchens knew. A woman like her would likely have a contact among the operators.

"When she spoke on the phone, she giggled like a schoolgirl. It's a sure sign of being boy-crazy. I should have dismissed her at once."

"Like I said yesterday, she seemed the same to me." Mr. Hitchens spoke sullenly. "Matthew is an eight-year-old boy. Things happen in a second with him."

"Not to our son!" Mrs. Hitchens glared at her husband.

"It doesn't make it Miss Littleburg's fault." Mr. Hitchens's voice rose.

"Of course, it's her fault!" Mrs. Hitchens's face resumed its pink hue. "We paid her to keep both eyes on the kids at all times."

"We should have given her a second chance."

"Oh no." Mrs. Hitchens faced him squarely. "I should have sent that little weasel off without references so she would never again have another child under her care."

"The girl is dead," Hitchens hissed. "Have a care what you say."

"Our boy almost died!" Her voice echoed in the café, bringing the attention of all the customers to the table. She clapped a hand over her mouth.

Detective O'Connor cleared his throat. "Where were you Friday night?"

"Do not answer, Liz," Hitchens growled.

"I was at a Ladies Social over in Hawk's River." Mrs. Hitchens looked from Detective O'Connor to her husband, a bewildered expression marring her face. Gone was the sophisticated woman of a few moments ago. Adaleigh almost felt sorry for her.

"And you?" Detective O'Connor turned to her husband.

"I'm not answering that." Mr. Hitchens helped his wife to her feet. "We're going now."

Detective O'Connor gave a slight nod. "I'll repeat what Chief Sebastian asked of you. Stay in town in case we have more questions."

"We're not suspects, are we?" Mrs. Hitchens glanced around at the other diners.

"We will discuss more at a later time." Detective O'Connor stood. "I'll take care of the bill. Thank you both for coming today."

Mrs. Hitchens pulled Adaleigh into an unexpected hug and whispered, "We need to talk. Thursday. My house. Twelve-thirty." Then she was gone.

CHAPTER NINE

D avid leaned against the fence surrounding the Wharfside, watching people go by. The afternoon sun blazed hot, and the humidity had risen since the morning. Or maybe the cloying air had more to do with his own annoyance.

As his boss requested, he'd put together the numbers. Two versions of them. Then the captain had failed to reappear in the shanty, and the *Tuna Mann* was gone. All the work, the missed lunch, the two sets of numbers—all of it left David in a sour mood, which meant he had no compunction about taking a break from work to take his uncle up on his offer to join Adaleigh and him after their meeting.

His spirits rose when Greg Alistar, team in tow, left in a huff. His curiosity piqued when, several minutes later, Lizzy and Mark Hitchens stalked out just as upset as the reporter. He could recognize the earmarks of Uncle Mike when he saw them. His mood dipped when he considered Adaleigh had also been in the Wharfside with them. He could only hope she fared much better.

"Waiting on your uncle?" Mindy pocketed her order book as she wove through the tables toward him.

"How'd you know?" He gave her a smile. Why couldn't he have been happy to settle down with a nice girl like her? They'd considered it once, years ago, but both knew they were much better as friends, and his choice felt even more right when he compared the cheerful Mindy to the mysterious Adaleigh. Nevertheless, he cared about Mindy and championed her like the older brother she didn't have.

"Word's gettin' around about Amy's burial." Mindy frowned, her usual light dimmed. David's protective instincts rose. "I know not many people liked her, but what a horrible thing."

"What are you working up to say, Mindy? You can tell me."

She blushed. "I'm not sure if I should say. He wouldn't like it, I know, but ..."

David swung a leg over the rope fencing and in a moment was inside the outdoor area of The Wharfside. He clasped her upper arm with his left hand. "Mindy, what's going on? *He* who? If you—"

"I saw Amy talking with Guy." She blushed a deeper crimson as she spit out her words. "You probably don't know him. He's new in town. Kinda handsome."

"Guy Spelding. We've met." He clamped down on the question of why Mindy used the scoundrel's given name so freely. "What about him?"

"Promise you won't tell him I told you?"

"Told me what? You haven't said anything yet."

She folded her arms across her middle.

"It can't be worse than my imagination is making it right now. You can tell me."

She tilted her head to one side, puffed out a bit of a breath. "Before she died, she and Guy ... I saw them together."

"Together?"

"You know ... together."

"He was kissing her?"

"Brazenly. And it was right before they say you found her, which means maybe he'll know something that would clear your dad. Now I need to get back to work. Don't tell anyone I told you, please?"

She appeared so flustered, all he could do was thank her. "You're a good friend, Mindy."

He'd never cared for Guy Spelding, but the more he learned about the man, the less he liked. And if his instincts were correct, Mindy Zahn knew more about Guy Spelding than was good for anyone, especially her.

Adaleigh spotted David as soon as she and Detective O'Connor emerged from The Wharfside. He stood at the entrance to the outdoor seating area and offered her a private smile before pointing his chin up the boardwalk.

"How'd things go with Alistar and the Hitchens?" David asked.

"Well enough." Detective O'Connor grumbled under his breath. "I strongly dislike that reporter."

"I've got until four-thirty if I'm going to set up for tomorrow and still make it home for supper. I never did get lunch."

Didn't get to eat? Questions swirled in Adaleigh's mind.

"Then how about I get us some ice cream to hold you over?" Detective O'Connor smiled behind his mustache.

"Aw, really, Uncle Mike?" David's eyes lit up, words and expression both resembling a little kid.

So Detective O'Connor was the crazy uncle who'd spoiled his niece and nephews? Adaleigh shook her head. His smile lines should have given it away.

"Why not?" Detective O'Connor led the way south down the board-walk. "How's Sweetie's?"

"Absolutely!" David's grin spread from his eyes to encompass his entire face. He turned to Adaleigh, barely able to keep walking as he talked. "Mr. and Mrs. Swensen opened Sweetie's around the turn of the century. Originally, they were only a soda fountain shop and sold penny candy. However, they quickly added sundaes and then, about ten years ago, they jumped on the ice cream cone craze."

Indeed, he looked the epitome of a kid in a candy store—a hard look to pull off when he stood over six feet in height with a weather-worn face. Adaleigh couldn't stop her smile if she wanted to.

"As children, my friends and I would spend every spare coin there. The most difficult part about going to Sweetie's is making a decision. There are so many options. Not just flavor choices. Cone or bowl. Sundae or float. And then the toppings!"

Detective O'Connor chuckled and pushed David to keep walking. "He's been like this since he was three."

David laughed. "It's the best place in Crow's Nest, and don't you deny it."

His smile was infectious, and the weight that had sat on Adaleigh's chest since the interview floated away.

In another few minutes, they arrived at a one-story building with a façade that made it look two stories. A railing separated it from the boardwalk, and a red-and-white-striped awning set it apart from the rest of the block. On the windows, white letters read, *Sweetie's Ice Cream Parlor.*

Detective O'Connor held open the door, and stepping inside felt like being transported to her childhood.

The black-and-white-checkered floor drew her gaze the length of the narrow room. The right wall held covered bowls of candy, maybe a hundred different types. On the left stood a solid oak counter behind which was the bank of fountain levers. An older man in an apron handed cones to the family seated on stools that bellied up to the bar.

"Grab us one of those, David." Detective O'Connor pointed to the far back where several tables had been set up for those who did not wish to sit at the counter. David obliged and Detective O'Connor looked to her. "What's your choice?"

Her choice? David was right. This would be a tough decision. Should she go with a cone or a sundae? Detective O'Connor ordered a float, then took David's spot holding down the table. David appeared at her elbow.

"Did you make your pick?" he asked.

"It's almost overwhelming."

"If it helps, I'm going sundae, with chocolate syrup and nuts sprinkled on top. Need my sustenance since I missed the lunch hour."

Adaleigh giggled. Giggled? That had to stop. She was not a mindless, flirting female. "I'll take a chocolate ice cream cone."

"Good choice." David's smile almost made her forget her resolve. Almost.

"David, tell me how you know Amy." Uncle Mike broke the easy-going conversation they'd been having since sitting down with their treats. He took a long draw of his float.

David pushed away his empty bowl, thinking through his answer before he said, "Not well. School was a long time ago, but I recall there was always a lot of fuss over her. Several of my fellow students had wished to call on her. I'm sure she considered most of them. Since then, I couldn't say."

"You two ever ...?"

Heat crept up David's neck. "No. She was too ... I don't wish to be unflattering, but she seemed too coquettish, and the other boys fell over themselves for her. It didn't sit right with me." He forced himself not to look at Leigh. "Eh, I liked the quieter gals."

Uncle Mike chuckled, but asked, "She a friend of Samantha's?"

"Sorry, I don't know." David let his answer trail into a frown. He'd lost many friends when he chose work over partying with them. Prohibition seemed to bring out the worst in his friends. Speakeasies and flappers. He wanted to say his choices had more to do with his convictions before God, but the honest answer was, he felt responsible for his siblings and grandmother. He bore the weight his father should have carried to support his family, which did not allow him to behave irresponsibly.

"I'll talk with her," Uncle Mike said, his direct glance expressing that he understood what David didn't say. He turned to Adaleigh, and David's hackles rose. "Your turn. Tell me again everything you remember from when Matthew fell into the harbor."

"Question first." Adaleigh dipped her partially finished cone at him. "You promised to tell me why you are interviewing us again after that other obnoxious man, the chief, asked us all these same things."

Uncle Mike's mustache twitched. David smothered a smile in his napkin. Maybe Adaleigh didn't need him to be her knight. Not that he would mind if she did.

She grinned. "You're not the only one who can spot more to a story, Detective."

Uncle Mike ran a bony hand along his face as if to wipe away his tell, but the crinkles around his eyes remained. "All right." He rested his forearms on the table and folded his hands. "The reason I was brought in on this case is because of my current investigation." He hesitated.

"Chief Sebastian has his own ideas and doesn't want you muscling in on a case involving your nephews," Adaleigh finished for him.

"You have a rare gift for putting pieces together." Uncle Mike shook his head. "Few people are as intelligently observant as you."

A delighted smile flared like a firework on her face, and David's heart emitted a quiet *ahhh*. He bumped her shoe under the table to tell her he agreed with his uncle. She refused to look at him, but he still caught the red climbing her cheeks.

"With that in mind ..."—Uncle Mike returned to his serious voice—"tell me what you observed of Amy. From the beginning of Matt's near-drowning."

"She ..." Adaleigh paused, a distant expression blanking her face. "The event scared her, really scared her, and I think she panicked because she didn't move to help. She just screamed."

"What else do you remember from the scene?"

She shook her head. "I didn't pay that close attention."

Uncle Mike held up a hand. "Close your eyes. Now try again. Describe everything until you can narrow in on Miss Littleburg."

Adaleigh took a deep breath and crushed the fabric of her skirt in her fist. "I feel the sun warm on my face. The seagulls cawing. Stashing my journal to respond to the scream. Staying focused on Amy, I remember blonde hair perfectly coiffed. Rouge and painted lips. Form-fitting dress with a deep-V neckline and a flirty knee-length skirt. Hand at her face while she screamed." Adaleigh blinked. "By the time I got there, she had already reacted to Matt falling into the water, so I don't know what happened prior."

David let out a low whistle. A smile peaked out from under Uncle Mike's mustache. Adaleigh gave a self-depreciating shrug.

"How did you recall such detail?" David asked. He wanted to know more, much more about this woman.

"I pay attention to what people communicate. With so much of our rhetoric not being the words we use, I tend to focus on those details."

"You noticed no other suspicious people around?" Uncle Mike brought them back to the matter at hand.

Adaleigh shook her head again. "Party trick won't work this time. There were plenty of people, but Matt's two friends were the only ones who seemed connected to the scene. Really, I was more surprised that it took a stranger to jump into the water. Most people preferred to gawk than help—other than the guy who performed rescue compressions on Matt."

"Silas Ward." David provided the name. "Local carpenter. Friend." One he should make time to go fishing with, soon. Too many of his friendships had been lost due to working for Captain Mann.

"All right," Uncle Mike spooned out the dregs of his float. "Back to the other night. You two were together?"

"Yes." Heat crept up his neck, but he answered regardless, not willing to let Adaleigh be embarrassed by something that was his idea. "I invited Leigh out to experience the light show. Suggested we walk."

"Uh-huh." A smile lurked under Uncle Mike's mustache. "Why?"

"Why, what?" David demanded.

"Why show a stranger the lights?" A hint of goading laced Uncle Mike's question.

David took the bait. Couldn't help himself. "Why shouldn't I have asked someone to go out with me? Why does that matter? How does it help my father?"

Uncle Mike's eye twitched. "Part of the process."

Adaleigh cocked her head. "You're after something specific."

"Then let me get there," Uncle Mike said. "Now, you two went for a nice walk along the boardwalk?"

David rolled his eyes, and Adaleigh clamped her lips in a straight line.

"Neither of you saw anything unusual? No people out of place? Nothing?"

They both shook their heads.

"Uh-huh." Uncle Mike narrowed his eyes, but a glimmer of mischief peeked through. "What did you notice?"

David leaned back in his chair and folded his arms. "We were talking, Uncle Mike." An edge crept into his voice. "I'm sure you've noticed Adaleigh is an interesting woman."

He snapped his eyes toward her when he realized what words, including the name he'd begun calling her in his head, had left his mouth. She bit her lip, but not fast enough to keep a smile in check. *Phew.* He hadn't messed things up.

"So you didn't notice anything until you saw your father?" Uncle Mike drummed his fingers on the table.

"We had a few interactions with people." Adaleigh saved David from finding words so soon after his outburst. "Is that what you want to know?"

"I want to know everything."

"We met up with Samantha along the boardwalk. We saw Miss Littleburg interacting with a young man Samantha said was her beau."

Adaleigh notably left out much detail from the night, like how Miss Littleburg had thrown out propriety by kissing Sean in public.

"Yes, her beau was Sean Green." Of course, Uncle Mike knew that already.

"Why make us say it?" Adaleigh frowned.

Uncle Mike raised his eyebrows.

Adaleigh emitted a sighing chuckle. "You want us to confirm what you already know. You're not interrogating us—you're using us to double check your facts because you trust what we have to say. We're helping your investigation, not a part of it. You could have told us that from the start, and maybe we'd be more willing to talk."

Uncle Mike laughed. "It took you long enough to piece it all together."

David leaned back in his chair, running his fingers through his hair, tired of Uncle Mike's games. There was another reason he asked these questions of David and Adaleigh together, and David suspected it had nothing to do with the case. He didn't need the man interfering with his ... relationship with Adaleigh.

"How is this going to help my father?" David snapped.

"That I don't know." Uncle Mike turned serious again. "There's something at play here, and I'm trying to gather all the threads so I can untangle it. Given the logistics of your evening, the likelihood that you saw the murderer before Amy was killed is extremely high."

Adaleigh shuddered, and David had to stuff his hands in his pockets to keep from comforting her.

"The murderer might think that, too, especially since you both are known witnesses. But as long as your father, David, is a suspect, the murderer will probably leave you both alone."

"Probably? What do we do now?" David subtly slid closer to Adaleigh.

"As you keep remembering people you met that night, tell me. For now, however, I want to revisit the moment you saw your father. How did he know you were there?"

"He turned around," David freed his hands from his pockets. "He must have heard us."

"Then?" Uncle Mike tapped his thumb against his spoon.

"He came over to us. I went to check on Miss Littleburg."

"No one else was around?" Uncle Mike asked. "No one said they would ring for the police?

"No. As I helped Leigh, my father just stood there watching as if he were in a daze. He smelled of alcohol, and he exhibited drunken behavior, after Leigh ..." *Swooned*. No, that was the wrong word for it. Hyperventilated. Panicked. David played with his spoon. He cast Adaleigh a concerned, yet grateful, glance. "He seemed quite shaken."

"Shaken, how?"

"As much as I'm still really angry with him, it's too unsettling to see that type of weakness and insecurity in my father. The only other time I've seen him like that was ... was with Mom before she died."

Uncle Mike gave the slightest of nods. He understood what David meant without him needing to put it into words. David's shoulders relaxed.

Uncle Mike turned to Leigh. "What about you?"

"I don't remember anything between what David told you about Miss Littleburg until right before you arrived."

"Her breathing was ragged before she collapsed. Thankfully, she responded to the treatments and quickly regained consciousness."

"All right." Uncle Mike stood. "That should do for now."

Adaleigh breathed a sigh of relief David felt to his core.

"My dad?" he asked.

"I hate to say it, David, but the other officers already have him convicted in their minds, so they won't consider whether he's even innocent. Unless I find a different killer, he'll take the blame for it. And you might not like to hear this, but I'm not perfectly sure he didn't do it."

"You know he's innocent."

"I don't, David. You found your dad with the murder weapon and a dead woman. It doesn't get more cut and dry than that. Much to Sebastian's irritation, I'm holding things up because we've found a connection to the Conglomerate. If that link gets severed, there's no hope for your dad unless someone else steps forward to confess."

David pinned down the hurt rising in his heart. "He might be a horrible father, but he wouldn't kill someone." Right?

Walking outside, Adaleigh had to shield her eyes from the sun. Heat rose from the planks of the boardwalk, and she longed for the coolness of the ice cream shop.

"David." Detective O'Connor stopped just outside the door. "When do you see Guy Spelding again?"

Adaleigh almost reminded Detective O'Connor about seeing Mr. Spelding the day Miss Littleberg died, but David answered his uncle first. "He's still commandeering the *Tuna Mann* every afternoon this week, but Mann's shut me out of the crew."

Detective O'Connor rubbed his face. "All right. I'll pay Buck a visit, see what he says. Tell your grandmother I'll be by tonight to pick up Samson." The detective touched the brim of his hat and disappeared down the alley between two of the buildings.

"He's got one dangerous job," David muttered and began walking back toward his shop.

"How long has he been working for the special investigation division?" Adaleigh kept pace, unsure whether David wanted her company, but having nowhere else to go.

"As long as I can remember."

"He must be good at it."

"He is, even if he threatens to retire every couple months."

"He'd get nosy if he didn't investigate for a living."

"That's for sure." David laughed. "He claims he'd just sit on the porch with Samson or go fishing, but he wouldn't be able to avoid sniffing out trouble or staying out of everyone's business. Especially while Buck Wilson roamed free."

Adaleigh smiled. She could picture Detective O'Connor fishing on the boardwalk while interrogating the children who fished beside him to be sure they hadn't cheated on their exams or gotten into other mischief.

She and David walked silently for another few moments, then he asked, "How was the interview with Matt's parents?"

"How'd you ..."

He grinned.

Right. Small towns. She folded her arms at her waist. Mom would have yelled at her to straighten her posture, but it felt more secure to wrap herself in a hug. "That reporter, Mr. Alistar?" Adaleigh shivered.

"He's the *Gazette's* hound dog. Thinks he's the bee's knees because he's their top beat reporter. He forgets the paper doesn't circulate beyond Crow's Nest."

"The strange part was that Mrs. Hitchens wants me to meet her on Thursday."

"Oh?" David's attention turned, snagged by a man in a cowboy hat. The one who helped her save Matt. Silas Ward. David waved him over.

"Good to see you again." Mr. Ward tipped his white hat.

She gave a polite nod. His deep voice had a honey quality about it, like the comfiest chair in the library. His broad shoulders made David look lanky, but they also made Adaleigh feel small.

"How's your grandma holding up?" Mr. Ward turned to David. "My mom wanted to stop by, but what with the funeral planning and then the girls came down with colds after being out for Memorial Day. They're recovering now, but between her and my sister-in-law, it's been a hen house." He chuckled, warmth crinkling the skin around his eyes. He might joke about the women in his life, but he was fond of them.

"I'll make sure she knows." David shuffled his feet. "You been out fishing lately?"

"Not enough for this winter." Mr. Ward dashed his eyes over to Adaleigh before they returned to David. "When things calm down, let's go together."

David agreed and Mr. Ward made his departure.

"I'm sorry about the interruption." David smiled at her and Adaleigh's insides warmed at having his attention to herself again. "You were telling me that Mrs. Hitchens invited you to visit?"

That doused those feelings. "Yes and I have no idea why. Do they live far?"

"No one lives far in Crow's Nest," David strolled forward and Adaleigh kept pace. "With Mann taking out the boat every afternoon, I can get free so I can escort you."

"That's not ... you don't—"

"If you do me a favor." He bumped her shoulder with his arm.

"Favor?"

"Come with me to see my dad."

"At the jailhouse?"

Sorrow drew lines on his face. "I need to get over there to see how he is doing. I know it's no place for a lady, but you seem the strong sort, and I'd appreciate the company. What do you say?"

She considered it for just a moment. "Deal."

"Adaleigh." David caught her hand. "I'm really glad you stayed."

So was she.

CHAPTER TEN

They parted ways at an empty slip beside a boat called the *Salmon Mann*—one of David's boss's boats—leaving Adaleigh with no idea what she should do with herself next.

Walking aimlessly up the boardwalk, she considered her position. The only reason she'd initially arrived in Crow's Nest was because she ran out of money for gas. And food. Now she was involved in a murder investigation while still trying to stay out of her sister's search radius. Panic rose but eased when David's parting words punctured through the haze.

He'd called her Adaleigh.

Hearing him use her real name, as he had at the ice cream parlor, was like being wrapped in a warm embrace. Like the way he held her after that horrid newspaper man took her picture. What would it be like for him to hold her without panic distracting her?

"You're David's friend, right?" said a voice behind her.

Adaleigh jumped and turned to find Mindy, the waitress from the Wharfside Café. She had a small purse over her arm, like she planned to go calling instead of taking orders.

"He's a nice person, you know," she said. "He's got a soft spot for you too. I'm Mindy Zahn, by the way."

"You can call me Leigh."

"I'm glad to meet you, Leigh." Mindy smiled and fell in step with Adaleigh. "How do you like Crow's Nest?"

"So far? It's pretty." And more adventurous than she wanted. Though, about David's hugs ...

"I've always wondered what it would be like to live somewhere outside of Crow's Nest." Mindy shifted her purse to her other arm.

Adaleigh's curiosity piqued. "Have you never traveled?"

"No. I've worked at the café since I turned sixteen and have never left."

"What about college?"

"What's the use of college? Or a girls' school? I'll be working until I marry."

"Is that all you want?" Adaleigh's dreams went well beyond that. Didn't other women dream too?

Mindy shrugged dismissively. "Are you looking for work? If you are, don't work at the café." She leaned close as if to share a profound secret. "The men can get handsy."

"Is that what happened with Amy Littleburg?" It seemed a natural segue. She couldn't solve the harassment for Mindy, but perhaps she could solve the murder of another woman.

Mindy brushed something from her skirt. "Amy didn't work at the café. I don't wish to speak ill of her, but she liked the male attention."

"Did you see her with anyone in particular?"

"Friday morning, Guy and her walked by the café, looking all friend-ly." Mindy's tone had an indecipherable edge.

"How do you know Guy?"

She blushed. "When he first got to town Wednesday, he came into the café, and we ... we went out on a date."

Responding to an instant surge of concern, Leigh placed a hand on her arm. "Was he good to you?"

"He was a charmer. At first. I didn't realize until he wanted more from me than walking me home that he's not someone I wanted to date." Mindy switched her purse to her other arm as they reached the end of the boardwalk. Then she pointed back the way they'd come. "My place is that way, but I liked talking with you, Leigh. You're really nice, and I see why you've caught David's eye. Would you want to get together again soon? I don't have many friends anymore, and David was right that we would get along."

David thought that, huh? A warm spot slowly filled Adaleigh's chest. "How about Friday?" She was getting to have a regular social calendar for a stranger in a small town! It felt comfortable. Good. And she ignored the worry nagging in her mind in favor of those pleasant thoughts.

Mindy brightened. "I get off at three on weekdays. I live above the bakery—it's on the south end of the boardwalk—let's meet at the The Wharfside and go there.

"Sounds delightful."

They said their goodbyes, and Adaleigh watched her walk away. If Adaleigh kept finding people like Mindy, David, and his family, perhaps staying in town wasn't such a bad idea. Starting anew, putting down roots ... the concept filled her with an unfamiliar sense of contentment.

All through dinner—another one with just Mrs. Martins and herself—the possibility of staying here distracted Adaleigh. She even offered to clean up for Mrs. Martins so that she could spend some time *doing* something in order to wrestle through her thoughts.

Truth was, she didn't know whether she could stay, regardless of what David, Mrs. Martins, or Detective O'Connor believed about her safety, or how she was beginning to feel about a certain first mate—who didn't return until after Adaleigh had retired. She spied him from her upstairs window as he trudged up the walk. His shoulders slumped, and Adaleigh almost redressed in order to see how she could help.

More sane thoughts kept her in her attic room. No reason to be forward, especially if she had to leave at a moment's notice. Even if she liked the roots she was putting down. Ugh! If her sister found her, leaving would be so hard, provided she survived the encounter. Maybe she needed to leave before then, then again, perhaps she could do some good before she left part of her heart in Crow's Nest.

"This is late for you, old man." Silas rounded the back of the house, where David sat with a cup of old coffee.

"Thanks for coming." David waved at the rocker, where Adaleigh had sat the night of Amy's murder.

Had Adaleigh still been downstairs when he arrived home, he wouldn't have called Silas. He'd prefer to talk with Adaleigh, but this was better, safer for his heart, at least. And Silas kept late hours after his time out west, working in his father's workshop, and since their telephone was located in there, David knew he wouldn't wake the rest of Silas' family by calling.

The chair creaked as Silas lowered his large frame into it. "What's on your mind?"

David rested his cup on his knee and looked out over the dark yard where Grandma's garden would provide food for the winter. The air was comfortably warm, if not a little humid. "I'm in trouble, Ward. I should have known it the instant I pulled her out of the water."

Silas had the nerve to chuckle as he rested his cowboy hat on his knee. "I was expecting to talk about your father, but okay, tell me about—what's her name, again?"

"A—Leigh." David corrected himself. "That's just it, I don't know much, but she's lost her family and needs a safe place."

"And there's your problem." Silas wagged a finger at him. "You can't resist helping people."

"It's different."

"I can tell. You're smitten." Silas's tone made it sound like he used the word *disgusting*.

David glared at him, seriously considering whether to toss the remnants of his coffee at him. It wasn't good for drinking. "You got something against the fairer sex?"

Silas rubbed his hands over his closely cut beard. "Family comes first and I get the impression that Leigh is ... progressive. Girls like her, who jump into water without thought to their clothes, don't become wives who grow gardens and pinch pennies to make ends meet."

"You've always thought I should marry Mindy." David's irritation oozed out.

"You two are close. Why not?"

"Because she's too ... safe." The realization struck with that word. Adaleigh Sirland was anything but safe. She was daring, mysterious, confident, and had survived being attacked by her own sister. Since that first day, all David wanted to do was find out more about her. And with how things had been going so far, it could take a lifetime to delve deep enough.

"I can see those wheels turning, Martins." Silas interrupted thoughts that were going way too fast. "You have your family to think of, too. Your father being suspected of murder is a big deal. Getting sidetracked by a stranger doesn't seem wise."

David glared at him. "Why did I invite you, again?"

Silas laughed. "Because you know I'm the voice of reason and you needed a heavy dose of it. You've got time to figure things out with Leigh."

But did he have time?

"For now, focus on your family. Your father's been absent for years, but this can't be easy." Silas swung his hat between his knees. "Your grandma and siblings need you, Martins. Don't get sidetracked by a pretty face."

"You admit she's pretty?"

"I ain't touching that one." Silas laughed again and stood.

David leaned his head back to keep eye contact. "You ever think about settling down? Especially since your brother ..." *died*. And left a wife and two sweet little girls behind.

Silas grunted, hiding his face as he replaced his cowboy hat atop his head. "I don't know that I'll find a girl who understands my responsibility to my family. I'm the father my nieces don't get to have and any girl has to understand that. I just don't see it happening. Especially with one of those progressive girls like you've got your eye on. Where'd I ever find a gal like that?"

"I pulled Leigh out of Lake Michigan." David chuckled. "No telling where you might find just the right match."

"Shut it, Martins. I came over to help you, not get relationship advice of my own."

"But it does help me because now I know I'm not the only one thinking about the future."

Wednesday, June 4

The next afternoon, after helping Mrs. Martins clean the house—something she had never done before—Adaleigh decided to revisit the seamstress shop where Sean worked to learn more about Amy's last night. If she could get Sean to tell her a detail Detective O'Conner didn't know, perhaps it would be enough to take the pressure off David's dad.

It took Adaleigh a couple extra, out-of-the-way blocks before she found the shop, but it allowed her to notice her surroundings more than she had before. She spotted the court house and city hall, even the Conglomerate headquarters across the street from her destination, Rose's Seamstress Shop. Perhaps she'd meet one of Mrs. Martins's elusive friends.

The shop door opened to her push. "Hello?"

Sean emerged from the backroom, eyebrows drawn into a V. "I thought I locked the door. We're closed. Mrs. Whittlebush will return in the morning. Unless you're interested in the dress I showed you yesterday?" He ran his eyes over her, as if taking her measurements.

"Can you show me fabric you could make into a similar style?" Maybe that would cover her real reason for being here.

He returned with a few choices, all warm colors that blended with her brown hair. He had a good eye, which he squinted at her while holding the bolts of fabric close to his chest. "Do you think Samantha would agree to go on a date with me?"

Adaleigh blinked. Where had that question come from? She folded her arms to study the young man using bolts of cloth as a shield. "Why didn't you ask her out before?"

He looked down, kicked his foot. "I had a girl. Amy." His jaw tightened.

"I know." Adaleigh watched him closely. "Were you guys close?"

"Not at first." Sean rubbed a piece of fabric between his fingers, fraying the edge. "Amy asked me and how could I say no? She's Amy Littleburg. I thought we were having fun ... until she began working for the Hitchens."

"Did she not want to go out on a date with you, then?" Adaleigh pressed, catching the bitter tone in his voice.

"Oh no, she did. She wouldn't let me out of her sight! A gal who wanted me—I'd be crazy to break it off. Then a week or two ago, she stopped talking to me, started avoiding me. I was desperate to understand."

A pit slowly formed in Adaleigh's stomach. Fully aware that she didn't want to hear a murder confession, she still had to ask the question. "What'd you do?"

"She finally agreed to go on a date this past Friday, then stood me up, so I came to the boardwalk searching for her. She assured me we were fine"—right, the heavy petting in full view of the boardwalk—"then, not twenty minutes later, I found her necking with this other, smart-dressed guy." Anger flashed in his eyes.

An image came into Adaleigh's head of a good-looking man in a suit waiting a few buildings down from the Lightning Bug. Guy Spelding. Could he have been waiting for Amy? The night after he tried to take advantage of Mindy? The creep.

His face clouded in a storm of anger and sorrow. "Some dope, I was."

"I'm sorry." She watched Sean's face for signs of guilt or anger, but all she saw was his drooping shoulders and downcast eyes. Either he was an exceptional actor or this poor boy wasn't a murderer.

"Did you want this?" Sean lifted his arms to indicate the fabric he still held.

Adaleigh shook her head, wishing she had the money to buy a few dresses from him.

"Martins!"

David popped up from checking the Hicks marine motor in the belly of the *Salmon Mann*, the second boat in Mann's fleet. "Captain Henegan. What can I do for you?"

The old captain swung himself onto the boat. "How's the engine repair coming along? Will I be able to take the *Salmon* out in the morning?"

"I think I fixed the problem, but I need to take her out to be sure."

"You'll be back in time for the meeting tonight, right?" Henegan frowned. "Surely, Mann told you?"

"No, sir." David wiped his hands on a towel. "What's the meeting about?"

"That's not like him. You're his right hand, so why would he leave you out of this?"

Of what? David wanted to shake the man. "I'm sorry, sir, I don't know."

"He feeling okay?"

"Captain Mann? The usual aches, I'm sure." David wasn't about to admit to the other issues. Not to an employee, no matter how much he liked Captain Henegan.

"We're meeting in the basement of the Catholic church at seven."

"Seven, huh?" Is that why Mann gave him tasks to keep him busy while he was out with Spelding? The ledger, the engine repair ... Did Mann want to keep David away from the meeting?

"And I'm sorry to hear about your dad, son." Captain Henegan slapped David's shoulder. "No one should have to deal with their father being a murderer."

David bristled at the expectation of guilt but kept his mouth closed.

Henegan left with an overly cheery goodbye, and David cranked the Hicks engine, his thoughts spinning as fast as the propeller. He wrestled with the news that his boss had shut him out of whatever meeting was happening. Why keep him in the dark? Did it have to do with the discrepancies he found? Or with the fact that everyone considered his dad a murderer?

Though David kept the bow facing east, he watched over his shoulder as the pink hues cast a warm glow over the scattered clouds along the western horizon. The spires of the two churches, one at either end of town, stretched into the sky. Trees beyond the small town—not to mention Crow's Nest Creek—cut it off from the rest of the state, giving Crow's Nest the sense of being a haven. Perhaps that's what caused Adaleigh to pause here long enough for him to meet her.

The wind whipped up a couple stronger waves. He wanted to kick up his feet and enjoy the colors as they changed from bright blue to the darkness of night, but he stayed alert, guiding the boat over roughening water. He wished Adaleigh sat beside him, enjoying the sunset and helping him think through the questions that filled his mind.

He liked her company—more than he realized after talking with Silas last night. He also liked the conversations they'd had over the last couple days. She made him think, made him feel. Deep places he'd long given up healing, now saw hints of hope—something he could use in large supply right now. Adaleigh harbored many secrets, however, and a past that caused her much pain. Opening his heart might backfire. He couldn't forget her sister had attacked her. A wrong move might send Adaleigh running. He had to think of her needs before leaning on her for his, if he wanted to cultivate her friendship.

A strong wave sprayed water over the deck, and David turned toward home, assured the engine worked fine. Yes, he was used to employing patience, waiting for fish to bite or the weather to cooperate, and then acting in a moment when the time presented. Perhaps he just needed to use the same skill to show Adaleigh she'd found someone she could trust.

Halfway down the block from Mrs. Whittlebush's tailor shop—outside a Dr. Thompson's clinic—Adaleigh heard her name. Her fake name and it took a few moments for it to register that whomever it was referred to her.

"Leigh!" The call came from across the street. Detective O'Connor.

He crossed quickly, meeting her on the sidewalk. "What brings you down here?" Detective O'Connor asked. The trace of a smile hid behind his mustache but peeked out through his eyes.

"Shopping."

Detective O'Connor's eye twitched. "I thought you said you had no money ... or did Samantha loan you some?"

Caught red-handed doing anything but shopping. Her mouth turned down.

"I suspected as much. Snooping into a case that isn't your business?" He lifted his hat and wiped his forehead with his sleeve. "You talked to Sean."

Adaleigh shrugged.

He cocked his head. "Best tell me what you learned."

She crossed her arms. "Guy Spelding is mixed up in this."

"Oh?" Detective O'Connor's eyebrows raised and his body tensed. This was something he didn't expect her to say. Interesting.

Adaleigh relaxed her stance. "Sean said Amy spent last Thursday evening with a man I believe was Guy Spelding. On Friday, David and I ran into him on the boardwalk, and Sean said Amy met up with a man matching his description. Did you find out more about him yet?"

His eye twitched again.

She smiled as sweetly as she could. It had never worked for her—not on Dad, not on her teachers, and certainly not on her swim coaches—but still, she tried, hoping for something she could share with David.

Detective O'Connor shook his head. "I can tell you I set up a meeting with Buck Wilson, the conglomerate boss." He pointed over his shoulder, toward the headquarters. "There's a lot of foot-dragging, so I suspect Spelding is one of theirs."

"That's good for David's dad, right?"

"Not necessarily." He studied her for a moment. "Sean opened right up to you, didn't he?"

"Yes." She drew out the word, knowing the detective had somewhere he was going with his observation. "Why?"

"Nothing for now. Go back to my sister's. I'll be there for dinner."

"Fine." Adaleigh gave him her but-not-because-you-said-so look and swiveled on her heel.

Mrs. Martins and Samson were the only ones home when Adaleigh arrived. The older woman stirred something in a pan over the wood stove, and Samson's nose hovered nearby. No wonder. A delectable smell met Adaleigh as she entered the kitchen. Her stomach rumbled, reminding her that coffee, toast, and ice cream did not make a meal.

"Welcome home." Mrs. Martins waved to one of the chairs on the far side of the table. "Have a seat and keep me company while I cook." Adaleigh agreed, and Mrs. Martins stepped away from the pan long enough to plop a plate of fresh cookies in front of her. "Milk's in the fridge."

Adaleigh asked her what she was making.

"Fish stew," she said over her shoulder. "A family favorite. Besides fish, it has carrots, potatoes, onion—or whatever vegetables are still in the cellar at this time of year."

Fish stew? Adaleigh had eaten various types of chowder, but never fish stew. Surprising, how delicious it smelled.

"Do you like to cook?" Mrs. Martins asked.

"I never had much opportunity. Our family cook didn't like me underfoot."

"Ah." Mrs. Martins chuckled. "Maybe you'll like cooking if you give it a try. Come stir this."

Navigating around the dog, Mrs. Martins handed her the wooden spoon but kept her hand on Adaleigh's. She had strong, albeit fingers.

"That's it. Slow, easy strokes. We're thickening it while adding the creamy flavor by mixing in flour, milk, and butter."

Around and around, the fish chunks tumbled over the brightly colored vegetables. Heat from the stove warmed Adaleigh, making her wish for a cool breeze. After Mrs. Martins added the milk, flour, and butter, she stepped back. Adaleigh risked glancing at her with a grin. She was cooking!

The older woman moved around behind her, gathering various things. "I'll make the rolls while you stir."

"You love to cook don't you?" Adaleigh asked, sniffing at the amazing smells wafting up from the pot. Garlic?

"Oh yes. My mother also didn't cook—my father did—very unconventional, I know. I would stand on a stool and stir for him."

"Did you grow up in Crow's Nest?"

"I did. My husband and I bought this place two years after we were married. Back then, it was only a one-story, one-bedroom house. When Maggie—my son's wife—got sick, I started the addition. My husband had passed by then and I knew the kids would end up with me since I was their only other family."

"How long ago was that?" Adaleigh cringed a bit after the question popped out. Hopefully, the older woman wouldn't find her intrusive.

"Let's see, Patrick is twenty-two, so twelve years now."

"Does it get easier?"

"What?"

Adaleigh swallowed. "Losing someone?"

Mrs. Martins pulled her hands out of the dough, dropping flour on the floor. "No and yes. The pain of loss does not, but learning how to live without them does get easier as time passes."

Adaleigh blinked back the tears. There was hope, then.

The older woman turned the conversation back to cooking while she separated the dough into little blobs for the rolls. While they rose, she freed Adaleigh from the pot so she could add the seasonings. Adaleigh watched, mesmerized, as Mrs. Martins sprinkled in a little of this and a little of that.

"While I stir this, can you slip the rolls in the oven?" Mrs. Martins asked. Adaleigh obliged. "How are you liking your stay in Crow's Nest thus far?"

Adaleigh hesitated. The answer seemed more complicated than she could explain.

"Hmmm." Mrs. Martins seemed to understand. "That fresh start you said you wanted? You might find—"

The older woman's words were drowned out as Samson leapt away from the stove with a howl. Somehow he got his four huge paws moving in the same direction, spinning his way down the hallway, barreling straight for the front door. The front door banged open, then slammed shut, silencing Samson's bark.

A beat later, a young man's voice echoed down the hallway. "Grandma! I'm starving!"

Adaleigh tried to relax the fists her fingers had formed.

"Don't holler, Patrick," Mrs. Martins shouted right back. "Come in here and talk to me." To Adaleigh, she lowered her voice and said, "They disappear all day, but they know where to find the food."

Patrick traipsed into the kitchen, Samson loping behind him as if neither had just taken two years off her life.

"It'll be ready in a few minutes." Mrs. Martins glanced over at him from the stove. "How was your day?"

"Fine." He plopped down at the kitchen table, and Mrs. Martins sighed. "Nothing interesting in hauling fish, Grandma."

Samson's howl prevented a reply. Once again, he lunged down the hallway. Adaleigh tried to keep herself from tensing. Failed.

"Grandma!" A female voice this time. "Is that your fish stew?" Samantha appeared in the kitchen, Samson at her heels.

"Who wants to set the table?" Mrs. Martins peered significantly at her adult grandchildren. "No food for anyone who didn't help with something."

"Aw, Grandma!" Patrick rolled his eyes.

"That's not fair!" Samantha crossed her arms.

"Family rules."

"Did she help?" Patrick dragged himself off the chair while glaring at Adaleigh.

"Leigh helped me quite nicely." Mrs. Martins whisked the buns out of the oven.

Seemingly out of excuses, Patrick pulled the plates out of the cupboard. Samantha moaned but joined him with the cutlery. Just as they laid the last place setting, Samson howled once again. This howl, however, sounded different than the others—three short howls. A bit of skidding and he was down the hallway for a third time. Curiosity overcame Adaleigh's anxiety.

"Hey boy!" Detective O'Connor's voice bounced down the hall. "Did you miss me? Yeah? Was Great Aunt Marie nice to my big boy?"

Who knew the gruff old man had a soft side?

"I'm surprised you don't have half the neighborhood knocking at your door, Em." He emerged into the kitchen. "I could smell that halfway down the block."

"I told the children no food without helping me, so reach me down those serving bowls."

In a few minutes, they had all sat down at the table, Adaleigh once again next to Samantha and across from Patrick, but keenly aware of

David's absence. After Mrs. Martins's insistance on saying grace, everyone dove into the food. It tasted even better than it smelled.

The stoneware and unshined silver would have been beneath Adaleigh's parents to eat off of, but Adaleigh liked it. More and more, the absence of those items her family and neighbors would have considered essential to a meal—bone china, candelabras, and dinner dress—were things Adaleigh had no interest in seeing again if it meant not being a part of a family, albeit a flawed one, like the Martins.

Second helpings had already gone around when Samantha broke the silence. "Uncle Mike, I heard you interrogated Sean today."

"Comes with the job," he answered, wiping his bowl with a bread roll. "How'd you find out?"

"I heard it from three of my friends who all heard it from someone else."

He paused with the roll suspended in mid-air. "Any of those friends got an idea of who killed Amy?"

"Michael!" Mrs. Martins swatted his arm with her napkin. "Not at the dinner table."

"We have odds on the guy Sean caught her with," Patrick said between bites.

"What did I tell you about gambling?" Mrs. Martins wagged her fork at him.

Patrick held up his hands in surrender. "I didn't say I had money down on anyone in particular."

Detective O'Connor swallowed his chunk of roll. "Just don't go near him, ya hear?"

"A killer?" Samantha wrinkled her face. "No way."

Detective O'Connor muttered something to himself.

"Michael!" Mrs. Martins glared at him. "Language. And stop talking about the case. And the Conglomerate. And all this nasty business. I don't want it at my table." She jumped to her feet with surprising youthfulness, disturbing Samson, and began picking up the serving bowls even though not everyone's plate was yet empty.

Detective O'Connor's bushy brows scrunched together as he straightened. "Marie, I know you're worried. But what about seconds?"

She waved a butter knife at him. "He's innocent, Michael. And until those officers stop railroading him simply because he's not some outstanding citizen, I don't want to hear any more."

Detective O'Connor raised his hands just as Patrick had done.

Silence descended. Patrick snagged a dinner roll from the basket before his grandmother snatched up the serving bowls, then followed Samantha as they dashed down the hallway toward the front door. Neither Mrs. Martins nor Detective O'Connor bothered to scold them into staying. Adaleigh offered to help with the dishes, but Mrs. Martins claimed she wanted to do them by herself. Detective O'Connor gave Adaleigh a nod, using his chin to direct her outside. She went.

Shadows stretched out from the front of the house. She breathed deeply, the muggy air clean and warm, easing the awkwardness of the past few minutes. Summer made for her favorite evenings. She could sit in the grass or a hammock and let the day fade into night. Let her troubles melt away.

Some of her favorite memories were from nights such as these. She and her friends would set homework aside to gaze up at the stars and dream about their lives beginning. At university, nightfall would bring out good-natured debates, driving convictions deeper into their beings. Adaleigh missed those days more than ever.

CONFESSIONS TO A STRANGER

The screen door opened, and Samson brushed past, headed for the lawn.

"He's her son, so I can't blame her for being uptight." Detective O'Connor eased himself down onto the top step, next to Adaleigh. Samson rolled in the grass as if rubbing in Adaleigh's longing for carefree days. "I hate to see her put through this, and those unruly grandchildren sure don't help. You'd think being adults, they'd act like it."

"She's a tough woman." Adaleigh leaned against the porch railing. The summer breeze wrapped her in a warm contentment she hadn't experienced in long while.

"That's an understatement." Detective O'Connor swung his hat between his knees. "She watched her husband waste away from cancer, nursed her daughter-in-law through the illness, then couldn't stop her son from going off the deep end. Now she's supposed to be retired, living a quiet life, enjoying coffee with the ladies, but instead she's chasing after ingrates."

Adaleigh stayed quiet, letting the old detective talk and watching Samson hunt down a flying insect.

"Life isn't always fair." Detective O'Connor rubbed his face before heaving a large sigh. "All right. I'm probably going to regret this. It goes against my better judgment, but hearing myself talk just now seals it."

"Yes?" Adaleigh half smiled at him, still a bit drunk on the summer air.

"My hunch was correct this afternoon. Somehow you get complete strangers to tell you things they won't usually say."

"Is this the theory you mentioned?"

"I had to prove it first. And Sean told you more than he even considered telling me."

"Weren't you the one who said people in Crow's Nest don't trust outsiders?"

"I thought so. Then, considering even I sat here sharing my deeper thoughts with you, who knows? Maybe it's just you."

Adaleigh laughed. "Like I cast a spell or something?"

"Your words, lassie."

She shook her head. "I think it's just human nature. We're more willing to reveal hidden parts about ourselves to someone we think won't see us again because the risk of judgment is lessened."

"I wouldn't have believed it without seeing it."

"We discussed some of these ideas in my psychology classes. It's human nature to not want to be judged, but we need to verbalize our thoughts. Sometimes it's because we sense a comrade-in-arms and other times it's because the stranger is the first person we see."

"All that is beyond me." Detective O'Connor waved a hand.

Adaleigh chuckled. "I find it fascinating. It shows how important revealing a part of oneself is to building relationships."

"Does that mean you'll be my informant?"

"Your what?"

"We might be able to get Frank off the murder charge if I can offer more reasonable suspects, or at least find out more about Amy's life, the type of things it seems I can't learn without dragging her friends into an interrogation as the big, bad, special investigations detective." He rolled his eyes. "If Sebastian will even let me do that."

"And you think I can learn things because I'm a stranger?"

"Who has an uncanny way of getting people to talk."

Adaleigh stared at him. She had the skills and told David she would help. This might be just the chance she needed.

CHAPTER ELEVEN

As the sun sank lower, David pushed the engine. A last test that would also get him home before dusk. He could either catch the end of the meeting Captain Henegan told him about or track down his boss. Perhaps both. The more the situation stewed in David's mind, the more concerned he became.

He had to close up the boat and the shop before he found his boss. The feeling that he would be too late urged him to work faster. Would Captain Mann fill him in? Or would pressing the issue cost David his job?

The question made David pause before leaping to the dock to haul in the boat by its mooring lines. He swiftly secured it, giving an extra tug as he prayed. *God, I need your wisdom. I can't lose this job, but I can't look the other way if something underhanded is happening.*

Whether God's direction or just an instinctual feeling, David decided not to go to the meeting. If Captain Mann was at the shack, he'd talk with him. Otherwise, David would take his afternoon off tomorrow to do some serious thinking about how to handle his next conversation with his boss.

Half an hour later, David locked up the shop with an uneasy conscience. Captain Mann had not shown up. He still had time to make the meeting if he hurried, but was his first impression to pray for a day before leaping into the thick of things the better choice? Sometimes a signpost would be easier than trying to figure out what God wanted.

"Explain something to me."

The voice behind David made him jump. "Spelding. What can I do for you?"

Still dressed in a way that made David feel like he wore aged castoffs, Guy Spelding smoothed his lapel. "What exactly do you do for this operation?"

"For Captain Mann? I'm his first mate and office manager. Why?"

"You pay his bills? Oversee his financials?"

"What business is it of yours?" David folded his arms. Questions swirled, but he kept a tight rein on them, not wanting to give Spelding any leverage.

"How much authority do you have over the business?"

"If you don't tell me what you need, then I can't help you."

"As a lawyer, I cannot divulge privileged information. However, I can say your boss has not been forthcoming with me regarding the financial situation of his company. Perhaps he does not know these figures?"

"You think I'm keeping him in the dark about the financial viability of the company?" David pushed back the worry that rose as he remembered the two different income numbers he'd found that morning.

"I am simply trying to give Mr. Mann the benefit of the doubt before my client enters negotiations on Tuesday."

"That's why you wanted our boat."

"Smart man." Spelding's expression said he thought anything but. "Do yourself a favor. Be willing to come clean. It will be of benefit to everyone involved."

David lifted his flat cap to run his fingers through his hair. What had Captain Mann gotten into, and did it have anything to do with the Conglomerate?

After explaining a few more details of his plan to Adaleigh, Detective O'Connor called for Samson and they left. Sitting alone on the porch, the reality of what he asked of her began to sink in. Being a stranger allowed Adaleigh to help in this particular way, but would that mean she would remain a stranger in this little town?

Staying a stranger went against the natural law of relationships. The more people tell others about themselves, the closer a relationship becomes. But supposing Amy Littleburg's friends bared their souls to Adaleigh as a stranger, would they ever want to interact with her again? She would know their secrets, which would give her a strange power over them.

She wagged her head, trying to shake loose the warring thoughts. Frankly, why did any of this matter? As the stranger, what did she care if people liked her after she asked these questions? Sure, this was a way she could help out this family, a way to say thank you for opening their home to her, but then what? Did she really see herself having a future in Crow's Nest? Did she want one, even if she could stay?

The warm summer air made the front porch homey and comfortable. She hadn't felt so like herself since her swimming days. Her fellow teammates had been determined to break the boundary set for them as women. Yes, women needed to know how to swim, how to save lives on the water, but they would compete too. It created a camaraderie between them, and they accepted each other as they were. Since her first day, they'd seemed proud of Adaleigh's bravery, her dogged determination, and adopted her right into their fold.

She sauntered down the front walk, aiming to wander the neighborhood while her thoughts meandered—she wouldn't make the mistake of going to the boardwalk alone again. She couldn't deny it felt good to be here in Crow's Nest. It didn't matter what she did or where she came from, she was the stranger, the newcomer. She didn't need a past, a dollar sign, or the right set of skills to fit in. People like Mindy and Sean and Samantha told her about themselves. Mrs. Martins took her into her home. David, well, yeah, David. Even Detective O'Connor was letting her peek under that hard shell of his.

How did she find herself in such a place as this? Walking among these homes bathed in the light of the setting sun. Front porch swings, stone pathways, and freshly planted gardens. Faded siding and towering trees.

The people of Crow's Nest were quite unlike the people she'd grown up around. They lived day-to-day, not thinking much past their little community or the work they had to do in order to put food on the table. It was a common, ordinary existence, but they didn't see it that way. It was just the way life was, and they made the most of it. Something about that idea felt secure and safe.

"You have an unfamiliar face." A male voice ripped that feeling right out of her.

Adaleigh spun to face the man. Before her stood the antithesis of the thoughts running through her head. Tall and likely in his late twenties or early thirties, considering he appeared of perfectly marriageable age, it was as if he had stepped from her past to remind her Crow's Nest was

CONFESSIONS TO A STRANGER

not her home. Dressed in an expertly tailored white suit, hanging open to reveal a starched white shirt, blue tie, and polished wingtips, he cut the perfect specimen of male wealth. Words failed her, and her cheeks grew hotter by the minute.

"Please pardon my manners." His smile dazzled like a finely cut diamond in the noonday sun. He held out his hand to her. "My name is Buck Wilson."

Adaleigh's jaw slackened, but she reined in all her Sirland power and managed to genteelly set her hand in his. "Adaleigh Sirland."

"A pleasure, Miss Sirland." He brought her knuckles just shy of his lips, then released her hand and stuffed his own in his pockets, looking the ever-casual man-about-town. "If I interpret your reaction correctly, you have heard of me, but I am at a disadvantage."

As much as Adaleigh clung to her past identity to give her strength, the knowledge of what she had just let slip—to Buck Wilson, no less—threatened to unnerve her entirely. Her identity and her name were tied too closely together. She could not be one without the other, no matter what she had attempted the last few days. And now this man of all men knew her real name.

"I seem to have caught you unprepared." He gave an understanding smile. "Come, let me walk you to a bench closer to the lakefront."

Adaleigh wanted to say no, to run as far away as the wind could take her, but he slipped her hand around his arm and led her around the corner, east, toward the darkening lake. He said nothing as they walked, and she slowly regained her equilibrium.

"Here we are." He unhooked her hand and steered her toward a bench along a walking path that followed the shoreline.

They must not be far from the boardwalk, but she couldn't see it beyond the houses to the right. Mr. Wilson sat down beside her, neither too close nor too far.

"I took you by surprise. I do apologize." A dash of worry flitted across his eyes in the waning light. "Are you feeling better now? There is more color to your cheeks."

Sure, there was. They had to be flame-red with embarrassment!

He grinned. "Before I stick my foot in my mouth any farther, tell me how you came to be in a small town like Crow's Nest."

"I'd prefer not to."

"Fine by me." He relaxed into the bench, pulling his right ankle over his left knee and placing his left arm on the top of the bench behind Adaleigh. "Then why don't you ask me something."

"Like what?"

"Let's see, a typical conversation could be about the weather. I, for one, am fond of such a beautiful evening." He nodded his chin out toward the water. "The stars as they begin to appear. The boats lined up as they return to the harbor. Gulls cleaning up after the humans."

At his description, Adaleigh's shoulders released their tension. "I could get used to seeing this view every night," she said.

"You did not grow up near a lake?"

"No. But I always loved visiting water. I guess that's what drew me here."

"And do you like it here?"

Mrs. Martins asked her that same question. Right here, right now, the answer seemed easy. "I do. I really do."

A corner of his mouth turned up in a smile. "Does that mean you are thinking of staying around awhile?"

"That seems a rather personal question."

He shrugged. "Since speaking of where you've come from upsets you, I'll ask where you are going."

"Are you from here?"

He chuckled. "My roots are, but I've spent many years away. Coming back felt like coming home."

"So this persona, did you come by it naturally, or did you build it?"

"There's a question by someone who has spent time among cultured people. New money or old money? I'll tell you, I came by mine honestly and worked my tail off for it, pardon the expression. I hope some of what I learned can benefit the hard-working people of this town."

Adaleigh frowned, attempting to reconcile what David and Detective O'Connor had said about Buck Wilson and the Conglomerate with the details the man himself now shared.

"I see you have already heard the rumors." He didn't appear troubled. "I mean no disrespect to Michael O'Connor or the rest of the police force, but they're barking up the wrong tree."

Unease slithered up her spine. "Then why are they investigating you?"

"Because I'm standing up for the little guy? I haven't a clue."

"I don't believe that."

Buck pulled his arm from behind her so he could twist to face her straight on. "You're a bold girl."

"Excuse me?"

"No one from around here would dare talk to me like that."

Hoity-toity scoundrel. "Perhaps it's high time someone should." Adaleigh folded her arms. "Did Frank Martins work for you?"

"I hire all sorts of people down on their luck for odd jobs. What's that to you?"

The steel in his eye irritated her even more, so that she blurted out, "Did you hire him to kill Amy Littleburg?"

He blinked. "What are you talking about?"

Adaleigh stood, keeping her disapproving tone. "I was there, Mr. Wilson. I saw Frank Martins standing over Amy's dead body. Did you have anything to do with that?"

"How could you even think I would?" He stood as well, but didn't tower over her as she expected. In fact, he seemed shocked. Had she found a second phenomenal actor—like Sean—or were both of these men innocent?

Nevertheless, taking a page from her father's practice, she wouldn't give Buck any room to negotiate. "Because I don't know you, but I do know that when a man is under investigation, he can do things to cover up what he doesn't want found out."

"Like why you're hiding your past?"

Adaleigh stepped back as if the words slapped her.

"You can't talk on both sides of this, Adaleigh."

His use of her given name stunned her. She shook her head as if doing so could clear the conversation out of her mind. "It was a mistake to talk with you."

Buck sighed as if he'd just lost a bet on the horses. "I'm sorry you feel that way. It's rare to meet a sophisticated woman such as yourself in a town like Crow's Nest.

"Oh, you do lay it on thick." Just like another well-dressed gentleman new to Crow's Nest. At least Buck Wilson had manners.

"I like your forthrightness. For that, I'll return the favor and put out feelers."

"Feelers?"

"To see if I can get you answers about Amy's murder. Witnessing it must have been terribly trying, and having the real murderer behind bars will give you peace of mind."

Adaleigh lowered her head. He'd spoken a bit too close to the truth.

"For the record, I did not order any murders, but I will find out if one of my men did so without my knowledge."

"Or whether it was someone else entirely?"

"That I cannot help with as much, but I will do my best."

Adaleigh stuck out her hand. "Thank you, Mr. Wilson."

"Buck, please." He sandwiched her fingers instead of shaking on it as she intended. "And the pleasure has been all mine."

She watched Buck walk back the way they'd come, one hand in his pocket and whistling a tune she didn't recognize. He left her conflicted, as if strung between two worlds. He represented her old world. The one that held pain and sorrow and fear. Yet she understood that world. The power, wealth, and drive. It might not be in her blood, but it had shaped her.

Money had never been a factor in her decisions before because her family never lacked it, but now, without it, it held her by a leash. Its lack kept her a stranger in a strange town, suspended between the compulsion to run for fear her sister would find her and the growing desire to set down roots in a new home. A home without pretense and façade.

CHAPTER TWELVE

D avid's mood instantly cheered when Adaleigh approached his grandmother's house ahead of him. He called her name, twice, but she didn't seem to hear him.

"Lost in thought?" he asked when he reached her.

"David!" She must have jumped as high as a rainbow trout as she turned around.

He laughed. "You seemed distracted."

She blushed. "The thoughts in my head get loud sometimes."

He bumped her shoulder with his arm. "What were those thoughts telling you?"

"Just puzzling out your dad's case."

He stuffed his hands in his pockets, his good mood fading. "Get anywhere?"

"No. Still lots of questions and no answers. I'm rather suspicious of Guy Spelding, though."

Spelding, huh? His name came up an awful lot. "If he did it and he is one of Buck's guys, Wilson isn't going to lose him over a dead girl. He'll gladly let a handyman take the fall. Has Uncle Mike questioned Spelding yet?"

"I don't know."

"Buck Wilson has really good lawyers." David's sigh betrayed the defeat he'd felt since talking with Spelding.

"Maybe Amy's friends will give us another angle."

David shook his head. "That's a rabbit hole. What are they going to tell us that will get Dad off?"

"We'll find something. Keep hoping." Her smile infused him with just the energy he needed.

The kitchen and downstairs were empty when they arrived. David spooned leftover fish stew into a bowl from where Grandma had left it on a warmer, then invited Adaleigh to join him out back. Thankfully, she agreed and he made her tea. He'd missed talking with Adaleigh the past few days, and he craved a quiet conversation with her.

The air continued to grow muggy, but the temperature dipped, making the dampness feel as if it could burrow under the skin. Adaleigh grabbed her sweater and laid it over her lap as she settled in the rocker, the cup in her hands.

He waited for her to settle, then leaned back in the lounge chair. "Do you ever wonder how many stars there really are? Some nights, when I'm weary, I take Uncle Mike's boat out and stare at the stars. With nothing but water in every direction, I can see the horizon on all sides, and the sky stretches like a black dome pricked with more stars than I can fathom."

Her voice came out a near-whisper. "As a child, I'd sneak out of the house with a blanket and find a dark corner of our garden to stare at the stars. I never fell asleep out there. I'd just study the sky, hoping to see a shooting star among the constellations."

He rolled his head to study her. "Did you have a large garden growing up?"

She nodded. "My parents had this gardener who could cultivate the most beautiful spaces. The roses were prize-worthy."

"Our little town must be so different to you." He spooned a bite of stew into his mouth.

"Yeah. Good different, though. Sometimes, money can feel like a burden." She cringed. "I'm sorry. I don't mean to sound ungrateful after hearing how many hours you work to put food on the table."

"Didn't cross my mind. Do you miss it?"

"The money?"

"All of it. Your home. Your lifestyle." He hesitated. "Your family?"

She nodded. "It wasn't always easy, but now that I can never have it again, I do miss it. At least some of it."

He took another bite while he considered his words. "You can't go back because of ... your sister?"

"I could probably press charges or something if I really wanted to go back, but what do I have to go back to? My parents are gone. My friends are scattered, starting their own families. My house is just a hollow shell of what used to be."

His heart hurt for her. "That's why you let her chase you away?"

"It's my fault that she came after me." Pain echoed through her words.

He set his bowl aside. "Tell me what happened?"

She pulled her sweater up to cover her arms.

"Adaleigh, my mom is gone too. My dad arrested for murder. I get it. You can talk to me."

"Promise to keep this to yourself?"

He placed his hand against his chest. "My word as a gentleman."

"It all fell apart the night of my commencement from university." She rubbed her arms.

"Okay." He prompted, more to keep himself from tucking her under his arm where he could chase away her fears.

"My sister and I were never on good terms, but our parents tried their best to keep the peace between us. But that night, as they drove to the ceremony, my parents ..." Her voice caught.

"Automobile accident?"

She nodded.

"And your sister thinks it's your fault because they went to your commencement ceremony?"

Tears dripped down her cheeks.

"And maybe you do too?"

Sobs silently shook her body. David placed a hand on her shoulder and slipped the tea cup from her hand, but she didn't look at him.

"I understand." David squeezed. He wouldn't take advantage of her emotion, but he needed to do something.

She sniffed and wiped at her cheeks.

"I get the 'if only.'" He squatted in front of her, letting his own pain show in hopes of helping her. "Perhaps my dad wouldn't be in jail right now. Perhaps we could have found a doctor who could've saved my mom. Perhaps your graduation would have been a different day or different place."

She raised her eyes.

"I'm not sure I ever quite believed what people would tell me," he continued, a catch in his voice. "That none of it was my fault. That there was nothing I could have done to keep Mom alive or keep Dad home. Doesn't make it easier."

"And then to have all these people at the funeral who were more interested in where my parents' money was going or how the business would survive. I didn't find a friend among the lot of them—the people we spent every social occasion with. They couldn't have cared less what happened to me or my sister, only what happened to the money."

David took her hand.

"The night after the funeral, when my sister came into my room ..." She clutched his fingers.

Was that when her sister tried to kill her? Should he encourage her to tell the story or would it be too painful to revisit?

Adaleigh rolled her eyes upward and blinked rapidly before continuing. "Why stay to fight? Fight for what? Best to run away. Best to find a new life. But she wouldn't let me go. She followed me. She tracked me to the hotel I had fled to. That's when I knew ..."

"That's why you think she'll follow you here?"

She looked down at him. "I can't even describe the amount of anger in her eyes that night."

He wanted to wipe away the fear and sorrow from her beautiful face but kept his hands still. "I know nothing I say will help you feel better, but you are safe here."

She took a deep breath, let it out slowly, as if it could clear the heartache from her body, at least for the moment.

"I wish I could show you that you're safe with us." David placed his other hand over hers, cocooning them. "People don't mess with Michael O'Connor's family."

That got a smile.

Later that night, after Adaleigh left David in the kitchen, she chuckled about the fishing stories he had told her to lighten the mood after their serious conversation. She also marveled at the differences between her experiences and David's, at how hard he worked. As a fisherman, winter was a time to repair the boats and equipment. This past winter, he also helped his friend Silas do odd jobs around town. The lumber camps up north were a possibility as well.

She knocked on Samantha's door. Buoyed by David's friendship and his commitment to his family, she wanted to return the good feelings by continuing to help him clear his father's name. Samantha had knowledge of the key players, so it was as good a time as any to talk with her, considering the young woman happened to be home.

Samantha opened the door, wearing a pink dressing gown.

Adaleigh showcased her warmest smile. "Can we talk?"

Samantha hesitated, then waved her inside. Adaleigh stood in the center of the room while Samantha closed the door. It was a simple room with a washstand, a dressing table, and a wardrobe. An old braided rug covered a portion of the worn, wooden floor. No adornments hung on the white plaster walls.

"Sit there." Samantha pointed to the green-cushioned dressing chair. She sat on her bed.

"I'm hoping you can help me." Adaleigh took the offered seat. "It's about Amy."

"Did my uncle put you up to this?"

Adaleigh crossed her ankles and tucked her feet under the chair. "He and your older brother want to help your dad."

Samantha folded her arms. "My dad doesn't deserve help."

Adaleigh clasped her hands in her lap. "Our courts are supposed to presume people innocent, but that's not the way of public opinion."

"Fine, but why you?"

"I get it." Adaleigh took a fortifying breath and went for shock value. "I've lost my own parents recently."

Samantha shed her cavalier attitude. "You want to help because of that?"

"Yes."

Samantha narrowed her eyes, then leaned back against the wall. "What can I do?"

Adaleigh's shoulders relaxed as the tension seeped out. "Can you tell me more about Amy?"

"Amy was Amy."

Adaleigh chuckled. "One of a kind?"

"You saw her. She was perfect. Everyone lived in her shadow. Vied for her notice. The girls got a few moments of her sun, and the boys got a few moments of her ... well, her affections. Everyone knew she cheated on everything from tests to ... you know ... but even the teachers stayed quiet."

Sadness washed over her. "Did her parents know?"

"No." Samantha picked up her comb and ran it through the silky strands of her bobbed hair. "She was their only child. They moved away after the crash last year and she stayed. That's when she began babysitting the Hitchens."

Adaleigh leaned closer, hoping to convey a conspiratorial spirit.

"She also began seeing Sean." Samantha tossed the comb onto the bed. "No one knew why she left Craig. He was our high school football star. He got a scholarship to some university out East, so we assumed she didn't want a long-distance relationship. How she picked Sean, I don't know. He was one of our group—the ones who weren't good enough for Amy. She chased him, and boys just can't—couldn't—escape her."

Adaleigh cocked her head. "Why watching children?"

"I know!" Samantha sat straight up. Adaleigh had her hooked. "She hated little kids, which I get, as they're slimy, messy, and whiny."

"You must have had a rumor of why." She kept her on track.

"Oh, we did." Samantha lowered her voice. "We think she and Mr. Hitchens ..."

Adaleigh's stomach twisted. "An affair?"

Samantha nodded. "She was always seeking a way up the ladder. That's why Sean made no sense. But dating a successful, married man would be exactly what she'd do. She'd get whatever she wanted that way."

"And he'd stay quiet." Adaleigh had seen it in her dad's company.

"Exactly. No one could confirm it was him, but we all guessed it. He made the most sense."

If that was true, Mark and Lizzy Hitchens could both be suspects. "She kept seeing Sean?"

"That's what makes no sense. What he saw in her ..."

"She might have picked him because he was loyal," Adaleigh mused aloud. "Perhaps she had him twisted around her finger to keep suspicion off her when it came to the affair."

"Now that sounds like her."

Adaleigh hated that Samantha had witnessed such goings on. "What about the new man, Spelding? She was with him the day she died."

"You're good." Samantha looked impressed. "Heard Uncle Mike mentioned his name, but no one can find out more. Amy always had an angle. Maybe she moved on since she got fired on Friday." She snorted. "Fired! Amy Littleburg was fired!"

"I take it everyone was happy about that?"

"Oh yes." She sighed contentedly.

Samantha had given her so much information already, but since the girl was in such a chatty mood, Adaleigh pressed for more. "Any ideas what she did from the time she was fired on Friday until she died?"

Samantha considered it. "Just that she met that Spelding person, whoever he is. Uncle Mike thinks he's bad?"

Adaleigh concurred. "Think anyone else would have an idea?"

"Sean."

Not helpful considering she already talked with him. "Anyone else who might be able to help?"

"Amy's best friend, but you'd have to talk to her yourself. She ain't in my circle. But I could introduce you to Sean's friend. However ..." Samantha twirled a short strand of hair. "What's in it for me?"

Adaleigh held back a laugh. "You, Miss Martins, get to be a keeper of secrets."

Samantha grinned. "You're not so bad."

Quite proud of herself, Adaleigh settled into bed a few minutes later. Not only did she have good information and solid leads, she'd won over Samantha. Maybe it was residual feelings from her talk with David, but Samantha's change in attitude toward her made her positively giddy. It was like having a little sister—the kind Adaleigh wished Ashley had been.

Adaleigh had never gotten along with her sister. People would tell their parents it was because they were so close in age. But Adaleigh knew the real reason for their fighting. Adaleigh was afraid of disappointing her family, conscious that she was an impostor. And Ashley continually showed her up, trying to win over their parents by putting Adaleigh down.

Perhaps a psychologist could have predicted that one day something would snap in Ashley so that she used something worse than words or fists to hurt Adaleigh. Perhaps Ashley's slew of boyfriends betrayed some deep, unmet inner need.

Their parents weren't oblivious to Ashley's attitudes against Adaleigh, but neither had they realized how deeply Ashley hated her. Adaleigh wasn't sure she did until Ashley tried to murder her. Yet, even though Adaleigh was through taking her abuse, she would always consider Ashley her sister. Adaleigh loved her and hoped that one day, Ashley could love her too.

Did Amy's murderer have a similar story? Did something snap inside him or her? Was it jealousy? Resentment? Adaleigh shuddered and tried to distract herself from those dark thoughts, to return to the cocoon of safety she'd felt a short while before. But as she drifted off, she kept seeing knives flung this way and that. Sometimes Amy was the victim—sometimes it was herself. Then a phantom of Ashley would appear, the anger in her eyes jolting Adaleigh awake.

Day after day, these waking nightmares had stolen her sleep. Finally, she took the quilt to the east window. The eloquent way David had spoken about the stars stirred an intense desire to stare at them as she had when she was a child. Since she was a guest here, however, Adaleigh settled for watching them from inside the house.

It'd been a month since she'd really looked at the stars. Ever since Ashley appeared like a specter in her bedroom, come for her accounting.

Stars had blanketed the inky sky then as they did now. The warm breeze caressed the curtains. Lightning bugs still dotted the backyard, and crickets sang in the night.

Adaleigh could almost hear the large grandfather clock at the base of the front stairs in her childhood home chime out midnight. A floorboard outside her bedroom creaked. The door scraped open.

The gleam of something in Ashley's hand made Adaleigh's greeting wither on her lips. Her chest tightened and she eased herself up on her elbows. Ashley left the door open as she tiptoed toward Adaleigh. Suddenly, she stopped, inhaling sharply.

"Ashley?" Adaleigh searched her sister's face, trying to understand her purpose. Even in the darkness, Ashley's eyes glowed with the malice that had multiplied for the last decade.

"You've never been one of us." Ashley's voice quivered.

Adaleigh reached out a hand as if that motion could calm her sister. "I know you're angry."

"You don't know anything!" Ashley's nostrils flared.

"It's going to be okay."

"It will be once you're gone."

Adaleigh's eyes followed the knife as her sister raised it. "Ashley!"

Ashley leapt toward Adaleigh, bringing the knife down over her stomach. Adaleigh twisted in her blankets to the floor. The knife sunk deep into the bed, and she let out a guttural scream.

CHAPTER THIRTEEN

A scream ripped David from uneasy dreams. Adaleigh!

Not wasting time to change out of his pajama pants or shirt, he yanked open his bedroom door. Samantha and Patrick stared at him with sleepy eyes from their doorways as up the steps he flew in bare feet.

The attic was dark. The bed empty. His heart raced as he scanned the room, ready for any threat. Then he saw her. Adaleigh cowered by the east dormer window, hand covering her mouth, eyes wide. She slapped away the blanket covering her shoulders, chest heaving.

David dropped to his knees in front of her, scanning for injury, for blood, for a reason for such a terrifying scream.

His siblings snuck into the room. Patrick stared at Adaleigh with wide eyes. Samantha clutched her hands under her chin. He turned back to Adaleigh. Her face pale, her gaze blank, tremors began to shake her body.

"It's not my fault," she whispered. Tears slipped down her cheeks.

David swallowed back his own emotion. The poor woman was living a nightmare she couldn't escape. If people knew about this, would they demand she go to an asylum? Not on his watch.

"Patrick." David cleared his throat. "Go downstairs and make sure Grandma hasn't woken up. Then stoke the stove and put her tea kettle on."

Patrick nodded and slipped from the room. Making an uncertain sound, Samantha swayed from one foot to the other like an upside-down pendulum. Too distracting to stay.

"Sam, go help Patrick get Leigh some tea."

Samantha ran from the room.

David gently wiped Adaleigh's tears with the pads of his thumbs. "I've got you. You're safe." He didn't trust his voice to say anything else, so he pulled her against his chest, holding her while she continued to tremble.

Finally, her breathing calmed.

"I scared them, didn't I?" Adaleigh peeked past his shoulder at the open door and dark stairwell beyond.

"Nah." David barely resisted resting his cheek against her hair. "Me, yes. Adaleigh, I thought for sure your sister had somehow gotten in here without any warning."

"Dredging it all up just made me remember it in all its horrifying detail." She shivered and tugged the blanket around her shoulders. "She came at me with a knife while I lay in bed the very night after we buried my parents. She was so angry. So determined to—"

"Shh." He pulled her closer and kissed the top of her head. "It's all over, Adaleigh, you're safe now. I won't let anything happen to you." *God, let me speak the truth.*

She pulled back to see his face, questions in her eyes.

"I've seen sailors succumb to fear on the water, but a damsel in distress? That I've never encountered." He winked to lighten the emotion between them, and Adaleigh's cheeks turned an adorable shade of red in the moonlight.

"Tea." Samantha appeared, her hair laying straight now, holding a tea cup with dozens of red roses. She glanced between David and Adaleigh. "Did I miss something?"

"Just trying to get her to smile." David helped Adaleigh to her feet. "And I do believe it worked."

Adaleigh shook her head but still smiled.

Samantha again shifted from one foot to the other. "Uh, I made a cup of Grandma's chamomile. I thought that might work."

"I didn't wake her, did I?" Adaleigh asked as she secured the blanket around her, covering her night dress. David rubbed his neck. Now that the initial scare was over, he realized the scandalous nature of the situation.

"No." Samantha handed her the steaming cup. That was a relief, at least. Samantha backed up a few steps. "So why'd you scream like that?"

"You've never had a nightmare?" David raised his eyebrows at his sister's insensitive question.

"Yeah, but—"

David made shooing motions at her. They needed to leave. "Let's let Leigh drink her tea in peace."

"But—"

"Go."

Thankfully, Samantha left the door open—not that him being in Adaleigh's bedroom alone with her would do her reputation any good, whether the door was open or closed. He needed to get her settled and get out. But he hated to leave.

Gently, he eased her down onto the edge of her bed, then David knelt before her and cupped his hands around hers as she held the tea cup. "You're safe here, so drink this and try to rest."

"How has a girl not snatched you up, David Martins?" Adaleigh's eyes roved his face.

Merciful heavens, he could imagine kissing her right now. He mentally strapped his knees to the ground to keep him in place. The last thing Adaleigh needed was him complicating the moment. He released her hands for good measure.

Adaleigh gathered the cup, holding it so the steam rose under her nose. "Thank you, David. This will help. I don't want to keep you up. You have an early morning."

Even after a nightmare, she was thinking of others. He nodded his agreement, knowing it was best to leave, but stopped in the doorway. Man, he didn't want to leave her. However, she was in too vulnerable a state, and he refused to do anything to take advantage of that or risk her reputation further, which meant he couldn't hold her the rest of the night.

Yet that didn't stop him from saying, "If you need anything ..."

Adaleigh tucked her knees under her and breathed in the scent of the tea. Its subtle, honeyed graininess wrapped around her, soothing, comforting, calming. Like David's presence had done so effectively.

How she wished he could have stayed. It would have been the height of impropriety, and only her care for him had allowed the words to send him away past her lips. What would it have been like if he'd kissed her?

Gracious. She couldn't think on any of that.

Instead, Adaleigh pulled out her journal, determined to do what she could for David, and wrote:

Project Mr. Martins. Notes.

She'd start with a list of suspects.

Frank Martins—Seen at crime scene
Sean Green—Jealous boyfriend
Guy Spelding—Seen with Amy; part of Conglomerate?
Mark Hitchens—Possible affair with Amy

That meant Lizzy had multiple reasons for not liking Amy.

Lizzy Hitchens—Angry at Amy for letting her son fall in
the water; angry about husband's affair?

Adaleigh thought for a few minutes, hesitated, then added:

Buck Wilson—Conglomerate connection

Should she include any of Sean's friends? He had a connection to Amy. A strong one. But what motive would Sean's friends have to kill Amy? In fact, why would Sean kill Amy Littleburg? Unless it was an accident. He seemed to know she was cheating on him, or maybe she finally decided to leave him and he got mad. Perhaps his buddy could fill her in tomorrow.

Friend(s) of Sean—Standing up for their friend

Adaleigh couldn't resist adding one more name.

Reporter Greg Alistar—Just because

Honestly, she wouldn't put it past Greg Alistar to manufacture a story, but he probably had nothing to do with Amy's death. He was just an opportunistic, self-satisfied, gigantic—Adaleigh stopped herself and took a cleansing breath. Mom would say there was no need to add colorful words when a more proper adjective would do. Sometimes even Mom was wrong.

Adaleigh rested her journal on her knees, studying the names while she sipped her tea. Her mind wandered to her sister, and she wrenched it back to the blurry page. The tea had worked its magic. Her eyelids grew heavy. Yet sleep held a chasm of fear. Prying her eyes open, she stared at her notes, willing her mind to find some clue that could repay David for his kindness to her.

All she could connect was that Mr. Martins, Sean, and Guy were the only ones seen with Amy the night she died. Mark and Lizzy Hitchens, and perhaps Sean, were the only ones with clear motive. And the Conglomerate connection, including Mr. Martins, Guy Spelding, and Buck Wilson, made things complicated.

There was still a lot of untangling to do, and she could do none of it with how spent she felt. Still, there had to be a way to convince the police David's father hadn't killed Amy Littleburg. Unless he did exactly that.

Thursday, June 5

David lay awake the rest of the night. He couldn't get his muscles to relax or his mind to stop thinking about Adaleigh. Would her sister really track her down? He couldn't imagine Samantha or Patrick being mad enough at him that they would try to murder him. Sure, they weren't always happy with him, especially when he had to be a parent. But stabbing someone was a whole extra level of anger.

Did that mean whoever killed Amy Littleburg carried that type of anger? Maybe he should discourage Adaleigh from helping him clear his father's name. No way did he want to put her in the sights of such an angry person. Who knew what they would do to someone who figured out their guilt.

That thought banished sleep for good, and even Captain Mann called him out for his irritableness while fishing that morning. All David wanted was to be home with Adaleigh, keeping her safe.

They'd barely returned to shore when Captain Mann sent him home, not bothering to wait until they'd cleaned and processed the catch. David didn't protest, stopping long enough to buy a paper after he caught one of the headlines.

Arriving home, he found his grandmother in the kitchen, preparing to clean strawberries. A large bowl sat on the table beside a basket full of the red fruit. She frowned before he could greet her and pointed to the newspaper in David's hands.

"Alistar wrote his article." David sank into a chair beside his grandmother. What had the man done? What would it cost Adaleigh? And David had promised to protect her.

He'd barely finished reading the article to Grandma when steps sounded on the stairs. So much for a chance to get his grandmother's opinion on what he should do. Should he tell Adaleigh? Hope she didn't see it and the trouble would pass over her? Did he have a right to keep something like this from her? After last night ...

"Morning." Adaleigh had her fingers tangled in the fabric of her dress as she entered the living room, her braided hair over her shoulder.

David's breath caught at her simple beauty. His heart was slipping away from him faster than most fish he failed to catch.

"I'd get you coffee, dearie, but my hands ..." Grandma smiled as she raised them. Strawberry juice stained them red, making David's stomach lurch.

"It's no trouble." Adaleigh headed for the stove, avoiding David as he tried to catch her eye.

"You make yourself quite at home." Grandma plucked off the green leaves, then pared out the stem.

"What are you making?" Adaleigh watched Grandma for a moment, hand on the handle of the cupboard where the cups hid.

"Rose Wittlebush had too many strawberries to use herself, so she brought them yesterday. Her strawberry harvest is almost over, and I still need to make my jam."

"You make your own jam? I'd love to know how to do that." Adaleigh selected a cup with a daisy in the middle.

"Oh?" Grandma's voice brightened considerably.

"You shouldn't have suggested that." David chuckled as he discreetly folded the newspaper. He needed to think about Alistar's article before he opened his mouth about it. Pray about what to say. His heart thudded at what the news could mean for Adaleigh.

"Hush." Grandma wagged a finger at him. "Jam-making is fun."

"Just make sure it's a day I've got to work late." David forced a wink and pushed back his chair, noting how Adaleigh's eyes followed the paper as he rolled it up. "Cleanup is a bear."

"Don't listen to him," Grandma said. "He eats the jam fine. It's just a messy, all-day process."

"You're a fine cook, Grandma." David pressed a kiss on her cheek, then risked looking at Adaleigh, hoping his emotion didn't show. "I understand if you don't want to come with me to see my dad." He'd been looking forward to the day together, but until he shared the article with her, he didn't know what to say. "If you'd prefer to stay and help Grandma, that's okay. Just let me know. I'd like to leave in half an hour." Then he dashed away before she could answer.

Adaleigh stared at her empty mug as David escaped upstairs.

"Are you all right, dearie?" Mrs. Martins's voice broke through Adaleigh's fog. The older woman rinsed her hands at the sink pump behind Adaleigh. "You don't seem quite yourself this morning."

"I ..." Where should she start? Did Mrs. Martins know about her breakdown last night? David sure was nervous this morning. Had he thought her crazy? She closed her eyes, remembering his comforting touch.

"Allow me." Mrs. Martins snatched the cup out of her hands and filled it with coffee from the carafe on the stove.

Adaleigh inhaled deeply before taking a swig. "Heaven."

"David makes the best coffee." Mrs. Martins went back to divesting her strawberries of their tops. "My husband taught him. Both early risers, they always had the coffee on the stove by the time I woke up. David still does."

Adaleigh nodded, still letting the coffee do its thing.

"He puts on a strong face, but I worry about him." Mrs. Martins glanced at the stairs as if looking to see whether David was on his way back down. "You've been a godsend. I fear he would have frayed at the edges had he been forced to face this thing with his father without such a supportive friend."

The nervousness boiling in her stomach turned to butterflies as it mixed with the coffee.

"You're the first person in a year or more to get him to do something other than work or fish." She put another cleaned strawberry in the bowl. "I also don't see you in a hurry to run away from here."

Heat bloomed in Adaleigh's cheeks. It might depend on how he felt after last night.

Mrs. Martins frowned, a disapproving hum coming from her throat. "Come sit here for a moment." She patted the table.

Once Adaleigh obeyed, Mrs. Martins set down her knife, wiped her hands, then clasped Adaleigh's hand in her frail ones. "I knew from the moment my brother brought you to my door that you needed more than a place to sleep. More than food in your belly or safety from what haunted you. You needed a sanctuary for your heart. A sheltered place where your emotional wounds could heal."

Adaleigh clenched her jaw against the feelings those words caused to rumble in her chest.

"I can recognize the battle-scarred. You, my dear, may have many scars, but you've managed to help David in ways you don't even realize yet. As I said, you've been a godsend to him—not to mention, to me. And, in turn, I believe David has gotten you to share more of yourself than you ever wanted to reveal. And that scares you, doesn't it?"

How did she know? Adaleigh swallowed hard, managing a tiny nod.

"David is a good man, and he'll keep those things to himself. I'm glad someone has been able to lower your defenses. It's good to get out of your head sometimes."

Overwhelmed and terrified at her hostess's words, Adaleigh only wanted to pull her hand away, run upstairs, and lock the door to her room so no one could find her. Ever. But she was in Mrs. Martins house, so that wasn't really an escape, was it?

Before Adaleigh could follow through on the impulse, David reappeared with a kind smile. "C'mon. Looks like a beautiful day for a walk, and I'd be grateful for the company."

That was a change of tune from his earlier uncertainty. What had he heard?

"Go on, dearie." Mrs. Martins patted her hand.

Adaleigh darted a look between the two, finally landing on the vulnerability shining in David's eyes. She took a fortifying breath, ran up to gather her things, and followed him out the door.

"All the municipal buildings are on the north end of Main Street." David cut through the silence with the statement two blocks from his grandmother's house.

As he led Adaleigh away from the lake, he quickly found himself disagreeing with his assessment of it being a nice day for a walk. The humidity made him feel like he breathed underwater. Even Adaleigh's gasps came short and quick as they climbed the hill leading toward the courthouse, adding to the uneasiness churning in David's stomach.

"Maybe it would have been better for you to have stayed back to rest?" He needed to tell her about the article, the one he clipped and carried in his pocket, and he also wanted her presence as he faced his dad, but was that only his selfish desires? Was he truly looking out for her best interests by inviting her along?

"I'm fine." Adaleigh blew out a breath laced with irritation. "It's this weather."

Taken aback, David stopped. In his personal battle over telling her about the article, he'd missed something.

Adaleigh halted beside him and clamped her arms across her chest, tears shimmering in her eyes. "Why are you so kind to me?"

What? "Are you angry with me?" *Why?*

"No!" She shook her head. "No, not at all. I'm not used to showing weakness, and I don't understand why you haven't used it against me."

"Against you?" His jaw dropped. "Why on earth would I do that?"

"Why wouldn't you?" The look on her face, so full of hope and fear, melted his heart and he realized this was about last night.

He bent close. "Because I want to show you I'm different from all those other people who've hurt you."

Adaleigh's lips parted. David ran a thumb over her cheek. Would a kiss show her he meant those words?

"David Martins and our mysterious visitor!" Greg Alistar appeared like a wraith out of thin air. The intensity of the moment evaporated, leaving only anger in its place.

"Keep walking," David hissed, pulling Adaleigh with him as he shouldered around the irritating reporter.

"I just need a statement." Alistar stayed right on their heels.

David increased their speed until Adaleigh suddenly stopped, her respiration rapid as she hauled wet air into her lungs. Great, he'd let his emotions cause her even more distress.

"For the record." Alistar held a pen and paper.

"No comment." David glared at him.

Alistar flashed a sly grin. "Your father murdered—"

David pressed a hand against Alistar's chest. "My father didn't—"

"David, don't." Adaleigh stepped between them.

David took a step back, her touch grounding him to reality. He needed to be careful around Alistar. Everything he said or did would end up in print. With a negative bias, most likely.

"Go." Adaleigh pointed behind Alistar. "The Martins have no comment, and I would thank you to leave them alone."

A gleam appeared in Alistar's eye. Oh no. He'd just moved his focus onto Adaleigh. David wouldn't let that happen. It was his fault—he'd brought her out into the open where Alistar could prey on her, which meant this was David's mess to fix.

Greg Alistar wore such a superior expression, Adaleigh raised her chin in an air of injured dignity, summoning her Sirland background to overcome the emotions boiling inside. "You print one word about David's father being guilty before it's proven in a court of law, and I'll—"

"What?" Mr. Alistar's laugh left spit on her face. "Cry to that detective?"

David stepped forward, but Adaleigh held up a hand, never moving her glare from Mr. Alistar's face. "Print it and your career will be over."

"You can't ..." Mr. Alistar hesitated, his bluster evaporating as he tried to discern if her threat held water.

Adaleigh gathered all of her father's thunder as she stepped into Mr. Alistar's personal space. "I will."

Mr. Alistar backed up, a touch of fear in his eyes. Then his jaw set. He spun around and marched back the way he came.

"Not good." She'd overplayed her hand. Once upon a time, her threat would have been enough. Now, she'd turned Mr. Alistar into a vengeful enemy. This would not end well.

"Wow," David muttered behind her. "Remind me not to get on your bad side."

"I should've kept my mouth shut." Rookie mistake. Why had she incited Mr. Alistar to turn his terrier instincts on her? How stupid could she be? She already knew she wasn't thinking clearly. Now she'd made things worse.

"You could really get him fired?"

"Once upon a time." Her confidence drained out of her. "My father was a marketing tycoon. He could make or break a company with a single ad campaign. Just mention my last name, and Mr. Alistar wouldn't get a job writing copy for a company selling ice in the desert."

David rubbed the back of his neck. "So when you say your family had money, that wasn't the half of it?"

Adaleigh shrugged. "It's all fluff without the authority of my father."

"I don't know about that. Just look at how you handled Alistar and even Spelding the other day. Not to mention how you've managed to hold yourself together after a series of incredibly horrible circumstances. The past few weeks would destroy most people, but you—"

"What do you call having your heart beat out of your chest? Your lungs feel like they'd suffocate you?" The words tumbled out of her mouth. "And the nightmare last night? You must think I'm completely insane. I mean—"

He grabbed her arms. "Those have nothing to do with how strong or weak you are."

Adaleigh blinked.

"Just because I didn't go to college doesn't mean I don't know anything."

"I didn't mean—"

"It's not that." His jaw worked and he wouldn't look at her. "In my mom's final months, she started getting the same kinds of episodes you had last night. Scared my dad into drinking."

Adaleigh attempted to cover her mouth, but David's hands held firm.

"Listen to me, Adaleigh. One day, a greenhorn lost it out on the boat. He jumped overboard but couldn't swim. It's a miracle we managed to bring him in safely. Once he made it back to shore, he was out of a job, but perfectly in control of himself. Turned out he'd been at the Battle of Jutland, in the Great War, being former Royal Navy. As thanks for saving his life, he took me out for a bite and explained his shell shock and the battle he's faced *since* leaving the navy. It's nothing to be embarrassed about. Many others fight these same battles, not just soldiers. Look at all you're overcoming. You rank among the strongest women I have ever met."

Words caught in her throat at the look in David's eyes. He'd moved beyond seeing her as a girl who needed help, as a woman who listened well, as a friend—or even godsend, as his grandmother called it. He truly cared about her. No one had ever looked at her like that before and the feeling soaked in, all the way to her heart.

Chapter Fourteen

D avid and Adaleigh sat at a table in a small room of the equally small jail. While they waited for his dad, David bounced his leg. He tapped his fingers on the table. Then blew out a long breath. "Why did I decide this was a good idea?" The words slipped out before he realized he spoke aloud.

Adaleigh leaned close. "Deep breaths."

"Do you wish you hadn't come with me?" Why had he asked that? He didn't actually want to know the truth.

She hesitated for a moment, then slipped her hand into his clammy one. "I'm glad I'm here."

His heart skipped a beat.

Several clanks came from down the hall. Voices. Footsteps.

"Just remember, no matter what he did, he's still your dad," Adaleigh said. "And you always respond to him as a son."

David gave a quick squeeze, then put distance between them as the door clanked open and an officer brought his father into the room. He shuffled as he walked, eyes downcast. His hair was wetted down, and at least a day's beard growth shadowed his jaw.

The officer secured Dad to the bench and left. Dad raised his eyes, then perked when he met David's gaze. "You came."

"I had to, Dad." David spoke softly, barely able to give voice to his words.

"Same gal from the other day?" Dad nodded his chin at Adaleigh. David felt her stiffen as his father's eyes wandered over her. It wasn't the leering of a drunken man, but a look of curiosity and challenge. Was Adaleigh good enough for his son? David didn't want his father's opinion on the matter.

"Dad." David brought the man's focus back to him. "How are you?"

His dad raised his eyebrows. "I'm in jail. What do you expect?"

"Tell me you're innocent." David leaned forward, needing to hear the words from his father's mouth.

"What good will it do?"

"You've got to fight this, Dad." David felt his control slipping. "Think of Patrick and Samantha."

"They already have me convicted." Dad flopped his hands, rattling his cuffs. "Even my lawyer thinks I'm guilty."

"Then tell me what happened that night." Desperation bled through David's words.

"What does it matter what happened?" Dad traced a scratch on the table's surface. "I'm not getting off. The sooner you realize there is nothing you can do, the sooner you can move on. It's better if your brother and sister forget about their old man."

"That's not good enough, Dad." David stood, leaning over the table. "You can't walk out on us again."

"I've got nothing to live for, David. Since your mom died ..." Dad lowered his head, eyes closed.

"What about us?" David's exclamation brought the guard.

"Just go home," Dad whispered, but the words felt like a dagger.

"I can't listen to this." David pushed himself off the bench. "You're so—" With a growl, he strode toward the exit. Tears burned his eyes. How could his father do this to them again?

The guard let David out of the dreary room, then looked back at Adaleigh. She held up a hand for the officer to wait. David needed to cool off, and Mr. Martins sat in a dejected heap, shoulders heavy, face filled with countless lines of sorrow. Her skills were best used here for the moment. The officer nodded, retreated, and closed the door.

Adaleigh took a deep breath. What could she say to get through to a man broken beyond hope? "Let me tell you a story."

Mr. Martins raised his head.

"It's about a little girl." She tightly clasped her hands together in her lap to control their shaking. "One day, she came home from school with bruises all over her body. Her parents, wealthy, upstanding citizens, immediately took her to the doctor and then instructed their lawyer to find the culprit so they could press charges. But he could not find out who had beaten the child, and no witnesses came forward."

"Why not ask the child?" Mr. Martins furrowed his brows. "She knew."

"No one could convince the girl to tell the truth about what happened."

"The child should have spoken up." Mr. Martins's voice rose. "It makes no sense."

"Doesn't it?" Adaleigh cocked her head, willing him to see her point. "She didn't think her life was worth as much as the person's who hurt her. The little girl already felt like an imposter, and since her tormentor was only reminding her of that truth, why rat on her?"

"What do ya mean by that?"

"Even if you know who the actual murderer is, why would you hand them in? Your life is over. People believe you are capable of murder. Why fight what everyone already thinks is true?"

Mr. Martins worked his jaw.

Adaleigh leaned forward. "Only, you didn't kill Amy, did you? But you were too drunk to save her, so you feel as guilty as if you'd actually murdered her."

He ground his teeth.

"You need to tell people what really happened."

His eyes turned hard. "If you didn't, why should I?"

Adaleigh froze.

"You're the girl in the story." His anger poured out of him. "You can't tell me my life has worth if you ain't thinking you've got any either."

"Then why act like a child?" Adaleigh shot back, her own anger getting the best of her. "Why not fight back? Tell someone the truth." A storm brewed in Mr. Martins's eyes. Heedless, she went for the jugular. "You're not scared, are you?"

"Shut up!" Mr. Martins leapt to his feet, slamming his hands on the metal table.

"Is everything okay in there?" The guard appeared at the door.

"Fine," Adaleigh called out loudly but didn't take her glare off Mr. Martins. Rage had replaced his despondency. Raw, sober, all-encompassing rage. Like a wild animal backed into a corner. She stared him in the eye and gave one last poke with her verbal cattle prod. "Don't let what you lost make you suffer for someone else's crime."

"Then don't be me." Mr. Martins loomed closer, his breath stale and hot. "My son deserves better than that."

Yes, he did. What was she going to do about that?

David was pacing the front steps of the jailhouse when Adaleigh finally emerged. She used her hand to shield her eyes from the sun and sucked in a mouthful of soggy air. It did nothing to stop the shivers that cascaded through her body. Though her plan succeeded, it zapped what little emotional energy she had left.

David bounded up the steps. "Where have you been? Are you okay? What happened?"

"Easy there." Adaleigh held out her hands to stop from colliding with him. Her hands still shook. She crossed her arms so he wouldn't notice. "I had a friendly chat with your dad."

David stared.

"I convinced him to fight the charges."

"And you? You look as white as a sail."

"Yeah." Adaleigh turned away. With Mr. Martins's words echoing in her head, Adaleigh needed time to think. David absolutely deserved better than his father. He deserved someone who would stay, who wouldn't break his heart. Adaleigh couldn't promise that. Not right now.

"Is it something he said?" David stayed in front of her, blocking her way down the steps. "Don't listen to him. He's a selfish—"

"But he is right, David. You deserve better than he gave you."

"Okay, so is it something I said? Is it because I left? I should have waited, I know, I—"

"Stop." Adaleigh grabbed his arm.

"If it's not me, then what?"

"You know you don't have to save me, right?"

"Oh, I know that. You can stand up for yourself just fine. But you don't have to struggle alone. You don't have to be strong on your own."

Adaleigh shook her head, thinking of the way he'd looked at her just an hour ago. "I'm a stranger here, a passing visitor. You deserve better."

He clutched her shoulders, stared directly into her eyes. "Adaleigh Sirland, you are no longer a stranger to me."

Adaleigh pressed her lips together to keep them from quivering, but nothing stopped the tears from dripping down her cheeks.

"Aw, Adaleigh, don't cry, please." He gathered her into his arms, right there on the jailhouse steps.

"It's not you." She rested her head on his chest, and security wrapped around her. "Well, it is, but it's because you're so good to me."

David raised her chin to wipe the tears from her cheeks, his eyes sad. "Come, sit with me. We need to talk."

He directed her to a shaded corner of the steps. From there they could see over rooftops until there was nothing beyond but sky. She hadn't realized they'd climbed what amounted to a hill from the Martins's home. They were not high enough to see the water, but it was there, a chasm beyond the houses. It yawned wide, threatening to swallow anything that dared get close enough. Adaleigh teetered on the edge. Emotions raw. All she wanted was to lean into David's strength.

"I've been selfish." David sighed, resting his elbows on his knees and staring out over the houses that sloped toward the lake. The memory of her in his arms made him want to hold her all the more. How could he when he was just like his father? Thinking only of himself. "You've been nothing but caring, and all I've done was get you into this mess."

"That's not true, David." Adaleigh spoke softly. "You were kind to a stranger."

"And walked you right into a murder scene." *Nor have I told you about Alistar's article.*

"Is that why you thought I should stay home today?"

"No." He puffed out another breath. He only wished to spare her more turmoil—and failed—but he could come clean now. "I should have shown you Alistar's article."

She startled beside him. A small motion that rocked against his heart like a rogue wave.

David rubbed his forehead. "I couldn't bring myself to ruin your morning before you even had breakfast."

"Is it bad?" She swallowed.

"It's why I was so mad when we ran into him." Another point he could chalk up against himself.

Adaleigh shifted. "I was afraid I'd scared you last night."

What? "Oh no, no, not at all. Adaleigh, after everything you've been through, you deserve a day of quiet or at least some semblance of normalcy. That's what I wished for you."

She gave a humorless laugh. "I don't even know what that is anymore."

He rubbed his hands over his knuckles. "Promise me that tomorrow you'll help my grandma with her jam."

"Why is it so important to you?"

Because he cared about her more than he'd ever cared about anyone. He wanted the best for her, this woman who so readily helped others while asking nothing for herself. A life of joy and peace and hope. Could there be any chance she returned the feelings building in him?

For a moment, she seemed lost in his eyes, then blinked. "What about Mr. Alistar's article?"

He held her gaze a moment longer, unwilling to break the connection, then pulled the article he'd clipped from the newspaper from his pocket. Adaleigh read it aloud.

"*Crow's Nest, WI—On Friday afternoon, eight-year-old Matthew Hitchens nearly drowned when he fell into the harbor while under the eye of his babysitter, Amy Littleburg. Miss Littleburg was recently found murdered, but it is assumed to be an unrelated case.*

"*Fortunately for young Hitchens, a visitor to Crow's Nest happened to be on hand to save the boy. We have been unable to ascertain much about this woman who jumped into the water after young Hitchens, but reports say she lives not far from here and is temporarily staying at the home of Marie Martins. Mrs. Martins was unavailable for comment. Other reports say that the woman arrived in Crow's Nest Friday and is going by the name Lee.*"

Adaleigh's respiration increased, and David clasped his hands together to keep from reaching out to her.

"*Young Hitchens is the son of Mark and Elizabeth Hitchens. Both parents expressed their gratitude to their son's rescuer by taking her to coffee. Later, Mrs. Hitchens explained that she will forever be indebted to her son's rescuer, even if she will never learn the woman's real name.*"

Adaleigh turned the clipping to read past the fold. There it was, her nightmare—a photo of her in front of a line of fishing boats, small and grainy, but with the focus on her alone. David had studied the picture and knew exactly when it was taken—that night on the dock when Adaleigh had been surrounded by a mob of drunken men. Alistar had snapped a photograph of her before David could break up the crowd.

Adaleigh let out a long, slow breath.

"You have to leave now, don't you?" David voiced the thought that had kept him from showing her the article all morning, the one he hadn't admitted to himself until now.

Adaleigh shifted to squarely face him. "You'd prefer I stay?"

Did he ever. But he could never ask that of her and that was the crux of the whole problem.

"You deserve better," Adaleigh whispered.

"Than you?" He met her eyes. She stared back, reading him like his grandmother and uncle did so well. He wanted to shut off the vulnerability she could, no doubt, easily see. Couldn't. He cared about this woman far more than he should after so few days.

Adaleigh swallowed, her throat constricting with the action. Her brown hair, damp from humidity, stuck to her temple. Her cheeks were redder than a number on the thermometer would make them. A warm breeze skated by, and she touched his arm. "It's been a month since I ran away, nearly a week since I arrived in Crow's Nest. Maybe she stopped looking."

His heart broke at her sacrifice. Just to give him a kernel of hope. He laid his hand on hers. "Please don't put yourself in harm's way because of me."

Her eyes widened as she gauged how much the words cost him.

The Hitchens family lived in a large brick home on a quiet street on the south side of Crow's Nest. Sculpted bushes and bright little plants enhanced an immaculate green lawn. On the long walk from the jailhouse, Adaleigh and David spoke of little other than the weather, which had been slowly growing warmer and more humid.

"Are you sure you want to do this today?" David asked when they reached the Hitchens' driveway. He wiped his forehead with his hand.

"Not really, but how can I reschedule? The woman almost lost her son."

David acquiesced. "Would you prefer I join you?"

"I should do this alone, and I hate to have you wait for me." Adaleigh patted his arm. "I'll be okay. I'm sure I'll find my way back to your grandma's house."

David scanned her face, as if assuring himself Adaleigh spoke the truth. That she wouldn't skip town without warning. Her heart twisted. Why did she have to meet a man who could read nonverbal signals as well as she could? She liked that about him, but it sure made it hard to hide her feelings.

Maybe that's not a bad thing.

"I told you you're one of the strongest women I know." David caught her hand. "Tomorrow is Friday again. Will you go out on the boat with me? Maybe this outing will go better."

Adaleigh nodded, not trusting her voice, but wanting to go along with him more than anything.

"I'll see you back home, all right?" David brushed her cheek.

Home. She liked that an awful lot.

With a last wave at him, Adaleigh walked up the drive. She needed to get this conversation out of the way, then she could figure out what came next. She took a calming breath and knocked at the door. No answer. She swayed from foot to foot, flapping the hem of her skirt in an attempt to dry off the perspiration that dampened it before meeting Mrs. Hichens. She should have freshened up, but there would be no way to do so without getting damp on the way here again.

Random, indiscernible noise came from within, but no one came. Should she knock again? Adaleigh had her hand raised when the door flew open. Mark Hitchens glared at her, dressed in tan slacks and rolled-up shirtsleeves, with bare feet.

"I—" Adaleigh couldn't get her words out.

"Kinda busy here." He glanced back into the house with a significant look. A woman giggled.

"Mrs. Hitchens?"

"She's not here."

"Oh." So who was ... oooh, dear! Adaleigh took a step back, her heel slipping off the stoop.

He smoothed out the wrinkles of his shirt, tucking it better into his pants. "Are you here for some kind of reward or something?"

"Huh?"

"For saving Matt?"

"No. No, I'm meeting your wife here in ..." She patted the pocket where she usually kept her watch only to remember she sold it for gas two weeks ago. Now she had no idea of the exact time.

"She won't be home until late."

Adaleigh firmed her voice. "We're meeting at lunchtime."

Mark Hitchens gaped at her. Then shook his head. "That has to be wrong. She didn't tell me anything about it."

Considering she'd whispered it, she must not have wanted Mr. Hitchens to know. Adaleigh attempted to cover for the woman. "Perhaps she forgot. I can wait out here. If she doesn't arrive soon, I'll go home."

"I can't have you waiting on my doorstep like a lost puppy. Come inside." He held the door open wider.

Uncomfortable was not a strong enough adjective to describe how Adaleigh felt walking into that house. She glanced around. To the left was a study, all dark wood with a large desk and piles of paper. To the right was a formal parlor, complete with austere curtains and two wingback chairs. Stairs leading to the second level rose directly in front of her. *Were the children home?*

From the left side of the study doors, a young woman about Amy's age peered out. For a minute, Adaleigh thought Amy had returned from the dead, but that didn't make sense. Adaleigh shook her head to clear her mind. The woman slipped past her and out the front door without meeting her eye.

Mr. Hitchens sighed heavily. "As you can see, I'm still conducting interviews for Amy's replacement. Give me one moment. Wait here." He waved her toward the parlor, then disappeared into his study.

Adaleigh's feet were frozen to the doormat. No way could she move if she wanted to. Interviews, indeed! What had Samantha said? That Amy and Mr. Hitchens were having an affair? Amy wasn't the only extra woman in his life, or Mr. Hitchens sure made a quick replacement. And in the house with the children home? Disgusting.

She rubbed her face as if that action could scrub the thoughts away. Motive. It screamed motive.

As if the thought conjured him, Mr. Hitchens reappeared in the hall, now dressed in a similar suit coat to the one he'd worn to Sunday's meeting, shoes on his feet. Adaleigh tried to keep the disgust out of her expression, but she couldn't look at him. He called her into his study office, but she hesitated. The closed door at her back, the silent house around her ... it weighted her down like cement bricks.

Mr. Hitchens crossed his arms, his eyes paralyzing her like a lion as it stalked its prey. "I called Mrs. Hitchens—she was at a Ladies' Aid meeting. She said to wait."

Like a car engine turning over, Adaleigh couldn't get her brain to function. She couldn't even summon her inner Sirland. She simply stared back at him.

"What you saw today ..." His voice was the low growl of a hunter.

That familiar squeezing started in her chest. She took in a few mouthfuls of air, but it didn't help. Finally, her inner voice—or maybe it was God's protective prompting—broke through the fog, telling her to run. The message traveled down her right leg, and Adaleigh stepped back. Before the directive could reach her left leg, Mr. Hitchens grabbed her arm.

With the touch, her instincts kicked in, and Adaleigh yanked away. But in one swift movement, Mr. Hitchens swung her into the study and slammed her against the wall. Breath flew from her lungs as her back hit the solid surface. Adaleigh inhaled, but no air seemed to enter.

She was an athlete, strong and capable. What could help her? Something, anything, that could get her out of his clutches. He gripped both of her wrists in one hand, raising them above her head. Adaleigh dropped her weight, but his other hand gripped her throat. The tightness in her lungs intensified. She opened her mouth for air, but it only made his grip tighter.

Her legs! They had always been her best weapon as a swimmer. Adaleigh shifted to her left foot to maneuver a well-placed kick with her right. She landed it on his shin.

He squeezed her neck. "If you breathe a word of this ..."

Blackness crept into the corners of her eyes. Adaleigh blinked, forcing them to clear. Mark Hitchens's flushed face hovered inches from her own. His eyes held no mercy. He would snuff the life out of her if it meant saving his own skin.

"Do you understand me?" His words slithered like a venomous snake. "I won't have my plans ruined by some nosy stranger."

No nosy stranger here. Just a girl at the wrong place at the right time. Or the right place at the wrong time. Or whatever place when Adaleigh didn't want to be there!

"Just because you saved my son doesn't make you welcome here." His grip loosened, and Adaleigh grabbed as much air as she could. "My affairs are my own. If you even whisper a word of this to my wife, I'll snap your little neck."

Adaleigh's eyes felt as if they would pop out of her head as his renewed vise-grip crushed her throat. The blackness she'd warded off flooded back. Adaleigh tried to inhale, but nothing happened. Her head swam. Her sight faded to mere pinpricks. *God, help me find a way out.*

CHAPTER FIFTEEN

David's thoughts buzzed like a horde of mosquitoes. Equally annoying, too. He couldn't focus on just one. Instead, his brain jumped from trouble to trouble. His heart didn't help matters. It simultaneously ached like it hadn't in years and felt whole for the first time in ages.

Taking Adaleigh out on his uncle's boat tomorrow night would help. He hoped. Being out on the water always did. Bringing her along would feel like a soothing balm on his soul ... or increase his longing for a relationship he might have to give up.

"David Martins." A male voice stopped his thoughts from spinning and his feet on Main Street. "Just the man I need to see."

"Buck Wilson." David held in a sigh. Just the man he didn't want to see. "To what do I owe the displeasure?"

"We need to talk."

"Why? Is this about my dad? I can't believe he would work—"

"It's about your boss."

"Captain Mann?" That surprised him. The captain wasn't a fan of Buck Wilson or the new Conglomerate, but why would Buck discuss that with him?

"Were you at the meeting he convened last night?" Buck kept pace alongside David as he made his way toward the lakefront.

"No." David considered not volunteering the rest of the situation. However, something in Buck's demeanor urged him to share. "Honestly, I only learned of it by chance. Mann made sure I couldn't attend."

Buck rubbed his chin. "I know what your uncle thinks I've done, but I need you to put that aside for the moment."

Unease tightened David's shoulders. "Why?"

"Mann is headed down a dangerous path. He thinks he's doing it to spite the Conglomerate, but he'll end up hurting his employees and losing his business."

Dear Lord, is that true? "The Conglomerate has put people out of business before, so why should I believe you?"

"Why do you believe everything you hear?"

"Seems like we're at a standoff." David stopped, folded his arms. "Why should I help you over Mann?"

"Because you want to keep your job. Because you have a conscience. Because he left you out of that meeting on purpose."

David lifted his flatcap and scratched his head. "Fine. What do you think Mann is up to?"

"He wants to ruin the Conglomerate. By doing so, however, he's misreporting his finances, taking unnecessary risks, and running his business into the ground."

"Explain the finance part." David ran the two different profit sheets through his mind.

"Members of the Conglomerate pay dues based on their income. If that is misreported, the dues are not calculated correctly. The Conglomerate may not appreciate the lower dues, but misreporting income can bring the Treasury Department and legal trouble. In the end, I aim to help this town, and Mann is treading dangerously."

David's thoughts ramped up their buzzing. "Mann's not part of the Conglomerate. He organizes his own co-op."

Buck raised an eyebrow. "He joined this last year, after the crash."

What? Why? And why didn't David know? Did that mean Buck was right? Did Mann misreport to just the Conglomerate or also to the government? David did not handle the company's taxes. Could that be the answer behind the two different spreadsheets?

"How can you tell when something is misreported?" he asked.

"When there's such a drastic difference between one year and the next, it makes the Conglomerate take note."

"Is that why Guy Spelding is meeting with Mann this week?" It was a stab in the dark, but it fit the situation.

Buck laughed. "I knew you were the right man for this. Spelding is a lawyer I brought in, and yes, he's meeting Mann to discuss the situation. I'll figure out a way to get you on that boat tomorrow."

"Why on the boat, not the office?"

"Negotiation tactics, my man. Best let Mann see what he has at stake."

David frowned. "And that's why I still think my uncle has a case against you."

"Think what you will, but best make sure you still have a job by the weekend."

David's gut clenched.

"Say hi to the lovely lady staying with you." Buck winked. "She's a fine one."

Jealousy reared its ugly green head, strangling any reply David could make. Buck clapped him on the shoulder and strode away.

"Liz is home." Mark Hitchens stepped away, releasing Adaleigh.

She coughed and tumbled to her knees. Her breaths came in gasps, but at least air filled her lungs. Blood rushed to her head. Adaleigh wavered, then caught herself with her hands.

"Pull yourself together, woman," he hissed, then disappeared.

Adaleigh wanted to burst into tears right then and there. She hadn't felt so trapped since she was a kid and Ashley had first physically turned on her. Adaleigh had sworn then that she would never let someone have that type of control over her ever again. She trained herself to outmaneuver, out-fight, and out-battle any physical, verbal, or emotional attack that ever came her way. But Hitchens had caught her off her guard.

Mrs. Hitchens's voice drifted from down the hallway. Adaleigh stood, caught herself against the wall, then took a deep, fortifying breath. She was a Sirland. She could do this.

She straightened her dress and met Mrs. Hitchens in the hallway. The lady of the house gave her a quick hug when she reached her. Adaleigh tried not to flinch.

"I'm so sorry to have kept you waiting. My husband says he was entertaining you as well as he could. We can sit here." She pointed to the parlor. Adaleigh sat where she had before Mark attacked her. "Now that it's just us, please tell me more about yourself. Leigh, I heard your name is, right?"

Adaleigh nodded.

"Where are you from? What do you do? What brought you to Crow's Nest? Please, I have been so curious." The woman sat primly on the edge of her chair, ankles crossed. The cut of her jacket gave her a professional look, but the shirtwaist beneath offered a lower neckline. No doubt this woman used both her looks and an aggressive manner to succeed at whatever she put her hand to. Weren't she and her husband just the perfect pair?

Adaleigh managed a smile. "I just finished university."

"What did you study?"

"Psychology."

"Ah." She tugged at her skirt hem and the conversation flagged.

"How is Mathew?" Adaleigh asked.

"Much better." She brightened. "And keeping us busy. It's really a lot to keep up with them without help. I thought Amy could manage, but obviously, she was too distracted. I hear they have someone in custody. Marie Martins's son." Her eyes narrowed. "You're staying at her house, aren't you?"

"Yes." Adaleigh drew out the word, warning bells clanking in her head.

"Such a shame. I don't understand why Amy was mixed up with Frank Martins. You have heard his history?"

"Yes."

"Tragic." Mrs. Hitchens waved her hand in the air. The gesture casual, the glint in her eye very much not. "Then to treat his family in such a way. And to think I was so hard on Amy the day she died." She gave a dramatic sigh.

Adaleigh bit the inside of her cheek to keep from demanding the woman get to her point. "It is understandable you were upset," she said instead.

"I've cooled some now. I'm realizing how much we asked of her. If I'd seen the signs ... She must have been a confused girl. It got her killed. I will not be allowing Sarah any of that behavior when she gets older."

Oh dear.

"But we found a replacement, I hope. She seemed quite promising. I met her this morning, gave her an intense interview, and then left her with the children until Mark came home."

"Wonderful." Adaleigh tried to sound enthusiastic. "I should really—"

"You must heed the warning as well."

"What?"

Mrs. Hitchens leaned forward. "The Martins are not to be trusted. They'll sway you over to their side, make you tell the police what they want you to say just to get that drunken man out of jail. I *saw* how the detective had you under his control."

Adaleigh's jaw dropped open. She'd become Alice, tumbling down the rabbit hole into Wonderland where everything was upside down and inside out.

"I asked you here to offer you a safe place to stay."

Adaleigh clapped a hand over her mouth to catch the laugh that nearly burst out.

"What other way can we repay you than by protecting you from that disreputable family? Chief Sebastian thought it a perfect solution."

Tears pricked Adaleigh's eyes. She needed to get out of here before she couldn't hold them back. "Thank you for your offer. Unfortunately, I have another appointment." Adaleigh lied.

"All right." Mrs. Hitchens seemed reluctant, but she stood and extended a hand. "You're always welcome here."

The woman showed her out, and Adaleigh could barely contain her unbounded relief at escaping that house. She nearly ran down the street. Free and safe. With no doubt in her mind that Mr. Hitchens had what it took to kill Amy, though he wouldn't have needed a knife, and that

Chief Sebastian was a fool of a man, if not a crooked one. She needed to stay far away from both men.

No one was in the common areas of the house when Adaleigh arrived, so she mercifully slipped upstairs to her room without speaking to a soul. Mark Hitchens's threat reverberated in her head. Lizzy Hitchens's suspect connection to Chief Sebastian unnerved her. Greg Alistar's picture had seared itself behind her eyes. And Frank Martins's warning weighed her down, despite David's protest. How quickly the dangers of staying in Crow's Nest compounded.

Adaleigh locked the attic door and went straight to the washstand. Red, blotchy skin, bloodshot eyes, and a puffy face stared back at her. Bruises in the shape of a hand had formed on her neck. She ran her fingers over the bluish-purple coloring, then splashed water on her face, pressing cold fingers to the swollen areas under her eyes. Then she scrubbed her cheeks so the pink blotches melded into a more normal pattern. The bruise stood out on her neck.

"Adaleigh," she said to her reflection. "What are you going to do now?"

A knock at her door made her jump.

"Leigh?" Mrs. Martins's voice came from the other side. "Would you care to help me with supper?"

Adaleigh's stomach grumbled, reminding her she missed lunch, but she stared at the bruises forming on her neck. She had no way to cover them and didn't want to discuss it, not right now. "I'm a little tired after the day. Is it okay if I rest first?"

"Of course, dear. Can I get you anything?"

"No, ma'am." *Please go away.*

"Come down when you're ready."

Adaleigh changed into a night dress, curled up on the bed, and closed her eyes, praying memories wouldn't keep her awake.

Friday, June 6

The next thing she knew, there was another knock at her door. Light streamed in the window, but it felt brighter than before her nap when she would have thought it would be darker as the sun set on the opposite side of the house.

"Coming." She jumped up and realized just how stiff she was. "Just a minute."

"Are you all right, Leigh?" Mrs. Martins sounded incredibly concerned. "You missed supper last night and have slept half the morning away."

She did what?

"The chief is here for you, too."

Adaleigh's stomach flip-flopped. She did not want to talk to the chief, not after Mrs. Hitchens bringing up his name yesterday. Still, she opened the door to Mrs. Martins and kept a hand over her throat to keep it covered, not knowing how it looked.

"Is she in there? I need to talk to her." Samantha's voice reached her like a jousting jab. The young woman pushed into the room. "Kyle is waiting for us down at the park." Samantha stuck out a hip. "You coming?"

Adaleigh sighed and leaned against the door edge. The last thing she wanted to do was interview more people.

"Have him come tomorrow." Mrs. Martins laid a hand on Samantha's shoulder. "I will make something I'm sure he will enjoy for lunch."

"But—"

"Out with you, Sam." Mrs. Martins shooed her away. "Leigh, I've already phoned Michael. He's on his way to join the conversation with the chief. So take your time coming down."

Before Adaleigh could reply, Mrs. Martins closed the bedroom door. Adaleigh sank against it, unable to catch up to her spinning world.

When she first arrived, she had left her motorcycle in a place it wouldn't be easily discovered. Unless she could come up with money for gasoline, it wouldn't take her anywhere. Right now, only her feet could get her out of this town. She'd have no trouble slipping out a window and skipping town. However, she doubted she could walk far before someone tracked her down.

Anyway, she couldn't do that to any of the Martins clan, especially David.

She put on her spare dress, thankful for the high collar, braided her hair into one long rope that hung over her left shoulder, and reviewed her reflection. It wasn't great, but it would have to do.

Gathering herself, she made her way downstairs. Recalling her three o'clock meeting with Mindy that afternoon and then her date with David that night—it was a date, right?—courage flowed through her. She had people who cared about her, so she could face one annoying Chief of Police.

"Ms. Sirland." Detective Sebastian set his coffee cup on the kitchen table. He did not stand. Mrs. Martins chopped something at the counter, each strike louder than the last.

"How may I help you?" Adaleigh perched on the edge of a chair across from him. Anxious energy battled to override her positive thoughts. *God* ... the prayer died away, and she rubbed her thighs.

Chief Sebastian glanced at his notebook. "Why did you visit Frank Martins yesterday?"

Adaleigh cleared her throat. She needed coffee. "David wanted to see his father."

"But why did you visit Martins?"

Adaleigh squinted at him. "What does it matter?"

He squared his notebook on the table beside his coffee mug. "You're a witness to him murdering Amy Littleburg."

"No wonder Mr. Martins feels railroaded." Had she spoken aloud?

"Railroaded?" The word jumped out of Chief Sebastian's mouth. "Martins is a murderer. You were key to putting him away, now you're putting my case in jeopardy."

No, she wasn't. At the crime scene, the chief had thought her a swooning female incapable of being a witness. How could a woman like that jeopardize his case?

"Maybe that's not a bad thing." Adaleigh crossed her arms. "Amy Littleburg deserves having her murderer behind bars. Her *real* murderer."

Before Chief Sebastian could answer, the front door opened, and padded footsteps lumbered down the hallway. In moments, Samson hung his slobbery jowls over Adaleigh's arm. She ran her fingers over his coarse hair and her composure returned.

"What are you doing here, O'Connor?" Chief Sebastian glared at the other detective as he emerged from the hallway and removed his hat.

"Don't let me interrupt." Detective O'Connor kissed his sister on the cheek. "Rhubarb, Em? You know I hate that in my strawberry jam."

She wagged a long reddish-purple stem at him. "My jam-making has been postponed until tomorrow since Marian Ward dropped off some of her garden produce this morning. Including rhubarb."

Detective O'Connor rolled his eyes and opened the cabinet where the cups were kept. "Well I'm here for lunch." At the word *lunch*, Samson deserted Adaleigh to discover what goodies Mrs. Martins might drop for him. Detective O'Connor glanced at Adaleigh. "Coffee?"

Adaleigh nodded and Detective O'Connor winked. Her shoulders relaxed knowing reinforcements had arrived.

Chief Sebastian moved his jaw up and down before he glared at Adaleigh. "Are you going to help me put a murderer away, Miss Sirland?"

"Of course, Chief." She didn't fully manage to remove all the condescension from her tone. Oh well. "But I don't believe Mr. Martins killed Amy Littleburg."

"What?" Chief Sebastian exploded from the chair, bumping the table and splashing coffee across his clothes. "But you saw him."

Detective O'Connor handed her a cup of steaming coffee, hiding a smirk behind his own. The pause to take a sip gave her a moment to collect herself, effectively banishing her unhelpful tone.

"Sir." Adaleigh focused on Chief Sebastian. "I saw Mr. Martins leaning over Amy. I never said I saw him plunge a knife into her. Or even hold or touch the knife. If you'd listened to me, you would know that, truthfully, I didn't see anyone actually commit the murder."

Chief Sebastian's mouth flapped like a fish out of water, whether from hearing a truth he didn't like or because it came from a woman, Adaleigh didn't care. Detective O'Connor patted her shoulder before giving it a squeeze of approval. She put her cup of coffee to her lips as the band around her chest fell away from the confidence of speaking freely.

Adaleigh stood, glancing from chief to detective. "Are we finished here?"

Chief Sebastian sputtered, but Detective O'Connor leaned close to her ear, said, "We'll speak later."

Without waiting for an answer from Chief Sebastian, Adaleigh headed for the stairs. Detective O'Connor took her seat, and Samson laid at his feet, his nose resting on his master's shoes.

"I told you to stay out of my investigation." Chief Sebastian's voice traveled up the stairs. "Your interfering is getting in my way."

"You're convicting a man who might be innocent."

"The two of them said ..."

Adaleigh didn't need to hear a repeat of how David and Adaleigh had ruined his investigation by merely reporting what they saw.

"What's going on down there?" Samantha opened her bedroom door as Adaleigh passed. "Is it about my dad?"

"Kind of." Adaleigh squeezed her forearm. "I don't think he's guilty, and I think he'll fight the charge."

Samantha folded her arms tight against her stomach. "The chief sure sounded like he already convicted him."

"You heard."

"How can he do that? Isn't he supposed to find who's really guilty?"

"On the surface, it looks like your dad is the obvious suspect."

"But you and David saw what happened."

"We didn't see who actually killed Amy."

Samantha turned away but not before Adaleigh caught the telltale glistening in her eyes.

"I know this is hard, Samantha."

"Hard?" She spun and spat the word at Adaleigh. "Amy was my age. Sean is my friend. Now my father is considered a murderer? My life has fallen apart. I can't face my friends. Most won't talk to me. And I hate my father. But he can't have killed someone. He's my dad."

"Sam, I'm so sorry." The words seemed pitiful, but it was all Adaleigh could think to say.

"Why are people so mean? And why are you so nice to us?"

"Why am I nice?" A humorless laugh escaped her. Adaleigh had asked David the same question. "It's your family who has been nice to me."

"You don't mind being in a house with the family of a murderer?"

"Don't doubt your father just because of what other people say. I believe he's innocent, but he needs to know his family stands behind him." Adaleigh squeezed the young woman's shoulders, getting her to look at her. "Anyway, friends who are only kind during the good times aren't friends. It's the hard times that show us the people who are really in our corner."

Samantha nodded.

As her own words echoed in her head, a picture of Mindy came to mind. They were supposed to have coffee together. The clock downstairs chimed the quarter hour, and Adaleigh paused. Did she dare wait for the detectives to clear out, or go to town, hoping Mindy might be free for lunch? Her stomach answered the question. "Samantha, think you can help me?"

Samantha tugged her ear. "Sure?"

Adaleigh glanced back at the stairwell. "I made a tactical error. I'm meeting Mindy at the Wharfside, but with Chief Sebastian downstairs, there is no way I want to go back the way I came. I'm sure you know an alternate way out."

Samantha grinned. "Right this way."

The humidity had soaked David's shirt by the time he reached Mann's fishing office after cleaning up the boat from the morning run. Clouds mostly hid the sun, but the air held its warmth. One couldn't ask for a more summer-like Midwestern day. If only his fisherman bones weren't telling him a storm hovered on the horizon.

"What are you doing here?" Captain Mann greeted David from behind the front counter.

What was *he* doing here? What was his boss doing there? And why did he have the financial records laid out on David's desk? He clamped down on the questions that clamored to spill out. Instead, he'd tread with caution. "There's a storm behind this weather. We may need to call off tomorrow, including the trip with Guy Spelding."

"No." Red mottled Mann's round face, making him look like a splotchy tomato. "We'll run the boats when I say."

"And if we lose the boat to a large wave?"

Mann's face grew even redder. "You youngsters think you know everything. I've been fishing these waters since I was a boy. This thunderstorm will blow right by us. Mark my words. We're running all three boats in the morning."

David clenched his jaw. "You're the boss."

"Don't you forget that, or you'll be looking for another job."

"Yes, sir." David spun for the door, Anger and frustration fighting for supremacy. Financial questions might have legal ramifications, but not listening to the weather could be deadly. He pushed through the door, the humidity smacking him in the face. His feet hit the aged boards of the wharf with a harder force than usual.

"Hi."

David stopped as the voice penetrated the dark clouds of his mind. Adaleigh stood at the corner of the Wharfside fence looking like a lake breeze in her green dress. His emotions immediately calmed. He hadn't seen her since he left her at the Hitchens's house yesterday.

"Hey, you. Grandma said you were tired last night, that that's why you weren't at supper."

She scuffed her toe against the ground and ran her finger along her collar. "I slept through till this morning."

Wow. Was she feeling okay? Had her visits to the jail and the Hitchens's left her that drained? David settled for stating the obvious. "You must've needed it."

She nodded but didn't meet his eyes. Hmm. Something was going on. No need to pry with the bustle of the wharf at midday. He'd wait until later. "So whatcha doing out here?" he asked.

"Waiting for Mindy." She gave a little shrug, more reserved than he had ever seen her. Could *he* be the reason for this shift in demeanor? "She invited me for coffee, but we're going to lunch instead."

"Good." David infused as much happiness into his voice as he could, given that he'd planned to go home for lunch so he could see Adaleigh. "How was your visit with Matt's mom?"

Her hand reached for her neck, but then she snapped her arms across her stomach. "Awkward."

David grimaced. He should have stayed with her. Adaleigh turned away from him. The movement was slight, and might appear as if she were looking for Mindy or out at the lake, but he had a feeling she was trying to hide from him.

"How was fishing?" she asked.

He'd play along until he could puzzle out what she was thinking. "Clouds are moving in, but if the water stays relatively calm, fishing should be good this evening. Would you still like to see what all the fuss is about?" His heart beat hard. Would she agree?

"I'd like that, David."

His poor heart. It was about to jump clean out his chest like a trout on a line. He cleared his throat to be able to force words past that traitorous, thumping organ. "Let's get you a fishing license. Follow me."

As much as David didn't like the idea of returning to the office, he wanted to spend time with Adaleigh more than he wanted to avoid Captain Mann. Fortunately, the rotund man wasn't behind the counter any longer, and the ledgers were filed away.

"You'll get one of these." David slid a pin across the counter. It was yellow and white, with *1930 Wisconsin* across the top, the license number in the middle, and *non-resident fishing license* on the bottom.

"That's it?" Adaleigh held the pin in her hand. "Doesn't it cost something?"

David gave her a wink. Adaleigh ducked her head. Heavens, he liked this woman.

"Still here, Martins?" Mann's voice boomed as he exited the back room. "Who's this?"

"Leigh, meet my boss, Captain Mann."

"Leigh?" Captain Man engulfed her hand in his meaty one. "You're not the one who rescued Matty, are you?"

"She is, sir." David answered when Adaleigh stuttered. "Been staying with us since."

"Impressive rescue. Not many of us old captains could have reacted so quickly."

David couldn't stop his grin and Adaleigh blushed.

"Brave thing you did, lassie," Captain Mann continued, all charm now. "You'd be a good addition to a crew with that quick thinking. Ever fish before?"

"No, sir." She glanced between David and his boss, and David had to wonder where Captain Mann was headed with his questions.

"I'm hoping to take her out on my uncle's boat tonight." David tapped a pen on the desk as he paused in filling out the paperwork.

"Be sure to have the business cover it." Captain Mann squeezed Adaleigh's hand. "As a thank you for your actions."

Adaleigh blushed an even deeper shade.

"Yes, sir." David came around the counter. "May I walk you out, Leigh?"

"Good, good. In fact, take the rest of the day." Captain Mann gave him a highly exaggerated wink over her head, and David held back a groan as he pushed open the door.

"There you are!" Mindy adjusted her shoulder bag as she met them outside. "Hi, David."

"Mindy." David gave her a smile.

As much as he'd prefer to walk Adaleigh home for lunch, letting the girls talk would be beneficial for both of them. He could look forward to having Adaleigh to himself later.

"You two have a fantastic time. Leigh, I'll see you back at the house whenever you get there."

He watched them walk away, but his mind was struggling to wrap itself around his boss's behavior. The extra free time had to be a ploy. He'd mention it to his uncle next time he saw him. For now, David would use the time wisely so he and Adaleigh could leave as soon as she returned home.

"He's one of the good ones." Mindy hooked her arm through Adaleigh's as they headed south down the boardwalk.

So many questions. Where to start? "Are you sure you're okay to leave work?" Adaleigh asked instead of prying into Mindy and David's friendship. But oh how she wanted to know more about it.

Mindy waved her off. "I switched half a shift with one of the other girls. We cover for each other, so no need to worry about me. My job is secure."

That eased Adaleigh's worry. Until another popped up. She'd been so thrilled to be invited, she forgot to mention she had only pennies to pay for coffee or lunch or anything. But how did one introduce such a quandary? Stall for info. "Uh, where to?"

Mindy pointed south. "I share an apartment with several other girls. It's above the bakery a block down from Sweetie's, so I thought we could make sandwiches there and sit outside. The owners let us use the tables if it's not too busy."

Phew.

"We'll have to go through the bakery, so you'll get to see it. It's cute, not like the Wharfside. It's decorated like a nod to the local dairy farms. But someday ... oh, I don't know, it's crazy."

Adaleigh cocked her head. "What's crazy?"

Mindy paused in the middle of the boardwalk. "Do you think a girl like me could open her own bakery or café someday?"

"I don't see why not." Adaleigh took a literal step back at the question. "A girl like you? I don't see why that matters."

Mindy started down the boardwalk again. "I mean, I don't have an education. I work at the Wharfside. How could I own a nice café?"

"You'd probably need capital, someone to invest in the project." Which would be difficult with the recent economic struggles. "You'd need a building to start with, then all the cooking and stuff to go inside."

"Stove? Tables? Cups?"

Adaleigh's turn to laugh. "Exactly. All that technical stuff. You'd have to get various permits, I'm sure, but once you're past that, what's to stop you?"

"You really think I have a chance at that?"

"Why not?"

Adaleigh and Mindy reached the bakery—The Barn, as it was called—and Mindy held the door. Just as she described, it had the perfect dairy farm feel to it from the bright red outside to the wood floors inside. Hay bales were stacked, and black-and-white pictures of black-and-white cows lined the walls. Adaleigh's favorite part was the stools along the counter that looked like tall versions of the traditional milking stool.

Adaleigh followed Mindy past a handful of customers, through a back door, and up the stairs. They put together sandwiches, then returned downstairs, Mindy waving at a plump older woman who shouted a greeting from the doorway to the bakery kitchen.

Then they found a small table outside, looking out over the harbor. The sun glistened on the water and Adaleigh smiled. She could get used to living here.

"You know." Mindy took a bite of her food, swallowed before continuing. "My mama keeps tellin' me I need to make better friends, and after that evening with Guy, it got me thinking. Maybe with better friends, I wouldn't pick guys who treat me like the dishes I clean up after customers pay the bill. But all my girlfriends have jumped ship, gotten married, or work jobs like me. I ain't educated, but I got dreams. I wanna be more than just a small-town diner waitress without a life. Then, seeing you with Mr. O'Connor and David, I can just tell they think you're a good person. If they do, then I think so too."

Adaleigh tried not to let her jaw hang open.

"Sorry." Mindy set down her sandwich. "That was too much, wasn't it? You haven't even taken a bite yet."

"It took me by surprise is all." It was so many words, so fast after sitting down. Honestly, Adaleigh was still sifting through them.

"It's just, you're different than people around here. Anyway, Mr. O'Connor wouldn't be helping you if he didn't see good in you. He's like that. You know, he comes into the Wharfside a couple times a week and is my best customer. He's a funny man, with that cute dog of his. And that mustache! But he treats me like a human being, a lady even, and not like the servant girl who is good only for getting his coffee or having a fling."

Adaleigh had no words, and even her books couldn't lend her one.

"And then there's David. I haven't seen him spend time with hardly anyone—maybe Silas Ward, but he was gone for years—let alone a girl, since his mama died. David is smiling again, laughing even, and you're the only person who could cause that. I see him every day, so I'd know. If you can do that to him ..." She let her thought hang in the air and studied her food.

Adaleigh waited, unsure whether Mindy had finished. Nor did she know what to say in reply. There was so much wrapped up in Mindy's words. But what stood out to Adaleigh the most was the thought that someone would want to be her friend without getting to know her first. Could a person really decide to like a complete stranger from first sight?

"Working at the Wharfside, I hear stuff and see stuff. All the captains have been talking about you since you saved Matt. You're the only girl who'd've jumped in that water. I betcha half the boys wouldn't've neither. Least not as fast as you did. That's some quick thinking. Captains like that."

"I simply reacted. Nothing special about it."

"See, you have good instincts. I don't have much going for me. I mean, I make bad decisions, and people think I'm dumb. And I know I talk a lot, but after a day of working at the Wharfside, I gotta talk finally, ya know?"

Adaleigh smiled, then looked away. "What if I can't stay in Crow's Nest?"

"I ain't never had a letter-writing friend. I wouldn't tell no one we still kept in touch if you didn't want me to. I'm sounding kinda desperate, ain't I?" She cracked a grin. "Well, I kinda am. Guy scared me. I need someone—a friend with good instincts—to keep me from doin' that again."

Adaleigh had never met someone as guileless as Mindy. She lived her life where everyone could see. Her eyes held no secrets. Her expression hid nothing. She probably wouldn't even know what an ulterior motive was. To her, the world was full of possibilities.

The positivity Mindy exuded reached into Adaleigh's soul, both convicting her and lifting the heaviness that weighed her down. Anyone who entered Mindy's orbit would leave a better person. Shouldn't Adaleigh, who believed in an Almighty God, leave others feeling the same?

"You still there?" Mindy waved her hand in her face. "I get lost in my thoughts too. What were you thinking?"

"That I envy you." Another unchristian feeling.

"Me?" She pressed a hand to her chest. "Why?"

"My life is so complicated, and you have such hope and brightness."

Her laugh was as lighthearted. "We all are born and we all die. Why not wholeheartedly enjoy what's in between?"

Why not, indeed.

CHAPTER SIXTEEN

M indy and Adaleigh talked for an hour more before they went their separate ways. She liked artistic activities, which Adaleigh did not. Mindy hadn't read many books—in fact, she blushed to admit she actually struggled with reading. So while they were opposite in many ways, as they parted, seeds of a solid friendship had been sown, whether Adaleigh would be able to stay in Crow's Nest or not.

Those good feelings evaporated faster than droplets on a summer day when Guy Spelding stopped directly in front of her as she reached the north end of the boardwalk. Dressed in a tan suit that made his dark hair stand out, he flashed her a smile that reminded her so much of one of her childhood neighbor boys, Adaleigh was momentarily taken aback.

"Swooning already?" Mr. Spelding closed the distance in two strides.

"You wish." Adaleigh glanced around for a way out, but she had mistakenly kept on the path that led along the lake and found herself near the same bench where she had spoken with Buck Wilson. To her right, the cliff fell away to the shadowed water below. Gentle waves lapped at the rocks like an old lady absently petting her cat.

He laughed. "You're a feisty one. I think we'd have a good time together."

Adaleigh squared her shoulders and focused on the crude man. "I don't know what island you're on, but your charms don't work on me." She thought of Mindy. Sweet, uncomplicated Mindy. Guy Spelding would have easily duped her, and it angered Adaleigh that he'd dented her new friend's happy personality. What about Amy? She didn't seem the same type. Was she playing him, or had she given into his charms like Mindy had?

"You're sizing me up." Mr. Spelding wagged his eyebrows. "Like what you see?"

"Oh, give it up." Adaleigh rolled her eyes and pushed past him. "I've turned down much better-looking men with much larger bank accounts."

"Is that what matters to you? Because I—"

"You don't understand the word *no*, do you?"

"Is that why Buck is asking questions?" He grabbed her upper arm. "Because you're trying to get back at me?"

"Let go." Adaleigh tried to shake him off. "You're not worth getting back at."

He pulled her closer, his voice a deep growl. "I came here because I have something to offer."

"Oh, shut it." Her anger boiled. Adaleigh had grown up around so many entitled males, she had no respect left for them.

"No one is around to hear you scream, so let's skip that part." He tightened his grip on her arm until Adaleigh was sure he could snap it in two. She clenched her jaw to keep from showing her reaction. He hovered over her, his suit coat lapels hanging limp in the humidity.

"You mean no one is around to hear you scream." Adaleigh stomped hard on his instep and he yelped. "Now let go."

"Why, you little—"

Adaleigh slapped him across the face, which effectively freed her other arm. She took five steps away from him when she noticed a house up the way, with smoke rising from the chimney and the flutter of laundry on a clothesline. It infused her with courage to ask what she wanted to know so she never had to speak with Guy Spelding again. "The night Amy died, is this what you did to her?"

"What are you talking about?" He pressed his hand to his cheek, his eyes darting over her shoulder. Good. He saw the house, too, and with the way he kept distance between them, he knew that whomever lived there would come to her aid, not his.

Adaleigh raised her eyebrows to encourage him to talk. "You were waiting for someone when David and I passed by."

"Like I told Buck, I didn't see Amy again after she went to meet up with her boyfriend. I don't usually get taken for a fool." A distant look overcame his usual suave expression. "Wasn't expecting it in a town like this." A door slammed and suddenly, his eyes sharpened to daggers, which he turned on Adaleigh. "You better watch yourself, little lady. Stop sticking your pretty nose where it doesn't belong." *Or else.*

She scrambled away, making haste up the path toward the home on the hill. Mr. Spelding didn't follow, but she waited until he was out of sight before finding her way back to the Martins's home. Her skin still crawled at his touch, but at least she wasn't shaking any longer.

How had she so quickly become a walking testament to people who had the means, motive, and opportunity to kill Amy Littleburg? She usually stayed quiet, but this was different than with her sister. Adaleigh needed to speak up, to tell the authorities about the threat Guy Spelding and Mark Hitchens posed to herself and others.

She rubbed her arm. Letting the bruises show would open the conversation. However, she knew Chief Sebastian wouldn't listen to her. No, she'd do better to wait until she could tell Detective O'Connor—and David, because David would get the truth out of her even if Adaleigh wanted to hide it.

"Sebastian is a bulldog, but I did not anticipate this." Uncle Mike leaned back in his chair. David sat across the kitchen table from him and behind David, Grandma chopped celery at the kitchen island. Samson sat on his haunches, his nose just below the countertop.

"Why is he after our family?" Samantha, who sat at the opposite end of the table, raised her head from where it lay on her folded arms.

"Amy's murder is somewhat high profile, as much as it can be in a town as small as Crow's Nest," Uncle Mike said. "'Young woman found dead on the wharf' is not a good headline for us. Frank is a convenient scapegoat that no one would complain about being put behind bars."

"For a murder he didn't do," David broke in. Grandma's chopping seemed to grow louder behind him.

"But it would silence the headlines." Uncle Mike scratched his mustache. "The biggest problem is that there is no better lead than your father."

David thought of Guy Spelding, then thought better of speaking up. Not while Grandma and Samantha were in the room. Behind him, Grandma paused in her chopping, Samson scrambled for something, then the chopping resumed.

"Kyle is coming tomorrow," Samantha said, resting her chin on her arms. "He's Sean's best friend. I tried to get Sean to come, too, but he's being sullen."

David's ears perked, but Uncle Mike spoke. "How so?"

Samantha waved her free hand in a circle. "Like a toddler, kicking stuff around because he didn't get his way."

David and Uncle Mike exchanged glances.

"And Kyle is coming here tomorrow?" Uncle Mike asked.

"So Leigh can talk to him."

Because David asked for her help.

Uncle Mike's mustache worked overtime before he finally spoke slowly, carefully. "Kyle isn't part of the investigation as far as I know. He's your friend, correct, Samantha?"

She nodded.

"And inviting a friend over has nothing to do with the investigation."

This time, Samantha and David exchanged glances. Sebastian wouldn't like it, but after hearing the latest way the man mistreated Adaleigh, David liked the idea of pulling one over on him.

"Until then" —Grandma's voice grabbed their attention. David turned in his chair as she scrapped a celery and carrot mixture into a large bowl— "no more talk of murder and suspects. I'm making vegetable soup for dinner."

"Oh, Grandma," David said. "I was planning to go fishing."

Samantha gave a semi-discrete cough, but Uncle Mike merely asked, "Need my boat?"

"Soup travels well in a thermos." Mrs. Martins poured the bowl of ingredients into a pot on the stove. "Take it with you."

Contentment dispelled the turmoil that had been roiling around his belly most of the day. Then a new feeling descended, a giddy nervousness that had his ears tuned to Adaleigh's return. This was no impromptu outing or a walk after coincidently running into her. No. This was a planned out, honest-to-goodness date with a very captivating woman. He couldn't wait.

Not forty-five minutes after Adaleigh returned home from her lunch with Mindy, Mrs. Martins handed her a picnic basket filled with more goodies than they could want, including two thermoses of soup. David drove his family's car down to the lakeshore where a single dock jutted out into the water and a tiny boat bobbed beside it.

"That's the boat we're taking on the lake?" Adaleigh asked as they parked on the gravel, feet from the water. The boat itself was a weathered wood, with no wheelhouse or covering, only three benches spaced inside. Two oars were nestled within.

David looked over his shoulder as he slid out of the truck. "Yeah, why?"

"It's so small!"

David laughed. "A twenty-footer is just fine for Michigan. We won't go that far out, anyway. Don't worry."

A small pit in her stomach told her to worry, but Adaleigh knew she had no need with David at the helm. Worst case, they would have to swim to shore, and that she had no trouble doing. As long as the water wasn't too cold ...

The air was noticeably cooler by the lake but still humid. The breeze blew by, ruffling the edges of her skirt, and she pulled her sweater closed. The lake stretched out like a wrinkled piece of deep-blue fabric. Adaleigh couldn't ask for a more gorgeous early-summer evening, especially since the sun had no thought of setting.

David helped her into the boat. It rocked beneath her feet, and Adaleigh quickly sat on the bench closest to shore. David sat on the middle bench, tucked the food basket under Adaleigh's seat, and took up the oars. The boat slid away from the dock and into the sparkling, open water.

A certain thrill crested within her as they bobbed through the waves, the shore growing in distance. She'd been on motorboats on a couple different lakes over the years, but never something like this. In front of them was nothing but water.

"How are we?" David paused his rowing to ask. He didn't appear winded, though he had to be working hard. His muscles bulged with every stroke.

"Great." Adaleigh smiled as the wind blew spray into her face. She nudged the picnic basket further under her seat, then settled to take in everything. Gulls swept down from the sky. Ducks floated in the water. If she wasn't mistaken, a pelican sat on a dock up the coast. But no, she must be seeing things since she'd never seen one outside of a book.

Farther from shore, Adaleigh gained a new perspective of Crow's Nest. The two large steeples on either side of town stood tall, as if marking the boundary limits. The lighthouse at the opening of the harbor flashed its light in a continual blinking pattern. The trees that made up the western boundary line appeared to surround the town in a protective hug.

The opposite horizon loomed before them, as if the water rose before it fell over the edge of the world. Although that edge always seemed about the same distance away, Adaleigh had a nagging concern that they might be getting too close. A large ship seemed to teeter on the brink, shrouded in shadow. She could understand how people in the olden days believed the world was flat.

Finally, David slowed his rowing. The waves made them rise and fall in a firm but gentle way. "What do you think so far?"

"It's breathtaking."

He grinned. "This is the life, isn't it?"

She nodded. "Now what?"

"We fish." He reached behind him to gather two rods.

A strange flutter filled her stomach. "Um ... I've never ..."

"I'll talk you through what I do. This is a steel rod." He handed it to her. It was a thin pole attached to a sturdy wooden handle, which also had a large metal bobbin with a crank. He tapped the bobbin. "This is a reel. When the fish bite, we use this to reel them in."

Adaleigh fingered the thread that went from the bobbin—reel—to the tip of the rod. "What's the line made of?"

"Silk. Sometimes it's cotton or linen, but this one is silk."

She nodded, acutely aware of his closeness as they both leaned over the rod.

David cast a glance at her, then reached behind him for a metal box. "In here are a few of our prized possessions. Uncle Mike and I share them since they're expensive." He pulled out a wooden object with eyes and two three-pronged hooks that resembled a fish.

"Why not use a worm?" Adaleigh asked. "Isn't that what most fishermen use?"

David smiled, making talk of worms and lures a rather romantic topic. "Fish in the Great Lakes eat other fish—I know, kind of gross—so in order to catch them, we use lures that mimic smaller fish."

That actually made sense.

"This particular one is called a Bass Oreno." He tied the lure onto the line, then raised the rod over his shoulder so that the lure swung behind him. With a flick of the wrist, the lure flew out over the water and splashed ten feet away. Then he set the rod in a round tube that rose up from the bottom of the boat. "You want to try?"

Adaleigh nodded. David secured another lure, this one with a red head and a white body, to the second pole. She took the wooden handle in her hands and raised it behind her.

"Easy, now." David knelt beside her. "There's an art to it."

Adaleigh swung it forward, and the lure clunked against the inside of the boat.

David chuckled. "You want to flick it, like you're throwing a ball." He took her hands and gently moved her wrists in the motion he described. She tried again, and this time the line sailed out into the water.

"I got it!" Adaleigh turned to grin at him, only to find him closer than she expected. It did funny things to her insides, and based on his slow swallow, it must be doing the same to him.

"I'll secure it." He set the rod in a holder on the opposite side of the boat.

The lines stretched out in the water, waiting for a fish to bite. He checked the fishing rods one last time before settling on his bench. He took the oars and gave them two tugs before letting them hang in the water again. He turned to stare at the horizon with the look of an experienced sailor. He seemed neither hurried nor uptight. It was as if this was his world and he was home. Some of the worry slipped off Adaleigh's shoulders. She felt incredibly safe with David Martins, a feeling she hadn't had for a long time.

Tears pricked her eyes. David deserved a friend who would stay. She couldn't. Her past left her no other option. Not once it caught up to her. Even if she could figure out how to stay out of Mark Hitchens's way. Keep her nose out of Guy Spelding's business. Follow Chief Sebastian's rules. Sure, then maybe she could see a relationship with David. But with the reporter set on announcing her identity to the world, how could she continue to hide from her sister while staying in Crow's Nest?

"Everything okay?" David's callused hand on her arm, more than his voice, brought her back.

Adaleigh swiped at the tears that escaped her eyes. "Just fine," she said and tried to smile as she ran her hand along the top edge of the boat. "We should see what goodies your grandma gave us."

David waited a beat, then mercifully pulled out the picnic basket and dug through it.

Adaleigh stared toward the northeast, where the boat was generally headed, trying to collect herself. The pain in her heart, the longing for the care David continued to show her, it turned into a prayer so desperate. Didn't she deserve to be happy too? Couldn't God grant her that? She'd settle for even a sliver of peace.

"You sure you're okay?" David stilled her hand, having left the opened picnic basket on the bench beside him. The boat rocked gently over tiny waves. "You keep telling me you're fine, and I believe it less and less each time."

He crouched so close, Adaleigh could feel the heat of his body beside her. "Have you ever wanted something so much you fought for it with everything you had?"

"What do you mean?"

"I haven't done it often." She stared at her hand nestled in his. "First time was when I joined the women's swim team. I was determined to prove girls could swim just as well as boys."

David's lips twitched as if he tried not to smile.

"I did it again when I stood up to my dad about going to university. I wanted to prove a woman could achieve academic success—whether other women already had or not. My dad said I couldn't make it work, but I did. He was so proud of me, he ..." Her voice cracked, but she refused to let it break. "You know what I've never stood up for?"

David shook his head.

"Me."

"How so?" His voice was so terribly gentle.

"I've stood up for others. For the greater good. Girls to play a boy's sport, women to achieve success, but never have I stood up for just myself."

"You mean your sister."

"For as long as I can remember, I've come up with every story in the book to cover for her. Now I've done the ultimate in not standing up for myself: I ran away. Literally left everything behind and tried to disappear."

"Sometimes that's what's better, safer." He swiped a knuckle over her cheek to wipe away a tear.

"But I'm not better or safer, am I? I'm still looking over my shoulder." Adaleigh massaged her arm where Mr. Spelding had grabbed her but thought of Mr. Hitchens's threat.

"Aw, Adaleigh, you've been a champion of others for so long. It's okay to let someone else stand up for you. To stand still and let God fight for you."

"When will that happen? When will someone actually stand up for me? When will God fight for me? No one, not a person, not God, has ever done that for me. I'm weary, David, and my heart is hurting."

David frowned but said nothing.

The churning in her stomach warned her she had said too much. "I'm sorry. You didn't invite me along to complain about—"

"Stop." David pulled her to her feet, somehow keeping the boat from rocking as they stood in its center. Her heart jumped out of her chest. Attraction washed over her at his closeness, yet he sounded so stern, so serious. She couldn't manage another man speaking harshly to her after the day she had. Sweat gathered on her forehead. Her surroundings dimmed.

Then David's arms wrapped around her. His warmth chased away the chilly wind. His sturdiness grounded them as the boat rode over a wave. She rested her head against his chest, feeling the strength of his heart beating against her ear. In that moment, it was as if the shelter of God's wings enfolded her. Her breathing slowed. And there, in the middle of a humongous lake, she felt perfectly safe.

CHAPTER SEVENTEEN

"Come." Loath as he was to let her out of his arms, David lowered Adaleigh to the middle bench beside the picnic basket, which he moved out of the way to sit next to her.

"David—"

"Focus on me for a minute." He pulled her chin back toward him so he could see into her hazel eyes. He needed her to hear him. "Never apologize for telling your story, especially to me. I always want to hear it. I wish I knew how to change things for you, but you have people who want to help. We'll figure it out. Together."

Adaleigh nodded, though he couldn't be sure his words soaked in. She looked so vulnerable, it reached into his heart. This woman needed someone to care about her. Unconditionally. No ulterior motives. He brushed her cheek with his thumb, then shook his head. He may want to kiss her right this moment, but he couldn't, wouldn't, take advantage of her vulnerability. He'd find another time to tell her how he felt. Right now, this was about her.

David used the oar on his side to adjust their course, keeping the boat close to the shoreline despite the relatively calm water. "Let's pull out Grandma's soup. I spotted a whole bowl of strawberries in there too."

Adaleigh opened the basket, her straw hat shading the heaviness lingering from the tale she'd just told him. She handed him a thermos, and he winked, hoping to lighten her mood.

"Tell me." He unscrewed the cap of the thermos and poured soup into it. "What is it that you enjoy doing on a quiet day?"

"Where did that question come from?" The gentle breeze played with wisps of hair that danced across her face. She brushed them away.

David looked to the hazy horizon so she couldn't see the depth of the emotion still churning underneath his skin. "I've told you all about my fishing, even convinced you to join me, but I want to hear more about you. Tell me what you'd be doing right now if you weren't on a boat with me."

Adaleigh fidgeted with the cover of her thermos, drawing his attention back to her. Was she afraid of what he might think of her answer? She needn't be. A blush crept into her cheeks. "I'd be reading."

"You enjoy books, do you?" David let a teasing tone infuse his words. "I should have guessed, you being college-educated and all."

"Oh, it started way before that." She perked up like a flower when given a cup of water after a drought. *Success!* "Ever since I was a school girl, whenever I saw a bookshop, I had the insatiable desire to go inside. They are like a land flowing with milk and honey."

"The Promised Land, eh?" He hid a grin behind a spoonful of soup. It warmed him as much as Adaleigh's presence did.

"Absolutely. But without the giants and walled cities. Except in the stories ..."

"And what do you buy in these bookstores?" He asked before she distracted herself into a daydream all her own, a habit of hers he was beginning to recognize.

"Books, of course." Adaleigh tossed a strawberry at him.

He caught it with a laugh. "Books, cooks. I need specifics." He wagged the strawberry at her. "Do you buy dime novels or great mythical tomes?"

"All and sundry. *David Copperfield* is one of my current favorites. I probably have seven different editions in the study back ... home." Tears jumped to her eyes again, but she sniffed them back in place as a particularly strong wave slapped the hull and she grabbed his arm for stability. "My family had a huge library that I cataloged and kept in order."

"Seven editions of the same book?" David scrambled for a way to keep the conversation lighthearted as he tried to ignore the feel of her hand on his arm. "For heaven's sake, why?"

A teasing glint flashed his way. "Sometimes I get two of the same title so I have the original language and an English translation. Like Alexandre Dumas' *Three Musketeers* or *The Count of Monte Cristo*."

He whistled softly. He knew Adaleigh to be an incredibly intelligent woman, but ... wow. "There's one bookstore in Crow's Nest. It'd be an honor to take you there."

"I'd like that." Adaleigh grew quiet, ran her spoon through her soup. David missed her touch, but the afternoon sun made the water sparkle behind her, as if she were a queen sitting on a wooden throne surrounded by glistening jewels and he the captivated peasant.

"I've never been a book guy. Love me a good story, though—and you should hear some of the old captains tell stories!—but reading them in a book was never something I enjoyed." David dipped his oar in the water, inordinately nervous about sharing a part of himself. "I did what I had to in order to get through school, but I prefer the real world. I like feeling the wind and sand and—"

The quick bend of the fishing pole beside him caused David to leap out of his seat. He grabbed the rod and let the silk line go until he gave a little yank, effectively setting the hook. He warmed under Adaleigh's study. This next bit was his favorite part of fishing. It was like a dance—reel a little, give a little, always drawing the fish closer to the boat until he could net it.

"Come here." David used his chin to beckon her to his side.

Adaleigh stumbled forward as the boat rocked. David stepped partially in front of her so she could use his shoulder for support.

"Hold this." He placed the rod in her right hand, the crank of the reel in her left. She hadn't worn gloves on their adventure, and he loved the feel of her hands in his. "Keep it taut. Just like that."

She bit her lower lip, feet planted against the pull of the line.

"Yup. Now keep turning the reel. Once around, then pause. That's it."

"I'm doing it!" Excitement laced her words.

He grinned at her, then grabbed a large net and leaned over the side of the boat. "When I say, take a step back. We want to keep the line nice and tight."

Adaleigh nodded.

David gave the signal. Adaleigh stepped back, turning the reel, as David swept the net into the water.

"Here we go!" He laid the net on the deck. Inside, a fish just under two feet long flopped. He held it up by the gills. "A ten-pound King! A salmon. Always feels good to know we won't go home empty-handed. Want to hold your first fish?"

"Hold it?" She stared at him, then her chin jutted up. "It's all part of the experience, isn't it?"

"You betcha."

She cringed, but held out her hand. Carefully, he set the fish on her fingers.

"Look at you! A right fisherwoman." David grinned.

"Okay, okay. You can take it back." She gave a little shimmy.

When he took it from her, he instructed her to close her eyes. Adaleigh sat primly on the boat bench in the stern and obeyed. Some parts of fishing were ugly, and he wanted to spare her that side today. Taking care of business, he stowed the fish before her eyes could pop open. Then he reset the rod and retook his seat across from her.

"We'll have fish for dinner tonight, thanks to you," he said. Once again, he felt her study. Tried to relax under the scrutiny and let the contentment he always felt after a catch settle like the gentle rocking of the boat.

"Tell me more about you?" Adaleigh cocked her head.

"You're much more interesting, I'm sure."

That received a smile. "Then tell me about younger David. What were you like as a child?"

Good question. "Let's see, ever since I can remember, I loved the water." He grabbed a handful of strawberries. "I'd try to chase the waves, and I always succeeded in getting wet."

"You haven't grown out of your mischievousness, I see."

"Not a bit. Though as I got older, I'd follow Uncle Mike everywhere, trying to walk and talk just like him."

"Did you ever consider joining the police force like him?"

"Nah." David stretched out a leg, his foot nearly reaching her bench. "I just liked Uncle Mike's swagger. It worked great with the ladies."

Adaleigh laughed. He loved that sound.

"In fact, my friends would send me to talk to their moms if they really wanted something. Dessert before dinner. The latest toy. A date with a girl."

"Cheeky."

David's turn to laugh. "I figured it never hurt to ask because nothing was ever lost by at least trying."

"Mindy has a lot of respect for you."

"Yeah." He drew out the word, not quite knowing what to do with her statement. *Wait.* "Do I detect a bit of jealousy?"

Her face reddened. "Don't you need to check the line or something?" She waved a hand at the pole leaning out over the water.

"Nuh-uh." Could she possibly return the feelings he felt for her?

"You're incorrigible!"

David grinned, then took a chance. In an instant, he'd crossed the space between them and taken the space beside her. "I'm guessing that means you left no fiancé or heartbroken beaux behind?"

"Back home, definitely not." She fiddled with the food containers, repacking his grandmother's basket.

David took a deep breath as if ready to dive into the water. "Then you like someone here in Crow's Nest."

Adaleigh gave a subtle nod as she tucked the basket under their seat. When she straightened, it seemed she'd moved a mite closer.

His heart thumped. Could that someone she liked be him?

David wanted to take her hand but feared pushing her. "Losing Mom and my dad leaving us with Grandma, it derailed me more than I realize sometimes. I've grown up before my time, so I've heard. The friends I had growing up, the girls I dated—none of them experienced what I did. They couldn't understand how hard life can be."

"'*To-morrow, and to-morrow, and to-morrow,*'" she whispered. "'*Creeps in this petty pace from day to day, To the last syllable of recorded time; And all our yesterdays have lighted fools The way to dusty death ...*'"

"That's Shakespeare, if I'm not mistaken." He remembered a few of the classics he'd been forced to read in school.

"*Macbeth*." Adaleigh turned back to him. "I've become a fan of Shakespeare."

"You *make* it sound beautiful." *Just like you.*

Adaleigh's eyes swung back to the horizon. "'*... Out, out, brief candle! Life's but a walking shadow, a poor player, That struts and frets his hour upon the stage, And then is heard no more. It is a tale Told by an idiot, full of sound and fury, Signifying nothing.*'"

David kept his eyes on her, a smile softly curving up the edges of his mouth as her words floated between them. This woman, who'd suffered more than any person should, shone like gold after being put through the refiner's fire. Never had he met a woman with her mix of strength and gentleness. Never had he felt this way about anyone either.

Her words faded as her gaze returned to his, pink coloring her cheeks. How long they sat like that, David didn't know.

He reached for her hand. "You've been like a reviving wind picking up tired wings. I know you think leaving is in the best interest of all of us, but, Adaleigh?" He leaned closer. His heart beat faster. "I hope you'll consider staying in Crow's Nest. It's a peaceful, quiet little town that lacks something important." He ran his free hand along the braid that hung over her shoulder. "A beautiful booklover—"

The zip of the fishing line stopped him. For the first time, it didn't send a thrill through him. He searched her eyes a moment longer. She'd have let him kiss her. Stupid fish.

Adaleigh watched as David caught two more small fish—rainbow trout, he explained—in rapid succession. While he reeled them in and tossed them back, darker clouds blew in, and the water grew choppier. It ended their fishing excursion and their conversation. They rowed back in silence until David moored at the dock.

Adaleigh tried not to read too much into her suspicion that he had wanted to kiss her. She would have let him—no, that was too passive a thought. She would have kissed him back, which was even more startling to her.

David leapt out of the boat and offered a hand. "Did you enjoy it?"

"Amazingly."

His eyes brightened with a mix of relief and joy. He squeezed her hand before he let it go. "This is my uncle's land. There's a spot up a ways where we can build a campfire and roast the fish you caught." He rubbed his neck. "Or we could just go for a walk."

Adaleigh bit her lip. The butterflies in her stomach wouldn't let her eat. "A walk sounds lovely."

David set the icebox by the wheel of his grandma's car and held out his arm for her to take. Strolling beside him, lake on one side, towering pines on the other, was like entering a fairytale. One she had no interest in ever leaving.

Adaleigh ran a finger along the bruise that hid beneath her high collar. She needed to tell David about Mark Hitchens, and Guy Spelding. However, the more she thought about Guy Spelding's warning, the more she remembered Mark Hitchens's threat, and the warmer she became.

The cloying pine scent choked her and the lake breeze chilled her. She tightened her grip on David's arm. Why did her memories assault her at the worst possible time? Why couldn't she enjoy a walk without flashing back to horrible circumstances?

"Adaleigh?" David's voice cut through. She focused on the warmth of his hand resting on hers. "What's wrong?"

She could tell him about Spelding, then they could return to their date. She was *not* going to ruin it. Simply start by giving information about him. It was just a chance meeting with someone who might have been the last person to see Amy alive.

"Who may have been the last person to see Amy alive?" David stopped them near the trunk of a giant evergreen. His brows pressed together.

Adaleigh blinked. How much had she just said aloud?

David's arm brushed her shoulder. "Talk to me, Adaleigh. Please?"

Adaleigh swallowed. "It was Mr. Spelding."

"What was?" David's voice coaxed and calmed.

"This afternoon." And that's when Adaleigh realized her mistake.

In an instant, she was there as Spelding grabbed her arm, invading her space. Now David's touch was like fire and she stumbled blindly away from him. Toward where, she didn't know, she just had to get away. The muggy air closed around her mouth like a hand and all her demons flooded back. All the doubts. All the fears.

She sagged onto a fallen log, hidden in the shadows. The quiet of the trees surrounded her in an insulating bubble. However, instead of creating a safe atmosphere, the piney stickiness clung to her throat, threatening to suffocate her. Humidity soaked her clothes, trapping her in stifling bands. The more Adaleigh struggled, the tighter they held her.

"Adaleigh?"

David hadn't deserted her. The concern in his voice tugged at her. She hugged her knees. She'd never shown this weakness to anyone, but David hadn't been scared off. Instead, he claimed *she* lifted *his* tired wings. How could that be when he had given hers the strength to beat again? To hope again.

She raised her chin, gathering her courage to meet David's gaze. She could feel him standing beside her. Waiting.

God had not given her a spirit of fear, but of a sound mind. She might not see a way to untangle her mess, her sister might not ever stop coming after her, the chief may not want to listen, but she'd had enough. She wanted to shed the worry, the fear, and fly free. God gifted her a chance to start over. He brought her to a town that slowed down enough to live, to a family who welcomed her into their home, to a kind-hearted man who treated her with a mix of care and respect she'd never experienced before.

Yet even that scared her. It had all happened so fast.

David touched her arm and she leapt to her feet. Restlessness charged her limbs and she paced away, then back again. Regardless of her feelings for David or his for her, how could she start over without settling old scores? She'd forever be looking over her shoulder for her sister, for Hitchens, for Spelding. That wasn't fair to David, and Adaleigh wouldn't hurt him. Running away wouldn't solve anything, but how could she bring the threats to an end?

She rubbed her forehead, turning the question into a prayer. When she'd paced the same section for the third time with no answer, she swung around to find herself staring up at David.

"Are you okay?" He studied her with compassion. "Will you tell me what happened?"

Adaleigh folded her arms. As if they could keep her feelings from tumbling out.

"Adaleigh, you can trust me."

"I do." The words came out as a whisper, a longing whimper. She pulled her arms tighter. The thing about trust was how small and defenseless it made her feel. She survived on her bravado, her independence, her ability to read another human. When it came to David, he could read her just as well as she could read him. He got behind her defenses—and he actually liked what he saw.

"Then what is this about?" He didn't move, didn't reach for her, just waited. Again.

Adaleigh leaned against the nearest tree. "I want to stop running."

"Then we'll figure—" His roughened finger traced the bruise Guy Spelding had left on her arm, visible where her sleeve had ridden up. "What happened?"

She cringed, waiting for the scolding.

"Adaleigh, what really happened with Guy today? Why do you have a bruise?" Sadness seeped through David's words.

No scolding? No anger? Adaleigh blinked.

"Why didn't I see this before?" His voice trailed away as his fingers moved to her neck.

She jerked away, bumped against a tree branch, and flashed to Mark Hitchens squeezing the life out of her. Fear gripped her lungs, taking away her breath. Adaleigh gasped the wet air and sank against the tree trunk. David knelt with her, concern showing in his rapid assessment.

She tried to tell herself David was safe, tried to pray, but all she could feel was Hitchens's hand around her neck. Adaleigh heaved in air, but none came. She tried to inhale again. Nothing. A hand touched her shoulder, sending alarms through her body. She tried to scramble away, but her back hit a tree.

Oh God, help me.

CHAPTER EIGHTEEN

D avid steeled himself against the emotions flooding him as
Adaleigh cowered against the rough bark of the pine tree. It'd
been torture to watch her battle whatever horrid image had her in its grip,
but when she jerked away from his touch it gutted him. He blinked away
the tears that smarted his eyes and made sure to speak calmly but firmly,
hoping to break through her panic-induced haze. "You're safe, Adaleigh.
No one will harm you."

She breathed rapidly, as if afraid the air would disappear.

"You're safe," David repeated and tentatively clasped her hands.
Touch could help ground her, but his touch had caused the attack in the
first place. "Breathe in. Breathe out. With me. Nice and slow. In. Out.
That's it."

He pressed his fingers to her wrist, felt her heart rate slow as her
breathing evened. *Thank you, God.* "There, some color is returning." He
brushed hair out of her eyes.

Adaleigh leaned her head back against the tree trunk, revealing the
bruise on her neck. "The ground is hard."

He forced a smile past the concern he knew was etched in his face.
Couldn't hold it. "You're shaking. Let me get you my coat from the car."

Before he could jump up, Adaleigh grabbed his arm. "Don't leave."

Never. As long as she'd let him stay, he'd never leave. He slid closer to her. "I won't go anywhere."

She leaned into his warmth, and he carefully wrapped an arm around her shoulders. Slowly, quietly, the story emerged. From Mark Hitchens's greeting her when she went to meet with his wife, to seeing the young lady he was with, to his physical threat. Then later to her meeting Guy Spelding, to his story about waiting for Amy, to his warning.

When the words finally stopped, Adaleigh rested her head on David's shoulder, and he tightened his hold, fighting the fury he felt on her behalf. How could these men use their strength to harm instead of protect?

"Thank you for telling me," he whispered.

Crickets chirped as silence settled between them. Then Adaleigh asked, "Why haven't you suggested I'd be better off in an asylum?"

David frowned. "What do you mean?"

She lifted her head and raised her eyebrows. Right. That's where many ended up when battling their demons.

He cupped her face in his hand. "I'm going to insist we tell my uncle because you were physically attacked and threatened today—" she flinched, but he held her steady— "As for the idea of insanity ... Adaleigh. You do not belong in an asylum. You need family and friends around you who will—" *Love you.* "Now, no more talk of asylums. I am here for you. Whatever you need." He ran his thumb over her cheek.

She closed her eyes and leaned into his hand. "Okay. I trust you, David."

He lowered his head and pressed a light, chaste kiss to her lips. "I trust you, too."

Saturday, June 7

The next morning, Adaleigh awoke feeling as though she'd been in a boxing ring. In the past, when she didn't have to get up on a cloudy day, she would have continued lounging in bed, likely with a book, but it was Jam Day, and she'd promised to help. Besides, she wanted to see if David was home—she pressed her fingers to her lips, the gentle kiss he placed there like healing oil to her heart.

Telling David, who'd then helped her tell his uncle about Mr. Hitchens and Mr. Spelding and the threats ... well, what should have terrified her felt freeing. She had people fighting alongside her now, and the fact that she no longer needed to carry her burdens alone had lifted a weight from her shoulders.

Remembering the stains on Mrs. Martins's hands after working with the strawberries, she put on her dirtier dress, then went downstairs. Her hostess was in her robe, sipping coffee and reading a book at the kitchen table. Adaleigh hesitated in the middle of the family room, .

The older woman spotted her and smiled. "How are you feeling this morning, dear?"

"Rested and much better. At least I will after I've had my coffee."

Mrs. Martins put aside her book. Her Bible.

"I've interrupted you."

"Nonsense. Get your coffee and come sit. You look refreshed. Did you enjoy your outing with David?" A twinkle danced in her eyes.

"The water was gorgeous." But she preferred to keep her time on the water with him close and not share, so she said, "Tell me about the strawberries. What all are we doing today?"

"Why, making jam, of course." Mrs. Martins spoke brightly. "Although I always have to make a pie too. Did you know strawberries are actually a member of the rose family?"

"No, I didn't. Very interesting. And I've never made—" A low rumble of thunder interrupted her.

Mrs. Martins pushed away from the table and moved aside the curtain to peer out the window over the sink. Adaleigh followed. Rain pattered the glass. The older woman's reflection revealed a furrowed brow and downturned mouth.

The same concern then darted to Adaleigh's midsection. "Is David out fishing?"

"Probably." Mrs. Martins turned away, but her worry stayed. "He's at the docks by three or four in the morning during the summer. Perhaps they have returned by now."

"Or maybe they didn't go out at all?"

Mrs. Martins shook her head. "It all depends on the water."

David had been doing this long enough that he knew when to return, right? Why risk their lives for a couple fish or a couple dollars? What unnerved her most, however, was how much she wanted David to return safely. It threatened to steal her breath.

Mrs. Martins rested her aging hand on Adaleigh's shoulder. "He's a good lad. He'll call to tell us he is safe as soon as he can. Give me a few minutes to get dressed, and we can start the strawberries."

Adaleigh had poured and finished her coffee and washed her cup by the time Mrs. Martins returned.

She tossed Adaleigh a faded blue apron. "Once that's on, climb on a chair and bring down that pot." She pointed to the top of the refrigerator. The pot she wanted was a type of stock pot Adaleigh remembered their family cook using when she stuck her head into the kitchen.

Mrs. Martins tied on her own fire-engine-red apron. "Fill it three-quarters of the way with water, then set it on the stove. I'll get wood to get it hot enough to boil that much water."

Adaleigh obeyed. After, Mrs. Martins stoked the stove, she set Ball jars and lids inside the pot. Then she handed Adaleigh a potato masher and a large bowl filled with five pounds of strawberries and told her to, quote, "mash 'em up good."

Five pounds of strawberries sounded like a lot, and it was. Adaleigh stood at the table and mashed until her forearm hurt. Then she switched hands and kept mashing. Somehow, it let her think while keeping any residual panic at bay. Or maybe her mind simply lingered on the kiss.

"You want all the chunks out, or we'll have chunks in the jam," Mrs. Martins explained as she fed the stove another log. A crack of thunder followed her words, and she frowned.

David hadn't called yet. Adaleigh's anxiety multiplied. His commercial fishing boat was larger than the one they'd been on last night, but he still took it far from land, in open water where a storm could ... She focused on mashing.

Once the strawberries were the consistency Mrs. Martins preferred, the older woman handed her a new bowl. "Six more pounds, dear."

Adaleigh stared at her.

Her face wrinkled into a smile. "We have to make enough to last year round."

In a small bowl, Mrs. Martins combined sugar and this powder she called pectin. Then she mixed it into the mashed strawberries. Looking like a chemist, she used tongs to remove the jars from the stockpot. Then, using a ladle, she filled the jars, wiped them down, and put them back into the boiling water.

"That's it?" Adaleigh asked. "That doesn't seem so hard." Mashing aside.

"I did a lot of the work the other day when I cleaned all the—"

"Strawberries?" Samantha wandered down the stairs, wearing a summery pink dress. "Kyle will be here around lunch."

"Why's he coming?" Patrick bounded down the stairs.

"None of your business." Samantha plopped herself at the table.

"Fine. I'll be home later!" Patrick headed for the front door.

"Wear a raincoat, young man!" Mrs. Martins called after him. "Samantha, help yourself to breakfast."

All fell silent, except for the bubbling water and the pounding rain. Every few moments, it seemed, Mrs. Martins would glance outside. Adaleigh knew she was thinking about David. Adaleigh was doing the same, starting at every rumble of distant thunder. Surely, he wasn't still on the water. But a conscientious man like him would have called by now if he was back on land. So, where was he?

David caught his balance as the *Tuna Mann* rode up one wave and down the other side. Rain and spray soaked him through despite his slicker. He swiped the wet off his face and sent a glare toward the wheelhouse where Captain Mann drove the boat.

He hadn't slept last night, his mind churning over what Adaleigh had told him, then dipping as he remembered the feel of her lips. David finally understood the allure of mutiny. Getting struck by lightning wasn't worth a few dollars let alone losing his life and leaving Adaleigh behind.

"Don't you dare take in those lines." Captain Mann shouted from the door of the wheelhouse. "The fish will be biting in droves in this storm."

The man was plumb crazy!

David stumbled, losing his hat over the side of the boat. And just like that, all the emotion he'd been bottling to deal with later rose up in David's chest. He was through being nice. Through sacrificing for everyone else. He wanted to get back to Adaleigh. Alive.

"Martins!" Captain Mann swore like the proverbial sailor. Thunder punctuated his words.

"Fire me, then." David shouted at his captain as he cut the lines loose. "I told you this storm was too dangerous to go out in. I warned you about it yesterday. We had ample time to change our plans. Take us back to the harbor, or I will."

Captain Mann's splutter ended in an *oomph* when Randell charged past him to lean over the side of the boat, losing his breakfast. The boat rocked on another wave, and David dove for the man's belt before he could go overboard.

"We're calling in our position and heading in." David stared down his boss.

Thankfully, Mann didn't deck him when he reached for the radio. He just yanked the receiver out of his hand. "I'm still the captain. I'll call it in."

David stepped aside. Thunder gave a deafening crack, and Mann mashed the button. The radio was dead.

A knock at the door interrupted their silent work. Adaleigh rolled her wrists to ease the soreness in her arms. Whiteness crept into Mrs. Martins face, and even Samantha sat at attention.

"Grandma?" Samantha looked from Mrs. Martins to the door, a quiver in her voice.

"I'll answer it." She wiped her hands on her apron, and they shook too.

Adaleigh left her masher to follow Mrs. Martins and Samantha to the door. Why would a visitor cause such a reaction?

Mrs. Martins opened the front door. "Hello?"

Buck Wilson stood solemnly on the porch, hands clasped in front of him. "Pardon me, Mrs. Martins."

"David?" When she barely whispered the word, blood pounded in Adaleigh's ears. This was how the community shared news of a fishing accident.

He pulled his wet fedora from his head, dripping water puddled at his feet. "We can't raise the *Tuna Mann*, ma'am."

Adaleigh's breath caught. Did that mean what she thought it meant?

Samantha clutched her grandmother's arm. "They're still ... out there?"

Buck gave a slow nod that felt more like a punch to the stomach. The memory of Adaleigh's professor pulling her out of the commencement line came back to her in a rush. Standing beneath an aged oak, she'd learned her parents were gone. Her world had been tipped on end, but it was also the moment that started her on the path that led her here, to this family. To David and his kindness.

"Don't lose hope," Buck was saying, a hand wrapped around Mrs. Martins's, his expression earnest. "We didn't get a distress signal from them, either, and just because we haven't gotten them on the radio doesn't mean they're in trouble."

"Of course," Mrs. Martins murmured, but she didn't sound convinced.

"C'mon Grandma." Samantha tugged her arm. "Let's finish the jam while we wait for David to come home."

Buck stepped back, rolling the brim of his hat. "I promise to keep you informed."

"Thank you, Mr. Wilson." Mrs. Martins allowed Samantha to lead her back toward the kitchen.

A muscle in Buck's jaw bobbed before he turned to Adaleigh. "Miss Sirland, a word?" Buck waved her outside. He half sat on the porch railing, his black suit coat dangling open, revealing a wet light-blue shirt. Rain sprinkled his rounded shoulders, but he didn't seem to notice.

"What does it mean that you can't raise them on the radio?" Adaleigh clutched her arms around her middle, chilled despite the humidity.

"We don't know." Lines marred his chiseled features. "This is the part of the job I like least."

Adaleigh nodded. "Why did the captain take out the boat if bad weather was coming in?"

Buck blew out a breath. "Captain Mann strongly supports the police's investigation into the Conglomerate. He's not my biggest fan."

"What does that have to do with the weather?"

"He is under the impression we don't have their best interest at heart." Buck rubbed his chin. "He thinks that if we urge boats to stay in harbor, it's because we don't want them making money."

"You wouldn't do that, would you?"

Buck's shoulders sagged. "You seem like you have a good head for business, so you can understand that running a business is more complicated than Mr. Mann makes it appear. But"—he straightened, stuffing one hand into his pocket, the other tapped his hat on his leg—"I wanted to speak to you privately regarding our conversation the other day. Since the police and I are not on good terms, would you pass along a piece of information to Detective O'Connor?"

"What about Chief Sebastian?" Not that Adaleigh wanted to tell him anything.

"He's a bumbling idiot. Anyone asking around can see Frank Martins has the least motive for the situation."

What a relief to hear someone else say it. "You believe he's innocent too?"

"I didn't say he couldn't have done it, just that there are other people with more to lose."

"Like Guy Spelding?"

"Guy." A shadow passed over Buck's face. "Guy has made a few missteps in his first days here."

Adaleigh bit back a humorless laugh. "Just a few?"

Buck raised an eyebrow. "You too?"

"He didn't like me talking with you." She rubbed her arm and also thought of Mindy.

Another strange expression passed over Buck's features but was gone before she could interpret it. "You, Miss Sirland, have caused quite the stir in Crow's Nest."

"That was the opposite of my intentions." Adaleigh took a settling breath. "What did you want me to tell Detective O'Connor?"

A thunderclap shook the porch, and Adaleigh couldn't stop the yelp that leapt from her lips. Buck jumped, one hand going to his empty hip, the other stretched out toward her as if he could shield her from harm. A blast of wind swirled a sheet of rain through the porch, drenching Buck. He muttered something unrepeatable and tried to shake out his sleeves. The drowned-rat look made his suit coat appear three times too large for him. Not nearly as appealing as the sharply dressed man Adaleigh first met.

"Just tell the good detective to come see me at headquarters," Buck said. "I'll return with more information on the *Tuna Mann* as soon as I can."

Another roll of thunder followed Adaleigh as she hurried inside. Mrs. Martins was removing the filled jam jars from the stockpot and replacing them with empty ones. Samantha shifted from foot to foot.

As soon as the filled jars lined the counter, Mrs. Martins grabbed the ear cone off the phone box on the wall. "I'm calling David's office."

Samantha and Adaleigh exchanged worried looks as Mrs. Martins spoke with the operator.

"No answer." Mrs. Martins tapped the ear cone against her other hand, then asked the operator to connect her with Detective O'Connor.

Lightning gave a deafening crack right outside the door. Rain pounded the house, and Adaleigh didn't like the pit developing deep in her stomach. She focused on breathing in, then out, praying panic wouldn't take root.

"Grandma?" Samantha pointed out the kitchen window. Past the white sheets of rain, a large branch of the tree next door hung by its bark. It waved in the wind. The right gust and it would be free to crash into anything, including the house.

"Michael isn't answering, either," Mrs. Martins said as she hung up. "And we could lose the telephone or electric lines any moment."

That's when Adaleigh realized the tree branch could be the least of their worries. The clouds were taking on a bumpy, swirling look that made the pit in her stomach turn into a boulder. Thunder rumbled like an earthquake, and another swift gust of wind rattled the window. Samantha stepped back.

"I don't like this." Mrs. Martins untied her apron. "I'll rummage for candles."

Thunder rumbled alongside another knocking at the door.

"That has to be Kyle." Samantha nearly skidded down the hall like Samson had done the other day. Mrs. Martins followed her slowly. Likely, she wanted to be sure there was no news before she began her search for candles. Adaleigh trailed at a distance.

A very soggy Kyle closed the front door behind himself. Not as tall as David, but definitely more lean, he had an easy smile and a freckled face. Water dripped down his shaggy strawberry-blond hair, his flat cap a soggy roll in his hand.

"I don't have news." Kyle hugged Samantha, wet clothes and all. "Wish I did."

"Samantha, dear, get Kyle a blanket so he won't be chilled." Mrs. Martins disappeared into her bedroom.

Samantha opened her mouth, and Adaleigh expected a complaint to come out, but Kyle beat her to it.

"I'm fine, Sam. Water doesn't hurt anyone." He ran his fingers through his hair, making it stand on end. A slender rope hung around his neck, something weighing it down hidden under his collar. Thunder rumbled again, and the clouds looked even more agitated.

"Samantha, call around to tell Patrick to come home." Mrs. Martins reappeared with a handful of candles. "Let's finish up the strawberries before the power goes out. We need to keep our minds busy."

She stoked the oven, and Adaleigh returned to mashing strawberries, though her heart wasn't in it. She kept glancing at the rain battering the patio window and hoping David wasn't outside in the middle of it. The storm intensified, and she craned her neck to spot the tree branch in the neighbor's yard. It hadn't fallen ... yet.

"So you're the new lass?" Kyle laid the now-damp towel across the back of a chair, the hint of a brogue lacing his tone.

"How do you know Samantha?" Adaleigh asked, reminding herself why he'd come. Perhaps the conversation would distract her from David's plight.

Kyle glanced over at Samantha. "We've been friends since we were wee ones."

"Samantha said you are also a friend of Sean's?" Adaleigh could've used more tact, but concern made her impatient. "It must be hard to watch your friend lose his girlfriend."

Kyle's innate cheerfulness faded. "He and I have been friends since before I can remember. He adored Amy, but Amy was crazy. He and I never fought about lasses before her."

"As in, got upset at each other?" A gust of wind slammed into the house, and Adaleigh shot a glance toward the tree branch. Still couldn't see it.

"Knock-out fight." Kyle frowned. "He couldn't see that Amy was using him, and when a knock to the head couldn't do it, I let him be. He's pig-headed. Once an idea gets lodged, nothing is going to shake it."

"Kyle, do you know anyone else who might be mad that Sean was seeing Amy?"

"I mean, just 'cause we're not in school any more doesn't mean all the lads weren't still jealous," Kyle said. "But why kill Amy, not Sean?"

Good point. "What about Sean? Anyone want to get even with him?"

"Enough to kill Amy? That's drastic."

Another good point. Adaleigh glanced at Mrs. Martins. What would she be thinking about this line of questioning? She screwed lids on the jars and added them to her growing collection, unlit candles ready on the counter beside them.

"There are the other boyfriends," Kyle said more to Samantha than Adaleigh. "Sean denied it, but yeah, she'd go out with someone else, then come back to Sean as if he was her lifeline. Anyway, I'd think they'd kill Sean, not Amy."

"Not necessar—" Adaleigh's words were cut short as thunder cracked right outside the house. A burst of wind followed. Then a tree branch sailed through the back door, breaking it wide open.

CHAPTER NINETEEN

S plintered wood flew through the kitchen as screams outmatched the howling wind. The familiar rushing filled Adaleigh's ears, but the need to help others managed to push the panic away.

"Is everyone okay?" she asked, coming out of her crouch by the ice box.

She took account of the room. The branch—really a small tree—had smashed through the window, knocking aside the table and crushing the chairs. Its branches reached toward the ceiling and filled the area where the table used to be. Rain poured through the open spaces, scattering leaves and debris.

"Sam's hurt." Kyle's voice sounded muffled. Adaleigh peered around the branches. He held Samantha close as she clutched her leg. A shard of glass stuck eight inches out of her calf. Samantha's breathing came quickly, and tears spilled over her cheeks.

"Leigh, dear, help me up. I'll call for the ambulance," Mrs. Martins said from by the stove. "Or Dr. Thompson."

Adaleigh jumped to her feet and helped Mrs. Martins to hers. Other than a few scratches and torn clothes, the older woman seemed okay. Adaleigh stepped carefully as she shifted to crouch beside Samantha.

"I have a little first aid training." Nevertheless, Adaleigh cringed at the wound. The piece looked well-embedded. She didn't dare remove it since it seemed to be stopping any blood from oozing out.

"The phone is dead." Mrs. Martins waved at the box on the wall, then grabbed the keys hanging beside it. "We're taking her to the clinic ourselves. Or the hospital if Dr. Thompson is not there, which I doubt he will be. Kyle, carry her to the car."

Adaleigh glanced at the angry clouds. The risk of traveling in this weather was nothing to take lightly, but not as great as the danger Samantha faced if she didn't get the glass spear removed.

"We'll make it." Mrs. Martins seemed to read her mind. Fear lurked in the back of her eyes, but determination overrode it. "Adaleigh, you find David and Patrick and tell them where we've gone. Make sure they're safe."

Adaleigh wanted to argue, but knew that not only would Mrs. Martins not hear of it, someone needed to tell her grandsons what happened. "How will I get a hold of you?"

"Call the clinic if you find a working telephone. If we aren't there, we're at the hospital in Hawk's River."

In a matter of minutes, Adaleigh stood in the doorway as Mrs. Martins drove away. She was alone. Alone in a strange town, in a house that was not her own, with a storm pouring rain through a broken window and, filling the room, a tree she couldn't move on her own. Her usual self-sufficiency bowed to her wish that David was here. Even more, she wished she knew whether he was safe.

As she stepped back into the house, emptiness closed in like a wet wool blanket. The storm wailed outside, and wind rushed through the broken window. The pounding rain sounded hollow, reminding her just how alone she was.

Thunder propelled her from her frozen state. Adaleigh left a note for Patrick in case he came back before she found a way to find him, grabbed a slicker from the coat stand, and stepped into the rain. A gust nearly knocked her over as she reached the sidewalk. This was not the smartest action, but she needed to find out if David was okay and she wouldn't disappoint Mrs. Martins. Maybe Buck could help her, too.

Adaleigh half ran toward the boardwalk. If people were looking for the *Tuna Mann*, a crowd might have gathered near Captain Mann's shop. Maybe David would already be there by the time she arrived. If she arrived.

The clouds swirled like an ugly cauldron of stew, black and angry. Lightning streaked across the sky, showing the enormous height of the thunderclouds.

"What in heaven's name are you doing out here?" shouted a male voice behind her.

Adaleigh yipped, her heart taking a leap. "Buck Wilson, you scared me!"

He hadn't changed from his sopping suit. "I repeat, what are you doing out here? It's too dangerous." He caught up to her. "I stopped at the Martins's house. Where is—"

"You have news?" She searched his eyes, hoping, fearing.

"They found the *Tuna Mann*." Buck pulled her arm to keep them moving. He grabbed the same place as the bruise Guy inflicted, and Adaleigh cringed. She dislodged his hand from her arm. "Is the crew safe?"

He studied her for a moment. "I don't know yet."

Panic made her walk faster. "What were they doing out there? Why did they wait so long to come in? Do you know why they couldn't radio?"

Buck kept pace. "Did you leave the house to find out?"

"Mrs. Martins took Samantha to the hospital and sent me to find her grandsons. Her phone is down, so here I am."

They reached the boardwalk as the rain lessened. Adaleigh swiped wet hair out of her face. The wind grew still, as if the world held its breath. Fear crackled through the air. Even the seagulls hid. Their shoes pounded on the wooden planks of the empty boardwalk. Then, in the distance, a distinct rumble began. The sound sent skitters of ice straight into her heart.

"We need to go faster. The Wharfside has a cellar out back." Buck grabbed her arm again, right on the bruise.

"Youch!" Adaleigh clenched her teeth. She couldn't spare patience for pain right now.

"I barely touched you." Buck looked at her as though she was losing her mind. Maybe she was. "Do you not see what's coming?" He pointed to the sky.

She didn't need to be reminded. Not with David possibly out on the open water and Mrs. Martins, Samantha, and Kyle likely still on the road to the hospital. The rumble grew louder. Closer.

Then she heard her name. She searched the boardwalk. There, hurrying toward them, herded by a group of grizzled men. David waved.

Tears of relief jumped to her eyes. David jogged ahead and pulled her into a crushing hug. He tried to speak, then gave up and hugged her tighter.

"We need to get to the shelter," Buck shouted as the rumble grew into a roar.

David released her, and Adaleigh got a glance over his shoulder. Her gaze landed on the one person who seemed more phantom than real. Feeling drained out of her like water through a cloth. Whooshing, like water through a dam, filled her ears. Her surroundings swirled like the clouds.

Ashley? How was she was here? In this storm?

Adaleigh blinked, but her sister was real. They locked eyes just a pool's length away and Adaleigh knew her sister had arrived to finish what she'd attempted the night of their parents' funeral.

Adaleigh backed away from David. Her eyes glazed, her skin white.

"Adaleigh—" David reached for her. His relief at being on dry land, at holding her in his arms, washed away.

"Into the Wharfside!" Buck shouted into the wind.

But Adaleigh was already in motion. Without sparing a word, she spun on her heel and ran.

"Adaleigh, stop!" David called after her, but she disappeared around a corner. Adrenaline coursed through his tired limbs. What had spooked her? She zig-zagged her way to ... where? Didn't she hear the tornado's barreling wind? Not that it would change his actions.

He dashed after her, footsteps following him. He didn't look back to see whose. Adaleigh ran north on Main Street, past the shops that lined the street. The air took on a greenish hue, as if a filter had been lowered over David's eyes to strain out the light. Above, the swirling clouds dipped menacingly. He needed to reach her, stop her, before those clouds turned into a second tornado. His own fear spurred him faster. With a lurch, he grabbed her. Adaleigh whirled around, eyes wide and terrified.

"I did not just survive on that boat to watch this storm kill you." David clutched her shoulders, his fear driving his words. "What is going on?"

"Adaleigh, are you okay?" Buck pulled up next to him, breathless.

Adaleigh? David glared at Buck. Buck squared his shoulders. Then, quiet at first, the wind rolled into a sound that seemed to fill his whole body. They needed to find shelter before the second tornado ripped them apart.

"We need to go back to The Wharfside," David tugged Adaleigh's arm.

"No. Conglomerate headquarters is closer," Buck said.

David clamped down on the ungracious words that wanted to slip out.

Buck glared. "We were the ones who found your soaking—"

"If you hadn't pushed Mann," David shot back, "maybe we wouldn't have been out there in the first place."

"We go to the headquarters." Adaleigh's quiet words stole David's anger.

"Follow me." Buck jogged to the one-story building directly across from Mrs. Whittlebush's seamstress shop.

The roar grew around them, as if a train had jumped its tracks and headed straight for Crow's Nest. David took Adaleigh's hand as Buck held the door for them. She glanced over her shoulder before blinking at the dim room, clutching David's hand tighter than he gripped hers. David wished he could comfort her, help her face whatever scared her, but they needed to take shelter first.

"This way." Buck took the lead. "We'll go to the old wine cellar. This used to be a booming saloon before Prohibition."

"Fitting," David mumbled.

"Saving your hide twice in one day should count for something," Buck snapped.

"Can we not argue while trying to escape a tornado?" Adaleigh's voice betrayed her panic level. She needed them calm, not bickering. David clamped his mouth shut.

Buck hauled open a large wooden door at the back of the room. David followed Adaleigh down the steps as the fury of the storm hit Crow's Nest but stopped abruptly when she reached the bottom. Sean Green swung to face them, a gun pointed directly at Adaleigh's chest.

Adaleigh froze. David pulled up right behind her. Buck swore ever so quietly at her side.

"What are you doing here?" Sean demanded. He moved the gun between her and two other men standing at the back of the low cellar—Mark Hitchens and Guy Spelding.

"He's crazy." Mr. Hitchens frantically waved his arms from his place in the far corner of the room.

"*He's* crazy?" Mr. Spelding glared at Hitchens. "You're the one he followed here."

"I wanted to know why the Conglomerate is asking questions about me." Mr. Hitchens turned his anger toward Adaleigh. "You! You're behind all of this."

Sean swung his gun back toward her. "You killed Amy?"

Adaleigh's heart pounded in her ears, deafening the roar coming from outside. She stared at the muzzle of the gun, the edges of her vision darkening so that it was all she could see.

"Breathe out," David whispered in her ear. Calm spread from his voice. She obeyed and was able to suck in a lot more air in the next breath.

"I told you she was responsible." Mr. Hitchens stalked toward her.

"Stop moving!" Sean shook the gun at him. Hitchens hesitated.

David shifted beside her. "Someone needs to go get help."

"We can't leave in this storm," Buck said, barely audible over the roar of the wind outside.

"Figure something out." Anger laced David's words. "You're the head of the Conglomerate."

"Oh, just go. Both of you," Adaleigh hissed at them. Boys. She rolled her eyes. Irritation usurping her fear, she stepped into the basement, facing Sean and his gun.

"We have a misunderstanding," she said to him. "Can we put the gun away so we can talk it out?"

"I want to know who killed Amy." Pain aged Sean's face.

Adaleigh held up her hands in a calming gesture. "But using a gun to get a confession isn't going to help."

Thunder shook the building around them.

"She's been sticking her nose—" Mr. Hitchens stepped forward again.

"Shut up!" Sean swung the gun back at Hitchens, effectively stopping him. He turned the gun back to Adaleigh. "Talk."

"You don't believe Mr. Martins killed Amy." Adaleigh had psychology and rhetoric on her side, the best defense to disarm Sean without causing anyone injury. As long as her own panic stayed at bay. She pushed thoughts of her sister away.

"The old drunk?" Sean gave a humorless laugh. "What would she be doing with him?"

"He's the one the police think—"

"What do they know?" Sean spat, then pointed the gun at Spelding. "That man was the last to see her alive. I saw them."

"She told me she broke up with you." Spelding waved his arms.

"Liar!" Sean cocked the hammer.

"Sean. We need to talk about this." Adaleigh tried to step forward but stopped when Sean turned the gun on her.

Adaleigh bit her lip. Fought the panic that threatened to rise. *Breathe out, Adaleigh*, repeated David's voice in her head. This would not end well unless someone could get through to Sean. The outside roar grew louder. Or maybe that was the roaring in her ears. Regardless, she needed to end this.

"You loved Amy." Adaleigh met Sean's wild and unfocused eyes.

"She was perfect." Sean leaned on his back foot and she caught the slight dip in the weapon.

She held his gaze. "Gorgeous. Fun. Popular."

"And the most beautiful ..." He choked.

The building above creaked against the power of the wind.

"No one thought she was good enough for you," Adaleigh continued.

"But she was!"

"I know." She stepped closer. "You gave her your whole heart."

"And someone took her away from me." The anguish came out of Sean's very soul.

Adaleigh could feel nothing but pity for the boy. He hadn't deserved Amy.

Then, like an ember bursting into flame, anger filled his eyes. He turned his gun toward Spelding and Hitchens. "Which one of you killed her?"

"Sean—" Adaleigh began, but he shoved her toward them. She stumbled on her heels, nearly falling onto her backside. When she looked back at Sean, the familiar panic gripped her chest. She'd seen that same look in Ashley's eyes before the knife nearly killed her. Adaleigh had failed, and now there was no doubt Sean would kill the person he believed caused him so much pain.

That's when Adaleigh noticed David had left his half-concealed spot on the stairs and inched along the front wall to come behind Sean. She tried not to watch him, to tip off Sean, but she was losing her own battle. The storm seemed to press down on them. It filled the basement with a tumultuous roar that felt as if the walls closed in. Before her was a gun in the hands of a wild-eyed boy who reminded her of Ashley, and behind her were the two men who had physically attacked her, leaving her bruised and threatened.

"If one of you doesn't tell me ..." The screech of Sean's voice sounded like a fork scratched on a plate, but it effectively snapped her attention back to the present. "I'll start shooting."

A beat. A frozen moment where all was still except the storm. Then everyone spoke at once.

"He did!" Hitchens pointed at Spelding.

"I didn't do it!" Spelding shouted.

David went for the gun.

"Put him down!"

"Pin the kid!"

"Stop!" Sean screamed and fired the gun at the ceiling.

David stepped back, hands raised.

An arm wrapped around Adaleigh's middle, but before she could react, a knife was pressed to her throat.

"Spelding, what are you doing?" Terror thrummed through David's body.

"Since you can't get the job done, I'm getting us out of here." Spelding adjusted the knife so it pressed up against the bottom of Adaleigh's jawbone. "Kid, drop the gun or I'll kill her."

Desperation clouded David's brain.

"You two battle this out," Hitchens mumbled as he edged toward the door.

"Stop it!" Sean pointed the gun at Hitchens. "I want to know who killed Amy before anyone leaves here."

"Can't we talk about all this like civilized humans?" David glared at all three of them.

"Just shoot Hitchens and get this over with, then," Spelding said, tightening his grip around Adaleigh's waist.

With her hands free, could she push him away? Only if she could get a good enough angle on the knife. David caught her eye and slowly shook his head. He didn't want her fighting Spelding if it risked her more. He glanced at Sean, then the gun. Adaleigh furrowed her eyebrows.

Hands low, David gave her a *sit still* sign and backed himself behind Sean. He planned a second attempt at disarming Sean, which should end Spelding's threat on Adaleigh. He cocked his head. Did she agree? Adaleigh closed her eyes—hopefully, her way of agreeing with him.

"You didn't kill her?" Adaleigh directed the question over her shoulder at Spelding.

David held in a groan. What was she doing? He wanted her to wait.

"Why would I?" Spelding growled. "But don't think just because I'm not her killer, I won't use you to get out of here. You're just a girl."

Heaven help us. That was the wrong thing to say to someone like Adaleigh. He could have predicted her stomp on Spelding's right instep. The man howled, his knife leaving her neck. Adaleigh leapt away as David and Hitchens both lunged at Sean. The gun skittered out of Sean's hands. Spelding and Hitchens dove for it.

A deafening roar drowned out their yells. Then, as if a giant used his bare hands to rip apart the building above, it came crashing down, beams snapping overhead.

David managed to slide Sean out of the way of a falling cabinet. Adaleigh ducked as debris fell around her. Hitchens covered his head as plaster showered him in white dust, using words that burned even a fisherman's ears, then stuffed the gun into his belt. Spelding took the moment to dash toward the stairs, only to have them collapse under him as the upper floor gave way.

Beams crashed through the ceiling, aimed for Adaleigh. David fought to get his feet under him in time to push her out of their way. Debris slowed him. Just out of his reach, a board hit her shoulder, knocking her to the ground. Another landed on her leg, trapping her ankle between two other boards.

"We'll get you out." David was at her side in a moment. He grabbed the two-by-four that pinned her leg. "Spelding, Hitchens, help me lift this."

"Just leave her!" Hitchens yelled over the din. He clambered up the debris, but Spelding yanked him off. Hitchens shoved the gun into his back. "Out of my way, idiot!"

Sean growled like an injured bear and tackled Hitchens, the gun flying out of Hitchens's hands. "Did you kill her? Did you? Did you?" he screamed.

"Get off me." Hitchens punched Sean in the jaw, sending him flying.

Spelding was piling debris to use as steps. Hitchens found the gun, aimed it at Spelding. "Move again and die." A soullessness filled Hitchens's eyes. David shivered. He would not hesitate to kill.

"Think about what you're doing." Spelding raised his hands.

"You killed Amy?" Sean asked, rising slowly, as if drunk.

David didn't dare move. Wouldn't draw the attention of these crazed men to where the boards had pinned Adaleigh, rendering her helpless to their whims.

"She deserved it." Hitchens took Spelding's knife and plunged it into Sean's side. "And so do you."

The air fled out of David's lungs as if the knife had gone into his own side. Adaleigh curled into a ball. David pressed her shoulder and swallowed down the emotion clogging his chest. "Hang in there," he whispered. "We're getting out of here."

The roar of wind settled to a gusty blow. Rain dripped through the broken building. The room filled with distant thunder. The tornado had passed.

Hitchens tapped the barrel of his gun on his palm.

"Just shoot us and be done with it." Spelding spit the words.

"This cannot trace back to me," Hitchens muttered.

Adaleigh stirred.

"Shhh." David tightened his grip on her shoulder.

"We need a plan," she whispered. "Before he shoots us right here."

"Don't draw attention. I have to get these boards off you first."

"Martins," Hitchens shouted. "We're taking your boat."

David cringed. "But—"

"You're not getting us on a boat," Spelding said.

"Oh, I will." A malicious gleam flashed in Hitchens's eyes. "Martins will make sure you get to the boat, or I'll kill his girl."

Cold ran through Adaleigh. Her life in the hands of these men? Perhaps if they could get Spelding on their side, they'd have a chance to get away before reaching the boat. Spelding must have realized that, too, because he agreed to help lift the beam that pinned Adaleigh. Pain shot up her leg, but she forced herself to hobble.

While David and Spelding freed Adaleigh, Hitchens climbed up the debris. From his vantage point, he instructed her to climb out first. Once she reached the top, Hitchens gripped her arm, keeping her close, and then demanded David climb next. Lastly, Spelding. Adaleigh hated to leave Sean alone in the basement. But if he was still alive—a big if—he needed treatment soon, and he was more likely to get it if he wasn't headed for a death trap on deep waters. She glanced around for Buck but saw no sign of him. Just when had he disappeared? Could he have gone for help? With no way of knowing, they desperately needed a plan.

They stumbled into the deserted street. Wind blew her hair into her face. Adaleigh brushed it aside. Destruction lay all around. No longer a charming row of buildings, Main Street had been reduced to a flattened mess of boards. A streak of lightning flashed in the sky. The storm wasn't over yet, and being stranded on a boat in the middle of a lake with a thunderstorm overhead was not the way Adaleigh wanted to die.

David stuck close to Spelding. Thankfully, the scoundrel was taking Hitchens's threat seriously. Perhaps together they could figure a way out of this. Or she could try to disarm Hitchens herself. But Hitchens's strength was something she could not beat, especially with a bum leg.

Just as Hitchens shoved her down a narrow street between two flattened buildings, Spelding pulled ahead of David and broke into a run. Was this their plan?

"Better stop him," Hitchens pressed the gun against her ribs.

David hesitated, looked to her, and Adaleigh shook her head. She couldn't get out of the line of fire if she could barely walk. Jaw clenched, David dashed after Spelding, taking him down before they reached the boardwalk. Spelding threw a punch, but David dodged it and flipped him over, knee in the back.

"I'm not risking her life," David hissed into Spelding's ear loud enough for her to hear. A strange flush warmed her even as guilt and gratefulness warred in her heart.

"Next time, she dies." Hitchens growled. "Let's move."

David hauled Spelding to his feet. They emerged onto the boardwalk, and Adaleigh searched for people, any people. They had to find a way to keep from getting on the *Tuna Mann*. The storm had left the streets deserted. Had there been any curiosity-seekers, the wind howled too loudly to call for help.

"Do we have to do this?" She stopped in the middle of the boardwalk, leg throbbing.

"Keep moving." Hitchens gave her a push, and had he not gripped her arm so tightly, she would have landed on the rough boards.

Her head kept telling her to find a way out, but pain clouded her thinking.

"She's right," Spelding growled. "Just finish the job already."

"Let's everyone calm down." David grabbed Spelding's shoulder, eyes pleading with Adaleigh to hang in there.

"Just shut up and keep moving." Hitchens propelled her forward.

Adaleigh stumbled. *God has gotten you out of tough situations before. He can do it again.* But will He?

CHAPTER TWENTY

A bout five slips down, David pointed to a boat. The *Tuna Mann* looked much larger than Detective O'Connor's little boat. Adaleigh guessed it to be over thirty feet long, and it had a large lean-to-like structure toward the front. The nose of the boat stretched away from shore. It appeared solid, despite frantically bobbing at its lines. Around the lean-to were piles of nets and other equipment. One large fan—the motor?—dodged in and out of the water at the boat's base.

Adaleigh's insides squeezed. What was Hitchens thinking, putting them on a boat in this weather? Maybe they could push him overboard and this standoff would be over? She considered the options as David and Spelding got on the boat.

"Martins," Hitchens shoved her after them. "If you don't get us moving—"

"Adaleigh? Adaleigh Sirland?" Bent double against the wind, a thin old man approached, gratefulness filling his wrinkled face. "Adaleigh, my dear! I found you!"

Her voice caught in her throat, her mind unable to comprehend. Not only had her sister found her, but their family lawyer, old Mr. Binitari, had as well?

"What are you doing out in this storm?" Mr. Binitari glanced at the men surrounding her. David was slowly untying the ropes holding the boat to the dock, an eye on Spelding, who appeared to be calculating his way off the boat, as only Hitchens and Adaleigh stood in his way to solid ground.

"Come back to the shelter with me." Mr. Binitari reached out an arm.

Hitchens's gun slid to a more inconspicuous, though equally dangerous, spot at her side, and Adaleigh caught her breath to keep from wincing as he pressed it to her skin.

"I'm sorry, sir," Adaleigh told Mr. Binitari, pretending she had no inkling as to his identity. She had to get him away from here, send him for help. "I'm on my way to meet my parents."

Mr. Binitari blinked. Adaleigh lifted her chin decisively, ending the conversation. She could feel Mr. Binitari staring at her. She could only hope he'd figure out the only clue she could think to give. Because if he didn't, she actually might see her parents before the day was through.

Fortunately, Mr. Binitari did not press the point. He stepped back to the boardwalk with a puzzled expression.

"Martins, let's go!" Hitchens readjusted the gun.

David cranked the motor, and the boat churned its way toward open sea, bobbing wildly in the choppy water.

Spelding gripped the boat's edge. "Why'd you let the old guy go?"

"I needed someone to see us." Hitchens's grip on Adaleigh's arm tightened. "Then I'll be the lone survivor of your plan to sink everyone."

"You're deranged!" Spelding scoffed, then caught himself as the boat nearly tipped sideways over a wave.

Hitchens slammed Adaleigh into the side of the boat. "Watch yourself!" he shouted at David.

Fear pressed in on Adaleigh. In an effort to not panic, she turned her eyes to the water. White caps sprayed water as they tumbled over themselves. Wave upon wave. The water was gray and angry and cold. The shoreline receded. A flash of lightning darted above the town. From here, she could see the whole path the tornado had leveled. Buildings crushed like matchsticks. Trees uprooted. A swath of destruction.

Death had left its destruction on this town, just as her life had been uprooted. But Crow's Nest would rebuild. The people would come together and breathe life back into the damaged buildings. They would replant trees. They would even heal from the murder that had ripped their town apart. Could Adaleigh do the same? If she got out alive.

"I know you're the reason Amy is dead," Hitchens said, his breath hot on Adaleigh's ear. Was he talking to her?

Spelding shrugged, wiping rain off his face. "Amy wanted a job, so I interviewed her on that Friday. End of story."

"Why would Amy want a job from the Conglomerate?" Hitchens squeezed the hand that held Adaleigh locked against him.

"Aren't you married, Hitchens?" Spelding's tone had been marinated in sarcasm.

"Amy was my true love."

Spelding rolled his eyes. "That's a load of—"

"David, are you turning?" Hitchens whipped toward the front of the boat.

David came out from the lean-to. "We don't dare go much farther, or no one will get back alive."

"Fine. Cut the engine. This will have to do."

David glanced at Adaleigh before he reluctantly joined them on deck. This was it. She could read in the slump of his shoulders that he didn't have a solution. Yet. She caught his eyes. His wheels were turning, and any distraction he could come up with would give her the chance she needed to escape Hitchens's grasp. She gave him an imperceptible nod. The gun barrel dug into her side, taking her breath away.

The boat tilted violently. Hitchens used his gun hand to grab the side of the boat, and Adaleigh whirled away, hopping on one foot as pain shot up her leg. David swung one of the handled nets from its holder on the side of the boat, over the water, and squarely into Hitchens's back. The man stumbled forward, dragging her with him. Adaleigh used the momentum to bring up her good knee.

The gun skittered away as Hitchens moaned in pain. David and Spelding leapt after it. Adaleigh shoved Hitchens off of her and watched, wide-eyed, as David and Spelding rolled on the slippery, pitching deck, tangled in the netting. It meant she didn't see Hitchens move until he yanked her out of their way, knife pricking her side and his other arm crushing the air from her stomach.

David delivered a punch to Spelding's shoulder that caused the man to recoil enough for David to grab the gun. Spelding launched himself, knocking David to his knees, and with a swift move, climbed on top of David and pinned his back to the deck. Equally matched, neither man could move without giving the other an inch. They stared at each other like two wild bulls.

"Keep quiet." Hitchens's whisper carried toward them.

Spelding glanced over, giving David the perfect chance to land a right hook. Spelding rocked backward, holding his bleeding mouth. Before David could adjust, Hitchens planted his foot on David's wrist, trapping the gun.

"Let go," Hitchens hissed, Adaleigh back in his grip.

David breathed out a silent prayer and released the gun. Hitchens kicked it to the far corner before Spelding could get to it. Then Hitchens retreated with Adaleigh at knife point.

"You idiot," Spelding spat.

"Then jump overboard," David shot back. "I'm not leaving without her."

Spelding glanced at the swells, which made a shot of fear cross his face, a look David had seen too many times to count. A deathly fear of water.

"Tie yourselves to the wheelhouse," Hitchens demanded.

"Not a—" Spelding writhed like a fish in David's hands.

"Sorry, man." David grabbed the rope hanging on the cabin wall next to them, secured Spelding's wrists, and lashed him to the wheelhouse.

Hitchens nodded toward the gas can secured near the wheelhouse. "Martins, spread that fuel around the deck. Come, come, this knife is sharp." To prove the point, Hitchens pressed it into Adaleigh's side, and she yelped.

David clenched his teeth but grabbed the spare jug of fuel, splashed it between him and them a couple times, then tossed it down. He needed to get control from Hitchens before he turned this radio-less tub into a fiery pile of wood. But how to do that without hurting Adaleigh?

"Sweetie." Hitchens's false endearment, directed at her, tightened every one of David's muscles. "Reach into my pocket and grab the matches."

His anger grew as red overcame Adaleigh's pale cheeks. David had never considered himself a violent person, but seeing Adaleigh squirming in Hitchens's arms made his protective instinct roar in his ears. He'd get her to safety if it killed him.

The boat rolled over a wave, but unfortunately, Hitchens kept his balance. Spelding, who had kept up a steady stream of swear words, paused and blanched as the craft tipped nearly sideways.

"Would you tie yourself down already?" Hitchens glared at David.

David hesitated, weighing his actions, and Hitchens dug his knife into Adaleigh's side, forcing her to whimper again. David locked eyes with her and wrapped the rope around his wrists. Could she read what he wanted her to know? That he would get her out of this even if he didn't know exactly how yet.

As distant thunder rolled, Hitchens touched a lit match to the fuel, and the deck burst into flames. The fire licked at anything it could devour. Hitchens pulled Adaleigh away. She looked through the haze to find David's eyes, pleading with him. He would find a way off this boat, but not without her.

The fire raced along the deck. Adaleigh's heart pounded an erratic beat. The wind kicked sparks into the air, and raindrops batted them away. Smoke rose to touch the stormy clouds above and choke her throat.

"How are you getting off this boat?" Adaleigh forced the words from her tightened lungs.

"I'll radio for help before I abandon ship." Hitchens kicked the life preserver by his feet. He didn't know about the radio, which meant there was no way to escape the flames except by jumping into the rolling water. Cold, rolling water. Did she tell him?

Hitchens's breath was hot on her. "Just waiting to see how you feel when you watch someone die, then you'll die too."

Nausea rolled in her stomach. "What did Amy see in you?"

"Love."

"You're demented. Real love is being willing to die for one another."

"Like lover-boy is willing to do for you?"

That hit her in the stomach. David had done nothing but show her great kindness. And how had Adaleigh repaid him? By attracting Hitchens's fury. Why did it seem she brought death to those who cared about her unconditionally? First her parents, now David. The very people who took her in when she had nothing to offer paid the steepest price. She met David's gaze through the flames. There was still time to save him from the same fate as her parents.

The fire had now consumed half of the deck and began climbing the cabin wall. It created a divide between her and Hitchens, and David and Spelding. She had to find a way to get away from Hitchens and stop this craziness before they all died. But how could she? Every idea ended with the knife plunged into her skin. However, if that was the only way to save David ...

David's yelp brought her out of her planning. His shirt had caught fire. Adaleigh instinctively stepped forward, wanting to help, but Hitchens's knife held her still. David sprung his wrists from the ropes and smacked at the flames, but the fire climbed down his pants. Tears blurred the scene. With one desperate glance at her, David yanked at the ropes holding Spelding to free him, and jumped overboard.

Adaleigh tried to pull away to see if David was okay, but Hitchens held her firm. Spelding stumbled to his feet.

"Had enough?" Hitchens shouted over the crackle.

"You're a dead man." Spelding narrowed his eyes at Hitchens. "Your leverage is gone. I don't care if the girl dies. The boat is burning. The radio doesn't work—"

Hitchens jerked.

"—and I'm going to kill you."

"Then you'll jump in the water, right?" Hitchens laughed, but it held a hint of fear Adaleigh had yet to hear from him. The radio had been his escape plan. Now what?

Spelding screamed and charged through the flames.

This was her moment. Hitchens pulled the knife away from her to offset the oncoming attack. The instant the knife left her side, Adaleigh used her good foot to stomp as hard as she could on Hitchens's instep. Then she dropped her weight, slipping out of his grip, planted on her bad foot, pivoted before her ankle gave out, and swung her other leg as if she were kicking the last five meters of a hundred-meter breaststroke. Her aim was perfect.

Hitchens crumpled to the boat deck as Spelding crashed into them. Spelding shoved her aside and tossed Hitchens into the flames as if he were a sack of flour. He screamed. Adaleigh screamed. Spelding grabbed her shirt, startling her into forgetting her nausea. He leaned over her, his face inches from hers. "How do we save the boat?"

"I—I don't know," she choked out.

He let loose a string of swear words. But in the midst of them, Adaleigh heard David calling her name. David! She twisted out of Spelding's grip, snagged the life preserver ring, clambered up the side of the boat, and dove off the end.

David met her when she came up for air. "You hurt?"

Adaleigh shook her head as she flung her arms around his neck, the ring dangling from her hand. David wrapped her in a crushing hug.

"Hey, lovebirds, how do I save the boat?" Spelding shouted from the deck.

"Toss down boards and rope. Quick," David called, pulling her to his chest again. The flames looked like they had already engulfed the lean-to walls. The man obeyed and David gathered the materials while keeping her at his side.

"Life preservers?" Spelding yelled.

"Already have one. The other is on the wheelhouse, probably burned," David shouted back, then turned to Adaleigh. "Where's Hitchens?"

"Spelding ..." Adaleigh's sob turned to a splutter as a wave caught her with mouth open. Her legs tangled in the fabric of her skirt and pulled her down.

Perhaps he spoke, but rushing panic filled her ears. *Breathe.* She focused on the feel of David's arms, then let her mind run through the life-saving courses she had taken in Chicago. One was particularly aimed toward women.

She looked up at David. "I need to get my skirt off."

"What for?"

"It will help me swim, but I have another idea. And don't worry, I wear bloomers." She grabbed his arm to keep from getting separated by a wave, then yanked at the seam between her skirt and bodice. It wouldn't come undone. "I need your help." If possible, his face grew redder, but he managed to split the seam, and Adaleigh pulled her legs free.

Her icy fingers struggled to tie a knot at both open ends, but she did, and it created a balloon of air they could hang onto until they figured out the next step, which they'd have to do quickly, before hypothermia set it.

David cast her a grin of appreciation before shouting, "Spelding, we have a life preserver, but you're going to have to jump."

"Can we help him if he does?" Adaleigh clutched the fabric of her skirt, her freed legs treading water more easily, especially as the cold numbed the pain in her leg. "I can pull an unconscious boy from the water, but a grown man?"

"We get him to jump first. Then punch him out if he keeps thrashing."

Adaleigh gave David a look that told him she thought he liked that idea a bit too much.

David didn't blink as he held her eyes. "He would've harmed you if it meant getting out of this."

Her heart tripped, but a wave drowned any reply she could muster.

"Is there another option?" Spelding's voice had a hint of panic in it now.

"You can stay there until the boat burns," David called back.

They remained barely within sight of shore, but with large waves, cool water, and no boat, it might as well be the moon. They had only a few more minutes before they'd be well on the way to going so numb, they'd drown.

"We need to turn these boards into a raft." David worked to tie the scorched boards together. "Spelding, now get down here!"

"You think help will come?" Adaleigh asked through chattering teeth as she tried to help him finish making the raft.

"The flames make the best distress signal, but ..." David's expression told her the same thing Adaleigh feared. It might not be enough. Only time would tell, and between the cold and the waves, they might not make it that long.

Spelding leaned over the side of the boat. It was disconcerting to see a good-looking smooth-talker nearly in tears because he was scared out of his wits. Facing death reduced a person to their most primal needs. She cast a glance at David. If her theory was true, what did that say about him? His whole concern seemed focused on everyone but himself.

"You've got to jump, Spelding," David shouted. "The boat's going down."

Spelding hesitated, but the fire was pushing him toward a decision—fiery grave or watery one. He chose, landing in the water a few feet from them. Came up thrashing.

"David, how are we going to do this?"

"Spelding!" David shouted at him, then tossed the ring. "Catch!"

The man's terrified eyes appeared just before a wave covered his head.

"Grab the ring." David reeled in the ring, tossed it again. Spelding just bobbed, his arms outstretched. David pulled the ring back. "He's drowning."

Adaleigh grabbed David's arm. "Let me do this."

"No."

She held his arm to make him face her. They rode a high wave. "You're stronger, so you can pull him off of me if this doesn't work." What she had learned about drowning is that when someone is trying to rescue themselves, they climb up anything they can get their hands around, their rescuer included. It was one of the most dangerous moments in a water rescue, which was why it was usually best not to touch a conscious drowning victim. She steeled herself from thinking about the ramifications if Spelding got too close.

David studied her, working his jaw, until he finally squeezed her hand and let her go. Adaleigh stuck her arm in the ring and swam toward Spelding. He barely moved, his mouth less and less above the water.

"Grab the ring, Mr. Spelding." Adaleigh tried to mix command with calm. She wasn't sure she succeeded, seeing that her own heart continued to pound in her ears.

Terrified eyes looked back at her.

"It's okay." She coughed out water. Her injured leg gave out just as a wave went over her head. "Spelding, you've got to try again."

She pushed the ring right up to his hand. No response. She shot a look at David, who towed the raft behind him, and he returned a solemn nod. She circled around behind Spelding, then wrapped an arm around his neck and lifted, helping his head stay above the next swell. On the downward side, he sputtered and flailed.

Adaleigh let go and swam away. Her injured leg kept her from escaping fast enough. Spelding lunged, clawing his way out of the water. She grabbed a breath just before she sank below a wave. She kicked toward the surface, but a vise grip clutched her bad ankle. She cried out, using the last of the air in her lungs.

She tried to pull away, panic making her forget about holding her breath. Pain sliced from her ankle up to her back. Her lungs burned. Hands only pushed her deeper into the darkness.

CHAPTER TWENTY-ONE

W hy had he let her attempt to rescue the drowning Guy Spelding?

Ever since David had met Adaleigh, his heart had broken at her pain, trembled at the possibility of her leaving town, and frozen at the danger hemming her in. Guns, knives, fire, all wielded in the hands of angry men, all threatening to steal Adaleigh's life from before his eyes. He knew from the moment Sean pointed his gun at her that he would do anything to keep her safe. And seeing her held hostage had showed how much she'd come to mean to him.

Now, in a moment, David's worst fears were realized. Adaleigh went under, pushed down by Spelding's frantic attempts to save himself. Fear propelled David over the water. He had seconds to keep Adaleigh from drowning.

Take a breath.

David pushed aside the prompting. Whether common sense or his Heavenly Father, he couldn't bring himself to slow his strokes. He plowed ahead and slammed a fist into Spelding's way-too-good-looking face. He tossed the unconscious man onto the raft and looked around for Adaleigh.

He spotted her, face-down on a swell that rose three feet away. The cold water slowed his reaction time, but he reached her in moments. He pressed shaking fingers to her neck, found a strong heartbeat. Tears stung his eyes. He blinked them away as he turned her onto her back and tilted her chin up to check her respiration. None.

He pushed emotion back as he leaned on his training. First, he made sure her mouth was empty of water, then turned her face toward him and closed his mouth over hers. Four quick breaths, then he turned her on her side to avoid letting her aspirate on lake water and vomit. Saving someone from drowning while still in the water was nearly impossible. Still, he pressed his forehead to the top of her head and he prayed like he never had before.

As if a cork popped, air burst out of her lungs. Adaleigh sucked in, half expecting water to fill her mouth, but no, it was air. Smokey, wet air, but air, nonetheless.

She coughed, choked, hacked, and gasped as much air as she could. A good, hard slap landed on her back, and she spit out a stream of whatever had been in her stomach. Arms pulled her away from the grossness. She tried to relax, but her body began shaking. Her lungs clenched. She wanted to cry but couldn't force her lungs to let in any more air. She spluttered, panic giving way to any good sense.

Then two strong arms came around her own, pinning her against a solid body. Adaleigh tried to kick, images of Hitchens flashing through her head like an electrical current.

"You're safe."

The words fell like a heavy blanket, dousing the panic, and Adaleigh was back in her library back home. The sun poured in the windows. She'd just had a big fight with Ashley, fled to the library, and now Mom wrapped her in a fleece and left a cup of hot cocoa on the table next to her. Her muscles relaxed as she sank into her comfy chair. Peace washed over her like a cleansing rain. A mist of—

"Adaleigh?"

She opened her eyes to find David studying her from over her shoulder. A cold splash hit her face. They floated in the middle of Lake Michigan, their boat was on fire, and both Mark Hitchens and Guy Spelding had almost killed her.

"You okay?" David's eyes told her how worried he was. Then she realized he held her against his chest. Propriety had flown away hours ago. She leaned against him. So solid, so safe, so close ...

Her ankle cramped. "Where's Spelding?"

David pointed his chin toward the bobbing raft a few feet away where the man lay. "I had to knock him out to get him off of you." He cleared his throat. "Let's finish the raft and get you out of the water."

David helped Adaleigh on board beside the unconscious Spelding, whom she tied to the raft to keep from falling off of it, while David added more planks to make a surface large enough for all of them. As David climbed up beside her, a swell raised one end, knocking her flat. David wrapped an arm around her waist to set her upright.

"Ready to paddle?" He handed her a board and kept one for himself.

She nodded. Her ankle throbbed, and her body ached and shivered, but she matched David stroke for stroke. The worry lines on his face were deeper than they had been all day. Thankfully, the rain had stopped, but the swells threatened to tip them each time the raft rose and fell.

Adaleigh sagged, and without David's quick reflex, a wave would have tipped her right into the water. As the raft swept down yet another swell, strong arms tucked her close. She wasn't sure how long they sat like that, rising and falling amid the swells, but warmth finally began to circulate through her limbs again.

Every few minutes, David's voice would wake her, or a hand would touch her cheek before she could drift off again. How many times he did that, Adaleigh don't know, but as her teeth stopped chattering, her ankle began throbbing threefold. It gave her brain something to focus on, bringing her out of her fog.

"Hey there." David smiled at her, relief soaking his features.

She tried to register how close he held her, but Spelding moaned at their feet, making her more aware of her surroundings. The raft still floated among the swells, but the clouds had lightened, and glimpses of sunlight peeked through.

"Any—" Adaleigh coughed, her throat incredibly dry. "Any sign of a rescue?"

"They should have noticed the boat was gone by now. And Grandma—"

Adaleigh smacked her head. "Your grandma took Samantha to the hospital."

"What?" David adjusted to fully face her, and she missed his warmth. "I'm sorry, I—"

"Why? What happened?"

"This tree branch came through the back door. Samantha got a shard of glass in her leg."

His muttered words dripped with anger.

Adaleigh blinked against tears. "I'm sorry, David, I should have—"

"No, no, not you." His voice softened, and he pulled her close again. "Mann. He was so bent on getting back at the Conglomerate, he insisted we go out before the storm. I shouldn't have gone. I should have stood up to him sooner, no matter the ramifications."

"You couldn't have known—" This time, a particularly big swell caught her off guard, and they clutched the raft, Adaleigh praying they stayed upright.

"Tell me why you came to the wharf today," David said as the raft settled flat again. "In the middle of a storm."

"Your grandma sent me to find you and Patrick."

"Okay. I guess I was just hoping it was your..." His turn to look away, only he did it with such a cute expression, Adaleigh couldn't stop herself from giving a quick peck to his cheek.

She could barely feel his weathered skin with her frozen lips. Before she pulled back, David whipped his head around and caught her in a deep kiss full of longing hope and desperate gratefulness. Adaleigh sank into it, letting it warm her soul.

David broke off after a minute, lifting an ear. "Do you hear that? That's a boat engine." He knelt, hands shielding his eyes. "That's the police boat!"

They were saved!

David propped his elbows on the boat railing and leaned back, soaking in the sun that poked through the clouds and trying not to let the kiss he'd shared with Adaleigh consume his thoughts. Wrapped in blankets, she and Spelding sat in separate corners of the police boat. They'd all suffered some degree of hypothermia, but they seemed none the worse for it. Even Spelding had fully woken.

One by one, Uncle Mike and Chief Sebastian managed to interpret their teeth chattering in order to record their official statements. The police boat captain made a pass around the smoldering wreckage of the *Tuna Mann*, but there was no evidence Hitchens had survived. David took a moment of silence for the boat that was his livelihood and for the father of two sweet children, even if he was a murderer.

The shore loomed as the police boat cut through the waves. The sunlight peeking through the clouds reflected off the wet surface of the boardwalk. The county ambulance stood ready. Only one person, wearing a trench coat, paced the north end of the boardwalk where the police boat was housed.

Guy Spelding was carried off in a stretcher. Adaleigh refused, and David helped her limp down the dock. As she reached the wharf, the man in the trench coat threw open his arms and hauled her into a frail embrace. David recognized the older man from when they boarded the boat under duress.

"I thought you were dead." The older man hugged Adaleigh even tighter. Emotions David didn't want to decipher tensed his tired muscles.

Tears dripped down her cheeks as she leaned into the man's thin body.

Uncle Mike appeared beside David and asked the very thing David wanted to know. "Who is he?"

A sniff and the man in the trench coat held Adaleigh at arm's length. "You shouldn't scare an old man like that, running away without asking for help. And then telling me you were about to meet your parents. God have mercy! I saw the gun that man was holding. What have you gotten yourself into?"

David shared a look with his uncle.

Adaleigh smiled despite brushing away tears. "You're always trying to fix things, Mr. Binitari."

"You girls will be the death of me." He shook his finger at her. "Your father charged me to look after you, then you go disappearing."

Father? Disappearing? Uncle Mike's steadying hand rested on David's shoulder. Tears ran down Adaleigh's cheeks. If only he could comfort her as he did on the boat, but he didn't dare intrude, especially after a medic took Adaleigh's arm and Mr. Binitari yanked her back.

"Unhand her." Mr. Binitari spoke with great authority. "I need to speak to her first."

The medic backed away.

Mr. Binitari glanced around. "Your sister is here."

David straightened. After all their efforts, it hadn't been enough to keep Adaleigh hidden.

Adaleigh hung her head. "I know."

She knew? Since when?

"I followed her," said Mr. Binitari, "hoping I could get to you first. We need to talk, child."

Pounding feet neared. Buck Wilson. *Great.* "Adaleigh, are you all right?" The man clasped her hands as if he was about to wrap her in a hug. Not on his life. David moved forward only to have his uncle hold him back. Why not let him have a few choice words with the man who'd left them alone in the basement of the Conglomerate headquarters to face off with a murderer?

"Excuse me?" Mr. Binitari's curiosity was evident in his voice. Inquisitiveness, not disdain. He ignored the rest of them.

Adaleigh pulled away from Buck, blushing. David didn't like it one bit.

Buck held her shoulders. "I know this mix-up put you in harm's way, so if there is anything—"

"Buck Wilson." Uncle Mike finally entered the conversation, giving David leave to follow him into the circle. "What are you doing here?"

"I'm so glad you are all safe." Buck extended a hand to David, but David crossed his arms, his jaw clenched.

"Went for help, did you?" David muttered.

Buck had the good grace to lower his head. "I returned too late for you, but not for Sean."

"Sean's okay?" Adaleigh asked.

"Maybe." Buck included everyone in his reply. "He was significantly injured and lost a lot of blood, but I understand major organs were missed."

Awkward silence followed.

"If you'll excuse me, I must speak to Guy." Buck shouldered past Uncle Mike. Spelding was being carried to a waiting ambulance, wrists cuffed.

Uncle Mike stayed in step. "We're taking him into custody."

"I need a word with him, first." Buck didn't stop. "He's my brother, detective. Step-brother, but my brother, nonetheless."

Uncle Mike's mustache bobbed. David had to consciously close his mouth.

"Who is he?" Mr. Binitari asked as Buck stepped up to the stretcher and gripped Spelding's hand.

"Adaleigh." Everything stopped as the female voice reached them. Adaleigh turned, whiter than a sail. David didn't need to guess that the black-haired woman who stood a mere ten feet away was her sister.

Panic clawed at Adaleigh's throat. Ashley looked mesmerizing in her knee-length black skirt and fitted black top. Her perfectly straight ebony hair stood out starkly against her pale face.

"Been looking for you." Ashley stood, a poised, stately woman, not three feet away.

Adaleigh suddenly grew conscious of her undressed state, despite the blankets that kept her modesty intact.

"Nice of you to arrange such a bothersome storm to welcome me."

"Girls, this is neither the time nor the place." Mr. Binitari stepped between them. "Remember, Sirlands do not make a scene."

"Get out of the way, old man." Ashley stepped forward until they were inches from each other. Adaleigh held up her hand to keep David or Detective O'Connor from intervening. This needed to end, and better it ended in front of witnesses than on a dark boardwalk like poor Amy.

"You left without leaving a forwarding address." Ashley's black gaze didn't leave Adaleigh's. "It was hard to track you down."

"Maybe I wanted it that way." Adaleigh matched her tone like only a sister could.

"You were always too good to be a part of our family."

"Maybe you should have treated me more like a sister."

"Girls!" Mr. Binitari attempted to raise his voice.

"You aren't my sister." Ashley spat the words, hatred flaming.

"Then why not let me go?"

"Because I read their will. They gave you everything. Everything! I was their blood. Me. Not you. And they left me nothing! Unless you die." Ashley lunged.

Adaleigh tried to twist out of her way, but her injured leg buckled, and Ashley was on top of her before anyone could stop her. Adaleigh's blanket fell aside, leaving her in only her bloomers and half a dress. She held her sister back by the shoulders, but Ashley pulled out a gun.

Instinct had her twisting away, only for the ground to drop out from under her. Ashley let out a terrified scream as the cold water shocked Adaleigh's senses enough to jerk free of her sister's claws. But her exhausted muscles refused to work. Tears burned her eyes as she sank. Not again.

"Grab this!" David shouted as he tossed a life saver ring directly in front of Adaleigh's hands. Relief swept over him as she clutched it. From the end of the dock, David hauled her to safety. To their right, Uncle Mike did the same with Adaleigh's sister.

Just like on her first day in Crow's Nest, David grabbed the back of her clothes and helped Adaleigh crawl onto the dock, wrapping a blanket around her and holding her close.

"No more water." She shivered in his arms. "Not today."

David's breath hitched as he ran a hand over her white cheek. He lowered his lips to her forehead, and his voice choked. "I'll keep saving you."

A medic approached, and while Adaleigh allowed him to check her over, she refused to go to the hospital. "Is my sister okay?"

"They took her to the hospital with Guy." Buck Wilson appeared next to them. "She doesn't look like your sister. Guy and I share a mother. Which parent do you two share?"

Irritation chaffed David at both the man's words and his intrusion.

Adaleigh blanched even whiter, if possible. "What do you know about my sister?"

"It doesn't take a genius to piece together the story." Buck looked at her with compassion, fanning a jealous streak David hardly recognized in himself. "You shouldn't have kept it all to yourself, Adaleigh. She had no business doing all that she did to you."

David looked between them, unsure what to do, but he couldn't hide his deepening scowl.

"He's right, you know." Mr. Binitari shuffled over. "Why didn't you tell me the whole truth, my dear? Way back when your parents had me begin the investigation into your injuries as a child. I began to suspect then, but you denied everything. You know I could have helped."

Adaleigh avoided David's eyes. Was she embarrassed? She shouldn't be. At least not with him. She'd already told him about her sister's abuse.

Mr. Binitari patted Adaleigh's arm. "As the family lawyer, I'm hoping to keep everything in-house. No newspaper attention, you know. I've already begun damage control here. That Greg Alistar is done asking questions. We need to make sure your image back home remains intact. Your parents have left you everything, except for a small allowance for Ashley. Now that you have inherited the money, house, business, every-thing, you'll have to manage all of that, plus their charities and ..."

Mr. Binitari's words blurred together. Was this why Adaleigh couldn't look at him? Because she was no longer the girl without a home, without money, without a future? Was he about to lose her, not because she ran away, but because she chose to return to her old life? Her real home?

Uncle Mike joined their group. "I think she's had enough excitement for right now. Best get her home."

"Yes," Mr. Binitari said. "You gentlemen may visit her later. She and I obviously have much business to discuss with the will and all, which would be better—"

"You're quite right." Buck clapped David on the back, and David wanted to slap his hand away. Buck gave Adaeigh a smile that felt like a dagger to David's heart. If anyone understood Adaleigh's real world, it was Buck Wilson. Not a first mate like David who likely didn't have a job any more.

"I'll take—" Mr. Binitari started.

"No. Go with Ashley," Adaleigh patted the older man's hand. "I'm going back to Mrs. Martins's house."

If only her words brought the assurance David's heart needed.

That evening, Adaleigh leaned on David as she half hopped into the Martins's stuffy sitting room. A small space at the front of the house filled with furniture that looked untouched. With the kitchen still a mess, this was the only other place to go besides her room.

Mrs. Martins pointed her to a comfortable chair and David settled her elevated ankle on a cushion. Such pampering felt all wrong in the Martins's house, especially since Samantha insisted on following Kyle to the kitchen.

"How's your leg?" Adaleigh asked before Samantha could leave the room.

"All sewn up." Samantha gestured to her bandaged leg with a flourish. "I guess we're twins now."

Adaleigh smiled, but half-heartedly.

"We're so glad you're all right." Mrs. Martins gave her a tight hug. "David told us all about it."

"I was worried about you, too," Adaleigh said into her shoulder.

"Oh, I drive fast when I need to." Mrs. Martins laughed.

"Have you heard how my sister is doing?" Adaleigh settled back against the cushion.

"Michael went with that lawyer." She sounded huffy.

"But she's okay?" Adaleigh pressed.

"Physically, from what I hear, yes." Mrs. Martins glanced between her and David, then speared David with a look. "Stay here with her while I get supper."

"I'll be fine, Mrs. Martins. David has had an even longer day than me."

"Medic said I'm healthy as a bear." David smiled, but it didn't reach his eyes.

Adaleigh chewed her lip, nervous for so many reasons. Front and center being David. "Buck was only partially right," she finally said when she couldn't take the silence any longer. "Ashley and I do not share any parents in common."

"You don't have to explain." He still didn't look at her.

Adaleigh adjusted her injured ankle on the cushion. "Our parents took me in as a baby, just before they discovered they were anticipating Ashley's arrival."

"So you're adopted?"

Adaleigh should have expected the lack of judgment, but it still took her by surprise. "Yes."

Finally, he glanced at her. "Do you know your original family?"

She shook her head, then told him something she had never told anyone else. "For years, I have felt like I wasn't good enough to be a part of the Sirland family. It's why I let Ashley walk all over me the way she did. I wasn't really a Sirland, I told myself. I was an imposter, a stranger, an orphan, and their way of life wasn't in my blood."

David squatted beside her, rested his hand on hers. Comfort and warmth traveled up her arm all the way to her heart.

"So now I just keep thinking," she continued, "why did they leave me everything? Did I even hear that right? I don't understand why I received any money. It should all go to Ashley. Frankly, it's probably the only thing we've ever agreed on."

He rubbed his thumb over the back of her hand. "You don't think your parents made the right decision?"

"I don't think they figured on being gone so young." Adaleigh sighed, then grasped her courage before it flitted away. "Do you see me differently now that everything has changed? Now that I'm not a runaway without a penny to my name?"

David sat back in his heels, studied her as if he could see into her soul. "The answer matters to you, doesn't it?"

Adaleigh nodded.

His hand grasped hers tighter. "When I first saw you, you intrigued me. You were confident yet mysterious. Not to mention, incredibly beautiful."

She flushed and lowered her lashes.

"Took me that whole dinner to work up enough courage to invite you out."

"I hadn't planned to stay." She whispered the admission.

He smiled. "I figured. I had one night, or my chance was gone." Silence stretched as David stared at the wall as if seeing a completely different scene in his mind's eye. Finally, he resumed. "Do I see you differently? After you listened to my agony over my father being suspected of murder? After you offered to help clear my father's name despite running from your own past?" A grin flashed. "Which we succeeded in doing, by the way. My uncle told me my father will be released in the morning."

"That's wonderful!"

"So do I see you differently? After all you told me about yourself? After the panic and nightmares? After seeing you trapped in a collapsed building?" His voice faltered. "Or held at knife and gun point? After watching you nearly drown? Yes, Adaleigh Sirland, I see you differently from that first day. You are even more intriguing, more beautiful, and someone I no longer see as a stranger."

"Money doesn't change your opinion?"

He shook his head. "You always had money, whether you thought you deserved it or not. You grew up with it, and it made you into who you are. But that's not what made me like you. Whether you have it or not doesn't matter to me."

"What do you ..." Was it too forward to ask what he meant by *liking her*? Yes, he kissed her after her panic episode and then on the raft, but that was after multiple near-death experiences. She needed to know whether there was something between them worth exploring or whether to focus on the job her parents had left her—a job Adaleigh hadn't wanted in the first place.

"What do I ... what?" David cupped her cheek, his thumb running along the bone.

She sank into his touch. Who cared about money or forwardness when she found a treasure right here in Crow's Nest? "When you say—"

The front door banged open. "Grandma!" Patrick shouted. "You won't believe the afternoon I've had!"

Adaleigh met David's gaze and joined in his laughter.

CHAPTER TWENTY-TWO

Monday, June 9

"What made you hide out in such a dirty town?" Mr. Binitari swiped crumbs off the table he and Adaleigh had commandeered in the corner of the Wharfside. That morning, her sister had been moved to an asylum in lieu of being tried for attempted murder. Her murder. The guilt weighed down Adaleigh's shoulders.

"You don't like it?" Adaleigh stared out at the bobbing boats and the glistening water. She found hope here. A place to start over. It wrestled against the darker feelings. She could understand Ashley's anger; didn't a biological daughter deserve more than an orphaned nobody like Adaleigh? Adaleigh had always thought so. But here, she wasn't that nobody. She wasn't a stranger any longer. She had found family, friends, people who cared about her.

"Before the tornado damage, it didn't seem to have much." Mr. Binitari huffed as he settled in his chair. "Now, it's pitiful."

The Wharfside had been open all night as people sought to recover from the storm. Electricity still hadn't been restored, but the people of

Crow's Nest were resourceful, and the Wharfside provided the town with hot meals. It had also become the impromptu headquarters for the recovery effort. When Mr. Binitari insisted they talk somewhere other than the Martins's home, especially since David and Kyle were working on cleaning up the mess, Adaleigh suggested coming here because she liked being in the middle of the town's community.

"What can I get you?" Mindy appeared, ponytail swaying. Dark circles rimmed her eyes, but she had a bright smile. "We just brewed a fresh pot of coffee."

Mr. Binitari handed her the menu with a sniff. "A salad. No onions. No tomatoes. Dressing on the side."

"Breadstick?"

"No."

"Something to drink?"

"Water."

"Certainly, sir." Mindy captured Adaleigh's hand. "How are you feeling? David told me all about your scare. Golly, I can't imagine—"

"You were going to order the salad as well, right, Miss Sirland?" Mr. Binitari cleaned his spectacles with a handkerchief.

Adaleigh squeezed Mindy's fingers. "We'll catch up later, how 'bout?"

Mindy leaned closer. "I want to hear *everything*." Her eyes widened as she emphasized the last word and Adaleigh suspected she wanted to know about things between her and David. "Now, whatcha want? Soup? Muffin? Coffee?"

Adaleigh grinned, heart warming at how well Mindy could guess exactly what she needed. "Perfect."

Mindy winked. "I'll be back with your beverages."

"So talkative." Mr. Binitari rolled his eyes.

"She's my friend."

"How can you have friends in, what, three days?"

A week. More. "She was nice to me."

"Fine. But now we're going home, and you have an image to maintain."

Adaleigh bristled. "I don't want that life."

"You don't have an option, young lady. The will left you everything. You're the face of the Sirlands now, especially with your sister—" He wiggled his fingers.

The guilt pressed in again. She was the reason for all of this, so of course she must follow ... wait. A memory surfaced. One she'd forgotten since it had no relevance at the time. When Adaleigh decided on her degree, her father brought her into his office to talk about the business. He always said she had the head for it, but that he wouldn't force her to take it over if that's not what Adaleigh wanted. She had options, he'd said.

Adaleigh leaned forward to meet Mr. Binitari's gaze, not unlike how she confronted David's father the other day. "I can hire a manager. I don't want to run it. Dad knew that."

"Then why did he leave it to you?" He yanked his spectacles from his nose. "He told me Ashley wouldn't handle it. He thought you could. Don't disappoint him."

Adaleigh clenched her fists, torn between expectation and the reminder of her father's true wishes. He wanted her to dream, not be tied down in an office until a husband took it over.

"Just the woman I need to see." Mr. Alistar pulled out a chair, joining them without so much as a by-your-leave.

"What do you want?" Adaleigh glared at him.

"You've been hard to reach, Miss Sirland." He smirked. "Care to make a statement? Did Mark Hitchens have any last words before Guy Spelding killed him?"

Mr. Binitari rose, yanking Mr. Alistar to his feet with surprising strength for his age. "I suggest you move along, sir. If you continue harassing my client, I will pursue legal means to end your career."

Alistar stared at Adaleigh.

"I hope you didn't doubt that I had that power." She gave just the barest of smiles. "I'm very ready to call your editor. Or should I go directly to the owner?"

Alistar stalked out, nearly crashing into Mindy.

"Where is he off to?" Mindy set down Adaleigh's coffee and Mr. Binitari's water. "I haven't seen him that speechless since, well, ever."

"It's a good sight, isn't it?" Adaleigh grinned.

Mr. Binitari grumbled, grimacing as he sipped his water.

"I heard Buck's lawyers argued for Guy's reduced sentence. They claimed he's the victim in all of this." Mindy's face turned red. "He's not an innocent party, but at least he didn't kill Amy. I'm glad for Sean's sake he knows the truth, and I heard Sean's moving out east somewhere. I don't blame him for wanting to disappear. Then there's poor Lizzy Hitchens. She is mortified over the whole messy affair, pardon the word. I heard she's glad Mr. Hitchens died at sea so she doesn't have to bury him. She's already taken Matty and Sarah and left town."

Adaleigh shuddered. Those poor children. Matthew's tumble into the lake had started the whole mess, dragging her in unwittingly.

"Is there anyone upstanding in this whole town?" Mr. Binitari sighed as Mindy hurried off to get their food. "It will be good to get you home."

Adaleigh swallowed. "I want to stay."

"Here?" He blew out a little breath. "That's the hypothermia talking."

No. "I've made friends."

"You mean that Mr. Wilson. He is a nice one." One of his thin brows arched up.

"Buck Wilson?" She'd known Mr. Binitari would like him. "What about David?"

Mr. Binitari patted her hand as he had ever since she was a child. "He's working class, my dear. Not good enough for you."

Adaleigh pursed her lips. How did Mr. Binitari know David wasn't good enough? He saved her life. Was more kind to her than anyone had ever been before. He even understood her quirks. Buck was handsome and had money, but that wasn't everything.

"Stop muddling your little head." Mr. Binitari tapped her right temple.

She withdrew from the gesture, somehow reduced to a floundering child. She firmed her mouth and added some sugar to her coffee. "How long will it take to get everything squared away at home?"

"A few days, some finalizing of paperwork, then we can get into the everyday matters. Plan for the future. And don't worry, we'll get you all cleaned up before you have to face the public. People have been quite concerned for you, you know." He squinted at her yellowing bruises. "No one has to know this whole episode happened. Once you get back home, it will all seem like a bad dream."

A bad dream. Yes, parts of it resembled a nightmare. But other parts ... Mrs. Martins's baking. Detective O'Connor's kindness. Samantha's discussions. David. Could she change her whole life without a promise of a future with him? She owed her family the time to at least settle matters back home. And then?

For goodness sake, she held degrees in psychology and rhetoric. She would have broached the question last night had Patrick not interrupted.

Tonight. Tonight she'd ask David if he saw a future between them. She had to return home for a few days, but after that, she'd follow her dreams, just like her parents would have wanted.

She took a deep, shuddering breath. "I won't leave until I say good-bye."

"Whatever you say, my dear." The water glass Mr. Binitari lifted to his lips failed to hide his smug smile.

"We need to talk." Not the words David hoped to hear from his boss as soon as he entered the shop around midday.

"Yes, sir." David followed Captain Mann into the back room, trepidation adding weight to his weary shoulders. He planned to see whether the man would fire him before he made the decision whether to quit. His family needed the money, but surely there were other ships that would hire him on.

Mann lowered himself to the chair behind his desk. Piles of papers, nets, and hooks littered the surface. The man himself looked as haggard as he did after they survived the storm. He leaned back and steepled his fingers. "I'll come right to the point. I'm too old for this, David. I've decided to retire."

Not what he expected. Not at all. David stared at his boss.

Mann pointed at him. "You've proved yourself, especially the last couple weeks. You were willing to stand up to me, even if it cost your job, when lives were at stake—and I wished I had listened. Now I know you'll stand up to the Conglomerate when it's in the company's best interest. You've reminded me that people come first. Not money. Not fish. Not the battle I have with the Conglomerate."

"Thank you, sir?" Utterly confused, David could only mutter the words.

Captain Mann waved him off. "I've decided to make you my partner."

What? "In the business?"

"I'll remain a silent partner until you can buy me out. I know it will take time, especially with the loss of my boat, but I have faith in you, son. You'll bring the business into its prime, and I know it will grow under your leadership. It already has."

David gaped at his boss as the words and ramifications snuck in. He hadn't lost his job. He'd received the ultimate promotion. There was only one person he wanted to tell, but it would have to wait until after he fulfilled his commitment to help his neighbors. Surely she would still be there when he arrived home.

Adaleigh helped Mrs. Martins clean up from supper. The kitchen had mostly been set to rights, though there was a chair or two to fix yet.

Mr. Binitari did not join them. Instead, he'd insisted on staying at a boarding house in Hawk's River, unharmed by the storm. Detective O'Connor had wanted to be at supper but was getting Frank Martins settled into his cabin. Apparently, the good detective offered to help his nephew with his sobriety. After David went to meet his boss, he'd sent word he would be late. Rose Wittlebush's seamstress shop was completely demolished and with Sean leaving town, she had no one to help her salvage her business. If Adaleigh's ankle didn't throb, she'd offer to help too.

Patrick disappeared as soon as the food was gone, but as he left, Kyle appeared in the hall. A light blush colored Samantha's cheeks as he took her hand. A wave to Mrs. Martins and Adaleigh and the pair disappeared out the door. Adaleigh hid a smile. At least Samantha appeared no worse for all she'd gone through.

"I haven't seen her that happy in a long time." Mrs. Martins hung up the dish towel, the kitchen finally spotless. "David either. You've been a balm to our home, Leigh. And Leigh is what I'll call you, no matter what your lawyer says."

"He's a stickler." A pain ached in Adaleigh's chest. She loved the older man who she'd known all her life, but she didn't appreciate how he looked down on the people of Crow's Nest. People she'd come to care about and call her friends.

Mrs. Martins lowered herself to the chair kitty-corner to Adaleigh, sliding over a cup of tea. "Are you happy to be going home after all of this?"

She grasped the cup's warmth. "I wish I could be here to help Crow's Nest rebuild."

"Don't you worry about Crow's Nest. We always land on our feet. You have some rebuilding to do yourself."

"That I do." She hesitated, then asked, "If you found yourself in possession of an amount of wealth that survived last year's market crash, what would you do with it?"

"Me?" Mrs. Martins fanned her face. "I can't imagine that ever happening to me, child. What do you think I would do with it?"

"Give it away." Adaleigh smiled. "Use it to help feed and house those who are out of work." She ran her finger over the lip of her cup. "I learned that there are more and more people losing their jobs around the country. You took me in when I needed a home, maybe there's a way I can help other women like me."

"I know you will be a godsend to whomever you are able to help." Mrs. Martins patted her hand. "And, don't you forget, you always have a home here."

That brought tears to Adaleigh's eyes and Mrs. Martins pulled her into a hug.

David wiped his forehead as he surveyed the work he and Silas had accomplished over the last few hours. Dusk had arrived before they finished, but they'd managed to clear out Rose Whittlebush's sewing machine, fabric, and baubles. It would be another day before they could assess what tables, shelves, and other materials could be salvaged from the destroyed shop.

"I'll make sure her parlor is turned into a suitable space." Silas slapped his cowboy hat against his thigh. "It's the least we can do for a widow without any family."

"Tell me how I can help when the time comes." David's heart rate quickened at the thought of finally being able to return home to Adaleigh. He caught Silas staring at him. "What?"

"You've been different today, I can't put my finger on it. An extra strength in your work and a new glint in your eye." Silas pushed David's shoulder. "It's that girl, isn't it. Leigh."

David knocked Silas's hand away. "What if it is? I like her." Maybe more than that.

"As your friend, I need to caution you on falling so fast for an out-of-towner. What do you really know about her?"

David bristled. "Enough."

"I was at the Wharfside today when she and that older man came in. The way he treated Mindy was abhorrent."

"Adaleigh and Mindy are friends."

"Martins." Silas rubbed his neck. "I heard her talking about leaving."

David's heart stuttered.

"She's been given her father's business and the older man wants her to return home to run it. I don't know whether she agreed to it or not, I didn't catch any more of the conversation."

David knew she was meeting with Binitari this morning, knew about the will, so the information shouldn't shake him as much as it did coming from Silas.

Silas scratched his beard. "Just think about what you're asking of her. I left my job out west to return home after my brother died to take care of my family. It was a sacrifice I needed to make, but it wasn't easy. She's having to make a similar decision as a woman during an economic downturn. You're asking her to give up her security to ... get to know a fisherman? Are you offering to marry her?"

Marry her? It was definitely too fast to be considering that option. But he couldn't ask her to give up her future without offering one with him. Then again, he couldn't imagine his life without her in it.

"It's been an intense few days, Martins." Silas situated his hat on his head. "I wouldn't be a good friend if I didn't ask you to think about more than how good she makes you feel."

"Thank you." David managed to say. He had the walk home to decide what to do.

Night had completely fallen by the time David returned. Adaleigh waited up despite the fact that Mr. Binitari was determined to have an early start the following morning. She paged through a book at the kitchen table, not really reading it, a candle her only light.

"How was your meeting with your boss?" Adaleigh asked as David stoked the stove.

He moved the tea kettle to a front burner. "He named me his partner and plans to sell me the company."

"What?" Adaleigh's smile hurt her cheeks. "That's wonderful, David!"

David ran his hand over his mouth, but it didn't hide his own smile. "From thinking I was about to lose my job to Captain."

"I'm proud of you." Such true words shouldn't hurt to say, but if she didn't stay in Crow's Nest, she'd lose him.

David's joy seeped from his face. He turned abruptly, setting the kettle back on the warmer. His action ignited a churning in Adaleigh's stomach.

"And you, did you reach your decision?" David lowered himself next to her. Did water and wind have a smell? Adaleigh soaked in his presence. If this conversation didn't go well ... even if it did and she left for only a few days, she would miss him.

She set the book aside. "Mr. Binitari is insisting I go home."

He bumped her shoulder with his. "Is that your decision?"

"There's paperwork I have to deal with, so I must return for a few days. He wants me to stay after that and be hands on with the company. I think I'd like to use the money to help other women who need safe housing, like what your grandma offered me."

"That sounds just like you. And, you know you're always welcome here." David hesitated, putting distance between them as he ran his hands over his head with a sigh. "I need to say this."

Adaleigh fought back the tears. She braced for what he would say. Could a girl like her hold out hope for a relationship? She was from a whole different world, whether she felt like she belonged to it or not.

He scooted out his chair so he could face her, though he rested his elbows on his knees, hands clasped, and kept his eyes down. "I think you should follow through on your dreams and your parents' wishes. You have a responsibility, a legacy. Do what you know how to do, what you've been educated to do. You will be brilliant at it because that's who you are."

Adaleigh's heart sank. His praise drifted past her as she wrestled with the meaning behind his words. Another rejection. Another place where she didn't fit.

"Adaleigh, I can't be the reason you stay in Crow's Nest." David's jaw tightened, then released. He finally looked at her, heartache in his eyes. "You are an incredible woman who would make a great leader of any company. Think of all the women you could help. You are amazingly smart, so you'll know what decisions you need to make. And with those psychology and rhetoric degrees, you'll win the hearts of everyone you meet. Like you did mine."

"I—"

He took her hand but squeezed his eyes shut. "This is even harder than I thought."

Her heart pounded in her ears, her brain tumbling through all the possible things he could say next.

When he finally looked back at her, tears glistened in his eyes. "It's too selfish of me to ask you to stay. Before, you needed a home, but now ...

Be honest with yourself, would you really be happy here? I need to send you home, to the home you know, where you grew up. You claim not to be a Sirland, but the way you've handled yourself the past few days, you are more capable than you realize."

Adaleigh blinked at the burn in her own eyes. "I thought you didn't see me differently now that I have money again."

"I don't. I'm ... I'm trying to think of what would be best for you."

At his expense? What did David really mean, behind the words he spoke? Could she take a guess? Perhaps say what was on her own heart before David decided her life for her? "David, are you giving me permission to leave because you don't want me here?"

"Heavens, no!" He shot up, desperation in his eyes. "I—"

"David." She pulled his callused hand to her cheek, memorizing the feel of it. "I don't need to return in order to manage my parents' company or build a house for women. My life from before is gone. My home is now a large empty house made up of painful memories and loss. But here in Crow's Nest, I've discovered new family and friends. Ones who like me for who I am, not for my bank account. If I stay in Crow's Nest, I wouldn't be staying here just because of you, but you are the one who brought life"—dare she say *love*? — "back into my heart."

She held her breath in the silence, hoping for a future she never expected to have. He studied her for several long moments, his thumb brushing her cheek bone, then seemed to come to a decision.

"Come with me." He helped her out the back door, and Adaleigh leaned heavily on his arm as he gently moved them to the center of the lawn. "Remember what we said about the stars?"

Adaleigh leaned her head back to stare at the expanse. The cloudless sky stretched above them, countless stars poking pinholes in a black canvas unhindered by electric light. "How we both I—"

"Love them?"

Adaleigh turned her eyes from the vast heavens and found David looking right at her, his face mere inches from her own. She caught her breath at what she saw there.

"Stay, Adaleigh," he whispered. "No matter what I said, no matter what logistics we have to figure out, I love you, and I want you to stay."

A hope unlike any before filled her chest. "I'd like nothing better because ... I love you too."

David's eyes lit up like a shooting star, and he captured her lips in a kiss.

Historical Note

The premise behind this story comes from how we often confide in strangers our deepest secrets. We share more than we might otherwise online, on airplanes, and in other places with people who we likely will never meet again. Yet we might have a hard time sharing with people we see on a more frequent basis. It's a fascinating phenomenon. If you'd like to read more, I recommend the article by Lydia Denworth and Brian Waves, "The Paradox of Confiding in (near) Strangers," *Psychology Today*, September 28, 2017.

In the 1930s, the central part of Wisconsin's Lake Michigan shoreline still boasted an abundant fishing trade. By then, the boats had motors, yet the waters had little regulation. With the start of the Depression, the work the labor unions had done prior to WWI was being undone as work became scarcer and workers became more transient. I tried to create as likely a fictional town as I could based on the various factors at play during that time.

An interesting fact about Memorial Day in 1930 is that the day was set on a date, not a day, so that year, Memorial Day landed on a Friday. It was originally a time to remember those who served and sacrificed during the Civil War. However after WWI, the holiday began to morph in name (from Decoration Day to Memorial Day) as well as to include those who fought in the Great War.

In the early 1900s, organizations like the YMCA took it upon themselves to teach life-saving techniques to women. With women competing in the Olympics, more opportunities for female swimming opened up. The Women's Athletic Club in Chicago is still around today.

The University of Illinois, as well as several other universities in and around Chicago, were pioneers in welcoming women into their programs. Before 1930, women attended U of I to graduate with degrees in scientific and mathematical fields. Psychology and rhetoric were also degrees offered during that time. Today, U of I's Communication Department, which absorbed the Rhetoric Department, is one of the top departments in its field.

One last historical note. As far as I could ascertain, there wasn't a tornado outbreak in Eastern Wisconsin in May of 1930. However, storms at that time were not often recorded. There was a damaging tornado that went through the area in 1921, and I used creative license to take some of the recorded destruction from that event for my story.

FROM THE AUTHOR

Dear Reader,

Thank you for joining me in the pages of *Confessions to a Stranger*. Adaleigh and David are a few of my favorite characters and I hope this story has been a blessing to you.

A huge thank you to the people who helped bring David and Adaleigh's story to you. A few I would like to mention by name: My friend and critique partner, historical romance author Ann Elizabeth Fryer. My editor, Denise Weimer. My proofreader, Lynn Owen. My cover designer, Roseanna White. My husband, Gabriel, who not only read through the story, but helped inform the fishing portions since he grew up fishing Lake Michigan. And to my boys who let Mama snag mini chunks of time to write. There are many more people I could list, friends who offered encouragement and readers whose excitement encourages me to keep sharing stories. I thank God for each of you.

One note ... we all come from different backgrounds and situations that color our everyday and bring out different responses in us. If your story has left you with scars like Adaleigh faces in *Confessions to a Stranger*, they may not manifest as hers did. We are each unique and yet we are not alone. I encourage you to reach out to someone—it is not weakness to ask for help. For more information and resources, you can visit https://www.mentalhealth.gov/get-help.

If you enjoyed Adaleigh and David's story, would you consider leaving an honest review on your preferred retail site? And be sure to tell a friend! Word of mouth is the best way to ensure an author keeps writing your favorite stories.

The *Harbored in Crow's Nest* action continues in July! David's cowboy-hat-wearing friend, Silas Ward, returned home for his family ... will he discover love as well? Find out in *Refuge for the Archaeologist*, book two in the series.

In the meantime, I'd love to keep in touch. Visit my website, danielle grandinetti.com, for my book blog, my author shop, and all the relevant social media links. While you're there, sign up for my Fireside News monthly emails where you can keep up-to-date on my writing plans and book recommendations. Or follow me on BookBub or Amazon to receive notifications on my newest releases.

Thank you, again, for reading *Confessions to a Stranger*. I'm grateful to have readers like you.

Danielle Grandinetti

CONTINUE THE SERIES

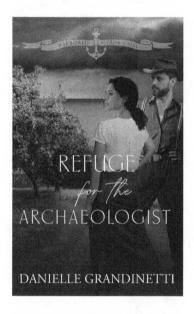

Refuge for the Archaeologist

Harbored in Crow's Nest, #2

Releasing July 2023

daniellegrandinetti.com/refuge-for-the-archaeologist

**Will uncovering the truth set them free
or destroy what they hold most dear?**

Wisconsin, 1930—With her health in shambles and her archaeological career on the line, Cora Davis retreats to Crow's Nest and the home of her great aunt to heal. She doesn't think much of the missing memories from between the earthquake that caused her dizzy spells and her trip home. Until she begins remembering the danger that sent her fleeing her last dig and the person responsible.

After a decade as a ranch hand, Silas Ward returned to Crow's Nest to provide for the women in his life. That same protective instinct propels him to Cora's aid. But when finances dwindle, the lies and greed of others threaten to ruin his family. Unless Silas can walk the thin line of compromise. A choice that might cost him Cora's affection.

As winter's chill threatens, will Crow's Nest prove a refuge, or will both Cora and Silas have no choice but to sacrifice their chance at happiness to save those they love?

**Welcome to Crow's Nest,
where danger and romance meet at the water's edge.**

Strike to the Heart Series

To Stand in the Breach (#1)

She came to America to escape a workhouse prison,
but will the cost of freedom be too high a price to pay?

A Strike to the Heart (#2)

She's fiercely independent.
He's determined to protect her.

As Silent as the Night (#3)

He can procure anything, except his heart's deepest wish.
She might hold the key, if she's not discovered first.

For purchase links, visit:
daniellegrandinetti.com/strike-to-the-heart-series

ABOUT THE AUTHOR

Danielle Grandinetti is author of the *Strike to the Heart* series and has won the University of Northwestern Distinguished Faith in Writing Award. She's fueled by tea and books, and the occasional nature walk. Originally from the Chicagoland area, she now lives along Lake Michigan's Wisconsin shoreline with her husband and their two young sons. Find her online at daniellegrandinetti.com.